FULCRUM OF MALICE

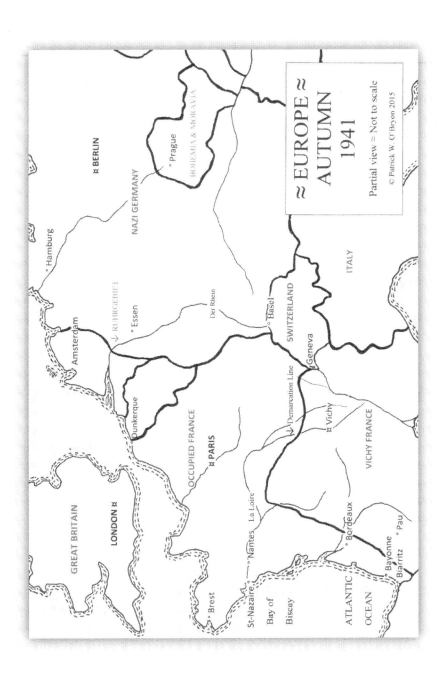

≈ EUROPE ≈
AUTUMN
1941

Partial view ≈ Not to scale

© Patrick W. O'Bryon 2015

GREAT BRITAIN

LONDON ¤

Hamburg

¤ BERLIN

NAZI GERMANY

Prague

BOHEMIA & MORAVIA

Amsterdam

RUHRGEBIET

Essen

Der Rhein

Basel

SWITZERLAND

Geneva

ITALY

Dunkerque

OCCUPIED FRANCE

¤ PARIS

Demarcation Line

Vichy

VICHY FRANCE

Brest

St-Nazaire

Nantes

La Loire

Bay of
Biscay

Bordeaux

Bayonne

Biarritz

Pau

ATLANTIC
OCEAN

FULCRUM OF MALICE

A NOVEL OF NAZI GERMANY

Patrick W. O'Bryon

Brantôme Press
NAPA, CALIFORNIA

Publisher's Note: This is a work of fiction. Names, characters, places, and incidents are a product of the author's imagination. Locales and public names are sometimes used for atmospheric purposes. Any resemblance to actual people, living or dead, or to businesses, companies, events, institutions, or locales is completely coincidental.

Cover Design by G. S. Prendergast
Book Layout ©2013 BookDesignTemplates.com
Author Photo by Ashley Urke Photography

Beacon of Vengeance/Patrick W. O'Bryon. -- 1st ed.
ISBN 978-0-9910782-7-1

To my dear wife Dani
and in memory of my father

CONTENTS

The truth is incontrovertible. Malice may attack it, ignorance deride it, but in the end, there it is.

—Winston Churchill

FOREWORD

The *Corridor of Darkness* trilogy spans a dozen tumultuous years from the onset of the Great Depression in Germany to the months before America's entry into World War II. In the course of the story the brilliant but initially naïve Ryan Lemmon gradually commits to countering the Nazi menace both covertly as an American spy and personally in a long-standing battle with a Gestapo nemesis. This concluding volume, *Fulcrum of Malice,* covers a few weeks in the waning months of 1941 as the United States prepares to enter the fray.

If you are new to the story, consider beginning with the first novel of the trilogy, *Corridor of Darkness*, so that you can better appreciate the characters, the intrigue and any surprises along the way.

For those already involved in the adventure, a short review of the concluding action in *Beacon of Vengeance* will ease you back into the story. A synopsis can be found on the last page of this book. I have included a glossary at the back to help readers with any unfamiliar foreign words or terminology.

And so we return to 25 August 1941 and a warehouse in Nantes, Occupied France, scene of a violent confrontation during the dark hours just passed...

RÉSISTANCE

1941

CHAPTER ONE

Nantes, Occupied France
25 August 1941

The gendarme was so focused on the field of carnage he hardly glanced at their identity cards as he waved the workers through. From front entry to rear gate the warehouse yard was littered with bodies, drained flashlights and spent weapons, all bearing witness to the bloodbath of the preceding night. Ambulance and morgue personnel scrambled about, searching for life, bandaging the few lucky ones, hefting bodies onto litters. At least eight uniformed men were down or on stretchers. Not one civilian casualty in sight.

Once beyond earshot Nicolas Bergerac nudged his comrade. "Can't say we'll miss a few Vichy cops, right?"

Marc Fermier looked back at the devastation. "Cut the strings on every fascist puppet, for all I care." He stuck a half-smoked cigarette between his lips. "I really don't give a damn." Marc plucked a fleck of tobacco from the tip of his tongue as the butt bobbed in the corner of his mouth. "Got a light?"

Nico handed him a matchbook. *Brasserie Fer Rouge*, Janine's favorite spot. God, what a night they'd had! He could still hear her breathless moans as she demanded more than he could give. Chantelle had already drained him an hour earlier.

The warehouse door showed no signs of forced entry. "Can't imagine what they wanted in this shit-hole," Marc said. "Who in his right mind would want to steal any of this crap?"

They hesitated just inside the threshold. With all the mayhem on the loading docks, Nico had expected a shambles. Instead, all appeared quiet, untouched. He took a second to listen and observe. First rays of sunlight pierced the neglected clerestory windows. High in the rafters a sparrow crossed the mote-filled space. Many got in when the loading bays were open, few got out. Nico was known to toss crumbs outside the office when closing up for the night. He kept a water dish filled. All the same, the weekend janitors often gathered tiny corpses with the floor sweepings, feet curled in death, eyes pinched closed.

"Tell you what," Nico said with a shrug, "you take the right while I head over to the office. Anything unusual, just give a shout."

"You got it, boss." Marc inhaled the precious smoke and took off, only to stop abruptly, turn and voice a sudden thought. "We find another belly-up *flic* in here, his tobacco's mine, *d'accord?* My ration's barely getting me through the week."

Nico gave a commiserating smile. Six kids, a nagging wife, that makes eight mouths to feed, not to mention his unquenchable demand for smokes. Couldn't be easy for him these days. "It's all yours, my friend."

Nico offered silent thanks for his own good fortune. His had indeed been a good night, and the slaughter outside couldn't dampen his spirits. Fiery Chantelle—yes, a firecracker in the sack, her pointy tits bobbing as she rode him, her cries of pleasure enough to wake the entire apartment house. But all the same a bit angular for his tastes—always the appetizer, never the entrée.

Then had come a quick wash-up at the sink, excuses made—early to bed, a new workday coming and all that—and out the door. A leisurely, quarter-hour stroll into the waiting embrace of his big, bouncy, blonde Janine, straining a negligee that had cost him twenty francs and worth every *centime*. Nipples like ripe cherries, and those soft, heavy thighs as she lifted her hips to his tongue. Yes, life was good. If he ever settled down it would have to be with Janine.

He entered the company office, whistling *Auprès de ma blonde*. The work table was strewn with diagrams, maps and blueprints. He squatted to run a finger through a congealed smear on the concrete. Tacky, rust-red. A shout rose from out in the warehouse and he stood again, cocking his head, distrusting his ears. There…a second call from Marc.

The sparrow took to the air as Nico ran up the cross aisle and headed toward the front.

The acrid stench of canvas bit at his nostrils, hampering already labored breathing. Tight quarters restricted all movement. Some hours before, Horst von Kredow had opened his eyes to total darkness, blinking repeatedly to confirm he lived. Now his lids remained closed with nothing to see in the pitch blackness. Repositioning his arms accomplished little. His toes barely reached the end of the crate, one foot managing to touch the lid above him, the other, twisted sideways at the ankle, immobile. By craning his neck upward he could feel coarse wood against his forehead.

His body inclined slightly, head down and throbbing. The attacks, first from Gesslinger and then Lemmon, had been severe enough, but Horst had long been immune to pain. Since the duel in Marburg his solace was in the all-embracing morphine. Seven years nearly pain-free, even in recovery from the trauma inflicted by his feckless wife. Yet now with the passing hours came a distress long forgotten, and he realized his body cried out for its trusted companion. He had skipped yesterday's injection in his haste to settle old accounts.

How long since Lemmon forced that poison between his lips? A cyanide pill was nothing new to him. He had once lost a British agent to such a capsule during a particularly enlightening interrogation. What fury and frustration in failing to spot the death pill tucked into that cheek! The moment he heard the Jew-bitch Erika call out for it, he knew he could turn it to his advantage. The game was only won through bold moves.

So he'd allowed the American his perceived moment of glory. A sham death came so easily to an expert in all things lethal, a man who had witnessed—no, caused—so many real ones. The faked convulsions were a body memory from all he'd suffered with the damaged facial nerve, the foaming at the lips easy for anyone with salivary glands restructured by a bullet, the gift of a loving wife. And the imbeciles hadn't known to finish the job. They could easily have shot him or crushed his skull or bled him dry, but impatience won out, or more likely squeamishness, the most dependable weakness of his adversaries.

His thoughts wandered, his focus straying, his mind not accustomed to the rising physical discomfort. To actual pain. If not freed soon, his damaged facial nerves would be the first to scream for relief, to weaken his tenuous hold on self-control, on sanity.

But that tiny insurance policy, the kill-pill, still rested between his jaw prosthesis and cheek. His tongue followed the slick contour of the steel implant, finding the gap left by missing teeth and exploring for the pill tucked between lower gum and jaw. He teased the deadly capsule onto his tongue and rolled it gently against his upper palate, relishing death so near, so accessible. How easy to crush the rubber, cracking the glass vial within and releasing his hold on life. *Wouldn't that please them all?*

What a risk he had taken in claiming to have destroyed his Marionette's infant! A weaker man would have dangled that gift of hope in such a desperate situation, using the child as a bargaining chip to spare his own life. Horst von Kredow had never shown weakness, and in that moment he'd felt strangely empowered by inviting his own death. Perhaps he had sensed it wasn't his time.

The hours passed and the pain grew relentlessly, yet he felt more invincible than ever. Eventually workers would come, would hear him kick against the wooden lid and call for help. The corpses of his incompetent squad were also likely crated up nearby. How useless they had been when confronted by amateurs, what pitiful excuses for German manhood. Where were all the strong, the capable? His hands cramped and he scraped his fingers into the canvas to restore circulation. At least the bastards hadn't made him share this coffin.

A jolt, a jagged tear in the fabric of his concentration, and he exhaled slowly. The game would continue. Must continue. A stalemate, but only for now. Plump fingers from that little girl—a nice proof of life—and his Marionette would return to do his bidding. Easy enough to track down Erika and her rutting mates. Right now they would be convinced of his death, relaxing their guard, congratulating each other. The fools.

His trembling fingers prepared to set the playing pieces back on the board. The final game of the tournament, and when the challenge no longer brought him satisfaction, checkmate at last. He drummed a staccato beat on the canvas. He willed the fingers to stop. They refused.

The hours throbbed on relentlessly, marked only by flashes of jolting pain. He followed the ebb and flow of blood coursing through veins and arteries, a pulsing tremor rapidly turning to a drumbeat, his temples threatening to burst. He had never wandered this far from the morphine, never sensed such a weakening hold over breath and muscle. And mind.

Dawn had to be approaching, perhaps already arrived, but only the sound of his labored breathing reached him. His jaw now trembled uncontrolled, and he forced the cyanide pill beneath his tongue to avoid inadvertently cracking its shell. He would leave nothing to chance. His safety valve.

Workers were sure to come anytime now, and he prepared to draw their attention. Some unsuspecting worker would fetch a pry bar to open the crate and witness Horst's resurrection in bloodied glory. The man would ask how all this had happened, and Horst would thank him politely, deflect all questions, and once the Good Samaritan turned to lead him away, that same crow bar would snap the man's neck, a swift *coup de grâce*, the man's body replacing his own in this infernal coffin.

Sweat now streamed from every pore and warm urine saturated his trousers. He cursed the loss of personal control, of self-restraint, his lifelong trademark. Every fiber of his being cried out for the drug, for the easing, for the calm and self-will. His foot kicked relentlessly on the crate lid until deep, agonizing spasms wracked his thigh muscles, arching his back and strangling the animal cry in his throat.

Nicolas ran to find his friend, wishing he'd first washed the tacky blood from his fingertips. "Nico! Over here! Come see this!" Nicolas spotted his comrade near the front of the warehouse. Surprisingly, no corpse sprawled at Marc's feet.

"So, what's so important you made me run?" Nico bent over, hands on his knees as he caught his breath. Last night's sexual exertions had taken more from him than he thought. Time to pace his activities.

Marc pointed to the highest crate in a stack. Its label read "tenting material," hand-printed in both French and German. "Just give a listen—our rats are doing more fucking than you and your two lady friends."

Nicolas heard only some distant commotion as a heavy vehicle entered the yard outside, its horn honking in frustration. "Cavalry arriving?" he asked.

"A bit late for that, I'd say." Marc pulled himself up on a cross-slat and pressed his ear to the top container. "There it is! Listen…and there again…" now he pointed, "and again…there!"

"*Ouais*, heard it that time. But what the shit do we care? Check the label—Priority C—this shipment will be underway for weeks, and that's assuming anything gets out at all today. Let the *Boches* on the Russian front sleep with the rats, right?"

"Let them eat them for dinner, for all I care." Marc fumbled in his pockets, his hands coming up empty, as usual. "But as long as you're here..." He showed Nico the crushed cigarette pack and mimed sorrow.

Nico handed over his pack of *Gitanes*. "Thanks for such an important discovery. Now come take a look at something of actual interest. There are papers scattered across the office that sure as hell weren't there when we locked up Saturday and there's blood all over the floor." He showed his stained fingertips. "Now that's worth a look, right?"

Now his body convulsed incessantly. For a few moments Horst thought he heard distant voices, but then all went still again. He struggled to maintain some last vestige of control, but hours had passed since his last fix, his mouth and tongue parched, his stomach clenching. He tasted searing bile. My God, it's too much!

He bit his tongue trying to position the capsule between his teeth. It stuck fast on his dry palate, and hard swallowing did nothing to dislodge it. He gulped repeatedly, willing the pill to his good side, to solid teeth, to shatter with a crunch. A new contraction coursed up his spine, sending his head ramming into the lid. He jerked in pain, light momentarily filling his field of vision before absolute darkness returned.

And then the pill was gone, the tiny lump descending whole into his roiling gut. He anxiously counted the seconds, but the capsule with its deadly toxin remained intact.

So he would not die by his own choice, after all, and this agony would defeat him. He thought to scream out in protest but knew no one would hear. His death would be tortured and beyond his control.

The exhausted police inspector took a cursory look at the plans and diagrams spread out before him, but his focus remained elsewhere. Roused at four that morning, trading disgusted looks with a wife who despised the bedside phone and never understood his unpredictable schedule, he'd listened to the report of gunfire in the warehouse district, six of his own men down. That would mean dragging himself into town, starting the investigation, filing reports and notifying families. Yet his only thoughts at that moment were of the warmth he'd just left and the way his wife's long hair framed her face, still lovely after all those years despite her look of disgust. He'd dressed and kissed her good-bye. Too much death, not enough time for life.

Releasing those thoughts he returned to dealing with the carnage outside. Two warehousemen waited by the door, caps in hand, exchanging glances. Having taken a closer look at the smears of blood on the concrete floor, he'd ordered two of his men to survey the entire warehouse. One now returned with a handful of Mauser 25mm shell casings. "Plenty of blood out there, too, sir, and smeared footprints, at least half-a-dozen involved. Plus drag marks, but no bodies."

"Hauled away, perhaps?"

"There's more to it, sir. A crate, with what appears to be blood smeared along the side. They may have stashed the dead in those boxes."

"So what's keeping you? Open them up, gentlemen, every one if you have to! Let's figure this out before the *Boches* come barging in and make a further mess of things." The men scrambled out and he turned to the worker who appeared to be the supervisor. "A phone?"

"Over there, sir," the man pointed toward the far corner, a hesitant look on his face, "in the right-hand drawer. But do log all your calls." Now he grinned. "Management rules, you know."

The investigator glared down his prominent nose and the man took an involuntary step back. The inspector turned to his lieutenant. "We may as well get this over with. Go ahead, notify the Gestapo."

Disgusted by the prospect of having his personal authority undermined, he stretched rubber bands around the maps and blueprints and made a neat stack of rolls at the edge of the table. Their military nature was obvious, as was the rendition of the port facility at Saint-Nazaire. The notations in French as well as German meant he'd stumbled upon trouble even worse than the loss of his men. Here was partisan resistance, not some black-market burglary gone awry. And now would come his worst nightmare, working hand-in-hand with the arrogant local Gestapo.

"They're involved in this somehow, that's for sure—" now mumbling to himself as well as the lieutenant. "Those Mauser rounds don't come from anything we've got."

The words to *Auprès de ma blonde* had abandoned Nico, and he wondered if his luck would leave him, as well. Gestapo on the way. The lieutenant was still on the phone, his carefully-chosen words unmistakably deferential. When the call was finished, the chief inspector took the rolled diagrams under his arm, signaled to his subordinate to follow, and headed out to oversee the opening of the crates. Nico exhaled.

Once the lieutenant had left the office, Marc lit up again, and Nico knew they faced a very long day.

CHAPTER TWO

Paris, Occupied France
27 August 1941

Ed had reminded him that hotel rooms assigned to foreigners were likely wired by the Gestapo and their phone lines tapped, especially those given to Americans now that FDR had further troubled the uneasy relationship with the Reich. So a public meeting place such as the discrete bar of L'Hôtel Paris on the Left Bank seemed advisable. Ryan arrived promptly at six to find Ed already at a corner table and deep into a bowl of crackers. An empty martini glass spoke to his early arrival. With few other patrons at that hour, there was little fear of eavesdropping.

Ed skipped any greetings as he rose to welcome his prodigal brother. "Just what the hell were you thinking, Ryan?" His voice carried a gravelly edge. "You promised close contact—you do remember that, right? Agreed more than once, I recall?"

"Yes, Mother." Ryan flashed a wry smile. He summoned the bartender with a wave. Ed ordered a second gin martini as the man removed his empty. "But things got a bit out of hand, so settle down long enough to hear me out." Ryan summarized his latest trials and successes, pausing only long enough to sample his whiskey. Ed listened intently, amazement in his eyes, his drink untouched. When Ryan came at last to the fateful encounter with von Kredow and his goons in the Nantes warehouse, Ed released a long breath. "So you finally finished off the asshole." Ed eased back on the banquette, draining his glass and signaling for a third. "You're one lucky bastard, you know. No disrespect to our parentage, brother."

"Quite an end to this thing, right?" Ryan couldn't hide his satisfaction. "A certain symmetry to it all—I'm forced to eat one stinking rat in Tours, then dispatch a second in that Nantes warehouse." He rubbed his right arm, still sore from the pounding he gave Horst. "And no worse the wear for either."

When he heard how Kohl and von Kredow had played them both for fools since 1938, Ed shook his head in disbelief. "Those sons-of-bitches!" His words slurred as he wrapped his mind around his brother's shoot-out with the French cops. "Just how hot are you now, brother? Should you be in hiding, or at least in disguise?"

"With von Kredow out of the picture, there's really no one to place me there or know my face, so I should be in the clear. I'm ready to take on whatever COI wants next." Ryan wrapped up the last loose end by explaining how he, René and Erika had settled the matter of looking after his son Leo.

Ed obviously had something of his own to share. "Glad those friends of yours are all doing fine now...no longer your top priority, because I've a bit of news, myself."

"Spill it! You get Grace pregnant again, or some new development in Washington?"

"Neither—the intrigue's right here on our Parisian doorstep. While you were traipsing across France on vacation, one of your old Berlin acquaintances insisted on making mine...a certain Rolf von Haldheim." Ryan's brow furrowed as Ed handed over the calling card. "He sends you his best, by the way, and wants to get together with you real soon."

Ryan scanned the elegantly embossed card and returned it to his brother. "That good ol' libertine, Rolf von Haldheim? You're sure about this?"

"Tall, lanky, almost too debonair? Impeccable manners."

"The one and only—what a character!"

"Believe it or not, your 'character' wants to do business with us."

"With us? What kind of business? Rolf was one of the early Nazi recruits from the upper crust, about '31 or so. In '38 he tried to warn his parents they were targeted by the SS. According to Erika back then, Rolf was still a regular at SS parties in Berlin. In fact, he was the one to clue her in on my return to the capital."

"Struck me as too fine a dresser to go for lightning bolts on his collar."

"Appearances can fool, brother. And I sure as hell plan to stay clear of the Sicherheitsdienst, given their open line to the Gestapo." Ryan considered what to make of Rolf's reappearance. "So how the hell did he run you down?"

"Not as big a problem as it might seem. I'm on both consulate and embassy rosters through Special War Problems. Claims he spotted our distinctive family name and thought of the good times you two once shared. Given German intelligence, you know damned well they have a who's who and who's where of everyone officially here in France."

Ryan bought the possibility. Lemmon a rare enough surname and Rolf might have recalled his mention of an older brother during those long nights carousing in the underbelly of Berlin. "So what's he proposing?"

"He spoke of finding common ground, you know, between his people and ours...and the Brits. All very hush-hush until we signal our interest. I met him in private on Isle-Saint-Louis." Ed reached for the last cracker. "He does know his wine, by the way."

"What did your embassy bosses say?"

"My "neutrality-first" desk chief wouldn't touch it—said to leave it to you and COI and keep my distance—but I rummaged around a bit on my own and learned that von Haldheim now works for Admiral Canaris."

"Rolf jumped ship to the Abwehr?" Ed was too dulled by the gin to catch the nautical pun, so Ryan let it slide. "Word back at COI was that Himmler hates Canaris' guts, but the Abwehr chief's simply too powerful for the SS to touch. Canaris seems to have the goods on all the Reich big shots, so his military intelligence operation is pretty much off limits to Himmler's boys in black."

Ed seemed uncertain of the next step. "So, do you intend to reach out to him?"

"Let's stick to channels on this one." Ed arched a brow, knowing that sticking to channels was never his brother's forte, and his odd look caused Ryan to laugh before continuing. "Find out how Bruce and Donovan want it handled, and then I'll move on it if COI give a thumbs-up. If Canaris really wants to talk with our boys, this could be major, especially if they're really seeking an intermediary to broker peace with the Allies...or even just an armistice." Ryan took a slug of his whiskey. Gullibility had recently nearly cost him his life and those of his friends. "But all this might be just some trap to test our American "neutrality."" He sighed and emptied his glass. "So, how do we reach our remarkable Herr von Haldheim?"

Ed slid over the calling card again and Ryan memorized the number. "So you'll wait here in Paris until I hear back from Washington?" Ed asked. "You had me on pins and needles holding nothing but that enigmatic postcard from Gascony. And now it seems I should have worried even more."

"Sorry, Ed. Who could have known von Kredow was manipulating everything from way back in 'The Group' days, and afterwards things took on a momentum of their own. Might never have made it without that Nicole. More than a bit disturbed after all that bastard put her through, but a helluva brave gal, and quite a looker."

Ed shook his head. "Don't you ever learn? You always go for the beauties who nearly cost you your life. Let's see, there was that brunette in Berlin dragging you into street fights and dives. Then your Erika, the dangerous blonde and mother of your kid. And now this unstable Nicole. Let me guess—a raven-haired knockout?"

"More kind of chestnut. Damned fine bouncing ponytail."

"We need to find you a stable wife, not another femme fatale, no matter how cute the tail."

"Not surprising advice, coming from a happily enslaved married man. God knows, I do need some down time." Ryan searched in vain for a cracker from the now empty bowl. "But I did put my hands on something to make you feel better after all that worry, something our Washington friends and the Brits should appreciate." He handed over the thin manila envelope.

Ed read the caption aloud, carefully enunciating past the gin buzz: *Proposals for Reform in French Secondary Education*. He dropped the report on the table, not bothering with the dozen or so pages. "Yeah, this is sure to delight Donovan and Company. About as exciting as warm milk."

"What did I just say about judging based on appearances? You never know what's hiding in plain sight." Ryan slipped the papers back in the envelope and stuffed it into Ed's inside breast pocket. "Courier only. What's hidden here is more valuable than you'd imagine, and will keep our paychecks rolling in. Which does remind me, high time to replenish operating funds. I'd lost what little I still had by the time I landed in that Tours jail."

"First things first, how about a change of clothes? Those duds are too small-town for the big city, and—brother to brother—could stand a good cleaning." Ed's shoe found the leather valise parked beneath the table and scooted it toward Ryan. "You'll find what you need in there. Once you've changed, let's grab a bite to eat. And replace whatever ID you're carrying with what's there, and quickly."

"Done. You pick the spot for supper, Ed, but I've got something on for later this evening. Marita doesn't know I'm back in town."

"Ah yes, I left your little Marita off the list, didn't I? Another brunette, as I recall. I see my sage advice to avoid *femmes fatales* still falls on deaf ears."

Ed shook a Lucky from the pack, lit up, then caught the bartender's attention and scrawled his signature in the air. The man immediately delivered the check to the table. "And incidentally," Ed pulled a small fabric sack from his side pocket, "here's a welcome home gift."

Ryan smiled at the sight of a new briar pipe. "Was I eyeing your smokes?"

Ed gave a throaty laugh. "And you'll need this, as well." Ed handed over a bulging leather pouch. "Virginia's best, because who can smoke the crap they're selling here now?"

Ryan reached over and clapped Ed on the shoulder. "Very thoughtful—you must have read my mind." Then the smile faded. "But one more thing, Ed."

Edward lifted an eyebrow, waiting. "Go on."

"Kohl."

"A dangerous bastard who's conspired to kill you, I know. But what can we do about it? He's high SD and Gestapo, and well outside our purview."

Ryan tamped tobacco into the pipe, giving a trial run to season the bowl. He lit a match. "You'll be seeing him again?"

"No doubt, he's local Kraut liaison for War Problems. And believe me, I'll have a devil of a time remaining civil and pretending to know nothing." Ed tried to add some levity. "But that's why they call us *civil* servants, right?"

Ryan, no longer in a joking mood, didn't look up. He only shook out the match once the flame reached his fingertips. "Mark my words—that son-of-a-bitch has to go, even if I track him down myself. They were a team, Kohl and von Kredow, both equally responsible for all those deaths. And now our war has turned real—"

"We're still neutrals, Ryan. Don't start America's war for her."

"As long as he's out there, he's a threat—to me, to you, to my friends. Damn it, Ed, he's a threat to our country. That's something you still don't get—it's not just personal. Yes, I've been bloodied, and now I've taken a couple of lives. And whether we accept it or not, we aren't going to turn our backs on this Nazi insanity much longer."

His cheeks burned with anger and he turned aside, rubbing the smooth bowl of the pipe with a thumb, admiring the glow of the briarwood in the soft light of the bar. He knocked the ashes into the tray and returned the still-warm pipe to its sleeve, then stood and squeezed Ed's shoulder. "Listen, Ed, we both have work to do. I'll let it ride for now, see where my next assignment takes me. In the meantime, the next time you see our friend Kohl, go ahead and be the swell, easy-going guy your Foreign Service demands. Just be aware that the bastard's in my sights. This is something I won't just forget."

The bluish glow of street lamps guided Ryan out of the subway. Against a sky of burnished steel the last rainclouds moved eastward. Some pedestrians carried flashlights masked by colored tissue paper to negotiate the dark and haze-filled streets of Montmartre. Others optimistically took their chances with the hard-to-spot curbstones and dimly lit street crossings. The neon signage of brasseries and night-spots remained shielded since the Occupation expected British bombers to appear any night in those metallic skies above.

The neighborhood pulsed to the musical beat of bars, clubs, and cabarets. Following Rue Pigalle toward Marita's club, Ryan overtook a group of late-evening revelers. With arms linked, the drunken celebrants sang *Lili Marleen,* the ballad of a soldier's faithful girlfriend. Listening to the rich voices, Ryan found himself back in 1934 Marburg, the tabletops smoothed by generations of steins and spilled beer, the easy camaraderie of fellow students toasting good health and eternal friendship. Then he thought of Erika's dazzling smile, the moonlit fog rising from the river into the *Altstadt,* and her demanding hips pressed to his, their excitement barely contained.

My God, he thought, *let it go and move on, Lemmon!*

Overtaking the rowdy group, he scanned their faces. For all he knew, one of the drunken men might have been an old university drinking buddy, but he saw only younger men with cheeks ruddy from alcohol and enthusiastic *Kameradschaft.* One officer eyed the American's stare with growing suspicion, so Ryan turned away and strode on. His nostalgia quickly disappeared as the strong voices joined in praise for the "swastika full of hope," and "a day of freedom dawning."

How hypocritical this Nazi Europe had become! He saw again the bloodied von Kredow struggling against the cyanide pill. Having rid the Reich of one sadist, the next should come more easily. At least so he hoped. The voices faded as he turned off Rue Pigalle. He decided to set aside such ugliness in anticipation of his reunion with Marita.

Over a decade earlier her sensual dancing and intriguing smile from the stage of the Folies Bergère had stolen his heart, or so he believed in the shared enthusiasm of the audience. For several nights he waited in the alley outside the club, the traditional Stage-door Johnny with bouquet of flowers. Dark hair slickly pomaded and blue eyes filled with humor, he happily endured the teasing jibes of the departing dancers. By the third night they all knew him by name, and two of the showgirls even volunteered to take Marita's place. But Ryan only had eyes for nineteen-year-old Marita Lesney, who left the club at closing with her older sister and fellow dancer Marie. Marita repeatedly declined his requests to speak in private, yet each time she accepted his flowers with a fleeting smile.

On the fourth night and at the urging of her sister, Marita had finally relented. Ryan and the stunning beauty spent the dark hours of early morning at a small café bordering the wholesale market of Les Halles. The scene was loud and lively: good-natured butchers in red-stained aprons shouldering massive slabs of beef, vendors hawking fresh produce to early-rising shop owners, and persistent cats fussing at the feet of the fishmongers waiting for hand-outs. But none of that mattered to Ryan. He focused solely on the young woman, inviting her with words and looks to surrender to his infatuation, and his interest proved contagious.

Several nights later, carried away by the sheer excitement of that victorious moment, he embarrassed himself by coming too soon in the warm embrace of the beautiful dancer. Thankfully, it never happened again.

Their romance had been short-lived, for he fell victim to a self-confessed addiction to new countries and new and willing girls. Marita's feelings for him however were far more true and long-lasting, with letters of love and concern trailing him across Europe and back to America. Occasionally he would respond, his words sincere but always noncommittal. At other times, her floral-scented envelopes disappeared unanswered between the pages of his journals, each missive well-creased from frequent readings.

In 1938 she welcomed him back to Paris. When he appeared at her doorstep buried in self-recrimination for having failed to rescue his friends, Marita buoyed him up at his lowest point and encouraged him to see beyond failure. But he knew he was the former lover holding a place forever in her heart but no longer in her bed.

Now he stood outside her club again, the lively music spilling across the sidewalk. He stopped long enough to remove his new hat and slick back his hair with a comb, then entered the smoke-filled lobby of *la Chatte bottée*. A revival of that decade-long friendship was all he would ask of her. If she offered more, he would gladly accept.

CHAPTER THREE

Paris, Occupied France
27 August 1941

The exotic dancers circled through the audience, their flowing scarves of gossamer silk giving teasing glimpses of breasts and swaying derrières. The audience marked time to the beat of the raucous orchestra. Most *Boche* patrons were already deep in their cups and rowdy after hours of salacious stage comedy and visual stimulation. As the dancers wound sinuously across the club floor, a remark from one officer brought a sassy reply from the showgirl. The Wehrmacht major attempted to pull her to his lap, missed his target and tumbled to the floor. She patted his balding head in faux concern, her hips never missing a beat before she strutted on. His comrades laughed uproariously at the involuntary slapstick. Almost lost in that sea of uniforms, the few business suits marked entrepreneurs and city officials enjoying one of the numerous privileges of collaboration.

Marita's venue had once been a cinema, but what motion picture could compete with such a sensual feast for the eyes? Ryan knew occupation marks were flowing freely into that cash box hidden behind the crowded mahogany bar. The club layout had greatly expanded since his last time in Paris. The Occupation was clearly paying dividends. Stairs accessed the mezzanine, where drinkers gathered at a second bar, and the balcony beyond allowed more intimate encounters for patrons and their guests. Another staircase led to the former projection room, Marita's office.

At the bottom step, Marita's gatekeeper Florian kept an eye on the crowd. The huge man with the shaved head plowed his way through the haze of smoke to offer the newly-arrived American a hearty handshake. "The years have treated you kindly, Monsieur Lemmon. You appear far healthier than when last we met." He offered a complicit wink. The bouncer's burly image hid a softer side, and the two men had come to a mutual understanding long ago—Ryan would treat Marita with utmost respect, and Florian wouldn't threaten him with his intimidating glare and wrestler's physique.

He was right about Ryan's changed appearance. When last in Paris he had sported a bandaged nose, badly swollen cheeks, and bruised eyes. Worse still, his left arm and hand had barely functioned after von Kredow's torture by fire. Now Ryan's nose merely hinted at the old break, and while his other features showed a bit more maturity at thirty-five, his good looks and dazzling smile could still turn a woman's head.

"And you, Florian?" Ryan found the bodyguard's massive shoulders and bald pate as daunting as ever. "Life treats you well?"

"As well as to be expected, monsieur. A couple kilo lighter in the belly, perhaps." He hitched up his trousers to demonstrate a looser fit, revealing a revolver in his waistband. Ryan frowned—the ex-pugilist bodyguard had always relied solely on brawn—but Florian only shrugged. "In truth, we've had our share of troubles lately, but who hasn't?" The experienced eyes of the bouncer darted again through the crowd by force of habit.

Ryan hurried along the reunion chat, anxious to get up the stairs and surprise Marita. "How are your wife and kids?"

"As long as food's on the table we get by. Mademoiselle Lesney scrounges a few extra ration cards each week to keep our brood in the basics." Ryan looked up the stairs again and Florian caught his impatience. "So, the boss expects your visit?"

"I thought I'd surprise her." Ryan saw some unexpressed worry in Florian's eyes. "Is she doing well? I really doubt she'll mind."

Florian surveyed the dimly lit mezzanine, its wall sconces losing the battle against billowing clouds of cigarette and cigar smoke. He was clearly troubled. "Head on up, but you'll only have a couple minutes for that surprise. She's just asked me to fetch a drink." He leaned closer to Ryan and his voice dropped to a whisper. "I know she'll be delighted to see you again, but things have been very difficult around here lately. You heard she lost her family last year?"

"Her family?" Ryan couldn't hide his shock.

"It happened when the city spread her legs for the mighty conquerors. I thought she might have written you."

"My God! Marie as well?"

"Sadly, both her parents and her lovely sister. The cowards mowed them down with those infernal Stukas as the family tried to leave town." Former boxer Florian rubbed his jaw as if he'd just taken one on the chin. "Mademoiselle blames herself for sending them out of the city but everyone thought the *Boches* would rape and pillage. Or worse. You do know her mother was a Jewess?"

Ryan nodded.

"She's taken it really hard, as you might expect."

Ryan remembered the beating Marita's father suffered from French fascists for having a Jewish wife. And of course, no one could forget Marie of the quick smile and beautiful legs. "What a tragic loss! How very sad for all of you. I'll help any way I can, and thanks for filling me in."

Florian turned his back on the crowd. "There's another matter, as well. Just in the last month we've faced serious difficulties here at the club."

"Financial?" Ryan's access to COI funds might help.

"Let's call it 'outside interference.' Everything's been extremely tense, but things now appear better again." He patted the revolver at his waist as if to make some point. "I'm sure Mademoiselle will tell you about it, knowing her trust in you." He nodded up the stairs. "I just wanted to forewarn you she's had a rough go of it, so be gentle with her."

"Thanks for that heads-up, Florian, and for looking after her so well." Ryan suddenly wished for a pistol of his own, the bodyguard's tension contagious.

He took the steps two at a time and gave a quiet knock, his heart beating faster despite outward calm, his buoyant spirits dampened by Marita's recent troubles.

"Come in." Her voice sounded distant, distracted.

He eased open the door. She sat in the Louis XVI chair with the worn rush seat, her back to him, her concentration on a stack of papers lying atop an open ledger. The cocktail dress revealed the curve of her graceful back. Thick auburn hair tied with a ribbon emphasized her slender neck. As expected, she wore ruby red. Always red.

Without glancing his way she gestured toward the divan. "On the coffee table please, Florian. Once finished here, it's off with these shoes and up with my feet." Her high-heeled pumps complimented legs as appealing as ever.

"Simply unbelievable!" she muttered as she set aside the papers. "That bastard Serge pissed off all our wholesalers. It'll take months to regain their trust!"

She turned, then immediately leapt to her feet and Ryan opened his arms to receive her. "*Mon Dieu,* Ryan, always when least expected!" She kissed him on both cheeks, then surrendered to tears and his embrace. "But why, Ryan? Why do you make my life difficult, just when I'm finally coming to terms with it?"

Ryan grabbed the hand thumping his chest and brought it gently to his lips. "Come on, my little Marita, I'm that bad penny that always turns up, right?" He kissed her forehead and used his handkerchief to gently blot at her smeared eye make-up. "Let's get you off those tired feet, I'll massage your toes, and you can tell me all about this 'bastard Serge' and anything else I've missed in the last three years." He led her to the couch. "You helped me at my lowest, so now I'm here to help you."

They sat down, her hand still in his, just as a knock rattled the door. Marita threw him a grin of apology and opened to Florian, waiting outside with two martinis. "I thought you both might wish to toast this reunion."

"You will join us, Florian?" Marita asked. She wiped away the last of the tears with Ryan's handkerchief.

"Non, non et non!" thought Ryan.

"Très gentille, Madamoiselle Lesney, but I must decline. Floor duties will keep me hopping till closing. Full house down there and more animated than ever, as you've surely noticed. Military successes on the Russian front inspire enthusiastic consumption, and our guests spend—and talk— freely." He set down the tray of drinks and turned to Marita. "Should you need anything…"

"I'll call," said Marita. "For the moment, Monsieur Lemmon and I have much catching up to do."

The door closed gently behind him and she returned to the couch. "Now tell me, my wayward love, to what do I owe the honor of another visit?"

Ryan's smile faded. "Florian told me of your loss, Marita." He took her hands in his. "Words can't express how sorry I am."

She seemed to retreat into memories before speaking, then her words came in a torrent: "It was all my fault, you know, I did it to them. I forced them from the city, sent them away with dreams of safety in Palestine." She leaned back against him, her eyes shut, tears streaming. "But that was all a lie, because I said I'd follow along, but I really wanted to stay, to use what Marie and I had built here as a weapon against the *Boches*, to find some useful purpose in these godforsaken times." Mascara streaked her cheeks. "And when Papa finally relented—he was the hold-out, *Maman* seemed lost already, and Marie knew full well what I was up to, so she played along—then all three of them had to die…and horribly." She fell silent for long moments, her eyes now open but unseeing.

He was at a loss, anxious to soothe her but knowing he couldn't. He understood the all-consuming sense of guilt that burdened her. He had once felt responsible for Erika and Leo's deaths only to learn they'd survived after all. His heart ached at Marita's self-inflicted suffering.

Ryan drew her close and waited out her sobs. He eyed the pipe he had set on the table but then thought better of it. Condensation pooled beneath the untouched drinks and the minute-hand moved across the face of his watch. When she calmed at last, he spoke again: "It will fade with time, you know—at least the guilt. Never the sense of loss, that will hurt forever if you dwell on it, but guilt only weakens you and can't bring anyone back."

She drew a deep breath and seemed to open to the words he spoke. "Marie would understand and want you happy, you know, and so would your parents. You need to be strong right now, Marita. Trust me, this horror has just begun and the suffering still to come will be truly unimaginable."

"How much more must we take from these monsters?" Her eyes demanded answers he didn't have.

"If we want to stop them, to punish them, we can't surrender to the sorrow and suffering they inflict. Instead, we fight with all we've got because the Nazis count on meek submission. They demand servants and slaves, and fear anyone they can't intimidate and control." He lifted her chin and she offered him a thin smile. "Let me help you, Marita, let me make things easier for you."

She inhaled deeply and straightened her shoulders. "You should know I've already made good strides. My weak moment is simply because you've known me so long and now you're here to comfort and reassure me. I've had to be strong for the others for what seems an eternity." She finally took a sip of the gin. "So go ahead and light up that pipe of yours. The smell will remind me of better times together while I fill you in on my latest."

She related the tireless efforts of her girls to covertly gather intelligence on German troop placement and movements. She told of carefully logging names, dates and destinations overheard in the club, and how she hoped the information was benefitting the Allied cause. He wondered how she passed this information up the appropriate channels, but didn't interrupt as she moved beyond her grief and self-recrimination. Finally she spoke of a gangster called Serge who had maliciously extorted control of her club. The brutal knife-branding of the young dancer set Ryan's teeth on edge. "But don't worry." she said. "A friend helped me put that asshole away for good."

"A friend?" He'd heard more in the word than expected. "Someone here at the club? I'm sure Florian's been a great help to you, and I see he now carries a revolver."

"Yes, Florian…but another, as well." A quick glance past smeared mascara to gauge his reaction. "Ryan, it's so silly for me to be this hesitant—I know we've had nothing serious between us for years—but I now have a close friend who helps me immensely."

Ryan sensed the change in direction and felt on uncertain ground. "I understand perfectly, Marita. We never made promises—"

"Well, at least one of us never made promises." The hint of a smile crossed her face. "And the other never gave up hope of getting one."

He shrugged, apologetic. "Marita, what can I say? I wasn't ready—"

She placed a finger on his lips. "Say nothing, my dearest, nothing at all. All I ask from you now is understanding, so let me tell you about someone very special …about Argent." Her words came faster now, as if she might lose courage and never finish. "He reminds me of you in so many ways, my darling Ryan, and he does love me, of that I'm certain."

"Argent? A Parisian?"

Marita observed him closely, hesitating. "No, not French…and he's young…a German," her lower lip quivering now, "and a Wehrmacht officer, a lieutenant."

"A *Boche*?" Ryan grabbed for his falling pipe, hoping to spare his new trousers damage from the glowing tobacco shreds. "One of the enemy?"

"Yes, a *Boche*, but one of the good ones, Ryan, someone who hates these Nazis with a passion as strong as mine. As strong as yours! And he's already proven himself to me, so please, Ryan, please don't pre-judge him."

Despite her words his first thought was unsettling. Treachery and deception raged across Europe, and no stranger deserved acceptance at face value. And that ragged jolt of jealousy had also made him wince. Marita continued in rapid bursts: "First meet with him, hear his story. You used to have German friends dear to you—"

He steadied his voice, his thoughts. "I still do, as luck would have it." He recalled Erika's final glance that very morning and René's warm assurances of enduring friendship. He pictured Leo in the garden, selecting flowers especially for him. "But more of that later, Marita." Ryan hesitated, uncertain how to proceed, unsure whether he even had any right to ask, then did so anyway: "You and this Argent…it's romantic?"

She nodded. "He makes me feel special, just as you once did." She placed Ryan's hand over her heart. "He reminds me so much of you when we first met—youthful, idealistic, determined to do only right and make your mark on this godforsaken world." She hesitated. "And he's devoted to me. Time turns back when we're together. Is that so wrong?"

Ryan felt beyond his depth. Never had he made a serious, lasting commitment to any woman, yet he found himself torn by the realization that his ever-reliable Marita was sharing with another the same passion he had hoped to rekindle. *God damn*, he thought as he refilled the pipe, *well,*

God damn! He struck a match, more to distract his thoughts than out of desire to smoke.

"Of course it isn't wrong, Marita. If you make each other happy and you truly trust him, then I'm happy for you. But I do owe it to you to ask: you're convinced he's worthy of your trust? Espionage thrives on subterfuge."

"I'm telling you this with good reason," she said. "You've certainly heard of the Abwehr?"

Ryan tensed, uncertain where this was headed. A romantic entanglement was startling enough, but a connection to military intelligence perhaps more so. "Yes, powerful and dangerous, from all I know."

"Well, this friend of mine, Argent—that's not his real name, of course—Argent works directly for someone in the Abwehr, someone who knows you personally!"

Oh, for God's sake, where could all this be going? Was he compromised? "You've got to be kidding, Marita! I purposefully never mentioned you in any report I filed, so who the hell even knows we're acquainted?"

"This gentleman knows. That's how he tracked me down. He's the one who passes along the information we gather on the club floor each night."

Ryan was stunned. "So you and your girls work for the Abwehr now?"

"*Mon Dieu, non!* These people—this man and my Argent, at least—are doing exactly what we seek, identifying sympathetic German officers, hoping to help put a quick end to this horrible war, an end to Hitler and his henchmen."

Ryan leaned back, his mind racing. "This man—not your Argent but the other, his boss—he's got a name?"

"Of course, but perhaps a *nom de guerre*," she said, avoiding his eyes for fear of reproach. "He's been here in person only once, posing as an army colonel to help us trip up that bastard Serge! I can describe him well enough if you wish. He's well educated and speaks excellent French. Fluent in English, too, according to Argent. Tall like you, but with thinning hair and going gray. Oh yes, one more thing, his nose suggests a dedicated drinker." As if reminded, she handed Ryan his untouched martini. "If it helps, Argent believes the man's an aristocrat. Impeccable manners, even when drunk. And last of all—how to put this discretely?—in all honesty, he may well favor women and men equally. You know, he has that certain air."

Ryan bolted upright, splashing his martini. "Did he, or rather did your friend, say how this man claims to know me?"

"He said he'd once shown you the shadier side of Berlin 'in all its diversity.'"

First Edward, now Marita. Ryan drained his martini, concerned by this new twist. High time for a chat with Rolf von Haldheim.

The phone on her desk demanded attention. "Probably just Florian checking up on us." Marita kissed Ryan on the forehead before leaving the couch and reaching for the receiver.

"Oui?" Her face went dark, her eyes cutting to Ryan before she spoke forcefully: "Stall as long as you can, then do it, but keep our people safe!" Ryan was already on his feet, shocked by her sudden pallor. She dropped the phone in its cradle and steadied herself. "Gestapo." Her words now in quick bursts: "Two cars, two agents already in the lobby, others heading up the alley."

Ryan put an arm around her trembling shoulders. "Keep calm, don't jump to conclusions. My God, it's wall-to-wall military and collaborationists down there—they could be after anyone in the place."

"Yes, anyone. But they're not, I just know it! My clients are powerful so the Gestapo would be cautious, wouldn't step on important toes with an open raid." She fumbled with the key to her desk. "No, they're here for me. Someone's talked." Her hand reached to the back of the drawer and withdrew a small pistol. She checked the clip and released the safety. "Should they take me, check under the carpet of the first step outside. No sense wasting the intelligence."

The clamor of a fire alarm suddenly interrupted, first on the ground floor, then across the mezzanine as a second alarm joined in. Marita appeared to barely notice, her thoughts solely on the arriving Gestapo. "But Ryan—they simply can't find you here!"

From below came muffled shouts and the pounding of feet as drunken patrons sought out the front exit. A few voices barked out commands for military order, but only Ryan seemed to consider how dangerous the uppermost room of a burning structure would be. "Come on, we have to get out of here! This place will be a chimney—the flames will be up here before you know it." He grabbed her arm, shaking her loose from her apparent lethargy. A person might outmaneuver the Gestapo, but a fire in a crowded club was uncompromising. "Now! Let's go, and hurry!"

She pulled back with a shake of her head. "There is no fire, Ryan, it's a diversion, Florian following orders, a sham to slow them down. The girls know—we've practiced for such a possibility."

Ryan slowly released his breath. "Good move, but what's the rest of the escape plan? Unless the cops buy the fire ruse they'll come knocking any minute."

"There's a hidden emergency exit from the balcony. A wall passage connects backstage but tonight's crowd's too big, we'd never get through to reach it and others would follow us down."

"If we go now we can fight our way through and at least attempt it!"

"Look, Ryan, I have connections within the Occupation, powerful connections," she grabbed a woolen overcoat from the rack, "but you just complicate matters. The Gestapo may have no interest in you now, but caught with me you're automatically a target. And for all we know, you may have also been compromised."

His eyes quickly swept the long, narrow room—two small shuttered windows out to the club, a closet in the corner, no escape hatch in the water-stained ceiling. He might be able to drop from one of the projection windows to the balcony, but could she make it in dress and heels? The screeching fire alarms made thinking difficult, and now the distant siren of an arriving fire crew added to the mayhem. "We'll have to chance the stairs, then."

Marita pointed to the closet door. "Get in there, now!"

"But there's no room."

"Inside and to your left, now! The shelving's been altered to make room for a watcher."

"Argent?"

"Yes, Argent. Because of Serge. But it wasn't needed—we found a better way. Now get in there," she handed him his coat and hat, "and keep your mouth shut, no matter what happens."

"They'll look inside." Ryan eyed the tight space warily. No claustrophobia, but he preferred any escape option, especially with Gestapo crowding the room.

"Just force your back to the wall—go on now, get in there! Huddle down and you'll be nearly hidden."

"Nearly?"

"No arguments, just hurry!" Alarms continued to rattle the building, but the shouting downstairs had eased. She gave his cheek a quick caress, then handed him the pistol and kissed him forcefully on the lips. "Now hide! I can talk myself out of anything, so don't feel you must be brave, and whatever happens, stay the hell out of it!" She shut the closet door with a final comment: "You're no good to me in a Gestapo cell." Ryan thought of Tours and followed orders. A shaft of light from the office caught his eye and he bent to the tiny spyhole.

Footsteps pounded up the stairs and Marita grabbed her business ledger and cinched closed her coat, feigning an escape from the fire. The door surrendered with a resounding crash and two men barreled in, sending her sprawling and exposing her long legs. One held a Walther, the other a Browning and a small suitcase. She attempted to pull down the hem of the dress now gathered at her hips. "Ah, the lady welcomes us with parted thighs—your typical French Jew-whore." The man with the suitcase laughed as the other agent dragged her to the couch. Marita cursed and growled, a cornered cat scratching for his face. The policeman backhanded her sharply and her hair fell loose from its ribbon tie.

"Get the hell out of my office, you filthy animals!" Her face flamed in anger. "You've no business here and my powerful German friends will make your lives a living hell if you don't get out of here right this minute!"

"And just who raised that fire alarm, *Mademoiselle Chatte bottée?*" The hatchet-faced agent sat on the coffee table facing her and placed one hand on her thigh, tightening his grip. "Perhaps you're unaware that a false alarm in a crowded building is a criminal act? Or perhaps some misguided attempt to keep us from our duty?" He grinned to his partner, who nodded eagerly. "First things first, you must learn to collaborate with your German masters." The agent shoved his hand between her thighs. Marita gasped and slid back on the couch.

Ryan had seen enough, he'd had enough. He tightened the pistol in his grip, calculating how best to take out both agents without risking her safety. Her eyes appeared fixed on her immediate assailant, but when Ryan lowered the handle of the closet door she shook her head and Ryan knew it was a warning not to interfere.

"Just what do you want, *cochons*?" Her voice was low and brittle.

"Well, *ma petite mademoiselle*," his French as harsh and brutal as his hand, "That should be obvious—we've come looking for you." He released his grip, sniffed crudely at his fingers, and sat back. "We have on good authority that you spy for enemies of the Reich and hide a wireless transmitter here in this office." He nodded toward the small suitcase at his partner's feet.

"That's absurd." She rose abruptly from his grasp, covering her thighs. The agent made no attempt to stop her. "I run a reputable club for the entertainment of your Wehrmacht officers and nothing else." Ryan could see her hands tremble. "Planting 'evidence' in my office will get you nowhere."

The Gestapo officer addressed his partner who now stood beside Ryan's closet. "Well, now that all those Wehrmacht friends have run from your fire, let's delve more deeply into your business. Perhaps a more thorough search is in order?" His attentive partner picked up the bag and reached for the handle on the closet door.

"I've nothing to hide, *messieurs*." She strode toward the exposed stairwell but never made it to the smashed door.

The sharp-faced agent shoved the Walther in his belt and dragged her back by the arms. "Let us be the judge of that, Mademoiselle Lesney. Right now it's time for a more intimate search, don't you think." He stripped off her overcoat and tossed it aside. With one hand at her throat, he traced the line from her neck to the small of her back before lowering her dress. The narrow straps gave way to expose a lace-trimmed brassiere as the red silk pooled at her feet. He ordered her to remove her underwear. She complied.

His partner abandoned the suitcase to get a better view. Marita shuddered but said nothing as the two men traded crude comments about how they would use her body were she worthy of an Aryan cock. The agents' aroused state was clearly visible with all their attention focused on the naked woman.

Ryan checked the safety, then clenched the pistol forcefully, determined to first put a hole in the man whose hand again slid between her thighs. With luck he could drop the voyeur partner before the first lecherous asshole hit the floor. Slowly lowering the closet handle, Ryan hoped against hope that the hinges wouldn't creak.

Sudden gunshots rattled the stairwell below and two agents barged into the room. Ryan's odds had changed for the worse. A heavy-set man, panting from the climb, lumbered over to Marita, who held her head up despite her vulnerable position. The newcomer smiled broadly. "Ah, we arrive just in time, I see. My turn yet?" He tweaked one nipple with his pudgy fingers. "Ah, a gumdrop, just the way I like them."

"What's with the gunfire?" Hatchet-face dropped his hands to his side and attempted to cover his groin by shifting his raincoat.

The sweating bruiser wrapped a meaty fist around Marita's breast and pretended to bite off her nipple. "We had to take out the bouncer. Big guy with plenty of guts, but wouldn't cooperate, so we popped him good."

The fourth agent, standing immobile at the ruined doorway, stared for a brief moment at Marita's nakedness before taking charge. "The bruiser put up a decent fight but couldn't say no to this." He held up his pistol. "Now wrap up the bitch and get her down to headquarters. Orders on this one come from the top, so it's the big boys who'll get the real entertainment out of this lovely thing."

The disappointment of the other agents was obvious, but they followed orders. The leader gestured toward the suitcase, still on the floor near Ryan's closet. "And don't forget that transmitter. Important evidence of espionage, *nicht wahr?*"

Once the agents had taken Marita away, Ryan finally relaxed his grip on the pistol and stuck it in his belt, then massaged his cramping fingers. He felt physically drained and his red-hot rage blocked rational thought. In the confines of the dark closet the shaft of light still penetrated the spyhole, a caustic reminder of all he had just witnessed—a woman dear to him, manhandled and misused, exposed to vicious depredation. He waited a few minutes, his teeth still on edge. They would surely have hustled her downstairs to a waiting sedan, carting her off to even worse humiliation. And likely torture. He knew first-hand the Gestapo's methods, and speed was paramount if he was to find a way to help her.

He cracked the closet door to scan the office, then moved cautiously to the edge of the ruined doorway and peered down the stairwell. Florian's body slumped against the wall at the bottom steps. The mezzanine beyond was silent and empty. A click of the light switch erased his silhouette from the door frame. Pistol ready, he slipped down the steps to examine the bodyguard. His fingers found a feeble pulse. Even unconscious, Florian was a bear. One bullet had found his arm, the suit jacket blackened by the spreading stain around the entry hole. He removed his necktie and wrapped the arm, cinching the fabric tight. Parting the coat, Ryan found the other wound, a clean shot piercing the bodyguard's barrel chest. He tore open the shirt and rolled up the undershirt, pressing the material against the wound to encourage clotting. Help was needed fast if Florian was to survive.

The cold barrel of an automatic pressed to Ryan's ear and froze all movement. Intent on helping the wounded man, he had missed the new arrival.

"*Votre nom,*" the voice low and menacing.

"Lemmon. Ryan Lemmon. *Je suis Américain!*"

"*Vos papiers,* monsieur Lemmon." The barrel eased off. "And quickly!" Ryan lowered his right hand toward his pants pocket, edging closer to the pistol he'd placed on the step.

"*Non,* monsieur. Left hand only. Jacket pocket first."

Ryan withdrew his hand and followed orders, fishing out the American passport Ed had given him just hours earlier. He handed it over his shoulder and began to turn around, but pressure from the pistol dissuaded him. The man ordered him to remain seated facing the wounded bodyguard, then stepped back to read under the dull light of the wall sconce. The pistol remained trained on Ryan's head. He managed to glimpse a Wehrmacht uniform.

When the man spoke again, the voice remained uneasy but all menace was gone. "*Enchanté*, Monsieur Lemmon. Or should I say '*Erfreut, Sie kennenzulernen*?' As the old American friend of Mademoiselle Lesney, you may call me 'Argent.' Now, shall we save poor Florian before it's too late?"

"Marita! She's—"

"I've already placed a call for help. There's nothing more to do until we learn who's responsible for this outrage. I put my driver on their tail so at least we'll know where they've taken her."

Ryan heard the anxiety in Argent's voice and felt immediate kinship with the young officer. At least for now he had a partner in rescuing Marita.

CHAPTER FOUR

Nantes and Bayonne, Occupied France
28 August 1941

"**P**lease tell me this is some sort of joke, René!" Her anger rising, Erika slammed down the platter of roasted potatoes. Chunks skittered across the table in a smear of oil and parsley and one dropped into Leo's lap. He gingerly bit off a corner, grinning as he caught René's attention. Erika shook her head in further frustration. "Leo's finally back with us. There's no way we're splitting up now!"

With a flick of a thumb trained by shooting marbles, Leo sent the potato wedge racing across the table into René's waiting hands. He gave the boy a wink and popped it into his mouth. "There's simply too much at stake and too little time." His words were muddled by chewing and he took a sip of wine. "The group's relying on me, the partisans in Saint-Nazaire are primed and ready to act, and you three will only be gone a few days anyway."

Erika glared at them both. "Leo, go see if Madame Nicole is ready for dinner?" She handed René a napkin and pointed to a fleck of food stuck in his beard.

"But *Maman*—"

"*Now*, Leo."

"Yes, *Maman*." Leo shot René another quick grin. Despite her anger, René knew Erika was pleased to see how close her "two men" had grown in recent days, and he was delighted with the new role of father bestowed by Ryan.

Erika picked up the remaining spilled potatoes and rinsed them in the sink. Food was hard enough to come by to waste any. "I just can't do this right now, René. This last encounter with Horst drained me. I need a rest, not new worries, and that means you help us get Sophie back for Nicole. Once the children are out of that cursed hostage house in Bayonne, we can all spend a few weeks recovering on the Morlanne farm. Together."

"It's not that easy." René rose cautiously from the wicker chair and joined her at the sink. She knew he was still in pain. Sitting was uncomfortable from the bullet wound just three days old, his limp worse after the fierce struggle, and his ribs and shoulder ached from the sadist's beating. Despite all that, he wrapped his arms around her. "Saint-Nazaire can't wait, you know. If we're to be effective there, we can't waste time—"

She turned in his arms and laid her head against his chest. "A couple of days won't end this damned war any sooner. Others can carry the load for a few weeks—I can't risk losing you, not now. Not ever!"

"I don't know whether this helps or hurts my case," René lifted her chin, "but we made a huge mistake in those last minutes as you and Ryan finished off Horst."

Her brow furrowed as she gingerly touched the lump on his head. It seemed to be healing nicely. "What mistake? We killed the bastard, crated the bodies, took the weapons and identity papers...oh my God!" She took a step back. "It's those damned plans for the U-boat pens! That's it, isn't it? We left the diagrams!"

René nodded. "Whoever cleaned up the mess will have handed them over to the *Boches*, and that means they already know we're planning something big. Not specifics, but they'll be more vigilant than ever. If we're to act, it has to be now, not weeks from now." Erika leaned into him again and he caressed her hair. "You know I'm right. You've no choice but to head to Bayonne tomorrow without me—poor Nicole won't wait any longer to find her daughter, and who can blame her?"

"I'm surprised she's held out this long. Sophie's the last family she has, thanks to that bastard, may he rot in hell."

"Doctor Ballineux says she can travel now. She walks without much flinching, but there's some infection so he says to keep an eye on her wound and he'll make up a little medical kit. Yves dropped off the forged travel documents a few minutes ago, and you certainly won't need my help getting to Morlanne. But I must enter those Saint-Nazaire pens before they button them up so tight no one sneaks in."

Erika pushed him away gently. "Of course, you're right. I'm being selfish. I'd imagined our having a few days for each other, and for Leo, a moment of rest before losing ourselves again in this saboteur business." She retrieved the platter from the table and scraped the rinsed potatoes back into the roasting pan. "I'll just warm these up a bit." Once the oven door was shut, she dropped to a chair and wiped at her eyes. René placed a hand on her shoulder.

Leo came in with Nicole. "What's wrong, *Maman*?" He ran over and put his arms around her neck. "What's wrong now?"

Erika stroked his cheek. "Nothing, nothing at all." She moved a lock of his hair aside. "Just disappointed that Uncle René can't go down to Bayonne with us."

"Why not, Uncle? It'll be fun and you'll meet Sophie."

"Business, Leo—important business. But you can be the man of the group, right? You take your mother and

Madame Nicole to rescue the kids, then introduce them to your animals at the farm. I'll come join you in a few weeks."

The Morlanne neighbor had been most understanding. Monsieur LeBlanc had immediately agreed to arrange a proper burial in the village cemetery for Jeanne. He also gave assurances he would look after the farmhouse for them. Erika knew René's grief would remain a deep and constant ache in his heart, but as usual he would suppress any emotional pain to stay focused on the greater battle. Jeanne had made a lifelong commitment to fighting injustice, so would be proud that she had raised their son to be selfless in the battle against social and racial intolerance.

"Will you be safe without us?" Leo gave his uncle a worried look.

"Always, Leo. But just in case I run into trouble, I'll remember that little trick of yours when you bit the policeman's hand. You saved us all with that one, you know." He ruffled Leo's blond hair. "Mighty clever thinking, young man."

Nicole had removed the potatoes from the oven and was slicing up the small chunk of roast pork, a welcome gift from one of the doctor's patients. She'd been so silent the last days that Erika was startled to hear her speak. "Yes, Leo, we're all extremely grateful for your help in ridding us of that monster. And for leading me to my little girl tomorrow." She bent to hug him, but instead flinched and pressed a hand to her bandaged side.

Erika was concerned. "Come, Nicole, you've done enough. Save your strength for tomorrow's trip and before you know you'll have Sophie back in your arms." She topped off the wine in the adults' glasses, diluting Leo's with an equal amount of water. "Quick, Leo, tell Doctor

Ballineux that we're about to eat. He should still be in his office."

"Yes, looking into his microscope again. This afternoon he let me help. You want to know what's swimming around in the drinking water?" Before anyone could respond, Leo left the room with a smug grin.

Erika shook her head and turned back to her husband. "Be careful, René. That warehouse was too close a call."

"That goes for the three of you, as well. Remember, the doctor's our go-between for messages. If there's any breakdown in communications we leave our coded notes, and I can always ask Monsieur LeBlanc to contact you at the farmhouse. Just let the doctor know when you reach Morlanne." He sipped his Bordeaux and settled back, obviously favoring his injured butt cheek.

CHAPTER FIVE

Paris, Occupied France
28 August 1941

More than anything else, it was the constant ache in her feet and legs. For long hours any slouch brought a slap to the face, and leaning against the wall to ease the pressure brought a suffocating blow to her belly. The nighttime hours passed under the harsh glare of an overhead fixture. At the desk in the corner sat a chisel-faced German woman, a study in gray. From time to time a man in uniform entered the antechamber, stood expressionless before her, and then wandered off. But that pig of an agent from the arrest made certain Marita stood stock-still to the verge of collapse. Argent had said that soldiers at attention should never lock their knees, advice which kept her upright during the long night. But now there was that incessant ache in her feet and cramping of the instep.

Only once did she receive permission to visit the latrine, but the dour woman from the desk had hovered over the stall, allowing her no privacy, and the moment she was done she was back in the antechamber. No washing hands or rinsing her dry mouth at the tap. Glancing at her image in the restroom mirror, Marita had been shocked by the toll of the long night, her eyes bloodshot and sunken, her hair in total disarray.

Back at attention, her request for water inspired the pig to offer "I've something for you to suck on if you're thirsty." The gray woman merely turned another page of her magazine, ignoring both crass comment and Marita's call for compassion.

Worse was surely yet to come, but she had prepared herself for months, knowing the work with Argent carried inevitable dangers. She had only herself to blame for what lay ahead, deserving all she would suffer. It had been so easy for others to forgive her—even Ryan had tried to reason away her guilt—but how could she forgive the destruction of her own family? As a miniscule cog in a giant espionage machine, it was time to pay the piper. How they had tracked her down didn't really matter now. Enough to know that she'd been compromised, and she would never reveal her contacts, no matter how serious the abuse.

She was a fighter, always had been. Others had belittled the sisters for wanting to have their own club. Few other women had accomplished such a feat in the face of tradition and male domination. Now she would prove herself the equal of any partisan who saw the evil in collaboration and preferred torture and death to squealing.

But oh, please spare my girls!

Too late for Florian—the horror of seeing his slumped body on the stairs tore at her heart. True to the end. But Ryan was resilient. He'd get out just fine, no doubts there. In '38 he'd been at his wit's end, weakened and devastated, yet she'd loved him all the more and he'd survived to fight again. Now he was back and stronger than ever.

There was so much she might have told him had the Gestapo never come. The man had lived in her heart for over a decade. She thought of those blue eyes that never wavered, the dazzling smile. He always made her feel special, and she knew he desired the quickness of her mind as well as the pleasures of her bed. He would enter her life and then leave again, time after time, and with each departure would go any hope of permanence, of commitment. Still, she loved him and gave no blame.

The agents at the club had allowed her the overcoat and little else. She hugged herself tightly, fighting for warmth. Hours without movement had set her teeth chattering. Oh, for a bath to wash away the filth of those groping fingers. Abandoning the red pumps would have made standing easier, but the obese agent had ordered them back on with a leer. "Your legs look far better in heels, but you can lose the coat anytime." He knew she'd been left with only her panties.

The woman at the desk made no effort to conceal her disdain, pretending not to notice Marita's suffering, her eyes glued to a magazine. A pre-war *Vogue,* it appeared. As if that frumpy *Boche* bitch could ever grasp Parisian fashion. From time to time she looked over, arched her brows and pursed her lips, "suitable treatment for a French slut" written in boldface. To throttle that scrawny neck, to rip those hideous eyeglasses from that smug scowl! Suddenly aware of her slouch, Marita drew back her shoulders as the pig waddled toward her. She wouldn't give him the satisfaction of another slap or crude grope.

The office just beyond the desk brightened with the first light of dawn. Again she thought of Ryan, of their last conversation, of the compromising paperwork in her handwriting hidden beneath the carpet of the office steps. Had the Gestapo somehow found them? No, impossible. As for Ryan, he would do his best to track her down, but the Gestapo was too powerful for any one individual to break its secrets, to thwart its plans. How much she still loved him. Always had, always would.

And Argent, that sweet boy with the kind heart— especially for a *Boche*—and that everlasting cock of his. He was supposed to have driven her home after closing that night. What a mess he must have found at the club, the place devoid of customers, her office in ruins, her favorite dress on the floor and—saddest of all—dear Florian staining the carpet with his blood. Florian, never to see his wife and children again.

She swallowed hard and wiped her eyes with her coat sleeve. Ever since the arrival of Serge she had feared his gang of thugs. Argent had stayed at her side to protect her, lain in her arms, and eased her longing whenever he could. But that Abwehr colonel, who obviously also loved Argent, had other demands on his young agent's time. Eyes shut, she shook her mind free of such rambling thoughts and worries. They would only weaken her. Let the bastards do their worst. She had done what she must.

A pudgy hand squeezed her ass, jolting her back to attention. "Head up, little lady," his breath as foul as his mind. "The big man's finally on his way." Activity in the hall drove the troll from the room at last, bringing momentary relief.

The arriving officer was tall and slender, perhaps thirty and impeccably groomed. His tweed suit appeared custom-tailored. She found this type so prevalent among the *Boches*—those finely-chiseled features and unnaturally ruddy cheeks, those eyes so bright when not soused to the gills. "Well now, what have we here?" Such a polite contrast to the ill-kept swine. "Your name, mademoiselle?"

"Lesney." Meeting his gaze, forcing herself erect, fearing to collapse in front of her interrogator.

"Your full name, *s'il-vous-plâit*." His voice cultured, his French perfect. Despite herself, she relaxed a bit, sensing some unhoped-for kindness after so much brutality.

"Marieanne Dominique Lesney."

"And called 'Marita,' if I'm not mistaken?"

"By friends."

"You are Jewish, Mademoiselle Lesney?"

"My mother yes, my father no. Neither particularly religious. You *Boches* make the rules, so you decide what I am."

He showed no reaction. "Mademoiselle Lesney, are you aware of the charges brought against you?"

Her rage surfaced despite herself. "Against me? *Monsieur l'inspecteur*, it was your brutes who entered my club, shot dead my friend and bodyguard and physically assaulted my person. They accuse me of espionage, then plant a suitcase in my office, suggesting an 'illegal transmitter' of some sort. As if I would know how to operate such a thing!" She drew herself up as tall as her exhausted frame allowed, her eyes piercing. "It is I who should bring charges!"

"My apologies, mademoiselle. Please calm yourself. Not all my men are capable of such boorish behavior, but a few could always use further training in good manners. Allow me to get to the bottom of all this." He offered a casual grin, his voice unnaturally gracious and accommodating. "Come along now—let's move into my office and make you comfortable? If you were treated inappropriately we will certainly make amends."

He guided her gently by the arm, her legs scarcely able to handle her weight. The sullen woman followed, a stenographer's pad under her arm, and dropped a file folder noisily on the desk. "Do have a seat, mademoiselle." He gestured to the solitary wooden chair facing his desk and the window, the daylight harsh on her eyes. The stenographer sat in the corner, writing block flipped open, pencil ready.

The man perused the file before taking a seat behind the desk, his back to the light. His features began to dissipate, his head haloed by the painful brightness. "Now then, we shall take our time examining the charges against you, and see what justification we might find, if any, for having disrupted your evening."

She flexed her legs and feet, chasing the pain from the soles and insteps. Her belly was bruised and swollen. She dearly wanted to massage her rear cheek where the pig had left his last fingerprints. Once the interrogator leaned back and lit a cigarette, she slipped off the pumps. The smell of the tobacco gnawed at her gut. "Genuine Turkish, you know." He offered the pack but she shook her head. He shrugged, "As you wish," and tapped off the glowing ash. "I am Detective Inspector Röttig, for the record. Now let's get to the root of this unfortunate matter."

The lengthy interrogation confirmed that the Gestapo knew nothing of her actual espionage activity. Röttig would surely have produced any real evidence, revealed a snitch or a breakdown in the network, brought up dates, times, and places. He would certainly have boasted of the arrest of her girls, or even of Argent. No, they had yet to turn up anything damning. Instead, he alluded to unspecified "treasonous acts" and always that damning transmitter "found" in her office. Who knew if that battered case contained anything at all? And the killing of Florian was already written off as self-defense.

Full daylight gradually turned her interrogator into a talking silhouette and made her fatigued eyes water. She looked for a wall clock but found none, though midday had to be approaching. Her wits felt rattled from exhaustion and her stomach grumbled from hunger and an unsettled gut. She placed a hand on her abdomen and flinched. The stumpy bully had done damage with those blows to her belly.

"Please consider the difficulty of my position, mademoiselle. Nothing would give me greater pleasure than to send you on your way with a satisfying meal and a quick lift back to your apartment. And, of course, our sincere apologies for any disruption to your life." He lit another cigarette. "You must be drained after such a trying night. But with charges as serious as these," one faultlessly-groomed fingernail tapped the file, "my hands are effectively tied." He rubbed his wrists together, miming restraints, before gathering the file contents and closing the folder. "You will, of course, receive a fair trial—we assure you of that. But your collusion with the enemy appears conclusive. And despite your claim to the contrary, the Gestapo does not manufacture evidence—your wireless transmitter was of English design. Very incriminatory, *n'est-ce 'pas?*"

"Am I to have an attorney?"

"Of course. The court will provide one should you have no one to call."

"And may I call my family to let them know I'm here?"

He held up the folder. "But, Mademoiselle Lesney, you have no family, remember? Unless you're inclined to put us in touch with some of your co-conspirators, then there's little more we can do." He crushed his barely-smoked cigarette in the tin ashtray and tapped another from the pack. "But do bear in mind—should you be open to revealing other partisans or spies, Jews or otherwise, anyone with treasonous intent against the Reich, then it's always possible that your charges could be lessened, your punishment made less severe."

Marita braced herself. "And what's to be my punishment, once your court finds me guilty of these charges?" The strain of the long, thirsty hours was beginning to tell in her voice.

"Why, I don't wish to be cruel, but you'll learn soon enough. The Reich punishes spies with something first developed right here in lovely Paris." He held the smoke in his lungs without exhaling. "Your Doctor Guillotin's famous machine." Smoke escaping from his lips and nostrils engulfed him in an aura of gray. "It's quick, relatively clean, and definitely effective."

She swallowed her gasp. "I wish to contact that attorney now."

"I regret you must remain in our custody for the moment, but we'll transfer you soon to Cherche-Midi for safekeeping. An attorney will contact you there. Marita cringed at the mention of the notorious Parisian prison for political detainees. "That's protocol for cases as serious as yours." He withdrew a small rectangle of cardstock from a paperclip on the inside cover of the folder. "But it's clear you must prepare a proper defense. Here is the name of one man who might offer help in this difficult matter." He slid over the calling card. Marita clasped her coat tightly to her neck as she bent forward to retrieve it, suddenly very conscious of her nakedness beneath the wool.

She read the name on the card and looked away, her gaze following the rising trail of smoke from the interrogator's cigarette. A chill chased up her spine. *Serge Bergieux*. And now it all made sense.

Despite efforts to escape the fear, she had little strength left to resist. After Röttig's hours-long interrogation, always posing the same questions and demands, always with the utmost politeness, Marita now knew that Serge held the Parisian Gestapo in his pocket. She would find no relief, and certainly no release. Her life was forfeit. Her seemingly clever trap for the extortionist, orchestrated with the help of Argent and von Haldheim, had somehow turned on her. Now it would cost her everything.

Röttig also appeared tired when he finally conceded defeat, stepping away from the light and revealing his long-hidden features. Marita had given him nothing and she knew her fate lay in the unforgiving hands of the man she'd condemned to Göring's wrath. "Well then, Mademoiselle Lesney, I regret your situation must now worsen. You will find few of my colleagues as understanding as I, or as well-mannered."

He spoke briefly into the phone: "She's ready." Standing beside her chair, he placed his cigarette to her lips. "Go ahead—you'll need it." She could no longer resist and drew the smoke deeply into her lungs. Coughing, she returned the cigarette with a nod and slipped back into her red heels.

Thankfully, the swine of an agent who had made her night a hell did not return to lead her away. Instead a matron responded to Röttig's call. She wore a long gray skirt, a black shirt with a Nazi Party pin and sensible black shoes. Coaxing Marita to stand, she gently clicked the handcuffs closed behind her back. "Please do understand, sweetie, we must treat you as the state criminal you are," the woman's voice not unkind, "and we can't have you trying anything stupid before you reach the basement. It's happened before, and what a mess, you see."

Marita was numb with exhaustion, her tongue so dry she could barely speak. "Just do with me as you will."

"But, my dear, we've no choice in the matter, do we?"

Röttig now stared out the window with her file beneath his arm. He didn't turn around. The sour stenographer folded her writing block with a grunt and left the room with a self-satisfied grin.

The gray-haired matron guided Marita through a maze of hallways to a lift. Two secretaries looked up and then quickly away when Marita caught their eye. At basement level they entered a long corridor with pea-soup green walls. The male guard unlocked a high, grated door and bowed with a sweep of the arm, as if inviting the women to join him for a dance. The matron returned his wink. But it wasn't the site of the cell block which clenched Marita's gut. As the door behind her slammed shut, heart-rending cries for mercy echoed up the corridor. The matron smiled sweetly and shook her head, as if to excuse the disturbance, then guided Marita onward.

She came to a halt outside an interrogation room, adjusting her thick hosiery as she complained of tired feet and having to deal with concrete floors. In the center of the open room a woman lay strapped to a table, her face lost in a mass of sweat-soaked hair, her sobs and cries agonizing to hear. Two brutes took turns clubbing the poor victim with rubber truncheons. Her body showed a mass of contusions, her breasts now shapeless, bruised flesh. The thudding of the bludgeons brought bile to Marita's throat and she tried to turn away, but the wardress held her firmly by the elbow. "It's always a bit hard to watch the first time around, my dear," the matron nodding in understanding, "but it gets so much easier with time. And believe me, that woman could end it all right now by confessing her guilt." She pushed the eyeglasses up the bridge of her nose. "Eventually they always do, you know." The matron offered a compassionate smile. "Now come along, we have a nice cell waiting for you." The victim's tortured cries had weakened to a pitiable whimpering with each successive blow.

Farther up the hall an equally-distressing sound evoked an animal held in a leg-hold trap. The matron prodded her into motion. Marita focused straight ahead as they passed the next door but the wardress pivoted her by the shoulders to face another open chamber. Agents had submerged a woman in a tub filled with water and ice. Only her head extended above the frigid surface. She suddenly slipped into delirium and her cries for mercy ceased. The men dragged her out onto the concrete floor. Her blue limbs shuddered spasmodically, her jaws chattered so loudly Marita thought they might break. She finally found the strength to turn away.

"Now don't you worry, little one," the matron patted Marita on the back, "it's rare to actually die this way. The cold just loosens the tongue, and that's good for the Reich, correct?" Marita bit her lower lip to control her anger and stared along the row of cell doors on the right side of the hall. She knew one was meant for her. She wondered which torture best suited her crime. What punishment for questioning a Führer's right to conquer the world at the expense of its weakest citizens? And what had she earned for condemning her own family to death at that same tyrant's hands?

CHAPTER SIX

Nantes, Occupied France
28 August 1941

"I need you back in Berlin." Reinhard Heydrich's voice rattled unpleasantly over the long-distance line. His words took von Kredow by surprise, causing Horst's mind to spin with possibilities. The thought of returning to the heart of the Reich, to Prinz-Albrecht-Strasse and Gestapa, brought both excitement and disquiet. He had spent three years with all of France at his disposal, a proving ground for testing the physical and mental limits of his enemies. His targets had shown themselves uniformly weak and easily manipulated. Even his underlings were often not up for the demanding rigors of his interrogation techniques. But above all, those three years had been his alone to control. Unexpectedly, now Heydrich was once again calling for personal assistance in support of the great work of the *Führer*. The timing was all wrong, but the opportunity immense.

The shrill connection with Berlin made a mockery of Heydrich's high-pitched voice. Horst bent forward in the swivel chair, ignoring its protesting springs and pressing the receiver tightly to his still swollen ear. He felt no discomfort, given the morphine coursing through his veins.

Beyond the glass partition waited three local Gestapo and their frowning captain whose shabby chair Horst now occupied. They feigned disinterest in the feared *Le Masque* with his badly mauled face. The deaths of two of their own agents in that warehouse fiasco three days earlier had soured the mood for further cooperation with the dangerous von Kredow. Horst didn't give a damn. Unreliable, poorly-trained agents assigned to this cesspool of a city deserved whatever they got. All fools deserve a fool's death.

Horst had phoned Gestapa to order new personal identity papers and a replacement badge. The bastards had taken everything before stuffing him in that damned crate. Surprisingly, his call had been transferred and Heydrich had come on the line with instructions for him to return immediately to Berlin. As Heydrich spoke of big changes occurring behind the scenes, Horst prepared his excuses, anxious first to destroy the bitch-wife and her two rutting dogs before turning to any new challenges.

The moment Heydrich permitted, Horst jumped in: "But my dear Reinhard, as delighted as I am to oblige, I'll need another week or two to tie up loose ends here. Pressing matters, you understand. Two weeks should definitely do the trick."

"Impossible, Horst. The locals can handle whatever you have in the works. Your efforts here in Berlin are far more important to the future of the Reich."

Horst assumed a subservient tone. "But of course, Reinhard. You've been most gracious in giving me free rein, and what an honor to work at your side again. You must realize however that this request does come as a bit of a surprise."

"Always the spice of life, right, Horst?"

"Indeed, indeed. But such a significant move demands preparation. I've been here for quite some time."

"Perhaps a bit too much time among the French, Horst? Am I hearing a trace of that *laissez-faire* attitude that makes for such a weak enemy?" Heydrich's laugh turned to a shrill whinny over the long-distance line.

Horst caught the implied slur to his Germanic sense of duty. "You do know me better than that, Reinhard."

"All the same, three years of the soft life in France can change a man. *Leben wie Gott in Frankreich, was?"*

Living like God in France, my ass! Horst thought, but he sensed danger in this questioning of his will to serve. "I remain the same devoted follower you first hired, stronger than ever in my dedication to you, the Party and our Führer."

"That's what I need to hear. You see, I'd hoped to tell you in person but time is too short. Confidentially, I have my eye on a powerful role suppressing dissidents in the Czech Protectorate." Heydrich hesitated, clearly awaiting praise.

"What a splendid advancement, Reinhard, and so well deserved!" Horst leaned back in the desk chair, the squeal of its springs mimicking Heydrich's distorted voice. Taking over operations in Bohemia and Moravia would be a stunning promotion for Heydrich. What personal benefits might come his way with his mentor's ascent into the most powerful echelon of Nazi power? "My heartfelt congratulations!"

"Now you'll see the need for returning here immediately. My special relationship with the *Reichsführer-SS* already invites the jealousy of those less gifted around here, and such a promotion will bring me even closer to the Führer himself. With me in Prague, my enemies will certainly feel emboldened to further scheme against me—against us, Horst, and all for self-aggrandizement rather than the good of the Reich."

Horst ignored the irony. He knew such advancement could leave Reichsführer-SS Himmler himself by the wayside.

Heydrich continued: "My friend, I need a trustworthy man to stay the course here in Berlin, someone whom the others will fear as much as they fear me, someone who will stay true to our shared designs and foil any enemies. He must keep me informed for my return, because I will return even stronger after putting the Czechs under the SS yoke." Horst waited for the pronouncement: "That person is you, Horst."

"Your trust and confidence honor me, Reinhard, but surely a few days won't matter?" It would be wrenching to forego the personal destruction of his enemies now that all three believed him dead. "As I said, even a week should do nicely, and then I'm all set for such rewarding duty in Berlin."

Despite the crackling phone connection, Heydrich's tone had clearly chilled. "When I agreed to mentor you fresh out of university, I gave you great latitude in return for your solemn oath that you would never question my orders. Perhaps that confidence was misplaced."

"Reinhard, nothing could be further from the truth!" Horst recognized a singular opportunity, but only if he momentarily surrendered his personal plans. "The next express will bring me to Berlin, anxious to do your bidding."

"Tomorrow's Friday and you won't get in until quite late. Better yet, fly from Le Bourget on Saturday. Have Kohl in Paris bring you directly to the airdrome once your train gets in. I look forward to greeting you in person first thing Monday morning, understood?"

"*Zu Befehl*, Reinhard! You will never regret this." Horst hesitated, unsure whether to mention the condition of his face and jaw. "But Reinhard, a quick heads-up in advance. I've had a rather violent encounter with local partisans, so don't expect me to cut quite as handsome a figure as the last time we met." He immediately realized Reinhard might have very low expectations. On Horst's last visit to Berlin in '38 he still bore fresh scars from Erika's bullet to the jaw.

Heydrich took a moment to reply. "These terrorists— they paid dearly for the insult, I assume."

"I've never forgiven lightly."

"Then forget about your looks. With that malleable mug of yours, I never know what to expect anyway. Perhaps just the ticket to intimidate our enemies, right?" Heydrich didn't wait for an answer and quickly signed off.

Horst set the receiver back in its cradle. His fingers explored the thick scabs clotting the hair at the back of his head. Was there more to this new development than met the eye? Nothing at all from Heydrich in months, and seldom more than occasional cabled praise for the successes of the extraction squads. He'd thrived on the independence, a Führer in his own French domain. Now came this invitation to be Heydrich's right hand in Berlin while he made Party history by annihilating the Czech rebels. But what wasn't Heydrich telling? Everyone had hidden motives, so why not Heydrich?

Horst had plotted for years to make his personal enemies pay the ultimate price. He knew such vindication would still come. The first night out of the coffin had brought a vivid dream with that promise. The vision had recurred nightly, almost the moment his head hit the pillow. His own blood was always the reddest of all, pulsing from the slashes on his thighs. The streams of crimson converged into a single, viscous flow as it moved across the tiles, sucking the life from the tortured body of Erika, from Gesslinger's shredded arteries, and finally forming a vast scarlet river encasing the fleeing Ryan Lemmon in its thick wave. All three victims shrieked in horror until they drowned, their mocking voices stilled at last. What fools to believe they could ever best him! If they weren't to suffer as a group, each would have to endure a fittingly painful death alone. He read the dream as assurance that time was on his side.

The materials found in the warehouse lay scattered before him on the Nantes bureau chief's desk. The saboteurs clearly plotted against the U-boat installation, so his Jewess and Gesslinger would act quickly now, knowing they'd left incriminating evidence behind. He would send agents to Saint-Nazaire to watch for their arrival. The moment Heydrich was off to Prague, Horst would find a moment to return and flay the bitch alive.

Ryan Lemmon would be back in Paris already, and Kohl could easily manipulate the brother into leading his men to the target. The next time Horst had his hands on that lucky bastard, they would bag up his body in pieces.

Now that he was off to Berlin, others would have to take up his work in France. The Bayonne children would lose all value to him as leverage, so Madame de Brassis could see to their disposal. He would phone her immediately. The woman shared his disgust with little Jewish worms.

How exhilarating it was telling those fools that his Marionette's girl was already dead and gone, a moment that could have cost him his life! But now those weak-minded dolts might seek out the remaining children. That half-breed Leo was surely bright enough to lead them back to the house in Bayonne, so why not set a trap there, as well? Time to teach his duplicitous Jew-bitch wife that, even from the grave, nothing could stop his vengeance.

CHAPTER SEVEN

Paris, Occupied France
28-29 August 1941

The cell door slammed shut and the wardress gave a double-turn to the key. Marita collapsed on the cot. Wrapping her bare feet in her coat, she whispered a mantra as she lay curled on her side: "So sorry. So sorry. So sorry." The distant cries ceased altogether as the afternoon passed. She didn't notice at what moment the brooding silence finally settled in. The resounding clunk from some heavy circuit breaker suddenly extinguished the lightbulb above her. The bluish glow of a streetlamp colored the frosted glass in the barred window above her bed, alerting her to the onset of night.

There'd been no meal, and the cell held only a toilet bucket, a small enameled sink and a pitcher of tepid water. No toilet paper, blanket or towel. Every hour the caged light on the ceiling flared again, the gated door up the hall near the lift clanged, and thudding boots and jangling keys announced the arrival of the guards. Laughing and joking, they strolled up one side of the corridor then down the other, opening each of the hooded spyholes to peek inside the cells and exchange jests about the prisoners inside. With bed checks done, the blessed darkness enveloped her again.

They came for her at first light, her legs barely able to comply with the order to stand. Her belly still ached from the repeated blows received prior to the interrogation. The matron was nowhere to be seen. Two hulking types in uniforms unlocked the door and tossed her a cloth bundle. Marita recognized the bludgeon-wielders of the preceding day. She readied herself as best she could, straightening her mussed hair, determined to keep her pride as she shed the overcoat as ordered and stood before them naked.

Men had first admired her publicly when she took to the stage at eighteen. She found no shame in her nakedness. She glanced down one last time in appreciation of the physical gift that had allowed her ultimately to gain recognition for her business acumen, knowing her lithe body would never be the same once these two had done their worst. A gift from Argent, her panties were stained from the monthly curse that had arrived during the long night. They laughed as she pulled the rough woolen smock over her head. Why wear anything at all with what they planned for her? Would the crushing cudgels disfigure her, or the ice water deplete the last of her energies? *At least with the bath I shall feel clean again,* she told herself. If only macabre humor could dampen the fear raging in her gut.

Once she was covered, the warders lost interest and ordered her into the corridor. Her eyes darted about, searching for anything to distract from the pain sure to come. Stained plaster where a pipe once burst. Cobwebs draping the bare bulb overhead. Crusted filth where linoleum met walls. At each doorway her step faltered. Which room ahead was reserved for extracting her confession?

But no cries of suffering or pleas for mercy shattered the silence. The portals to terror remained closed. Instead the men led her through the barred gate to the lift just beyond. An SS sergeant stepped forward to take charge, handing her a quarter loaf of dense brown bread and a mug of water. Her eyes misted in gratitude. For a few minutes she stood at the guard's desk, tearing off chunks of the stale bread and gulping them down with water, ignoring her filthy hands. *Why? Why?* With the last crumb consumed, handcuffs closed around her wrists. She found the cold steel oddly comforting knowing it meant she was leaving the torture cellar. A quick stop on the ground floor to sign her out and the sergeant hustled her into a sedan waiting at the curb.

They shot through the rues and boulevards as they approached the Seine. She stared out the side window memorizing the city she so cherished, the streets appearing less familiar when seen at such speed. Over a year had passed since she'd been in an auto, a privilege now reserved for the chosen few.

The Occupation presence was everywhere—a line of tanks idling in clouds of diesel smoke, a squadron of bicycle soldiers with packs and rifles strapped to their backs, and everywhere street signs in German. Stone walls were plastered with rows of identical propaganda posters, some overlapping others. They screamed for *Victory over the Bolshevik Hoards*. The Russians all bore a striking resemblance to the caricatured Jews on the posters lining the previous block.

She felt somehow relieved to see the grand monuments and beautiful bridges standing proudly against a blue sky despite the crimson swastikas floating on the breeze. And the Seine still flowed relentlessly north to the Channel. She knew she would likely never see the clock tower of Rouen, or the charming boat basin at Honfleur that her father had so admired. But long after she was gone, Paris would somehow survive.

The building at the corner of Rue de Raspail and Rue de Cherche-Midi was massive, a four-story structure with an ivy-laced façade, louvered shutters, and a mansard roof sprouting numerous chimneys. It seemed more a grand private mansion than the foreboding last stop for political detainees. Walls five meters high were interrupted by quoined columns and gabled guard huts.

The Mercedes stopped outside the metal gates. Her sergeant, silent but polite, sprang from the vehicle to take her arm, then abruptly held her back as a military lorry rumbled in and parked just ahead of them. Two soldiers with machine pistols leapt from the back, herding five disheveled, shackled men into the grounds. A city policeman signaled passing traffic to keep moving.

A stubble-faced citizen, sleeves rolled past his elbows and a briar pipe in his hand, observed the new arrivals from a bench in the shade of tall trees lining the traffic island. He shouted to her as she waited to pass through the metal gates. What she first believed to be a call of support lifted her spirits. Then she grasped his words. He had called her a treasonous whore.

Once inside the prison compound her guard pressed a bell to gain entry to the women's wing. A warder led them down white-washed halls to the admissions office where her sergeant removed the handcuffs and wished her "*bonne chance.*" She took a seat on a bench between two other women awaiting registration, knowing that luck would do her little good now.

Her rough smock clashed with the discordant red heels. The other two detainees wore everyday clothing, undoubtedly chosen that morning with no thought they might enter prison before the day was out. She looked at them warily. Could either be a police plant hoping she would incriminate herself? The younger bore an inflamed bruise beneath one eye, and her coarse blond hair in a fashionable short style showed streaks of dried blood. Her fingers clenched and stretched in an endless cycle of nerves, her eyes never leaving the linoleum tiles at her feet. The other prisoner had an impassive face and no obvious signs of mistreatment, but her eyes danced constantly from point to point. Only the finger twining a long lock of red hair suggested inner agitation.

Marita was first to stand before the woman in charge of admissions, a starchy brunette in the same drab skirt and black blouse with Party pin she'd encountered at Rue de Saussaies. Her chignon was drawn back so tightly it gave a feline look to her eyes. In a bored monotone the woman posed the obligatory questions, duly noting Marita's personal data in the prison registry: surname and given names, date and place of birth, father's given name, mother's maiden name—she looked up when Marita said 'Levi'—place of residence, marital status and profession. Again that subtle look of surprise when Marita claimed ownership of a Montmartre night club. Once listed in the prison rolls, Marita eavesdropped on the registration of the other two women. The bruised blonde was Claire Levallier, twenty-three years old, salesgirl in a textile shop, unmarried. The impassive redhead was Denise Duchamps, thirty-five, widow and photographer's assistant.

Officially now residents of Cherche-Midi, the inmates followed a female guard along a filthy hallway and through grated doors to a windowless room. A wooden bench hugged the wall beneath evenly-spaced hooks. The wardress ordered them to disrobe, and the prisoners numbly obeyed. Once their clothing hung on the white-washed wall, two additional female guards joined their colleague.

On orders, the prisoners lined up, placed hands on knees and bent over facing the bench. The head guard directed them to cough several times as the wardresses impassively checked private orifices for contraband. With this humiliation behind them, they moved into a tiled room to stand beneath rust-stained showerheads. The water ran lukewarm as they applied the obligatory lice-medication to all hair on body and head. Marita managed to scrape some hardened residue from the empty soap dish affixed to the wall beside her shower. Her fellow prisoners followed suit.

As the women left the showers, their thread-bare towels landed in a wicker basket. In the dressing area Marita's crude woolen sack and Claire and Denise's civilian garb were gone. Only their undergarments remained on the hooks. On the bench lay utilitarian smocks in black-and-white prison striping and bulky wooden clogs.

A middle-aged woman waited at the end of a hallway lined with brown metal doors. Her deeply-creased face wore no makeup. Though the ever-present swastika decorated her black blouse, her manner was surprisingly polite and respectful as she addressed the new arrivals in decent French. "*Soyez les bienvenues, mesdames.* I am Frau Biermann, director of your women's wing. I understand your anxiety, but the sooner you understand our house rules, the easier your lives here will be."

The wardress standing beside her handed each prisoner a list of regulations and a timetable. "Go ahead, have a look. You can memorize them later." Marita quickly scanned the printed schedule. At eight in the morning the cell doors would open for inmates to empty slop buckets, refill water jugs, and sweep out cells. At ten a.m. breakfast on the cell block and at four p.m. a second and final daily meal. Prisoners were to stand immediately if addressed by any German. No personal items were permitted other than linens, soap and a comb, all to be provided by the inmate's family. Reading and writing materials and outside food items were allowed only at the discretion of the warders, and again, only if provided by family.

"Frau Biermann," Marita felt encouraged by the director's pleasant manner, "My name is Marieanne Lesney and I've no family to care for my needs. At my arrest I was left with nothing but the undergarment I wear and the coat taken from me this morning. In addition, I'm having my monthly. It's most distressing—as a woman, you might well imagine?"

The director flipped the papers on her clipboard and gave Marita a frown of regret. "Mademoiselle Lesney, your case is marked for special handling and your trial to be expedited. The regulations permit no special treatment for you. You are to be isolated from the others as well as from the outside, meaning family would do you no good, and you are not allowed reading or writing materials of any kind. As for your menstrual period, you must do your best with things as they are."

"But madame, if it were you—"

The woman's patience abruptly reached an end. "Mademoiselle, given these charges, I would be pleased they hadn't shot me on the spot and saved the expense of incarceration, no matter how short." She gave all three a stern look. "You French must learn to be more grateful for all the Reich provides." The guards nodded in agreement. Marita flinched, but thought she saw some look of understanding before the prison director offered her closing advice to the inmates: "Follow the rules, keep yourself clean, and respect the guards. Do that, and your stay here will pass without undue pain or suffering." She handed a clipboard with cell assignments to the nearest guard and marched off.

Marita's spirits reached rock-bottom as she entered her cell. She dropped to the edge of the bed. Having eaten nothing but bread in thirty-six hours, she felt a knot in her stomach and the clogs were already aggravating her sore feet. Now she faced an uncertain future in a filthy box barely as wide as she was tall. Less than three meters deep, its walls were scarred with graffiti, heart-rending messages from previous occupants.

She bent forward to run a finger over the cracked and stained surface, sensing the anguish of past prisoners. At eye level she read: *My beloved babies, forever in my heart.* On the wall beside the cot: *Dearest Jacques, I never meant to leave you.* Under a carefully sketched set of angel wings: *Papa and Maman, I shall greet you in Heaven with open arms.* Marita lay back, cradling her head in her hands, and stared up at the cell door. In finely-worked calligraphy, scratched painstakingly into the flaking brown paint, she read a heartfelt *Fuck off, mein Führer!*

On the water-stained ceiling a fan light wobbled. The metal bedframe supported three wooden planks, a straw *paillasse*, and two coarse blankets. She found little else to hold her attention. With nothing to read or write, there would be no use for the stool and small table. She rolled to her side on the straw mattress, hands to her face, willing the tears to stop, but it had all been too much. Now totally alone, she quietly sobbed herself to sleep.

CHAPTER EIGHT

Ermenonville, Occupied France
29 August 1941

Deep in the night a car came for Ryan. Rolf's driver picked him up on a pre-arranged street corner several blocks from his Left Bank hotel. With spies and snitches everywhere a meeting in the city was simply too problematic. Each policing department of the Occupation was jealous and suspicious of the others, and foreign "guests" drew close scrutiny from the many intelligence authorities. Within hours of hotel registration, the particulars of any identity—false or real—became a new file card with the secret police and the metropolitan gendarmerie. Someone, somewhere, was already questioning what business had brought the French educator Raoul Diderot, his latest and now-abandoned alias, to the occupied city.

Edmond Brédeaux was a terse but polite young driver in a felt cap and wire-framed eyeglasses. His eyes lifted repeatedly to the rearview mirror, making clear his primary concern was reaching their destination without a tail. Twice they detoured onto narrow country roads when hooded headlamps suggested another vehicle might be on their trail.

Edmond apologized to Ryan for losing track of the arrest vehicle after the raid on the club. Though the man's regret appeared genuine enough, Ryan still felt bitter. He kept to himself, his thoughts on Marita's ordeal.

The Château d'Ermenonville lay on the outskirts of a small village near Roissy. The Renault rumbled across a moat and entered an ornate double-gated portal. Beyond the elaborate wrought-iron loomed a U-shaped classical structure of pale stone. The graveled courtyard separated the two wings, and a figure in a dark trench coat and wide-brimmed fedora closed the gate discretely behind them. They parked behind a dark Citroën. Rolf and Argent already waited beneath the lamps flanking the main portico. Even in the dull light Ryan saw worried faces and knew at once that the hours of desperate searching since Marita's abduction had been unproductive.

As expected, all talk centered on Marita. Despite Rolf's many contacts throughout the city, her whereabouts remained unknown. Rolf revealed to Ryan his role as inebriated Wehrmacht colonel in helping save Marita's club from the extortionist Serge Bergieux. Von Haldheim had obviously fallen for her charms and seemed genuinely concerned for her. But beyond that there lay a practical side to his involvement—Rolf had been the Abwehr conduit for the intelligence Marita so diligently gathered. With her arrest his entire operation was now at risk.

Argent remained adamant: "It has to be Rue des Saussaies. It's the main Gestapo headquarters, and they always take them there first for interrogation—and worse. The whole city knows it."

Ryan toyed with his pipe. He'd lost all interest in smoking. "But I have heard of other stations around the city, Rue Lauriston being one. That complicates matters." He turned to Rolf. "Don't we have a trustworthy source at Rue des Saussaies?"

Rolf wrinkled his brow and shook his head. "It's Dannecker's headquarters for rounding up Jews, but from what I hear our girl may already be in La Santé or Cherche-Midi. They often send them to the prisons for interrogation, farther from prying eyes." He crushed out a just-lit Gitanes. "Or she may already be in Berlin at Gestapa." Rolf patted Ryan's hand. "Don't worry. Our people in the capital are looking into that possibility."

"Planting that wireless smacks of desperation. Any real proof of what she's been up to—what you three have been up to—and they wouldn't need such a phony measure. There's something very suspicious about the whole matter." Now Ryan began pacing again.

Rolf tamped a fresh cigarette on the cover of his silver case. "Knowing the nature of her purported crime would help immensely. It would tell us just who put them on to her. On to us, actually." He fumbled with his cigarette holder. Ryan recognized the nerves. "God help us all if she spills what she knows."

Argent was adamant: "She'll never talk." He strode over to the tall windows.

"It's true Marita will fight—to the end if she must," Ryan conceded. "But God willing, that won't become necessary. I know her and she's tough. She was naked when those bastards toyed with her, but she stood proud and never flinched."

Argent looked down, his fists now clenched, his knuckles bloodless. "I swear I'll tear them limb from limb, those gutless sons-of-whores!" He turned on Ryan. "Why the hell didn't you come out of your damned closet and drop those pricks? You had a weapon! You and Marita could have used the balcony exit to get away!"

Ryan met his damning glare. "You weren't there." He felt his own guilt, still seeking excuses for his failure to act despite the odds. "I might have plugged them both, but she would have met the cross-fire and two more of the assholes were already coming up those damned stairs." He rubbed his jaw, forcing his voice to soften. "She shook her head, she signaled me to stay hidden. She thought she could talk her way out of it and protect me, as well."

Rolf stepped in. "Let's forget all rancor and recriminations, *meine Herren*. Done is done, and now only decisive action will spare her. We all know what these Gestapo types are capable of." Ryan and Argent nodded in surrender to his logic. "Look, I've strong connections. I work with someone who can ferret out the true reason for her arrest, but regrettably that man's in Berlin. It may take him a day or two, so we all must be patient, at least for now."

Argent paced before the windows, speaking to himself as much as to the others. "She may not have 'a day or two.' For all we know she may already be dead."

Rolf joined him. "Let's agree our hands are tied for the moment and work with it as best we can." He put an arm over the younger man's shoulder and gave a reassuring squeeze. "Look, Argent, I know your feelings for her, and waiting for an answer will be hard, but we've simply no choice. If we surrender to blame—to guilt and sorrow—we lose focus. There's too much at stake here."

Rolf guided him back to the table. "As for us, as selfish as it sounds, we can only hope she holds out no matter what they throw at her. Despite confidence in her strength, she is human. Should she reveal everything, they'll be coming for both of us, Argent."

The young officer gave a look of disgust and flopped into an easy chair, his shoulders slumping. Silent minutes passed before they renewed the fruitless discussion, only to exhaust another hour with "what-ifs" before all three lapsed again into silence. They finally agreed that Argent would arrange day-and-night watches on the prisons and on Gestapo headquarters and auxiliary stations. Ryan would contact Edward to explore any possible consular paths to determining her whereabouts, and Rolf would make further inquiries with his people in Berlin.

Ryan looked out over the vast lawn behind the Château d'Ermenonville. Two rows of ancient trees stretched from the eighteenth-century castle to a distant pond, a scene from an old painting. A walking path in deep shade bordered the green expanse. No one strolled at this early hour. Ryan's fellow conspirators remained inside but he saw no point in further discussion on how best to rescue Marita. He ignored the brilliant fall foliage contrasting so starkly with the verdant lawn and the duckweed glowing greenish-yellow in the sluggish moat below. Beauty lay far from his mind after the raw ugliness of the Gestapo raid he'd witnessed from the spyhole.

His head throbbed mercilessly from the long hours of futile discussion. He found no relief in the fresh air of the terrace as he paced past stone balusters and potted evergreens. On the far horizon Paris caught the first rays of the sun, but Ryan focused inward, determined to solve Marita's desperate situation. She had been there for him over the years, a loving reminder of the stability and commitment he wasn't ready to face. Now she was gone, and he felt deep anger and even deeper responsibility.

His mind wouldn't release the searing images of her shameful mistreatment. How high she'd held her head while he hunkered down in that damned closet. He leaned his brow against the cool limestone of the wall, mentally forcing aside the worry, the fears for her safety, clearing his mind for action. Any action. And still he had no plan.

Back in the salon he grabbed his overcoat and hat. Argent still sulked in the leather chair. He gave only a desultory wave to acknowledge the American's departure. Ryan, his mood grim, quietly thanked Rolf for his hospitality and aid. Their reunion had been soured by the demands of the moment. In any other circumstance Ryan might have shared old times, but Marita's arrest was too pressing. This was also not the time to bring up Rolf's overture to Ed and the question of how America might covertly deal with any disgruntled military leaders of the Reich. For now Ryan was simply grateful that someone working for German military intelligence was intent on releasing Marita from captivity.

Edmond waited in the courtyard beside the sedan, its rear door open. Ryan climbed in with a nod of thanks, but the driver hesitated as Argent, striding across the gravel, shouted for their attention. The young officer's voice was serious but somewhat friendlier. "A moment in private, Herr Lemmon?"

"Of course. Ryan gestured to the empty seat beside him. "Shall we talk on the way into town, or would stretching our legs be in order?"

"A stroll suits me better," he said. "You may have noticed I'm having a difficult time controlling my anger and frustration. Some exercise might do me good."

Ryan joined the young German outside the iron gates. The porter was nowhere in sight. "So what's left to discuss?" Ryan asked. The throbbing in his temples plagued him and he had no interest in a lengthy rehash. "It seems we can do nothing substantive until we've news of her whereabouts."

"Look, Herr Lemmon—and please know that this is a difficult subject for me to bring up—we both have our reasons for mutual suspicion and frustration." They walked the shaded levee above the moat. "First, my apologies for the outburst upstairs. I know you did all you could for her, given your situation." Ryan accepted his offered hand in truce. "Rolf assures me you're a man of integrity, and he has already made clear to you my personal reasons for despising this regime. Marita's arrest and maltreatment is symptomatic of all I loathe in my own countrymen, so suffice to say we share the goal of putting an end to these horrors."

Ryan nodded but kept silent.

The younger man's eyes stayed on the château, obviously hesitant to say what was on his mind. "Herr Lemmon, you must realize just how important Marita has become to me." Avoiding Ryan's eyes, he continued. "You're her friend of many years, and she's always spoken highly of you, so I'm obliged to ask this now—is your interest more than that of an old friend?"

The question out, Argent's eyes shot to the American. Ryan caught the look of heartfelt distress. My God, he thought, he genuinely loves her, but what do I truly feel? Ryan suddenly sensed a deep personal loss. Marita had always been part of his European life, someone whose clear love for him had been too easy a gift, someone to bed but perhaps never adequately treasure, knowing she would always be there without a commitment. Now she was in mortal danger, and his complacency was rattled to its core.

He strode ahead without responding, lost in his own troubled thoughts before abruptly returning to the officer, his decision made. "Herr Argent, my friendship with Marita spans more than a decade and at one time it appeared something deeper might come of it. You should also know that I do indeed love her." Ryan cleared his throat, his emotions rising. "But over such distances and after so many missed opportunities—after a mellowing of our early romance, shall we say—it's clear to me that she's taken you into her heart. I won't stand in your way or interfere. Rest assured I'm not here for that—just to see her free again…and finally happy."

Argent sank to the stone-capped wall with a smile of relief and gratitude. Ryan felt only disquiet. Had he just surrendered any emotional claim to Marita, actually lost her forever? Perhaps years of procrastination had made that decision for him, driving her into the arms of this handsome German.

"For the moment," Ryan said, "let's set all this aside. Until she's free from these barbarians nothing else matters. For this to succeed, we'll need the best your Abwehr and my people have to offer. Any consideration of Marita's love and affection remains meaningless should we fail to rescue her, and soon."

Ryan suggested they meet for a drink later in the evening at a secure spot of Argent's choosing. Only by developing mutual trust could they work closely to gain Marita's freedom. But hardened by von Kredow's treachery, Ryan was not about to offer his confidence blindly, no matter who guaranteed the loyalty and motivation of another.

CHAPTER NINE

Saint-Nazaire, Occupied France
29 August 1941

The partisans gathered in the former shipping office at break of day. Scorch marks and soot all but obliterated the signage high on the front brick wall reading *G. Moulin et Cie, Maison d'Expédition*. The abandoned warehouse was a skeletal derelict in the otherwise intact port district of Saint-Nazaire. Several of the men wore soft-brimmed caps and worker's blues, everyday wear in this proletarian district. They fit right in with the stevedores, warehousemen, and streetwalkers at the bottom rung of the town's social ladder. The men passed around a battered pack of cigarettes. Maurice's wife Laura, absent due to her advanced pregnancy, had nonetheless sent along vacuum bottles of roasted-barley coffee. With Erika and Nicole heading for Bayonne, today's meeting to determine roles in the sabotage of the U-boat pens would be all male.

Looking past the grime on the window glass, René scanned the bank of warehouses crowding the port facilities. Early-morning haze still drifted in the streets below, and he spotted a few laborers heading toward the docks and basins. It was nearing seven a.m., and smokestacks already puffed white clouds into the still air as steam whistles drew laborers to their work stations. In the distance the broad Loire estuary opened to the Bay of Biscay, the shallow mudflats speckled with late-departing fishing trawlers heading out to sea. The saboteurs' target, the massive concrete bulwark of the *Kriegsmarine* submarine pens, lay dead center with the huge Bassin de Saint-Nazaire just beyond.

The Moulin warehouse reminded René of an arm raised in protest at the devastation below. In the first autumn of the Occupation the Germans had used this space as a supply depot until a suspicious fire gutted the facility. *Boche* quartermasters were left to face the oncoming winter with nothing but a framework of charred and twisted beams and ruined materiel. In the past year someone had salvaged the easily-accessible metal. Others had probed the scorched and abandoned crates for anything of black-market value. Now only cracked bricks, incinerated crates, and the occasional corrugated panel littered the concrete floor. The warehouse opposite had remained shuttered and abandoned for months after the arrest of its Jewish proprietor, and only an occasional curious rat explored the dingy street separating the two structures.

The office had somehow survived the arson, towering over the rubble and flanked by three partial walls. A metal staircase with several twisted and warped treads made access difficult and the office thus well-suited to their clandestine meeting. The saboteurs from Nantes had joined forces with the local partisans. Maurice spoke highly of the Saint-Nazaire leader, a man not yet known to René. They awaited his arrival any minute.

René still felt uneasy. The proposed plan to infiltrate the U-boat bunkers seemed sound. He had rushed his study of basic structural engineering under Maurice's tutelage to permit speaking intelligently when portraying a visiting naval officer. But the Nantes affair had left him doubting their preparation. The recent confrontation with von Kredow had raised numerous questions. Where had their security failed? How could they have avoided the trap? Others of Horst's ilk were surely out there, not lusting for personal vengeance, but equally determined to destroy anyone having a go at the Reich.

He thought of Erika and Leo, by now in Bayonne on the trail of those kidnapped children. He missed her. Years spent together fighting and fleeing had left him incomplete without his wife. And now also his son, thanks to Ryan's blessing. He massaged the shoulder still bruised and swollen from the dislocation. He ignored the pain of his battered ribs. He'd suffered far worse working the Rhine boats in his youth. The officer's cap he would wear during his charade would cover the healing scabs on his scalp.

He fought back memories of his late mother Jeanne as he listened to the small talk of the others. Never hesitant to make suggestions, she would have loved to help with the major strike they planned. Her greatest wish had been to witness the end of the Nazi tyranny and he would make her proud. Before emotion could overwhelm him, he returned his attention to the group. Erika and Leo would be safe on the farm, so time to concentrate on the task at hand.

A coded knock rattled the door and the local leader entered, a tall, slender man who carried himself like a confident street fighter. René approached him with caution, remembering the treachery of Nicole. Von Kredow and his machinations had made him extremely wary. The man introduced himself as Malraux, and René pegged him close to his own age, early thirties. Some would say his good looks were given character by the tweaked nose over a square-cut jaw. A boxer, perhaps. The prematurely salt-and-pepper hair was short on the sides, longer and slicked back on top. His lips were thin but his smile friendly.

René's appraisal stumbled over the faded scars on fore-head and temple. Those were clearly *Schmisse* so similar to his own, unmistakable marks of a German university dueler. A *Boche* should never trust another *Boche,* not in this war. He met Malraux's handshake with a fierce grip of his own. "*Sehr erfreut.* Always a surprise to find a countryman fighting on behalf of France. He squeezed even harder. "What are the odds, *mein Herr?*"

René spotted an unexpected twinkle in the man's eye. "*Guten Morgen, mein Herr,* the pleasure's all mine." His accent spoke of northern Germany, likely Prussia. The man pretended to massage his fingers to restore circulation after the vigorous handshake. "If you fight the *Boches* with equal strength we'll definitely come out the victors." Maurice alone laughed.

René turned to Maurice, the Nantes group leader. "You might have warned me I would meet a fellow citizen of the Reich."

"Sorry to disappoint, Rénard." René's *nom de guerre* still sounded strange to his ears. "Our friend and colleague here is anything but *Boche.*" He clapped the newcomer on the shoulder. "Despite all appearances, Malraux here is a Briton…on His Majesty's Secret Service."

Jean-Philippe's face immediately darkened. His close-ly-spaced eyes bored into the new-comer. "*Un sale anglais?*" He turned to his compatriots. "These filthy English cowards abandoned my father and brother at Dunkerque!" As hot-headed as ever, he spat on the plank floor and headed for the door. René had often heard the complaint that the "filthy English" turned their backs on the French soldiers during the disastrous rout of Allied Forces in 1940. Hitler's Wehrmacht almost wiped them out at the Channel, and only a valiant British effort managed to save many of the soldiers to fight another day. Most of the late-arriving French had literally missed the boats.

Maurice again intervened: "Hold up, Jean-Philippe, there's still more to Malraux here than meets the eye." He intercepted the angry partisan at the door. "We need this fellow's skills and guidance, and he can be trusted." The partisan resisted as Maurice took his arm to guide him back. "Just hear him out, then decide—you owe the group that much."

Jean-Philippe shook himself free and moved to the corner nearest the stairs. He slid to the floor, his back to the fire-scarred wall. "*D'accord*, messiurs—convince me."

Malraux addressed the group. "Before we begin, might I bum a smoke off of one of you gentlemen?" Henri shook a cigarette from the crumpled pack and René offered his lighter. Malraux inhaled, then released a cloud with a resounding cough. "Pretty strong stuff passing for tobacco these days, eh?" He cleared his throat again. "Now, where to start? You find before you a Londoner by birth but a German by heritage. My parents emigrated from Hannover in 1910 to establish an import-export enterprise in the capital of world commerce. In that spirit I grew up tri-lingual with a strong affinity for my heritage, for Germany. But only as it once was. I read law at university in Hannover, watched those megalomaniacs corrupt all that was good in German law, society and culture, all to found this brutish Reich. So when the call came from MI6, I was well-prepared for undercover work, so there you have me."

Malraux's story left René intrigued by its complexity. It sounded absurd enough to be true. His personal adventures as a *résistant* made as little sense in the crazed world of Nazi Europe, but such a cursory overview didn't satisfy all doubts. "Might I ask about those *Schmisse*? He pointed to the dueling scars. "Quite rare for a foreigner to fight a *Mensur*, wouldn't you say?" René himself had fought in Marburg on Ryan's behalf in the very duel that led to a decade of von Kredow treachery.

"Ah, my scars." Malraux ran a finger over the thin raised lines on his brow and cheek. "Self-inflicted, I'm obliged to admit, rite of passage to validate my status as a true son of the new German empire. A special assignment, and the chaps back home couldn't believe I was up for it. Few fellow Englishmen would ruin an otherwise acceptable complexion by adding the scars, but these did establish credibility with the *Boches*."

His expression went grim as he turned to Jean-Philippe. "But to you, sir, I offer my sincere regrets for family still in captivity. I, too, was at Dunkerque last year. Let me assure you, we did our very best to get them all out, both English and French. Time was simply too short and vessels too scarce to rescue everyone."

Jean-Philippe glared at him from his spot against the wall, obviously unappeased. "And yet, most of you English made it out just fine, right? Barely got your feet wet, right?" He drew arabesques with the snout of his pistol in the sooty grime on the floor.

René's interest was aroused. "You were there, Malraux, Dunkerque? At the end? Which unit?"

Malraux looked sheepish and responded in English: "Ah, a sticky wicket, that." Maurice nodded his agreement, obviously already aware of where the story headed. "I was with the 18th Division, X Corps."

All eyes shot to the newcomer. The 18th was a *Boche* division. Maurice grabbed the pistol from Jean-Philippe's grip, his other hand holding the struggling young man as he tried to rise with fire in his eyes. The delay allowed René to speak. "You fought for the Germans? For the enemy?" His voice a growl. "I believe you owe us more of an explanation."

"Not *for* them—just working *amongst* the Huns on London's orders." Again came that look of subtle amusement, of playing with matches without intending to start an actual fire. "That was my last exciting assignment, to return to the fatherland as a newly-reborn German reclaiming my Teutonic heritage. Volunteer early, swear allegiance to the glorious Führer, then infiltrate the officer ranks any way possible." He clicked his heels together with an exaggerated Hitler salute. "Thus this stunning—albeit self-inflicted— scarring." Again his finger wandered down his cheek. "So I was there, all right. Intelligence officer on the general staff of Hansen's X Corps, doing my best to mess with the *Boche* advance. Ironic, isn't it?"

Henri now spoke up, no longer able to hold his peace. "So you slaughtered our men as you drove us into the sea, all in the name of His Majesty's Secret Service?" His eyes glowed with hatred.

"Actually, *mes amis*, I did my best to misdirect communications, to slow things down on the *Boche* end. Everyone knew the Allied push on the continent was already lost, and the Wehrmacht commanders were impatient for Paris. So once we turned south, my contact gave me a new cover, I pinched a motorbike and headed for Brittany, and here I am."

A long hour and much interrogation later, the younger men from Nantes finally settled down, conceding that their friends in the local cell had always spoken well of the leader, just never mentioned his colorful past. Maurice pointed out that experienced Malraux had spurred partisan recruitment in Brest, as well. And in the final analysis, Malraux sold himself well. René, still a bit dubious, finally felt enough at ease to help in merging the two groups for the coming challenge.

CHAPTER TEN

Bayonne, Occupied France
29 August 1941

The women's false identity papers had easily passed scrutiny from French railroad officials and German controls. The inspectors had taken pity on the pale young woman, asking few questions of her before moving on to the mother and boy beside her. Nicole had claimed a stomach upset to explain her unease. In truth, her bullet wound showed signs of rising infection. Once the inspectors moved on, Erika wanted a closer look. In the lavatory at the rear of the coach she applied sulfa powder and a fresh plaster. Neither could miss the stench of septic flesh.

Luck remained with them at the Bayonne station. The SS official waved them forward. Leo remained quiet as his mother handed over the documents, answering questions for all three with quiet reserve. The pale young woman was a cousin suffering an unsettled pregnancy. They were heading south to stay with relatives near St. Jean de Luz. Yes, those were the family names and the location of their village. No, there was no phone for direct contact. Yes, she had documentation of employment as a nurse. She handed over the employee card for a Tours hospital.

The dour official never asked to see inside their two small suitcases, a waste of time anyway. Nothing there but clothing, undergarments and a few toiletries. Nevertheless, a small loaded pistol lay hidden beneath a false bottom in each bag. René had been proud of that handiwork.

Satisfied at last, the young SS officer waved them through the gate and the long line moved silently forward. No one dared show either impatience or relief. The three then passed an SS guard shouldering a carbine and two men in long overcoats. Clearly Gestapo. Erika and Nicole stared straight ahead while Leo returned their glares with a grin.

Relying on Leo's memory to guide them, they walked south toward the bridge spanning the Adour. Bayonne glowed like a rose-colored jewel under a setting sun dissolving in the fogbank to the west. Erika spoke at last. "Leo, you drive me crazy. For a minute I thought you might stick your tongue out at those policemen!"

"I know better, *Maman*. They just always look so serious. Don't they ever laugh and joke around with their kids?"

"Their children are undoubtedly back in Germany. Perhaps they miss them."

"Well, it wouldn't hurt to smile once in a while." He was walking backward now and looked up at the troubled face of Nicole. "We're going to find Sophie now!"

Nicole smiled. "Yes, Leo, let's not waste another minute! Hurry, lead the way!"

Erika was pleased to see renewed signs of happiness in Nicole, and was almost equally anxious for the coming reunion. In the troubled woman she sensed a cracked glass on the verge of shattering. Poor Nicole had lost the rest of her family to Horst's sadism, and now she bore guilt for having betrayed trusting partisans to save her daughter. Since Horst had taken the toddler for the sole purpose of tracking and destroying her own loved ones, Erika also felt responsible for her personal role in the horror. Sophie's safety might restore Nicole's mental state and even help with her own peace of mind. Such a relief to know the man was finally dead and gone.

Halfway across the bridge Erika came to a halt. "Here, Leo." She took a fold of waxed paper from her basket, last evidence of the sandwiches from the long train ride. "Feed the seagulls and stay clear of bird droppings!" Laughing, he shrugged his shoulders and raised his eyebrows. "If you say so, *Maman*." He raced to the railing and scattered the crumbs into the river below. Several birds dove for the water, others raising a raucous chorus around him and demanding more.

Nicole turned on Erika, her words edged with anger: "What are you doing? We've no time to feed birds!"

"There's good reason." She touched Nicole's arm in reassurance. "The bridge is clear for the moment. Open your suitcase and move your pistol to your coat pocket. Mine comes next. No telling what we'll face with that old bitch Leo described. The nursemaid sounds easy-going enough to handle." Nicole favored her injured side as she burrowed deep in the suitcase. Erika stooped to help.

Leo was back. "Look!" he pointed to the shoulders of his jacket, "no bird poop!" He eyed his mother and Nicole suspiciously. "Are we going to shoot people again, *Maman*?"

Erika rolled her eyes. "Let's hope not, *mon petit*, but no more surprises, right?"

Leo jutted out his chin and scissored his jaws back and forth. "Remember, I'm always ready to bite!"

"Then let's get to it. Which direction at the end of the bridge?"

Leo pointed right and excitedly took the lead. After a false turn or two he shouted excitedly when he recognized the correct street. Huge bronze wall lamps under cloth shielding barely defined a massive entry of oak and iron with leaded-glass sidelights. The stone lions guarding the stoop were as impressive as Leo had described. An amber glow escaped the heavy drapes of a room to the right of the portico, most likely the flat of the concierge. Clearly old wealth resided here.

The new arrivals huddled in the deepening shadows across the street from the townhouse. Nicole scanned the façade and wondered whether von Kredow had set a watchman, whether the matron and the nursemaid alone were caretakers for the children on the second floor. For Sophie. The mothers had agreed that Leo shouldn't witness further violence. He'd endured enough in that horrid warehouse. Despite the boy's incredible resilience, it would do him no good to see more bloodshed.

Nicole descended a stairwell while Erika and Leo remained hidden above at street-level. She changed into a nurse's smock that had belonged to Dr. Ballineux's deceased wife. Nicole remembered the melancholy look in the physician's eyes as he handed her the garment. She thought of the death of her husband Antonio, but just as quickly pushed those memories aside. The overcoat would remain unbuttoned, revealing the nurse's guise. She pinned up her hair in an institutional style and took her pistol off safety. Comforting.

Erika and Leo crouched at the top step, peering through the wrought-iron railing, alert for passers-by. Nicole whispered up to them: "How do I look?"

"Suitably severe." Erika's voice low and tense.

"Pretty, but quite strict, I think." Leo waved her up the steps.

Erika raised a hand in warning. Nicole saw the bicyclist rattle by, hunched forward as he managed the tricky cobbles with a baguette on his bike rack. Another rider approached from the opposite direction. The men exchanged a quiet "*bonsoir*" in passing. Once the clatter had faded, Erika signaled all clear.

Nicole lost no time in racing across the street and up to the front entrance, her heels clicking on the stones. She buzzed three times in rapid succession, her other hand cradling the pocketed pistol. No response. She tried again, this time depressing the button to maintain a constant trill beyond the door. A latch clicked, hinges squeaked, and eyes appeared behind the grate of a small door in the massive portal. "What is it? What do you want?" The concierge, a woman, growled her displeasure with the disturbance.

"I'm here to help with the children." Authority in Nicole's voice, entitlement.

"Not here anymore—they've all left." The barred window started to close.

Nicole trembled in frustration, her nails digging into her palm, the other hand steadied by the pistol. "Listen, madame, I have my orders, and you surely know the people I work for. Orders are orders. Let me in, and now, or things will get ugly." She tasted blood on her lower lip where she had bitten it. She forced her jaw to relax, shook loose her clenched hand.

The woman's face disappeared and Nicole heard the lock turning. The heavy door groaned and she forced her way in past the concierge, an older woman in a flowered housecoat who began to protest vehemently. The foyer was unheated but elegant, its hardwood flooring gleaming. Light from the open door to the caretaker's flat showed tiles cracked with age, matching the older woman's face now twisted in anger. "How dare you? I said they're all gone!"

Nicole was in no mood. "Just listen, madame—you will fetch the keys to the upstairs rooms, understood?"

"But—"

"No buts—" She grabbed the woman's elbow and steered her into the flat. "The keys!" The concierge offered no resistance. An older-style telephone with its upright receiver sat atop a demi-lune table just inside the entry. A wall rack above it displayed numbered hooks. Nicole shouldered her captive aside and gathered all the keys. "Get back to your supper," she peered into the cooking alcove, "your *cassoulet* is burning." Distracted by the smoke escaping the oven door, the woman turned to rescue her meal. Nicole yanked the phone cord from the wall and out in the foyer assured herself the front door remained unlocked. From an upstairs window she would signal Erika and Leo to join her.

The grind of the old cage lift might betray her arrival so instead she opted for the stairs. Her pistol hand braced her injured side as she climbed. Leo had said the children were in a flat off the first landing. She slowed her pace, her back to the wall, each foot carefully placed. Reaching the final step she checked for movement in the hall. At the end of the dark corridor a door stood ajar, a faint bluish light defining its frame. With pistol clutched in both hands, Nicole edged closer, then entered and cautiously headed toward the source of the light.

Her heart sank. The concierge had not lied. The children were missing, her Sophie gone. There would be no vindication for having betrayed all who had trusted her, no redemption for having become everything she despised in a world corrupted by hatred and violence. She moved slowly across the heavy carpet, her eyes drawn to some brighter object draped on the dark sofa, ignoring the overturned game boards and the children's playthings strewn across the floor.

Watching for Nicole's signal coming from an upper window, Erika and Leo saw instead a sudden flash of light followed by a muffled pop. No other noise could mimic a sound they knew too well. With Leo on one hand and her weapon in the other, Erika was in motion. Limited only by his stride, she reached the front door just as it opened to reveal the fleeing concierge. Bundled in a ragged fur coat, the woman drew back and swung her handbag. Erika wrenched it by the strap, binding her attacker's wrist. "Let me go," the woman screamed, "I'm late!"

"You're going nowhere." Erika dragged her back into the vestibule by the scruff of the coat. The door to the concierge flat was open. The smell of burned food pervaded the foyer.

Leo, grimacing, muttered under his breath: "It stinks in here."

With every nerve was on edge, Erika was in no mood for delays. "The nurse who arrived a few minutes ago—where is she?" She shook the concierge so hard her poorly fitted dentures slipped loose.

"I told her they were gone but she went up anyway." The woman's words slurred clumsily, her eyes glued to the pistol in Erika's fist. "I can't be responsible, you know. I must go now, I've an appointment." She readjusted the false teeth.

"Inside!" Erika was losing patience. "I'll be the one to decide who's responsible around here." Leo nervously eyed the lift and stairs, Erika sharing his worry. "Get in there!" She shoved the woman ahead of her, freeing the torn phone cord from the receiver. She ordered the woman to the wooden chair by the stove and quickly bound her hands and feet.

"I'll scream!"

"Be my guest," Erika stuffed a potholder into the woman's mouth, securing the gag with apron ties. "Leo, keep an eye on this woman while I go find Madame Nicole."

"But I can help—"

"Leo, you will stay down here and keep an eye out! If a vehicle comes, if someone rings—anything unusual outside at all—call for the lift and I'll hear the bell upstairs, d'accord?" Leo nodded meekly.

She took the steps two at a time while checking the safety on her pistol. On the landing she spotted the open door leading through to the main room of the suite. She approached stealthily, senses alert, vaguely aware of a distant police siren and a clock ticking somewhere within the apartment. She eased into the grand salon. Dim light from an outside streetlamp silhouetted a table and wooden chairs centered on the carpet. A sofa backed to the high windows, the spot where Nicole should have signaled with a match. Not a gunshot.

Barely discernable against the dark fabric of the divan, the young mother lay slumped, unmoving. Erika rushed forward, ignoring the toys at her feet, unable to look away yet wishing she could. Nicole's hair was ratted and damp, the right temple glistening purple in the pale light. A pistol lay on the cushions.

Erika set aside her own weapon and fought back the tears. She moved the body upright and closed the sightless eyes. Just moments before, so much tormented beauty, and now only this raw ugliness, the strings of Horst's "Marionette" cut by her own hand.

Tears now raced unchecked down her cheeks. *Pull yourself together, dammit!* She spotted a wad of cloth clenched in Nicole's left hand and released the fabric from the dead woman's fingers. She held it toward the window. A bullet had pierced the tiny dress of a toddler. Unlike the smears on the couch and the splatter on the window panes, this blood was dark and fully dry.

Erika removed the pins and arranged the damp hair to cover the wound at the temple. The young mother deserved a last shred of human dignity. She wiped her fingers on the couch and took Nicole's pistol and false identity papers. She could only guess the authorities' reaction when they found this scene, what story the concierge would tell.

Even from the grave, Horst continued to torment with new suffering, new sorrow. What of the other children—had Horst manipulated their parents just as he corrupted poor Nicole's mind? Were they also his latest and youngest victims? The timing had her baffled. Had he committed this atrocity himself days earlier, when he picked up Leo on his way to Nantes? Or had he left orders for associates to carry out the monstrous act? Question upon question. She closed the door behind her as she left the flat, ready to demand answers.

Leo waited expectantly on the bottom step. "Where's Sophie, *Maman*? Where's Madame Nicole?" He was already on his feet and rushing up to meet her.

Erika raised her hand to stop his progress. "No, Leo, you stay there. I'm coming down." With each step she gathered her thoughts, resolving how best to explain Horst's final vengeance. Her son's baffled look meant no putting off the inevitable. Leo would pester and pester until he knew the truth. "They're gone, Leo. They're—"

"What do you mean 'gone'?" Leo moved to get past her. "I know this is the right place! Where else could they go?"

Erika pulled him into her arms. "The children have all left, and poor Madame Nicole is dead, Leo. There's nothing we can do."

"But how?" his voice plaintive, "how could she be dead, *Maman*?"

How to explain suicide to a seven-year-old when she herself reeled at the thought? "You remember what I told you about how sad she was? Sophie was all she had left, all she lived for. She found Sophie was gone, and it was simply too much for her. She...she shot herself." Leo looked toward the landing as if Nicole and Sophie might somehow still appear. What was going through his young mind, having already witnessed so much violence and tragedy? She held him at arm's length, forced him to look in her eyes as he began to cry. "We must both be strong, Leo."

"Did I do it, *Maman*, did I make her do it? I told her about Sophie, and she was so excited, and now Sophie's not here and Madame Nicole..." His voice drowned in sobs of self-blame.

"Of course not, Leo—you mustn't ever think such a thing! Sadness is a terrible sickness. She was already sick with it when we met her, and now she thought she had nothing more to live for."

"Sophie's dead, too? And Pierre and Jacqueline and Jakob? Are all my friends dead, *Maman*?" He buried his face in her coat.

Erika felt the burden of the dead woman on the sofa above, and the tiny dress, once pink, now caked in red. And this immense challenge for her young son, who had already witnessed so much suffering and violence. A convenient but misleading truth seemed the best answer for now: "I don't know where the others are, Leo, but they're not upstairs and I intend to find out what's happened. Come on, let's go see the concierge."

"*Maman?*"

"Yes?"

"I want to say good-bye to Madame Nicole." He started up the stairs.

"No, baby, no!" She grabbed him, fearing he might make a run for it. "It isn't something for you...for anyone to see. It's simply too sad, and we've already had enough sorrow, haven't we?" She guided him down, an arm around his shoulders. "Come on, I'll ask the concierge about the kids, right? She must know." At the front door she turned the lock. This was no time for unexpected visitors.

The woman glared from her chair under muffled grunts of protest. Erika wouldn't have Leo witness the interrogation in case it revealed some further horror. "Leo, I need you to go back in the bedroom and watch the street from the window. Anyone approaches, let me know right away. Someone may have heard the gunshot and called the police. Meanwhile, I'll learn what I can about your friends."

She waited for him to disappear behind the heavy window drapes before closing the door to the bedroom. "Listen, madame—I will remove the gag, but only if you truthfully answer my questions. I'm not going to hurt you, is that clear?" Accepting her nod of acquiescence, Erika set aside the saliva-soaked pot holder and freed her hands. The concierge seated her teeth properly and rubbed her jaw, then glared as Erika posed her first question. "Listen, madame—why were you running?"

The woman's voice was low, calculating, looking for advantage as she massaged her wrists. "I heard the shot... upstairs...that young nurse?"

"She's dead—took her own life." The woman's eyes widened, but she said nothing. "Is anyone else in this building?"

She shook her head. "They all left."

"When?"

"Days ago. In a big hurry."

"Tell me what you saw." Erika's eyes narrowed. "Exactly."

"I saw nothing. I keep my door shut and follow orders."

"You see everything, madame. A good concierge knows all that happens in her house, and you are a good concierge, aren't you?"

Her chin rose: "One of the best."

"Tell me everything or you'll tell it to the police later, understood?" A nod. "So speak—"

"They came a few nights ago—"

"Specifics now, don't waste my time! Who came?"

"The tall Gestapo, the one called *Le Masque*."

Erika's time to nod. "Alone? Was he alone?"

"Two others, and that ridiculous Madame de Brassis." She spit the name with such venom her dentures slipped again.

"This Madame de Brassis, you don't like her?"

"A *Boche* and a bitch, that's all I'll say. Full of herself. Married into old family and thinks that makes her a countess, gives her the right to lord it over us all." Her hand shot to her mouth to reposition her teeth. "And now with Monsieur de Brassis dead and buried, she sleeps with the Gestapo to keep herself in food and fine clothes. This building was his, you know, from before, from his first marriage.

That wife, now she was an angel. Treated me with respect until this one came into the picture."

Erika moved her along. "Tell me exactly what happened when the Gestapo came."

"They locked me in here with my cat." Her eyes shot to a shelf above the stove. Erika hadn't noticed the two golden eyes observing them, and the sleek black creature began to rumble loudly. "But I listened at the door anyway. It *is* my house, you know, my business what happens here."

"Of course. And heard what?"

"*Le Masque* and another agent took away your boy there." She gestured to Leo, who now stood at the threshold, eavesdropping, ostensibly watching the cat groom itself. "And the other agent took the youngest boy of the group."

"Leo, take the cat back in there with you and close the door. And keep your eyes and ears on the street, not on my discussion with this woman, is that clear?"

"Yes, *Maman*." No grin despite the animal. It told her just how much the suicide and missing children disturbed him. He eased the long-bodied cat down from the shelf. It melted onto his shoulder and its purr grew louder with the attention.

The door again shut behind him, Erika returned to the interrogation, her voice lowered. "And the other children?"

"My ankles?" The woman gave what passed for a smile. "They're very stiff and uncomfortable, and I do have a touch of arthritis."

"Tell me the rest, then you go free, so hurry it up. What of the others?"

"Three remained with their governess. They took them away in the bitch's grand limousine." She opened and closed her fists, stretching her fingers. "That's all I know."

"And that was the last time anyone went up there?" Erika's eyes shot to the ceiling, shuddering as she remembered what she'd just seen, picturing the beautiful woman so alive with hope and anticipation less than an hour before.

The concierge hesitated, thinking or maneuvering, Erika wasn't sure. "A man came back the next day, alone. Had keys, went upstairs briefly, then left again." She stomped her bound feet on the floor, ostensibly restoring circulation. "That was it."

"The nanny, she lived upstairs full-time?"

"She did."

"Her name?"

"Haven't a clue." Hands planted firmly at her knees, stockings slumped to the cord binding her ankles. "Now, what about my legs?"

"Soon enough, but that doesn't add up—a woman living full-time in your building, and you never learned her name? She had to come and go for groceries and ration coupons and the like, yet you never inquired, never met her in the hall to chat?"

"No, never. I keep to myself."

Erika stood up. "In that case, we shall also leave you to yourself." She took one corner of the saliva-soaked gag, ready to return it to the concierge's mouth. "You and your cat, entirely to yourself, just as you prefer. The house is now deserted but for a dead woman upstairs. Your Gestapo friends appear done with you. How long before someone drops by? Days? Weeks, perhaps?" Erika watched the woman maneuver the dentures with her tongue, her eyes fixed on the cat bowl beside the stove. "Oh, don't worry about your cat. I'm sure it will find something to eat around here once she's hungry enough. Turn-about is only fair play, you know. In Paris they had to eat their pets, what with food being so scarce under our *Boche* friends."

The woman's hands began to tremble. "Agnès. Her name was Agnès, she was my friend, alone…like me." The woman's chin dropped to her chest.

"You said *'was'* a friend."

"Is. *Is* a friend."

"So you went upstairs after they left."

"No. What happened up there was none of my business."

Erika lifted the woman's chin to look directly in her eyes. "You saw it, didn't you? That little dress with the bullet hole?"

The woman's shoulders began to shake and Erika took pity at last. She dropped the gag back on the sideboard. "Fine, all we need to know is where they went and we'll be out of your hair."

"Don't you understand? Are you totally blind?" The woman's eyes glistened. "They're all gone, Agnès too. Who cares where they took them? They're gone, all dead, as I told that young nurse before she barged upstairs anyway!"

"Let me share something with you, madame. I knew *Le Masque*, the one with the scars responsible for all this." Erika's broad gesture encompassed the entire building. "Nothing was ever as it seemed with him, every move devious, always some hidden motive. He lived for manipulation and cruelty. Give me some proof that all those children are truly gone and I'll get out of your hair."

"What would you have me do? How should I know where they took them?"

"Your beloved Madame de Brassis. She didn't live here anymore?"

"No. Only before they brought the children. She despises kids, thinks them worse than cats, messy and unmanageable. When he brought the children here she moved out."

"Where to?"

"How would I know where the harpy lives?" She kneaded her hands, clearly working out a new falsehood.

"Surely your friend knew. This Agnès had to have a way to reach her boss."

The woman fell silent, unconsciously shifting her jaw. At last she spoke again, now with resolve, her decision made: "Agnès spoke of a fine house directly on the coast, between here and Biarritz. A summer house on the strand, far too good for that woman."

Erika digested this information, crafting a plan. "You can find this place, this 'summer house?'"

She nodded. "Agnès reported there weekly, bringing the mail. "She described it to me well enough. But I'll need money. Who knows if she'll let me stay on, now that all this has happened."

"I can pay. We leave now, all three of us."

"But my cat—"

"Get us to that summer house and you're free to return." Erika loosened the phone cord. The woman massaged her ankles, moving stiffly. Erika helped her stand. "Now, madame, tell me your name."

The man in motorcycle leathers settled back in the armchair. He'd been stuck for almost twenty-four hours in that apartment, whittling down his supply of stale food, drinking ersatz coffee boiled on the hotplate, chasing its bitterness with brandy. He supported the binoculars with one hand, his elbow braced on the worn velvet of the chair as he observed the mansion across the street from the unlit room.

His vigil had paid off with the appearance of the first young woman. He'd seen the flash of the pistol at the upper window, and the slender blonde and the boy disappearing behind the huge front door. There was no sign of the two men he had also expected to see, one taller, the other a bear of a man with a limp. He'd briefly seen the blonde at the windows, wiping her eyes, and knew she would have found the bloodied dress of the little girl. Minutes later, the young boy appeared briefly in front of the drapes, watching the street. And that was it. Eventually they would all have to leave, and his instructions were clear. It would be good to be on the road at last, looking forward to a real dinner and the rich payback for all their troubles.

CHAPTER ELEVEN

Bayonne and Biarritz, Occupied France
29 August 1941

Just shy of the train station they spotted an occupied taxi stand. The driver was a stubby, poorly-shaven man with his cap pulled low. He curtly acknowledged his availability as he stoked the fire. Leo thought the *gazogène* engine a swell machine. The driver became friendly enough when *Maman* paid him in advance for the ride south.

Leo wished he could sit at the window rather than wedged between his mother and the concierge, this Madame Trouget with the frightening loose teeth. He tried to keep some distance as he thought about Sophie. He was worried. *Maman* looked away at any mention of the children, and spoke only to his reflection in the dark window. Perhaps they wouldn't be finding his friends soon.

Other than a few lamps burning behind private drapes, the city slept. Businesses were already shuttered for the night and traffic consisted mostly of *Boche* military trucks. On the outskirts of the city the roads narrowed and the woods encroached. Once he thought he saw a deer bound into the foliage beside the roadway, and later a badger disappeared into a ditch at their noisy approach. But then the taxi neared the coast and the fog thickened, making it hard to spot anything.

Other vehicles became rare. A fast-moving police car warbled toward town with red light flashing. They came up on a military transport, glowing cigarette tips flitting about under the canvas cover. Soon a motorcycle overtook them. The cyclist peered into the rear of their cab before accelerating on.

Leo remembered huddling in a sidecar, encased in a wool blanket and tucked between his mother's legs. Herr Lemmon was with them, goggles masking his eyes as he guided the motorbike into the onrushing night. Then the image faded, and once again that scariest of thoughts returned to haunt him. *Maman* now carried two pistols—he had seen her quietly check them back at the city house. He forced the disturbing idea from his mind, staring instead at the blurry roadway ahead, hoping to see another animal despite the fog. Moments later they passed the motorcyclist parked on the shoulder. The man looked their way and brought a match to a cigarette as they rattled by.

They had left poor dead Madame Nicole upstairs. "There's nothing more we can do for her," *Maman* had said, and he believed it was so. He had made certain the cat had fresh water and a few scraps from the burnt casserole, and promised the kitty it wouldn't be home alone for long. He hoped he was right. The cat wove around his ankles, trying to distract him from leaving, then meowed plaintively when the old woman shut the door in its face as they locked up the mansion.

Madame Nicole had finally seemed more cheerful on their way to find Sophie. Despite his mother's protests he felt personally responsible for what had happened, and a troublesome suspicion tugged at his mind. He tried to bury it in a field of other worries. Then there it was, back to nag him. He dared not ask, at least not out loud. But still it troubled his thoughts. He had seen the flash in the window and heard the pop of the gun, but why would she shoot herself simply because Sophie wasn't home? Maybe she shot at someone else. And then *Maman* came down without her and had both pistols in her pocket.

Did *Maman* kill Madame Nicole?

There, out in the open, shoving other thoughts aside. She might have. He remembered how angry she was with Nicole at the warehouse when his Gestapo father and those secret policemen tried to kill them all. She did carry that blackjack hidden in her clothes. He knew *Maman* always did what she must to protect him, so maybe Madame Nicole had been a danger to them both, so she had to die.

But how was that possible? She seemed so nice. So pretty. It made no sense—why would she have killed herself? If she'd only waited a little longer she'd be with them now in the cab, about to find her little girl at last. Or so he hoped, despite his mother's strange attitude. Then he wouldn't be avoiding this unpleasant old woman with the bad breath, and Nicole would still be smiling. And alive.

Life was terrifying. You went about your daily business and then people chased you, or arrested you, or even tried to kill you. Without his mother and his uncle René and Herr Lemmon, he'd probably be dead already. That's just the way life was.

Leo had told the grown-ups everything he knew about the kids at the Bayonne house. It wasn't that much. Pierre was older and shy. He claimed to be ten, but Leo suspected maybe only nine, short and very quiet. One day the police took away his parents while he was in school in a city called Pau. And then a secret policeman brought him to Bayonne to live with the other three kids and the governess. Jacqueline was Leo's age and had one missing tooth. Leo's teeth wouldn't even budge yet. A matter of time, *Maman* would say. Jacqueline said her family was in a camp somewhere.

Her schoolmates in Foix said it wasn't a fun kind of camp. Leo liked her blond pigtails and freckles and might even marry her someday. Together they had looked after Sophie until Leo's Gestapo father took him away. He knew the least about Jakob, the youngest other than Sophie, except that he wet himself and cried himself to sleep at night and never said much about anything.

Maman had said nothing at all about the kids when she questioned Madame Trouget, and that was very strange. She always did that, asked all the questions, demanded all the answers, and clear answers, too, not fuzzy ones. Uncle René said she was 'mining,' digging and digging and never happy until she knew all there was to know. So why didn't she ask about the children? Right then she was 'mining' the concierge again, this time in hushed tones, asking about the mean Madame de Brassis. Leo would be happier never to see the woman with the pinching fingers again.

The taxi eased slowly onto gravel as it left the paved provincial road. At a break in a high wall of hedges, stone columns supported heavy iron gates. Only garden tools crowded the guard house beside the entrance. A broad circular drive curved up to the main structure silhouetted against a bank of encroaching fog. The stone porpoises decorating a large fountain no longer sent water into the chill autumn air. The three-story mansion dominated a steep escarpment above a long beach.

The estate spoke of old money now depleted by Occupation and war. Erika pictured fine carriages gathering in prosperous times of old when attentive servants encouraged guests to join the festivities and dance to waltzes. Several meters beyond the gate she asked the driver to stop and handed him an extra hundred francs. "Please wait. You'll be well-rewarded."

"Yes, madame." He tipped the bill of his cap and stuffed the bills into his vest pocket. "I'll keep this beauty fired up for as long as the fuel holds out."

She had barely stepped from the taxi when Leo was at her side. "I'm coming with you—"

"No, you're not. You'll stay right there with Madame Trouget." Erika left no room for argument, and Leo pouted as he slunk back onto the car seat. "Don't worry—I shouldn't be long," she assured him.

She buttoned her coat against the strong breeze and headed up the drive. The evergreens swayed and dried leaves scudded underfoot. The grounds appeared deserted in the muted light of a veiled moon. Once beyond sight of the cab she made certain the safety was off, then slipped the smaller pistol into the top of her right stocking beneath the garter clip. Nicole's handgun remained in her coat but firmly in her grip. The house was clearly occupied—lamps burning at windows on two floors and the entry door illuminated—but nothing stirred behind the drapes, and no guards patrolled the front of the property.

The image of the blood-stained child's dress drew her on. She would get to the bottom of this monstrous act and punish those responsible for the horror. She would avenge Nicole. Having circled the mansion and satisfied herself that the coast was clear, she felt strong and ready as she returned to fetch the concierge and Leo.

She had them wait beside Madame Trouget at the foot of the steps while she ascended to the front terrace. The taxi still idled down the drive, its rumble barely audible over the howl of the rising wind. Erika rang the bell and within moments the front door swung inward. Leo greeted the woman with enthusiasm: "Mademoiselle Agnès!" He gave her a big smile and raced up to greet the governess who had treated him kindly in Bayonne, but she ignored Leo and spoke instead to Erika: "Please enter, madame. What took you so long?"

Erika saw the governess looking past her and followed the woman's gaze. A Browning automatic gleamed under the portico lamps. The weak-seeming concierge was now armed and a threat. Erika understood the danger in the blink of an eye but kept calm, her hand tensing on the weapon in her pocket. "My word, what a surprise, Madame Trouget! I'm sure you've many more up your sleeve!"

"More than you can imagine, my dear, but do come on in. You, too, Leo." Erika felt the Browning in the small of her back and duly raised her arms. Now the old woman spoke clearly to the governess, her teeth in full control: "You'll find a pistol in her right pocket—felt it when she roughed me up at the flat."

Erika surrendered her handgun to Agnès.

"Now let's go make ourselves at home in the parlor," said the governess, taking the lead. The two women appeared related, sisters perhaps, too similar for chance.

"But Mademoiselle Agnès—" Leo eyed his mother's raised hands nervously, his brow furrowed. "Aren't you glad to see us?"

"Of course we are, Leo. More than you can imagine." She smiled and patted his shoulder with one hand, the pistol snug in the other.

As they crossed the foyer, Erika reassured him: "Everything's fine, Leo. Don't worry, we're just going to have a little chat." She kept Leo on her left, her right hand free to go for the pistol in her garter. "Isn't that so, ladies?"

"That's correct, Frau von Kredow, but your little chat will be with Madame de Brassis, not with either of us." Agnès led them down the hall, the concierge bringing up the rear.

Ornate double doors opened to a grand parlor flanked by two curved staircases. Seascapes hung on walnut-paneled walls, architectural moldings framed the space, and an immense crystal chandelier accented the coffered ceiling. A massive stone hearth anchored the far wall, and French windows would reveal an impressive view of the Bay of Biscay in good weather.

The infamous Madame de Brassis held court on a damask-covered couch in the center of the room. "Welcome," she said, her smile vacant and bitter. "Forgive me if I don't rise to greet you, but I'm feeling a bit out of sorts, and we've wasted an entire day awaiting your arrival." She adjusted her silk skirt. "But you're here at last and we must make the most of it, so please be seated." She gestured to an armchair and Erika pushed aside an embroidered pillow to make room. Leo chose a camel-skin footstool. Unbidden, the two armed women assumed posts at either end of the sofa. "Now Agnès, were we not told to expect another woman and a couple of men, as well?"

De Brassis ignored the concierge, obviously of lesser rank in her little team of kidnappers, so Erika gave the sad news. "The other mother is deceased. She killed herself when she found the little dress." Erika thought she heard the governess gasp. "I'm sure your concierge can fill in the details."

"All the better she's gone, I suppose. And the men?"

"Occupied elsewhere."

"Well, can't be helped. Meanwhile, I'm sure you're wondering why you're here and what's to become of you."

Erika sensed the pistol at her thigh, tempting her. But how to shield Leo? *Keep the bitch talking.* "An all-female operation you're running here, is it?"

"Not quite. We have a couple of soldiers at our beck and call." De Brassis turned to Agnès. "By the way, what's keeping those handsome brothers, dear?"

"Herbert is down in the kitchen, madame, preparing a late supper, and Heinrich just came in the back way."

"Well, we'll introduce you later, I'm sure." Madame de Brassis took a look at Leo and grimaced, then turned away. "But the boy can't possibly stay. He must join the others. Children are a nuisance, in general, but I find these racially impure ones especially off-putting." She took a sip. "They offer nothing but future headaches." As for you, Frau von Kredow, you shall be our guest until your husband returns to look after your needs."

Erika, feeling her way blind: "But you must not have heard—my dear husband recently passed—something he ate, I'm told."

"*Au contraire.* I'm pleased to say you're misinformed." Her lighter flared and cigarette smoke streamed from the side of her mouth. "Why, I spoke with him just last night when he told us of your possible arrival."

Erika's heart missed a beat. "Impossible! You spoke with him?"

"Indeed. He mentioned some unfortunate mishap up north, something about unreliable men and treacherous women, but you'll be delighted to know he's doing just fine, although now headed back to Berlin." Her pronunciation was impeccable, her German heritage clear. "But he intends to make your experience with us unforgettable. And he gave explicit instructions on disposal of the boy. Such a considerate man, don't you think?"

Erika cautiously drew her hand along her thigh, slowly coaxing looser in the garter. "You're sure it was my husband you spoke with? Horst von Kredow? We all believe he's dead…" She was barely able to get the words out.

"The man's practically immortal, don't you know." She emptied her glass and signaled for a refill. "One more as a nightcap, Agnès." The governess fetched the Scotch whiskey from the sideboard. "It all tastes bitter to me lately, no matter the brand. Quality does suffer during war, you know, and the imported stuff becomes so difficult to obtain. Perhaps I should switch to vodka?" She set down the drink, her hand trembling. "But then, I'm being a poor hostess. Allow Agnès to offer you a glass."

Erika struggled to calm her breath. Incomprehensible that Horst could have survived the cyanide.

De Brassis asked again, "A drink for you, Frau von Kredow?"

"No, no thank you, I'm fine." Erika straightened her shoulders, setting aside the incomprehensible riddle. A dreadful mystery for later. But for now, she had to save herself and Leo. "You mentioned the children?" She prepared for the worst, and it came.

"Ah, yes, the children. Well just consider this—they had no further value to Herr von Kredow, what with his returning to Berlin as we speak. And it's not as if we really have a choice. Surely you must understand. These mongrels burden the purity of our race and Reich. They're vermin, actually, and just as troublesome. So our two young men helped them on their way." She took another drag. "The others are off to join their families, you might say."

The alcohol was taking its toll, the woman's jaundiced eyes blinking rapidly as she observed Erika. The cigarette ash threatened to fall and Agnès set an crystal dish on the cushion beside her. "It was Herr von Kredow's suggestion that our men leave you a little clue in town, just to bring you out here to find me." Her lips appeared to tighten, accentuating the wrinkles of her upper lip. "A pink pinafore, as I recall? A bit worse for wear when you found it, perhaps."

Erika steadied her voice: "All of them, then?" Leo was listening, watching, far too intelligent not to understand.

"Indeed. Well, at least the remaining three. One little Jew-boy left the same day your husband picked up this one." Her hand languidly pointed toward Leo. "But the other three are long gone now. My soldier boys said it was quite painless, if that means something to you. One here—" she pointed to her head, "and a second here." She tapped her chest. "A simple process, and—*pouf*—all nuisance gone, and our Aryan race all the better for it." De Brassis threw Leo a dismissive glance.

Erika saw Leo's glare and willed him to remain silent, to bide his time. She suppressed her tears in the face of this callous barbarity. Strength was needed now. "How did you…how did von Kredow know we would come here?"

"Oh, he wasn't completely sure you would, but the man's always a step ahead, you know. He suspected the other one might hunt her daughter down. And Herr von Kredow said your boy here is clever—for a mongrel, that is—and might remember enough about the Bayonne house to find his way there. So he set up a watch, and now here you are."

She gestured again for a refill and the liquid disappeared in three long gulps. "Now, if you'll excuse me, I'm feeling a bit off and will head to my rooms. Agnès and her sister will deliver your boy to the soldiers for proper treatment and then make you comfortable in the wine cellar." The woman moved unsteadily, working her way forward on the couch. "Such a pleasure to have made your acquaintance," she crushed the cigarette in the ashtray, "albeit short." Madame de Brassis rose on unstable legs, drew herself up and then lurched to the floor in convulsive spasms.

Erika saw her opportunity in the unexpected collapse of the drunk. She was shouting to Leo before the woman hit the carpet: "Run, run!" He disappeared through a side door without looking back. In one motion Erika grabbed for the pistol at her garter, slid from the chair and crouched low, ready to drop both sisters during this sudden distraction.

Her effort was wasted. Neither woman had even flinched as de Brassis plowed face-first into the Persian carpet. Instead, they exchanged self-satisfied smiles before breaking loose in unbridled laughter. Erika's jaw dropped. Agnès spoke first: "Please relax now, madame, and forgive us our little charade." She slipped her pistol into the pocket of her smock.

Louise Trouget explained: "Our detested Madame de Brassis has now consumed sufficient wood alcohol to send her to hell. She'll be dead within the hour, at least if there's any justice left in this godforsaken *Boche* world." Erika was stunned by the sudden reversal of fortune. The woman came over and placed a hand on her shoulder. "Sorry I made you pump me so hard for information, but it was necessary to bring this all about. We couldn't risk this taking longer than hoped and having von Kredow show up unannounced." She gestured to the jerking body at her feet. "It's high time this one dies, but we do so regret the tragic suicide of the young woman. It was never meant to happen that way. Sophie's mother, I presume?"

Erika could only nod as she sat down again, her legs trembling.

"Nothing we could have foreseen, I'm afraid. Von Kredow ordered us to set the trap and we had to do everything as he demanded to disguise our plan."

The dying woman continued to retch repeatedly, spewing cords of vomit on the expensive wool rug. "My God!" Erika suddenly remembered, "Where is Leo?" She scrambled to her feet and lunged for the door.

"Don't worry, madame. He can't have gone far, and Leo's perfectly safe now."

"Safe?" Erika pulled up short, horrified by the thought of Leo somewhere in the huge house with two dangerous soldiers around. "We must find him, and now! Those SS thugs killed the other children!"

Agnès smiled. "Heinrich and Herbert are party to our little deception, so no worries there, either, and they aren't actually SS, they're army. The men may appear a bit simple, but they're trustworthy fellows."

"You women astonish me! What about the others? The baby girl?" Erika stood up, nauseated by such heartlessness. "How could you allow them to slaughter innocents in your care?"

"Oh, not to worry, dear," Agnès placed a reassuring hand on her arm, "all of our little ones are hale and hearty. That's what makes the young mother's death especially tragic." Erika recognized a look of true compassion and regret. "These soldier boys of ours faked everything, even that bloodied little dress von Kredow demanded. Neither your husband nor the old witch there was any the wiser. As far as he knows, we disposed of the bodies in the furnace, just as ordered. But all the little darlings are safe, sound and well-fed, and I'm sure they'll be delighted to see Leo once again." She suggested they all move down to the hearth to escape the smell of vomit and the sight of disturbing death throes. "And by the time anyone comes looking, my sister Louise will be back home with her cat and the rest of us long gone."

Erika had barely wrapped her mind around Horst's survival and now this complicated deception seemed equally astounding. She took a closer look at the dying woman. Despite her loathing, as a former medical student she thought she should either ease the woman's suffering or dispatch her more quickly. She recognized the bluish tinge of lips and nails, knew the convulsions would soon lead to coma and death. "Just how long has she been drinking methanol?" The throaty gurgling was turning to choking gasps.

"Madame here is often in her cups, so helping her along with the wood spirits was a natural choice. We started about twenty-four hours ago. Young Heinrich and his brother grew up on a farm, so they know their way around chemicals found in a caretaker's shed. Madame was already complaining of a headache and vision trouble by bedtime last night, so we upped the dosage with her first drink of the morning." Agnès appeared very pleased with their successful plan. "She thought it would do her good."

Louise Trouget spoke up, her tone reassuring. "Your arrival late this afternoon was perfect! My sister and I had already decided to act—to protect the dear children—so we were all set to put our plan in motion. Our young soldiers are trustworthy, decent, so orders to slaughter children didn't sit well with them either."

"It wasn't difficult convincing them we could offer a better future elsewhere," Agnès added, "and now they've settled on heading back to the Sudetenland. We've offered a sizeable monetary inducement to help with such a dangerous move, since we know where Madame keeps her safe."

Agnès hooked her arm through Erika's. "But your being here will make things even easier!" The governess steered her toward the door Leo had taken. "Please come with me, madame. You and Leo must be famished after such a long day, and I'm sure Heinrich has prepared something delicious for us all. He's quite a chef, you know."

Louise took a final look at the matron, now almost still. She nudged the matron with her foot. "They'll assume she drank herself to death, which is true in a way. We just helped her along. Our soldiers won't be missed for a while since they're on assignment to de Brassis here and the Gestapo. Later they'll be deserters, of course, so it will appear they did away with de Brassis before absconding with the family treasure. But for now, we've plans to make. You and Leo are about to lead us out of this *Boche* nest and into the Free Zone. But first, why don't we send that cabdriver back to Bayonne?"

CHAPTER TWELVE

Nantes, Occupied France
29 August 1941

The governess blathered on incessantly and Horst fought the urge to smash the phone receiver on the desk. The imbecilic woman whined and wheedled, offering feeble excuses for failing at the simplest of tasks. He would gladly strangle her with the phone cord if only he could.

Most of what she said went unheard after the first staggering news. Years of planning, murder and manipulation, all for nothing—his Jew-bitch of a wife was dead. Erika, the bane of his existence, destroyed by accident rather than by his design, stolen away by the incompetence of underlings. First those inept agents from Nantes who bungled his grand finale at the warehouse, and now these feeble-minded sisters in Bayonne had bungled a second opportunity. She had escaped his exquisite tortures after all, would never pay the price for duping him into *Rassenschande* and polluting his noble bloodline by bearing a *Mischling* son. She would never compensate him for screwing her way out of the Reich, first with the American and then with that hulking Alsatian.

Those Bayonne morons had foiled a perfect plan. He had considered it possible, if not probable, that Erika would show up at the townhouse. It was simply her nature to attempt the rescue of hostage children. Having his Marionette there was a bonus. How he wished he had witnessed her discovery of the blood-smeared dress of her infant daughter, had heard those cries of anguish! Instead, the weak-willed bitch had gone over the edge and put one through her own head. And he hadn't been there as it all played out.

The rest of the plan had gone equally sideways. Madame de Brassis and those doltish soldiers were charged with shattering his wife's mental and emotional composure. They were to display the charred carcasses of the hostage children, then hold her for Horst to complete a task he'd plotted for years. Instead, the liver of old de Brassis had surrendered to that ungodly amount of alcohol she consumed day and night, and Erika had somehow overpowered the old biddies with a hidden pistol. Regrettably—so the sobbing governess repeated ceaselessly—both wife and the boy perished in the exchange of gunfire with the soldiers.

Horst ran his hands through his hair, then allowed a finger to follow the contour of the dueling scar on the deadened half of his face. He exhaled deeply, releasing the fury. His flaring temper finally under control, he spoke calmly to the hysterical woman, consoling, easing her conscience, allaying her fears. "I understand, madame, it simply couldn't be helped. An unfortunate turn of events, but unavoidable under the circumstances and certainly no fault of either you or your sister." He would find time later to punish them both for such moronic behavior.

Her voice quavered and he heard the disbelief. His reputation for cruelty and retribution was widespread along the Atlantic coast among those who had dealings with the Gestapo, and such leniency was unheard of. "Yes, sir, most unfortunate but unavoidable…you're absolutely right, sir—"

Horst interrupted: "Done is done. Here's what happens next—the three women and the boy join the children already incinerated, understood? The soldiers know the drill."

He imagined the hag's head bobbing up and down, so determined to please or perhaps simply to actually escape his wrath. "Yes, sir, the soldiers will do as you command," she said. "Not a single trace, just as you wish."

"*Au contraire*, madame. There will be a single trace, for I have a special instruction for you and you alone. Had that fool de Brassis not drowned in her own alcoholic puke she would handle this for me, but now it's all up to you."

"Whatever you say, sir."

"Need I speak of penalties for you and your sister should you fail in this matter?"

"Of course not, monsieur, of course not. We'll do exactly as you say—"

Horst interrupted again, disgusted by her fawning manner. What good were stupid women, especially the plain ones? He steadied his voice, a model of calm. "Now, pay close attention, madame. Write down the following—" Horst gave the address for Gestapa in Berlin. "Now, read it back to me."

"Yes, sir. Prinz-Albrecht-Strasse 8, Berlin."

"Very good, madame. Now listen carefully. Before the bodies enter the incinerator you will remove one finger each from my wife and the boy. Place them in alcohol and seal them in a tidy package. And from my wife it must be the ring finger, understood?"

"Yes, of course, sir, the ring finger."

"Send them to me by *Luftpost* at the address just given." Horst allowed his order to register on the woman's feeble mind before prompting her again: "You will do as I say, madame?"

He heard a nervous exchange of whispers as she shared his demand with her sister, the concierge, and then at last came a timid answer. "Just two fingers, monsieur…am I correct?"

"Indeed, madame. And if they don't arrive in good condition, I shall pay you and your imbecilic sister a personal visit when next in Bayonne and take a few of yours, as well."

He dropped the phone in its cradle and allowed himself a few moments to surrender to the new reality. Three years of dogged pursuit, three years of deception, trickery, deceit, all to bring Erika under his knife, to feel the blade slip beneath the yielding flesh, to watch the blood surface as she screamed for mercy, the life force draining slowly from her wracked body and mind. What a cruel twist of fate to forego her final despair, to lose out on her cries for compassion for that insufferable brat.

He slid his hands beneath his thighs to still the tremors. With eyes closed, he leaned back, consciously relaxing his limbs. The trembling had bothered him now for days, ever since the endless night in the crate, ever since he'd stared down death until it flinched. Each morning he awakened drenched in sweat, his fingers beyond his control as they worked at the scabs on his thighs.

He would display those proofs of death in his Berlin office. It was an inspired idea. Such blood trophies were sure to break the will of Lemmon and Gesslinger. Perhaps he would castrate them both first. He had once broken the will of a traitorous Jewess by presenting her with the severed cock of her husband. "I improved his circumcision," he had told her. "If a little off the top is good for you Yids, imagine Jehovah's pleasure in seeing so much more removed."

Erika might be gone, but the game remained his to win.

CHAPTER THIRTEEN

Paris, Occupied France
29-30 August 1941

Two memorable events occurred those first days in Cherche-Midi prison. Only one would make her stay there more bearable. Well before the morning meal of vegetable soup and coarse brown bread, a warder had stopped outside her door. Dutiful to the rules of the house, Marita sprang to her feet upon hearing the grate of the key. The guard immediately stepped aside for a female non-com who set a bundle wrapped in brown paper on the table and left as quickly as she had come.

Marita hesitated to move until the lock clicked shut. She watched the peephole to see if anyone would slide the metal tab aside but the cover didn't budge. She then tore open the bundle to reveal two pairs of blessed underwear, a cotton chemise, a handkerchief, rough woolen socks, and a comb. But most welcome of all was a stack of bandage wadding, palm-sized cotton squares. Frau Biedermann was a woman, after all.

Between noon and two, the guards disappeared for their break. The women of the cell block began calling out to one another, sharing rumors picked up from family visitors or from notes hidden in linen deliveries. Official reports of *Boche* victories on the Eastern Front were met with jeers and remarkably foul language, even for Marita, who thought she'd heard it all. Reports family members had garnered from illegally-heard BBC broadcasts received rousing acclaim.

The hourly interruptions throughout the long night established a steady rhythm: just as at Rue de Saussaies, the sudden glare of the overhead bulb, the march of jangling keys and screeching locks toward her cell door, the scrape of the spyhole cover and that single eye peering in to remind her that privacy was only found in her rudely abandoned dreams. The prisoner across the way said the predictable routine would surely keep her sane.

By early morning her fellow inmates awakened and did a make-shift wash, with shouts of *"bonjour!"* and *"bien dormie?"* passed from cell to cell and across the aisle. She returned those greetings while lying face-down on the floor, calling back through the gap under the iron door. Once all were awake, the women joined together in a chorus of "la Marseillaise," followed by shouts of "Vive le général de Gaulle!" But the exuberance faded promptly at eight, when the guards reappeared. Then the prisoners entered the corridor with slop pails and water jugs and used the small brushes provided to sweep out their cells.

She learned that blonde Claire, now occupying the cell to her right, was accused of partisan activity in complicity with her boyfriend, secretly relaying messages and funds to support a local Communist cell. The Gestapo had caught her leaving underground flyers on *Métro* seats. Her sentence was ten years, most likely in a forced labor camp in Germany.

It took more of the group's encouragement to learn red-haired Denise's sad story. Her husband Jean-Louis was stranded by the *Boche* invasion while picking up a wholesale dry goods delivery in Chantilly in June of '40. The poor man had inadvertently insulted an SS colonel. Standing on the sidewalk to stare at the long, tight column of armored vehicles and marching troops, Jean-Louis failed to doff his cap as the colonel passed in an open car. His punishment for such lack of respect was a bullet to the back of the head. His body remained on the pavement as a warning to honor the new conquerors. A week later the wholesaler used Jean-Louis' own delivery van to return his corpse to their doorstep in Paris. The old friend hadn't dared brave the roads until the Occupation was a *fait accompli.*

To support their two young girls, Denise had hastily found a job assisting a photographer. The man was doing well financially taking portraits of men in uniform for parents, spouses or fiancées back in Germany. The sudden increase in orders with the influx of soldiers on leave required a clerk who could greet arriving customers. However, unbeknownst to Denise, her boss was also forging documents for an underground resistance group, and she was rounded up as an accomplice. The police arrested her at work, and she hadn't dared make calls to neighbors for fear of implicating them. With no surviving family in Paris and no phone of her own, her daughters would return from school to an empty apartment. She had begged to be allowed to alert them, to find someplace else for them to stay, but to no avail. She now faced a sentence comparable to Claire's but the fate of her children remained unknown, tearing at her heart and gnawing at her conscience.

The other news on that first day was far less welcome than the package sent by the *directrice.* It showed what little hope she had of ever escaping the descending blade. Marita and the new-arrivals had quickly learned the warning codes used when guards approached: the first inmate to spot a warder at an off-hour would whistle *Au clair de la lune.* The popular tune *Cadet Rousselle* alerted everyone once the coast again cleared. So that afternoon, after the second daily meal—dense sausage and margarine accompanying any bread that survived breakfast—Marita recognized the signal for a surprise visitor on the block. She heard footsteps stop outside her cell and the turn of the key.

The guard led her to a meeting room where her state-assigned attorney waited. *Avocat* Bertin was young—perhaps in his mid-twenties—and his recently acquired Doctor of Law degree undoubtedly decorated some nondescript office in a poor *arrondissement*. Anxious to appear professional, his officious manner covered an obvious lack of expertise, and from the sound of it, experience. He reviewed her story and the Gestapo interrogation notes, and when she still denied any wrong-doing, advised her that the government's case was air-tight. "There can be no doubt you were caught with an English wireless transmitter." He promised to plead her case to the best of his abilities—little consolation there—but felt she would do better to admit her treasonous acts and beg for leniency from the judge. "If you only had something to share, the name of someone else complicit in your crime? You should be aware the court favors those who help carry out its judicial duties."

How dreary and boring her fate now that it was only a matter of time before the blade fell. The daily communal time in the courtyard allowed the women to see each other but talking wasn't allowed as they paraded around in an endless circle, each with a hand on the shoulder of the woman ahead. No other human contact was allowed. She found little solace in the long hours alone in her cell. She had already memorized the graffiti on the walls, imagined the individual writers as her companions in misery, crafted in her own mind a personal history to accompany each heart-rending comment.

Now her thoughts wandered to all who had been closest to her. Despite her best efforts, she could only revive her parents in dreams, never in waking hours when the guilt surfaced with a flood of emotions. The spirit of Marie, however, was always there at her side, telling her to remain strong. And how painful to remember Argent, holding her in his arms, asking awkwardly if he wasn't too young for her. *Mon Dieu, a few years' difference is nothing!*

And then dear Ryan, ever confident Ryan, smiling up from the pillow as they found pleasure in bed. How he loved to have her ride him. She would grip him tightly as she met the thrust of his hips, her back arched to show off her youthful breasts, then bend over to frame him in a hood of dark hair and press her lips to his. How sweet to feel again the gentle touch of his hand.

The guards periodically led prisoners away, sometimes for further interrogation, other times for torture. Upon their return the women all shared the suffering and sorrow. Marita guessed the torturers might leave her in peace because her only known crime was daring to cross powerful men who now demanded her death.

Worries about the club filled the long nights. With Florian gone they had surely closed its doors, so who would help with his family, and where might her girls find other places to dance? Though only a decade older, she thought of herself as their mother. Had her two trusted bartenders found other employment? What would become of Pascal with his club foot, or poor damaged Colette? What other club would hire that lovely child whose belly bore the permanent autograph from that venomous Serge?

CHAPTER FOURTEEN

Biarritz, Occupied France
30 August 1941

Once at the Colmar estate back in 1938, René had driven Erika to Strasbourg to pawn the ring symbolizing her marriage to Horst. Every piece of von Kredow jewelry smuggled into France was to aid Jews moving toward Marseille and on to Palestine. Erika was determined that some fraction of the wealth of a man determined to destroy European Jews would help the fugitives escape Nazi persecution, and ridding herself of that ring would sever her last tie to a despicable tormentor. Or so she had believed.

With Horst again in pursuit the following year, René proposed marriage and she had accepted. His mother offered her own wedding band to commemorate the union. "My dear husband remains forever in my heart and my dreams— I'd rather you two have this ring," Erika immediately protested, insisting Jeanne keep the ring on her own finger. For several moments his mother remained silent, finally continuing with a catch in her throat: "He would have grown to love you as much as I have in the last few months, my dear, and I couldn't imagine a better wife for our René." She patted his hand. "So let this be our wedding gift to the two of you." They had sized the band for a perfect fit. In lieu of an official marriage, the ring had become a constant symbol of her commitment to René.

Now faced with a chilling task, she removed the simple gold band from her finger and set it on the porcelain plate. A chill raced up her spine. Suddenly she felt the tie to René broken and grabbed for the band. Sliding it onto the finger of her right hand, she exhaled deeply and braced herself on the edge of the kitchen table to steady her nerves.

A heavy cutting block sat before her, the butcher's knife alongside. Its handle showed the wear of years of daily use. She had honed the blade to a scalpel's edge, remembering her medical studies in Marburg, where fascination with the workings of human and animal bodies had inured her to dissection. This blade could not possibly cut as cleanly and precisely, but it would have to do.

Erika had requested Agnès be present. Her nurse's training was a godsend in such a difficult situation, for she could apply pressure to the stumps should Erika faint or lack the strength. She laid out a small sewing needle and thread to suture the wounds as needed.

They had secured the rooms where the children played so no one would burst in to witness her terrifying act. The concierge Louise had asked Heinrich to drive her back to the Bayonne townhome. The group agreed that suspicions would be raised should she also disappear from the Bayonne area. De Brassis wouldn't be missed for a while since she came and went at her leisure, and few visited the mansion above the beach. But cleaning up the site of the suicide and removing the body of Nicole was a priority.

Horst had demanded her ring finger, of course. His abject cruelty insisted on taking the concept of final severance literally. He hadn't specified which of Leo's fingers would satisfy his blood lust so she would also sacrifice her smallest finger in the hope it would pass for her son's.

"Proof of death," Agnès had repeated with tear-filled eyes after that fateful phone call. The group was stunned. Even the two young soldiers seemed to pale at von Kredow's demand. Unlike his orders to kill and dispose of the children, this act couldn't be faked, and Erika knew Horst's sadistic mind, knew he wouldn't accept the "deaths" of wife and son without that tangible proof.

"Perhaps we can..." Agnès' voice had faded into silence, and she wrung her hands in frustration.

"Let's just finish up here, burn the two bodies in the basement furnace, and then all of you make a run for the Free Zone." Agnès smiled encouragement. "Then you can forget that deranged man altogether, right?"

"It's no good," Erika replied with a shake of the head, "he's every bit as powerful there as here. His squads know no boundaries." Her knees had weakened and she sat down. "There's no point in fleeing if he suspects Leo and I live. We simply can't run forever with his sword suspended above our heads."

The two brothers had never found a home in the Wehrmacht. Their impoverished Sudeten family was ethnic German, but centuries of farming outside the *Altreich* had made them Czech at heart. When Hitler annexed Czechoslovakia in 1938 the Federbach family holed up on a rural farmstead, but the young men soon came to the attention of the conquerors. Before long they were German soldiers, but adjustment to army life had been difficult. Their comrades in arms treated them as second-class citizens, ridiculing their ancestry. It led to frequent brawls. With no fear of getting their hands dirty, the brothers often came out the winners. His bored troops found hazing "sub-humans" a pleasant enough pastime, but the local commandant found having to punish the instigators along with the victims undermined troop morale.

The brothers' only farm-acquired skill of value to the German army was keeping heavy equipment functioning properly. The Federbachs eventually found themselves working side-by-side in a maintenance battalion near Biarritz. When Horst demanded some obedient muscle from the local commander, the commandant was happy to rid himself of those troublesome Federbachs. Best for all concerned to send the two belligerent brothers on special assignment, one demanding brawn rather than intelligence. Once they were under de Brassis' direction, Horst had given the matter no further thought.

Winning first their trust and then their complicity had been easy, according to Agnès and Louise. And Madame de Brassis' obvious contempt for the brothers helped drive them into the camp of governess and concierge. From the moment the young soldiers arrived to oversee the hostage setup, the sisters had begun planning. Raised in poverty, Heinrich and Hermann marveled at the trappings of de Brassis wealth and social standing, and Agnès had gradually convinced them they deserved to "inherit" some of the de Brassis fortune. The sisters thought the men should head for Spain rather than return to the Bohemian Protectorate, but the men were homesick. They refused to consider that showing up at the family farm as wealthy deserters would fail to ingratiate them with the German authorities. "We'll make do," they said.

Erika had requested a few quiet hours to think. She hoped against hope to find some other way but with every passing hour Horst could forget Berlin and suddenly show up, determined to complete his mission of vengeance. In fact, all this might be some new ruse on his part, the bastard coming through the mansion door any moment. She needed to get the blood trophies into the mail. They needed to flee with the children. She stilled her inner voice, seeking distraction in the distant sounds of hide-and-seek organized by Leo. Such a joy to hear him laugh, and little Sophie, so adorable, her high-pitched giggle a delight to any mother's ears. Erika forced back the memory of Nicole, dead without reason.

Her decision felt right yet still she questioned her own strength and will. She lifted the butcher knife, felt its heft and balance before extending her two fingers over the edge of the cutting board. Sweat beaded on her forehead. She stilled her trembling hands by sheer force of will. With the knife tip pressed to the wooden surface, she lowered the blade until the edge met skin. A single drop of blood welled up. She gave a nod to Agnès, who stood ready with gauze and bandage, then steadied herself and shut her eyes. Her grip on the handle tightened and the blade came down.

"Frau von Kredow, wait! Don't do it!" Heinrich burst into the kitchen. "Please wait!" The swinging door barely closed before the concierge hurried in on his heels. Her ill-fitting teeth showed a broad smile. Startled by the sudden interruption, Erika lost all focus, releasing the knife as it entered the flesh of her small finger. The blade clattered to the cutting board and Agnès sprang forward to compress the wound. Erika sagged to the floor, her body shaking. Agnès kept one hand clamped to the bandage as she helped Erika to a chair.

"Why the hell did you interrupt? My God, now I must start over!" Erika trembled, fury in her eyes. "Wasn't all this hard enough?"

"Relax, madame," Louise's eyes sparkled, "we've a solution!" Heinrich handed over a small package as if presenting a gift. He made a polite bow. Filled with dread, Erika gingerly unwound the cloth. Two delicate fingers lay encased in waxed paper. One long, one short.

Louise beamed. "I trimmed the fingernail on the small one to look more like a boy's."

Erika held her breath, knowing now what they had done, torn by both horror and relief. "Oh my God, you've mutilated Nicole's body!" Tears rolled from her eyes.

"But madame," Louise protested, "the young woman had already mutilated her body with a bullet to the head! My pruning shears won't affect her future, but certainly can make yours easier." She gave Erika a perturbed look. "Madame de Brassis' fingers were simply too old and wrinkled so they would never have done the trick! If these won't satisfy you and your brutal husband, carry on with what you were about to do." She turned to leave. Heinrich looked on, clearly baffled by the quick verbal exchange in French, while Agnès beamed with pride at her sister's ingenuity.

Erika steadied herself. She took over applying pressure to her finger and called after the concierge. "No, please wait, Madame Trouget. I'm so sorry—do forgive me. I'm simply a bundle of nerves and need a moment to think."

The concierge turned back begrudgingly, avoiding Erika's gaze and looking to her sister. Agnès was already wiping down the blade and cutting board. Erika examined the two pitiful fingers, already stiff and darkening. Memories of the young woman who had sacrificed herself needlessly overwhelmed her. She swallowed hard, seeking new strength, but sobs overwhelmed her.

"Come, come, it'll be fine." Agnès dried her hands on her apron and squeezed Erika's shoulder. "Just consider this, my dear. You were determined to save your son from that evil husband of yours, whatever it took, including crippling yourself by severing your own fingers. Why? Out of love, correct?"

Erika accepted the offered handkerchief.

"The young woman shot herself last night out of love for her child, *n'est-ce-pas*? She couldn't bear what she thought the final loss, the end of all she'd lived for." Agnès drew Erika closer. "She has no further use for these fingers, so don't you think she'd have gladly sacrificed them to save Sophie's life. You, Madame, will now use them to save that little girl as well as your son."

Erika managed to nod.

Agnès held Erika's chin and looked directly into her eyes. "It's now up to you to be strong and make our plan work. Louise and I love these children. We never had a chance to bear our own, but we've done everything to provide a decent life under horrifying circumstances for these innocents. Your job—our job—is to release us all from that man of yours and his Gestapo."

Erika looked from sister to sister, seeing for the first time the love and generosity which had brought them to this moment. She felt ashamed of her own hesitation in the face of all they risked for the children and slowly re-wrapped the "proof of death." When she was done she gave them each a half-smile, even poor Heinrich, who appeared embarrassed to be present.

"No, you're right, you've all done well, and I thank you. Years from now all the children will remember and thank you." She rose from the chair. "Your decision was right. My mutilated hand might have drawn attention on our trip east. She held out the bundle. "Send them off. These should satisfy the bastard and win us all our freedom."

Feeling light-headed, she dropped back into the chair, a vow forming in her mind, a promise from one mother to another: *I swear to you now, Nicole, your daughter will know of your love and sacrifice.*

CHAPTER FIFTEEN

Paris, Occupied France
30 August 1941

Horst's career move could mean many things and Richard Kohl knew the risks. Von Kredow had distanced himself from Berlin for three long years, acting alone and with no direct supervision from Heydrich. His extraction teams had received praise from Berlin for extraditing numerous traitors, spies and saboteurs, but no one really knew what currents of favor or disfavor might now flow through Gestapo headquarters. A command appearance couldn't guarantee a pleasurable reception in Berlin, so Kohl chose his words carefully. "So, Horst, seen enough of beautiful France for now?"

"Heydrich calls and I answer." He checked the clock under the glass-and-steel canopy of the Gare de Montparnasse before stepping off briskly toward the station hall. "So what time's my flight?"

"I've an airplane standing by for you at Le Bourget," Kohl offered a wry smile, "for you alone, my dear Horst." Kohl handed his partner the briefcase placed in his charge only a few weeks before. "It's clear he needs you in Berlin in a hurry."

Kohl had always envied Horst's height, his intense blue eyes and that bold mark of courage on his left cheek. Unlike Kohl's corpulent build and relaxed demeanor, von Kredow's slim physique and carriage embodied the ideals destined to bring glory to the Reich. In truth, Richard Kohl had always been more the clever thinker than a strong physical specimen.

His German parents had instilled in him great pride in his heritage, and his mental acuity won him a scholarship to Princeton. But his middle-class, mercantile upbringing isolated him from the well-heeled elite he'd hoped to emulate. The young student soon blamed his social troubles on a suspected cabal of wealthy Jewish students determined to block his upward mobility, and the pudgy, oftentimes smug young man found nothing but rejection from the Ivy League coeds. So Kohl swore off educated women and quietly joined the local German-American *Bund* where he felt at home promoting a National Socialist party destined to lead the world at the expense of the inferior races.

Recommendations from supportive university faculty opened doors at the State Department. Kohl's manipulative talents and insight into the German mind quickly moved him up the ladder in German and Austrian Affairs. In 1935, while attending an international law seminar in Berlin, he fell in with Nazi students who shared a vision of restoring Germany's greatness on the world stage.

Tasked with expanding the Reich's secret police powers, Reinhard Heydrich found an easy recruit in Kohl. Flattered by the Nazi leader's recognition, he eagerly volunteered to become an SD mole in Washington. Here at last was an assignment befitting his intellectual talents, and once he took command of the German desk at State, he helped dupe Americans into exposing anti-Nazi cells in Germany.

But it was von Kredow who took all the glory in Berlin by rounding up the actual traitors and bringing them to justice. Richard Kohl had always dreamed of hands-on secret police work rather than remaining desk-bound in Washington. The loss of his State Department position had been a blessing in disguise. In Paris he finally found himself in the thick of the action, and despite his lacking the physical attributes of his aristocratic colleague, Kohl knew himself to be von Kredow's equal in manipulating anyone who got in his way.

Now times had changed. Horst von Kredow appeared much the worse for wear, his face bruised and tattered. The notorious visage remained as intimidating as ever but bore a purplish-green cast and a half-moon of pock-like scabs beneath the left eye. Kohl suspected damaged cartilage in that formerly straight nose, and his colleague carried his head a bit more stiffly. The staged escape of Ryan Lemmon, so carefully planned for months and initiated just weeks prior, had clearly misfired. Kohl hesitated to test his colleague's limits by inquiring directly, but his curiosity was getting the better of him.

He fell in beside von Kredow as they forged a path across the concourse. Uniformed men and women made way for their passage. Despite his battered face, Horst's bearing spoke to his authority and the Gestapo control officers waved them through with little delay.

Kohl finally felt compelled to ask. "How'd the Lemmon decoy work out? Did you bag your prey?"

Von Kredow's cold eyes never left the crowded concourse, and Kohl wondered if his words had failed to register. Horst came to an abrupt halt. Other detraining passengers slipped clumsily past them, a surging river of field-gray to either side of their stationary island. Horst tore open a fresh pack of Aristons and brought a cigarette to his lips. His "*Feuer, bitte*" was barely perceptible. Kohl obliged with a match. "We'll discuss all that at the airfield, understood?"

"Of course, Horst." Kohl felt the suppressed fury in his partner's words. "No hurry, no hurry at all." Things had definitely gone sideways. Perhaps a bite of lunch might calm von Kredow. He checked his watch. "I hear the café on the square serves up a decent enough lunch if you're hungry."

"Get me to Le Bourget, and quickly." Smoke streamed from his narrow lips and nostrils. "No time for idle talk."

Bristling at the dismissive tone, Kohl led the way along the front arcade to a waiting sedan on the Place de Rennes. If his colleague was truly about to ride Heydrich's coattails to the summit of Party power, Kohl needed to stay in Horst's best graces. Yet he bridled at the thought von Kredow's career might soon overshadow his own.

Running the German desk at State had spoiled him, ruling over his own fiefdom, manipulating American foreign policy in favor of Reich and Führer. He had never learned which of Roosevelt's patsies had pulled the plug on his charade. No charges, just an abrupt dismissal with orders to clear his desk within hours. This current Paris duty was a genuine opportunity to lead again, but this time in the heart of the action. The Special War Problems program made excellent cover as he assembled his personal team of espionage agents to stifle the covert flow of Allied operatives through the city. His secondary assignment was to simultaneously block Abwehr interference in SD intelligence-gathering. Now at last he could shine in field work, the realm where von Kredow had always stolen the limelight.

The Gestapo driver closed Horst's door and hurried around to open for Kohl. Pedestrians took one look and moved on, feigning disinterest in the official car and its stern occupants. A squad of soldiers waited for dismissal, ready to explore the city on the Seine. A few trams rattled by. Another black sedan and some *gasogène* taxis waited curbside for passengers. A troop of soldiers pedaled past on bicycles.

Once clear of the square the Mercedes headed northeast. Traffic remained relatively light and Horst seemed lost in thought. Kohl wondered what was coursing through his comrade's mind. He himself would have personal misgivings were he the one summoned back to Berlin after an absence as long as his colleague's.

At Le Bourget the driver ignored the busy air terminal and customs buildings and circled around to a side entrance to the airfield. An SS non-com swung open the gate at a signal from the driver and the sedan shot across to the waiting plane. The black swastika on the tail stood proud against the shiny metal of the fuselage. Both engines revved loudly as the pilot tested ailerons and rudder. When the driver reached for his door, Horst ordered him away. He saluted and went to stand under the wash of the nearest propeller, his head bent low, hat pressed to his head with one hand.

Horst turned to Kohl, his voice without inflection. "You've surely gathered that all didn't go exactly as planned, Richard. No need for details, but suffice to say my primary goal is accomplished—I'm free at last of that Jew-bitch and her spawn." Horst ran a hand through his hair and put on his hat. "Both dead and gone, but sadly all occurred in my absence. I had special plans for those two, you know."

"Still very good news, Horst, and a tremendous relief, I'm sure. It's been such a long and fruitless pursuit until now." Kohl took some pleasure in bringing up the years of failure. "And what of the two men you pursued?"

"The Alsatian's gone underground with Nantes partisans. They've some plan for sabotage in Saint-Nazaire in the works." Horst removed a dossier from his briefcase. "The fools abandoned maps and diagrams when I sent them packing."

"Such incompetence!" Kohl chuckled aloud, wondering how Horst had managed to "send them packing" without eliminating them once and for all. And what was the story behind the new physical damage to his colleague's face? "And yet they think themselves smart enough to outwit us?"

"The ineptitude of such inferior minds accrues to our benefit. We can take down all the saboteurs when they make their move."

Kohl fussed with his fountain pen, ready to take notes. "That's the 'Gesslinger' fellow, as I recall."

Horst handed over the folder. "He's surely using a *nom de guerre* for the moment. The full physical description is in here along with a photograph taken in '34. He's the big one all done up in dueling kit. He still looks much the same but wears a full beard. After our run-in a few days ago he'll be the worse for wear, his arm and shoulder possibly in a sling or cast. Those *Schmisse* on his forehead can't be hidden, and he favors his left leg. A brute of a man—not a trace of Germanic refinement."

"I'll see to it." He returned the pen to his breast pocket. "Most important—detain or eliminate?"

"Alive and back in Berlin. No formal arrest. I intend to peel that asinine grin from his face personally." Horst appeared distracted before turning his attention back to Kohl. "Sometimes things go awry. If for any reason you must kill him, make sure it's done slowly and very painfully, *verstanden*?" Kohl nodded. "And then there's Ryan Lemmon, your old patsy in Washington. He was somehow involved with that Nantes saboteur group, but now that he thinks me dead he's likely returned to Paris."

A surprise for Kohl. "Thinks you dead?"

"A very close call, Richard. I only survived thanks to my own quick thinking. I feel like Lazarus. And no thanks to the incompetent Nantes agents tasked with supporting me. Enough to know that the remaining targets believe I'm out of the picture for good. It'll make them careless."

"Lemmon's still assigned to State and listed with the local consulate, without doubt a cover for espionage activity. He'll link up with his brother, a fool as naïve as the day I first hired him. He should be grateful his father-in-law's rich and influential enough to keep him employed in Washington. That being said, a tail on Edward will net us Ryan."

"When the son-of-a-bitch pops up, he's all mine. He's to believe me dead until this 'immortal' Horst von Kredow severs his balls at last. Again, ship him to me in Berlin as quickly as possible. Cut his damned Achilles tendons, if you must—the bastard has a knack for escaping—but keep him otherwise sound, understood? I assure you, when I'm done with him this time, he'll be singing alto soprano."

Kohl laughed. What a feather in his own cap should he finally accomplish the one goal which had eluded Horst for many years. "Will do, my friend. Anything else?"

"That's all for now. Don't disappoint me, stay in touch, and call immediately when you have either man. I trust you can handle this adequately, but I must say I've run into nothing but disappointment recently with the caliber of Gestapo support. Our secret police seems to attract nothing but imbeciles of late."

The implied incompetence galled him but Kohl hid his true feelings. "You've got it, Horst. Smooth flight, and my very best to Heydrich." He signaled the driver.

With von Kredow on board and its engines roaring, the plane rumbled toward the runway. Kohl didn't follow the plane's progress as it took to the air. Instead he instructed the driver to return directly to the center of the city. Plans to outshine his colleague already formed in his mind. High time for Horst to learn he wasn't the only one capable of effective action.

CHAPTER SIXTEEN

Biarritz, Occupied France
31 August 1941

With one hand securing a hat from the de Brassis' wardrobe, Erika turned to face Agnès and Louise. She kept her back to the stiff breeze off the Bay of Biscay. The four children chased around the dry fountain out front, enjoying their freedom at last. The women had pored over every room in the mansion, determined to keep any trace of their presence out of Gestapo hands. The brothers were now shuttering windows, a major task. Once the group was away, any curious observer would assume the place battened down for the coming winter and its owner off traveling.

"It's very lovely country over in Gascony." Erika still hoped to keep the children together as a family. She had no expectation that their parents would ever be found alive. "And there's plenty of room on the farm for the two of you, as well."

"We thank you for the generous offer, but Louise will hear nothing of abandoning Bayonne—she returns to the townhouse this morning, come what may." The concierge confirmed with a nod.

Erika looked up at the rooftop. The brothers had consigned the bodies of Madame de Brassis and Nicole to the basement furnace and the tall chimney released thick braids of smoke into the onshore wind. The memory of lifeless Nicole haunted her, of that ugly wound oozing purple in the pale light. She recalled her own mother's death and that last embrace before Erika's train left the Giessen station. A suicide done of love for a doomed husband now mirrored in a young mother's tragic mistake. Horst's malice knew no bounds.

She shook her mind clear and picked up the thread of Louise's last comment. "But the Gestapo will come to Bayonne looking for Madame de Brassis."

"Of course they'll drop by eventually, my dear. That's why Louise must remain at her concierge post, feigning ignorance of all that's happened so they don't get suspicious."

"But you and the children could still come with us to Morlanne, right?"

Agnès refused to give in. "That would be lovely, but we'll be safer in Pau. I've family connections there and perhaps I can reunite Jacqueline and Robert with their own relatives. They deserve family who'll love them as much as we do." Her voice turned hoarse. "Hard enough having just lost Jakob to who-knows-what, and now having to part from little Sophie." She dabbed at her eyes. "But she and Leo get along so well, and at my age I'm not sure I'll be up to the challenges of handling one so young for much longer."

"All the more reason to join us, and we could certainly use your help."

The governess patted Erika's sleeve. "You three go on to your farm and wait for your man. I'll just disappear into the city with my young charges." She squinted into the wind but Erika knew the tears had a different cause. "First we'll see the three of you off at the bus terminal tomorrow, of course." Agnès was again all business. "Give me the directions to that farm of yours and I'll commit them to memory. If things are less than welcoming in Pau we'll seek you out, *d'accord*?"

The soldiers now appeared inside the glassed-in conservatory. They struggled to heft the safe brought down from the upstairs master suite onto the wooden table. The women went in to oversee the operation. The men set to work with sulfuric acid, a machinist's drill and cold chisels and hammers taken from the work shed. Soon the stench of the acid became nauseating, and the sisters chose to wait outside in the wind. In less than an hour the strongbox finally gave up its small fortune in cash and jewelry. While the brothers cleaned up the mess, Erika laid out each find on the heavy oaken table and Agnès assumed the duty of paymaster.

Heinrich and Herbert happily took their shares in francs. As they stuffed much of the bundled money into their boots, Erika insisted they also take some of the smaller jewelry for the hazardous trip east. Always good for bribes, she assured them. Erika and Agnès' shares disappeared within the satin lining of two suitcases, much heavier now for their hidden caches. Louise bundled hers into a dishcloth and placed it at the bottom of a woven bag alongside the package destined for von Kredow in Berlin. Once the treasure was distributed, the battered safe disappeared beneath the sands at the base of the cliff.

With the safe-cracking tools back in the shed, Herbert drove the motorcycle of the late Monsieur de Brassis into an overgrown ravine near the edge of the estate. Then Heinrich brought the Ford limousine around from the carriage house and all piled in for the short drive north. At the outskirts of Bayonne they pulled over. Louise kissed her sister goodbye, bid the others adieu. Erika watched her lively step fade to the shuffle of a tired crone as she headed away to catch a local bus. "Louise always was the better actress," Agnès said. The concierge would drop off the "proof of death" at the post office, preserved in de Brassis' liquor and carefully wrapped for the next airmail delivery to Berlin.

Sheltered from the harsh onshore wind by the river estuary, Bayonne was rapidly warming. The queue to get through the gate and onto the platforms was long and stationary. Only a gentle breeze off the Adour made the wait tolerable. Now in street clothes, the brothers joked around with the children. They laughed at her mention of the risks involved in deserting. "We're not actually abandoning our duties, Frau von Kredow," Herbert explained quietly and with obvious tongue in cheek. "Our orders were to keep an eye on these youngsters, *nicht wahr*? Well, we can't watch over the brats if we're stuck here on the coast, now can we?" The women shook their heads at the brothers' air of calm. With such casual confidence, perhaps all would actually work out for the best.

Erika excused herself to use the public phone. The long-distance operator was unsuccessful in reaching Doctor Ballineux outside Nantes. Erika insisted on placing the call again. Both her men needed to know Horst still lived, and the doctor was her sole contact. René knew how to get a message to Ryan's brother in Paris, who could then pass along this shocking news. Her frustration grew with each distant ring of the doctor's phone. The operator asked tartly if Erika wished a third attempt. Just then the crowd began working forward toward the checkpoint and she hung up without a response. She would try again from Pau, but knowing the two most important men in her life remained in danger tore at her heart.

The border control officers moved methodically through the train occupying the neighboring track. From her window Erika watched the men appear and reappear as they moved from compartment to compartment, checking papers, questioning, sometime interrogating, often badgering. The express carrying affluent passengers took natural precedence over Erika's three-car local, but the many hours on board had not been easy and she wished the *Boches* would hurry it up, forget worrying about those priority travelers and come harass her and her fellow sufferers instead. *Anything to get this over with!*

Tall metal fencing rose out of woods on either side of the double rail bed. A striped barricade arm blocked the vehicle roadway to the right, where uniformed guards periodically depressed the counter-weight to allow the passage of cars, trucks and horse-drawn wagons into and out of Vichy territory. German and French armed soldiers slouched in the oppressive heat, sweat blotching their uniforms, exhaustion souring their faces. Those currently off-duty found shelter beneath the overhanging eaves of the two guard sheds. Less fortunate were the men controlling the vehicle crossing, forced to suffer the full assault of the afternoon sun beneath steel helmets. Fifty meters ahead stood a second barrier manned by the French *Douane,* whose custom inspections would further delay all travelers.

The hard wooden benches of third class had become devices of slow torture. Even the upbeat mood of the older children had turned sour in the debilitating heat. A tin of cookies from the de Brassis pantry was all that kept Sophie from her next tantrum, but Erika figured she'd find the time and energy to teach the toddler better manners once this trip was only a bad memory. She wished she too could drop to the floor, kicking and screaming, if only to distract herself from this misery.

From time to time a caged rooster on an old man's lap expressed similar aggravation at the delay. Nearby passengers attempting to doze in the oppressive atmosphere bolted instantly awake every time the bird crowed. Despite the open windows the stagnant air betrayed unwashed bodies and unchanged diapers, and a steam pump on the neighboring locomotive recharged its brake lines with monotonous regularity—ka-thump ka-thump—a dull, rhythmic beat echoing the throb in Erika's head.

They had purposefully chosen the local rather than an express, anticipating a trip of a few hours at most. A slow train stopping at every waystation seemed far less likely to harbor fugitives seeking escape from the Occupied Zone. Two wicker baskets held foodstuffs from the Biarritz pantry, since neither drinking water nor provisions were available en route. But the women hadn't counted on many stifling hours side-tracked in a third-class rail car waiting for the arrival of a replacement locomotive when theirs suffered some mechanical failure.

Their suitcases in the overhead rack contained clothing, a few diapers for Sophie, and basic toiletries. Should an inspector ask for a look inside, they intended to lift down the cases themselves, since the added weight of the gold, currency and precious stones could easily betray them. A small fortune traveled along under the most ordinary and trying of conditions. They had agreed to leave behind all pistols rather than risk discovery and unavoidable arrest.

Erika had chosen a bench close to the rear of the last carriage. Leo and Sophie sat beside her, facing Agnès and her orphans. The two groups pretended to be strangers, but the children began mugging and giggling at secret jokes almost immediately. Leo and Jacqueline were the instigators, and despite her stern reaction, Erika could understand their frustration and boredom. The expected two-hour trip had already consumed much of the day, with both temperature and humidity climbing as the afternoon progressed. Now she secretly longed for a bit of naughty behavior to replace those glum faces and mumbled complaints.

Agnès' identification papers would pass any muster, since they confirmed her true profession as a state-licensed nursemaid. A letter from a private pediatric clinic in Toulouse authorized her to accompany displaced orphans moving between Occupied France and the Free Zone.

Erika's forged identity card was less convincing. Far from her documented "home" in Nantes, she also carried a few forged letters from "grandparents" requesting she travel to Pau for family medical reasons. Expired ration cards issued at the Morlanne city hall were her one verifiable connection to Gascony. The coupon booklet would leave her handbag only should things get sticky at the border.

Her rigid posture borne of worry aggravated the ache in both her tailbone and head. The knife cut on her finger throbbed. From time to time she shot a furtive glance to Agnès in unspoken commiseration. The nursemaid smiled back bravely, nervously smoothing imaginary wrinkles from her skirt. Erika found the gesture increasingly annoying.

Behind them sat the young brothers, now officially deserters. From time to time Erika noted their hushed conversation in Czech. Occasionally they laughed or sent cigarette smoke wafting forward to aggravate her headache. The men wore expensive civilian clothing taken from the closet of the late Monsieur de Brassis—tan trousers, open collars with loose neckties, well-cut tweed jackets. Their forged papers passed inspection at the Bayonne checkpoint so would likely present no difficulties at the Demarcation Line. *If those damned inspectors ever finish with that damned express!*

On their way at last! Erika watched the inspectors descend to the rail bed, glance over at her track, then move forward between the trains. Two men in their mid-twenties, clipboards in hand, pistols holstered, exhaustion written across dour faces. The taller man signaled the engineer of the express with a dismissive wave of the hand and the locomotive responded with a screech of the whistle before chuffing forward to enter Vichy France. The customs shack awaited just meters ahead. The Germans hesitated below her window, stealing a quick puff or two before flicking away the still-burning butts and approaching the forward carriage of her train. At the step they brushed their caps free of cinders and climbed aboard. The inspection ritual began again from the top.

The headache and heat had gotten the best of her, robbing her of focus on the task at hand. An eternity passed before the inspectors reached her carriage. The men moved with painful slowness from bench to bench, one to either side of the aisle. Occasionally they traded comments, exchanged documents for second opinions, or laughed at some inside joke. She tensed each time an inspector compared a traveler's identity card to the list on the clipboard. Only then did she nearly forget the pounding between her ears.

Now they came to Agnès. The nursemaid smoothed out her skirt, stood in deference to their authority and dutifully offered her papers to the taller officer. The man took in Erika and grinned in obvious appreciation, then returned to vetting the nursemaid's identity.

Agnès put confidence in her voice. "I believe you'll find everything in order, sir."

"When I last looked, that was still my decision to make, madame." His French carried a Bavarian accent. His cool blue eyes sought out Erika's and she realized he'd meant it to be humorous and was anticipating her acknowledgement of his wit. The officer briefly scanned Agnès' letter from the clinic, compared it to entries in the nurse's identity booklet, and returned the papers. "Your final destination is Toulouse?"

"Yes, sir. These two," her hands on the shoulders of Robert and Jacqueline, "head to an orphanage. Then it's back to Bayonne for me." He nodded dismissively.

Turning, he focused on Erika, his smile returned and she could read his thoughts. It was an attitude she knew all too well. Blood rushed to her cheeks, now from both anger and nerves rather than the debilitating heat. "And just whom do we have here, madame?" He ignored the two children at her side.

She fished about in her handbag. *"Ma carte d'identité, monsieur."*

"You are very far from home, madame." He whistled for the attention of his colleague and displayed her with a sweep of his hand like a prize filly at a horse auction. "Reason for crossing the border?"

"The children haven't seen their grandparents in a good long while and now they both are ailing."

The man hesitated, one finger at the dueling scar on his cheek, the others at his chin. She thought of Horst. "Do I detect a hint of German in your French, *madame*?"

Erika silently cursed the liability of her native tongue. "I lived in Hesse as a child, *monsieur*, and was bilingual by the time my French parents returned to Gascony."

"I'm sure the fatherland is poorer for your absence, *mein Schatz*. But as for me, I am all the richer in making your acquaintance." The inspectors exchanged sly grins. "So where is the father of these handsome children?" The officer's eyes ran the length of her body. "And what man allows such a desirable wife to travel unattended? Just imagine the possible consequences!"

Erika kept her anger in check as she sought a way out. "My husband has yet to return from the war, so a woman has to make do, wouldn't you agree?" *A despicable little game now, and with children at my feet, yet!*

"Indeed, madame." He ran his fingers through his straw blonde hair and replaced his cap. "A tiring journey for the three of you, given this unseasonal heat. Have you considered a relaxing evening here at the border?"

She lifted Sophie to her hip and placed her hand on Leo's shoulder. "It's unlikely we'd find anything suitable nearby, and their grandparents await our arrival in Pau." She hoped the obvious presence of children might cool his ardor.

Leo intervened. "*Maman*, it's—"

"Hush, darling, let *Maman* talk to this considerate German officer." She held out her hand for her papers. "As I was saying, we can rest when we reach our destination."

Had she not been so fatigued, had her head not throbbed incessantly, Erika might have realized she'd entered a trap. Now she heard the door slam shut. With a chuckle the officer turned to his companion. "Stefan, this adorable creature is clearly weary and needs a break. Do you suppose we might find her lodging nearby?" The tip of his tongue followed the line of his thin mustache, as if savoring some fine liqueur on his upper lip. "Think you can handle the rest of this one by yourself while I do my chivalrous duty and find her a suitable bed?"

His partner fixed his gaze on Erika's body. "Make the Führer proud, comrade!" He gave a quick Hitler salute and snapped his heels together. "Émile up the street will have a room available, and his old lady will mind the brats while you help this one to 'relax.' "

Erika stepped back abruptly, realizing she'd lost control of the situation. This man had full authority to force her off the train and he was giving no time to object. "Please come with me, *mein Schatz*." He took her elbow, his forearm pressing into her breast. "How very lonely having a husband away for so long. A nice bath, a pleasant drink or two and a little spoiling will make a new woman of you." He raised his voice for his partner's sake. "Though I doubt there's much I'll wish to change once I've had a closer look."

She went numb as the man guided her toward the carriage door at the rear. Leo hurried to catch up. The small blackjack in her bra would be useless until she found herself alone with this man. Agnès watched them exit while the two older children tugged at her sleeves, demanding an explanation. Erika shot a look at the brothers as she passed by. Their eyes met hers but remained unreadable.

Other nearby passengers stared down at the floor, desperate to remain uninvolved, private lives and personal secrets likely hanging in the balance. No one wished to fall under the crosshairs of the remaining officer, who leered appreciatively at Erika's ass with an envious smirk on his face.

With no warning, Heinrich lunged past the children and brought the first officer to the floor. They fell in a tangle of luggage and baskets as passengers jumped aside to avoid the struggle. The officer fought for his pistol but Heinrich wrapped the man in a body hold, one forearm over the officer's throat in an unrelenting chokehold. The moment Heinrich left the bench, Herbert dropped the man's partner with a powerful right to the jaw, then bent over and pounded him viciously until he lay still. The brothers shouted to each other in German, confirming both officers were down for the count.

Horrified mothers pulled children close and passengers close to the brawl pressed to the windows. Erika held Sophie tight and dove with Leo to the back wall of the carriage. The child bawled loudly in protest and other small children joined in, and the disturbed rooster flapped his wings rapidly and crowed repeatedly, finding new excitement in all the activity. Most travelers remained silent, leaving this internal *Boche* problem to the feuding Germans.

Even with both inspectors unconscious, only a few dared to make whispered comments. Erika retrieved her identity papers and quickly rejoined the children, huddling down beside Agnès.

Heinrich and Herbert ordered the aisle cleared and no one protested. The brothers dragged the inspectors into the narrow passage alongside the WC and set to work removing the uniforms, leaving the inspectors in nothing but their underwear. They rolled their civilian garb into parcels cinched tight with belts for ease of carrying , then stuffed their cash and jewels into every available pocket. A stooped *grand-mère* hobbled back to offer them a spool of knitting yarn for trussing up the downed men. Once that was done and Herbert had returned the skein, the grandmother went back to her knitting.

Now fully outfitted as German officers with holstered pistols and uniform caps, the grinning brothers saluted the children. Heinrich then addressed the passengers: "*Mesdames, messieurs,* our apologies for the disruption, *bon voyage*, and we'll be on our way." They stepped over the bodies and dropped the bundles, then swung down to join them.

Heinrich gave a lazy wave to the locomotive engineer up front. The train whistled sharply and rolled forward. The guards in the shack didn't look up as the local rattled past. In the brief moment when the carriages hid them from view, they grabbed their bundled clothing and loped across the rail bed, disappearing from sight in the dense foliage of the ravine.

Like a Victrola suddenly turned to full volume, the crowd broke loose in conversation and animated gesture, strangers questioning strangers about everything just witnessed. Erika turned to Agnès: "But why'd they step in? They could've let that idiot take me and been safely into the Free Zone!"

"To help you and the kids, of course," she patted Erika's hand in reassurance, "but also for a more selfish reason. The control in Bayonne never spotted a mistake in their papers, but we knew this border could give them serious trouble. You see, the counterfeiter must not have cared much for *Boches*, or he was an idiot. He listed both their birth years as 1941. They are indeed young, but that's a bit of a stretch, don't you think?"

Erika collapsed onto the bench and pulled the children to her side. "So what will they do now?"

"Find a border guide once they've ditched the uniforms, I suppose. I've heard *passeurs* make a good living around here. At least the boys now have money and pistols." The train was already squealing to a stop on Vichy soil. Agnès encouraged everyone to find seats. "After an inspection like that, French customs should be a snap."

Erika looked back at the unconscious officers. "Should we just let the *Douane* find them lying there?"

"Let's give our boys a solid head start before we tell the customs officials about how those nasty young men attacked the *Boches* without provocation."

CHAPTER SEVENTEEN

Pau to Morlanne, Vichy France
31 August – 1 September 1941

The oppressive heat was long gone by the time they finally detrained. Erika insisted on trying to reach the doctor again, but still no one picked up. One more worry to add to the mix. Agnès arranged for all to spend the night with her niece, who graciously made do with an apartment full of tired children and exhausted adults. In the morning, a clearly refreshed Agnès led Erika, Sophie and Leo to the bus terminal and saw them off with best wishes for a safe journey.

The decrepit regional bus constantly backfired as it left town and headed north on the country road. As with all public transport, the passenger compartment was filled to overflowing. Erika held Sophie on her lap. Leo hadn't been able to contain his excitement all morning, telling Sophie repeatedly about each of his animal friends on the farm. Despite many scheduled and one unscheduled stop—the haggard driver fiddling with the carburetor, his head buried beneath the hood—the ramshackle bus ultimately deposited them in front of the *mairie* in Morlanne.

Erika led the children into city hall. Regretting the lack of a public phone, the clerk took pity and agreed to call for the local taxi. Within minutes a derelict Citroën sat waiting at the curb. The young driver with a missing left arm ran around to stow their suitcase in the trunk. "And where are we off to, madame?" he asked.

His cheerful demeanor was contagious. Erika was curious to see how he managed steering while manually shifting gears. She instructed him to follow the provincial route heading northwest. "Perhaps you're familiar with the LeBlanc farm?" Erika pictured the helpful neighbor who had recently handled burial arrangements for Jeanne.

"Yes, madame, Monsieur LeBlanc is very well known around here."

"Well, his place adjoins ours, so as we get closer, I can give you specifics?"

"Of course, madame. And what brings you to Gascony?" He bent to brace his shoulder against the steering wheel with every change of gears. "You speak fine French, madame, but I catch the trace of an accent." His brow furrowed. "German?"

"Raised in Germany." Erika hesitated. "My mother-in-law recently passed and we're here to stay at her cousin's farm. The children and I will tend to the place while we wait for my husband."

"My deepest condolences on your loss, madame."

"Thank you."

The man's eyes returned to the road. "Your husband…he is also a *Boche… Allemand*?"

"Alsatian."

"Ah, I see." He nodded when he caught her eye in the rearview mirror. "Ours is a close-knit community and I believe I know just which farm you seek." He described it in detail before adding: "Word is the animals went free. It took Monsieur LeBlanc a day to round them up."

Erika could think of nothing to add. Leo, now dozing beside Sophie, couldn't offer his perfectly logical explanation. The driver also fell silent but his eyes repeatedly met Erika's in the mirror.

The old car shifted in fits and starts along the undulating road. Nearing the farmstead, the driver came to a halt a hundred meters short of the gate. Looking over his shoulder, he smiled at the two sleeping children, his sympathy apparent. "Forgive my presumptuousness, madame, but some around here may blame you for attracting unwanted Gestapo interest to our area." Erika said nothing. "So I wouldn't expect too warm a welcome hereabouts. If I were you, I'd take those children elsewhere before the secret police show up again."

"Thank you for your concern, monsieur." Erika stroked the damp hair from Leo's forehead and gently nudged Sophie awake. "You may drop us off up ahead and we'll walk in. But if you wouldn't mind, please wait up the road just beyond the gate." She removed several larger franc notes from her handbag and passed them forward. "I'll make it well worth your while."

The young driver pocketed the bills and grinned. "Of course, madame. Always glad to be of service."

The car lurched to a stop and the young driver sprang from the cab, opened Erika's door and fetched her bag from the trunk. His brow wrinkled. "Do take care, madame." He sounded sincere. Erika watched for a few moments as the taxi made a U-turn at the next curve in the road and pulled onto the shoulder. He tipped his cap to her.

She hefted Sophie onto her hip. Leo, still rubbing sleep from his eyes, looked around in surprise. "But *Maman*, we're here already!" He became exuberant, tugging at his mother's arm, urging her to hurry before setting off on his own up the hill. "I want to see Musette, I'm sure she's missed me!"

"Come back here right now, and stay at my side!"

Leo reluctantly retraced his steps. "But *Maman*, she'll want to see me again! Cats are like that, you know."

"All the same, we stay together until we reach the house."

Leo appeared worried, sensing her mood. "Will there be trouble, *Maman*? I can help, you know."

"I don't think so, Leo. But we have learned to be careful, right?" He nodded, suddenly very serious.

The dirt road curved to the right. As the farmstead came into sight, all appeared normal. A few cows grazed in the pasture below and a hen in the coop announced the arrival of a new egg. But reaching the picket fence, Erika spotted something amiss. All of Jeanne's flower plantings and rosebushes formed a wilted mass atop the compost heap. The house itself appeared vacant, but the bench and chairs normally found on the porch were stacked to one side. And most disturbing, the rear bumper of a truck protruded beyond the far side of the house.

Just then the screen door creaked and Monsieur Le-Blanc strode out to join them under the midday sun. A scowl creased his face and Erika briefly spotted a shadowy figure lurking inside just beyond the threshold. Someone at the *mairie* in Morlanne had obviously sent word of their imminent return to the farm.

Erika put on a gracious smile and greeted the neighbor with a handshake. "Monsieur LeBlanc, quite a surprise to find you here. Has there been trouble?"

"We never expected to see the likes of you around here again, madame."

"No? I believe my husband spoke with you about the interment of his mother. Did he lead you to believe we were abandoning her property?"

The farmer took a moment to light his pipe before choosing his words carefully: "Let me assure you that your mother-in-law received a proper Christian burial. No real ceremony, of course, but your husband said she wouldn't have chosen that. You may visit her at the cemetery should you wish."

"We are most grateful for that, sir. But what's going on here?" She pointed to the devastated flower garden. Leo eyed it nervously, questioning her with his look. He started to walk toward the rabbit pens and Erika called him back.

LeBlanc continued confidently: "Your family left under unusual circumstances. The gendarmes were here along with the Gestapo." Now Leo glared at the man. "In fact, they have started an inquiry after the suspicious deaths of two older women at this farm."

"Just what are you implying?"

"I imply nothing, madame, merely state the obvious. The owner of record passed away a short while back. Now your mother-in-law up and dies in the same house within months. I come over to find the place untended, the animals on the run." He pointed at Leo with the stem of his pipe, "and the boy there was missing. You'll understand the official concern."

Erika was unappeased. "So you tear up the flower garden?" Her voice dripped sarcasm. "Searching for more bodies, perhaps?"

"Making room for more livestock, madame." He released a stream of smoke. The figure in the shadows of the living room remained a silhouette. "This property is now fully in my care."

She dropped the suitcase at her feet and took an angry step toward him. "We asked you to keep an eye on it, not turn it upside-down."

"Where's my cat?" Leo glared at the man. "Where's Musette."

The man laughed at the distraction. "Take a look at the barn, kid. Usually down there."

Leo looked to Erika, who nodded approval. "Keep close." She straightened his jacket collar while whispering in German. "Danger! Hide close-by until I call you." She watched Leo head down the path lined with upturned earth, then turned back to LeBlanc. "So this is how you care for another's property?"

"That's just it, madame—I'm afraid the farm doesn't belong to you. It's now the property of the local authority based on an abandonment claim. The village authorities found it sensible to put me in charge until further notice, since my properties adjoin this one. Farm production is in too short supply to have these fields sitting idle."

Erika couldn't hide her contempt. "And, as I recall, the 'authority' in such matters is a relative of yours?"

The man laughed again, a good-natured card player caught cheating at the neighborhood tavern. He beckoned toward the house with a wave of his hand and the local constable emerged into the sunlight. Erika had only met the man once and taken an instant dislike to the lawman's supercilious grin. "Madame, allow me to reacquaint you with my brother-in-law, Constable Graves."

The official stepped down off the porch. "Madame," he touched the brim of his cap, "I'm afraid I must detain you here. I have orders to hold you for interrogation."

The situation was clear. She had stumbled upon the last vestige of Horst's widespread manhunt. If unchecked, it could mean her incarceration and, far worse, the loss of her children. Options limited, she assumed an accepting calm.

"Very well, sir. I've nothing to hide. But I must get my little girl out of the sun. May we all go inside?"

"Be my guest." The constable made a gentlemanly gesture toward the open door. Erika spotted Leo crouching low beside the rear bumper of the nearly hidden truck, awaiting her signal. She casually put a finger to her lips as she entered the farmhouse. The men followed closely behind. Setting Sophie down on Leo's old cot, she turned to her captors. "My daughter needs a change of diaper. Would one of you gentlemen bring in my valise?"

She looked to LeBlanc and the farmer agreed with a nod. "Of course, madame." He went out into the sun, the screen door slamming in his wake, leaving her alone with the constable. She removed the soiled diaper, the rank odor pervading the small living room. Sophie giggled in relief and kicked her naked legs in the air. "Good!" she said. "Good!" The constable stepped to the open window, seeking escape from the sight and smell of the child's dirty bottom.

In one quick move Erika dropped him with her black-jack. He exhaled as he hit the planks. She gave another blow as added insurance before positioning herself behind the open door. Moments later LeBlanc stepped back in. He came to an abrupt halt at the sight of the little girl on the daybed, now freed of her diaper and lying unattended. The cudgel dropped him, first to his knees, then the ground. She grabbed the suitcase and threw it on the cot beside Sophie.

Erika called for Leo and quickly diapered the child. His footsteps pounded across the wooden porch and he ran inside. The sight of the downed men brought a smile to his face. "You've done it again, *Maman*!"

She put Sophie on her hip. "The suitcase, Leo! Close it and we're out of here!"

They hurried to the main road, slowed only by Leo's difficulties with the heavy valise. Erika had her arms full with Sophie hanging on her neck and protesting the sudden departure. She waved to the waiting taxi driver. Crunching the vehicle into gear, he rumbled down to pick them up, then made a U-turn and put the accelerator to the floor. "Where now, madame?"

"Farther north. And thank you." He smiled before turning his concentration to the curving road ahead. "And will we be followed, madame?"

"I suspect so, monsieur. There was a truck and quite possibly an auto, as well, though I can't be certain of that."

Leo piped in, "Oh yes, *Maman*, an automobile, too. But don't worry about those." He settled back with a smug expression. "I took care of everything."

Turning her attention from the rear window, she gave him a curious look. "What do you mean, Leo?"

He offered an impish grin. "Uncle Rénard taught me how."

"How to do what?"

He bent closer to her, throwing a quick glance at the cabdriver, who appeared to concentrate on his one-armed shifting. "It's actually very simple. You put stuff in the fuel tanks—you know, sand, dirt, whatever's handy. Uncle says they can try to follow you but won't get very far!"

Erika was less than convinced. "Will that really be enough to stop them?"

"Don't worry, *Maman*. I also let air out of the tires." He laughed. "Those men will be pretty mad when they wake up."

She couldn't resist another look back. The road remained clear and she hugged her son to her. "You're as clever as your father," she said, but thought "fathers."

"I know." Leo sat back in the seat. "And *Maman*?"

"Yes, love?"

"Musette was at the truck and she's nice and fat, so she must be finding lots of mice."

The driver chuckled as the taxi slowed to a more reasonable pace. They rolled to a stop where the road forked. "So, where's it to be, madame?"

Leo settled down to teaching Sophie the names of objects and animals spotted from the taxi, then confusing her by giving the German equivalent. The young driver agreed to a substantial sum for driving as far as the Demarcation Line. Fuel was scarce, but a gold bracelet with tiny emeralds convinced the proprietor of a crossroads service station to fill their tank, despite her lack of ration cards. He would surely find a way to short his next customer.

Doubts plagued her every thought. Why didn't Dr. Ballineux answer his phone? How else to reach René? She had tried calling the previous evening and several times from the bus depot that morning. Still nothing. What if René tried to contact her by way of that traitorous LeBlanc. The man would surely draw him into a trap in Gascony. Her only solution now was to track down René, and quickly.

As the hours passed, she considered who she'd once hoped to become. She explored paths taken, mistakes made. The endless questioning of her motives and decisions soon left her devastated. When young, her desire for high society and adventure had shaped her direction, and how much suffering that naïveté had brought to those around her! Both parents had paid with their lives. She'd exposed Leo to violence and fear, and all her loved ones to incredible risk. But

worst of all, she'd failed to save millions of suffering innocents. The theft of Horst's horrifying protocol had come to
nothing. She fought back tears of self-recrimination. This
ache was too great a distraction, itself a threat to these price-
less children and the loving man relying on her in the face of
adversity. And if that weren't enough, an unexpected and
troubling development was now on the horizon.

"What's wrong, *Maman?*" Leo's worry reflected the
distress in his mother's eyes. Sophie began to sob in commiseration. Leo sidled closer to his mother. "Please don't
cry!"

"It's nothing, my darlings, nothing at all." She blew her
nose and hugged the children closer. "I miss Uncle René so
much. So now we're going to head home to be with him, all
right?"

Leo assumed his favorite role and comforted Sophie,
drawing her attention to spotted cows in a pasture beyond a
passing fence. He looked over at his mother and whispered:
"I'm helping you, right *Maman?*"

Home. Such a curious word. She'd had so many since
Marburg, each temporary, each fraught with danger and
abandoned under threat of death and cover of night. Would
she ever find a sanctuary free of upheaval and cruelty? They
had often spoken of crossing into Spain to seek a calmer life,
but to go it alone now would mean accepting the possibility
of never again reuniting.

No, her decision was final. She'd had enough separation in the last days to fill a lifetime, enough incessant worry
about René's safety and their own. Her husband was mentally sharp but trusted too willingly. She would track him down
in Nantes or Saint-Nazaire. They would attack the U-boat
pens before moving on to more stable ground. Then René
would continue to fight the Nazis, seeking vengeance for

having surrendered his Rhine birthright to bastards like Horst.

Yes, René was set in his role, but she was changing from fighter to mother. Wasn't tending the children and teaching them right from wrong equally important as fighting evil with a blackjack or pistol? She was tired of fleeing, of the struggle, exhausted by the prospect of shielding Leo and now Sophie from the dangers ahead in such a tormented world.

Leo—such a devilishly complicated boy, and so determined to be her protector. No wonder, given what he had witnessed, all he'd overcome on his own. Leo was strong, a survivor. His was the precocious mind of Ryan tempered by the same down-to-earth determination of René. Leo would prosper. How she loved the boy!

And Sophie, with those dark curls and blue eyes, was quickly winning her heart. The little girl who had lost so much had a bright mind. She adored her new brother and gleefully mimicked him, even when clearly wondering what he was up to. But the child was also quick to voice her dissatisfaction in the loudest of terms. Strong-willed, as had been her mother. That trait might benefit her in a world turned upside-down by war and deprivation, but soon she would need potty-training and become even more demanding. She would need some semblance of a stable home.

It was up to Erika to make sense of this little family, and she willed herself to be strong once more. As long as Horst lived, René and Ryan remained at risk. Vigilance on her part was vital, and she wouldn't let them down. Only in protecting those she loved could she atone for the damage and hurt already done, for all the suffering.

The fault truly lay with her. Once, in a moment of indecision, she had held in her hands that morphine syringe and chosen not to put a definitive end to Horst's cruelties. They all paid a price for that moment of compassion. They would do so until someone, somehow, sent that brutal monster to his death.

This time for good!

CHAPTER EIGHTEEN

Paris, Occupied France
2 September 1941

The sergeant's well-cut uniform suited his luxurious post. He sat ramrod straight behind an ornate walnut desk and screened visitors to the Occupation's administrative offices in the Hotel de Crillon. Many of the grand hotels now did similar duty throughout the city. The non-com held court behind a leather-bound appointment book embossed with a bold black swastika. To his right stood an equally impressive soldier at parade rest. Ed's three-piece suit and burgundy tie had seemed suitable enough for any diplomatic purpose that morning, but now his tweeds appeared rumpled and déclassé amidst such military finery.

The sergeant greeted him respectfully in French. "The purpose of your visit, sir?"

Ed slid a calling card across the polished surface and replied in American-accented German. "Edward Lemmon, United States Department of State, here to see Herr Richard Kohl."

The non-com switched to English, his tone a bit less cordial. "You have an appointment, Mr. Lemmon?"

While America remained ostensibly neutral, many in the Reich recognized the lay of the land. This soldier had quickly assumed a combative stance more suited to addressing a future adversary, and Ed knew better than most that "neutrality" was on borrowed time. Congress already provided materiel and moral support to the Allies under the Lend-Lease program, and the shift was obvious at high governmental levels despite the Charles Lindberghs, Ham Fishes and Rush Holts who campaigned ceaselessly for isolationism back home.

"Yes, Herr Kohl set this appointment himself," Ed consulted the mahogany clock on the wall. "I'm now running late. Can we hurry this along?"

The sergeant opened his log book and ran a finger to the appropriate entry. "Yes, here you are—room 233." He nodded to one of the enlisted men crowding a satin-covered bench across the vestibule. By the time a soldier appeared at Ed's side to lead him away, the sergeant had already beckoned to the next visitor in line, greeting him respectfully in French.

The enlisted man stepped off smartly with a "Please follow me, sir" and guided Ed to the lifts. Outside 233 the soldier knocked and stepped aside to allow Ed to enter. Kohl rose from his chair and shook his former subordinate's hand. He gestured to one of the upholstered chairs facing the broad desk. Kohl's supercilious grin was as annoying as ever as he adjusted his wire-rimmed glasses and made a notation before looking up. "So, Edward, once again we find ourselves working toward a common goal."

Ed held himself in check. "Repatriating foreign nationals may be beneficial for both countries, but our personal goals remain far apart." Ed ached for a smoke but refused any distraction, his curiosity too strong. "You requested a private meeting so let's get on with it, Kohl."

"Years of cooperation and fellowship and we're no longer on a first-name basis, Ed?"

"We both now know your true loyalties, Kohl." Ed abruptly leaned forward, his tone cold and measured. "So let's not pretend things are any different than they are. You have revealed yourself as a traitor and are thoroughly despicable. You and von Kredow have undermined American interests and plotted to kill my brother." Ed glared, his knuckles white. "So let's put all cards on the table, shall we? You're a double-dealing, homicidal bastard, and you think me a weakling unworthy of licking your fascist boots. All well and good. The only reason I'm here is the SWPD requirement that I deal with you, so get to it."

Taken aback by Ed's spurt of venom, Kohl leaned back and shifted papers until he had regained his composure. "So how is the ever-saintly Ryan doing?" Using his necktie, Kohl carefully rubbed fingerprints from his lenses. "Word is he met a bit of trouble with some partisans over in Nantes. Pity—the man's never been a great judge of character." He set the eyeglasses back on the bridge of his nose, "Or shown any real understanding of global politics, actually. Really, Edward, no one seriously buys his assignment to Special War Problems."

Ed held his gaze.

"No, our boy Ryan's now one of Donovan's do-gooders, out to save the world from the Reich." Kohl swiveled away from the fuming Edward, turning his attention to the view beyond his tall window. "Oh, yes, my friend, we have Ryan's number down, and spies are always fair game, not like diplomats, right? You'd both do well to note his days are numbered here in beautiful

France." Kohl put his feet up on the sill. "Or anywhere else, for that matter."

Ed steadied his voice. "Again, show me a purpose for this meeting or I leave now." The temptation to throttle Kohl was growing, but he'd recognized in that smug grin someone hiding a matter of mutual interest. He dared not risk losing the opportunity.

"Ah, but I believe I've just made the reason clear. Our association goes way back, and despite my seemingly abrupt change in political allegiance, you both still hold a warm place in my heart. So how about some friendly advice from your old boss at State?" Kohl braced his hands behind his head, staring across the *Rue* Boissy *d'Anglas* at two pigeons strutting along a stone cornice.

Certain that Kohl was considering what a fine meal of *pigeon rôti* they would make, Ed felt he was in Kohl's sights, as well. "It's your move, Kohl."

"For old time's sake I'm doing both of you a service, so be grateful, Ed. You can let our beloved Ryan know the Gestapo is on to him. I admit my late colleague von Kredow was a bit zealous at times and things haven't been easy for Ryan, so the least I can do now is give him a heads-up."

Kohl abruptly swiveled back and placed both hands on the desktop. "And while you're at it, tell him it's time to forget that woman and child he was so obviously fond of. An unfortunate personal loss, I'm sure, but they're both out of the picture now." He casually spat a hangnail toward the waste basket. "One less distraction for a spy, right?"

Ed felt the hairs on his neck rise. "Out of what picture?"

Kohl's smile broadened. "But of course, there's no way you could know that, is there?"

"Know what?" Ed tensed. "What about Erika and Leo?"

"So sorry, my friend, but some partisan business down in Bayonne, a real Wild-West shoot-em-up, I'm told. The woman and child came out the losers." Kohl gave a self-satisfied smirk. "A mother ought never involve herself with terrorists, right?"

Ed sat back, stunned. "That's a damned lie!" Residual evil from that bastard von Kredow, of course. "Who could possibly wish an innocent mother and child dead?"

Kohl feigned surprise. "Innocent, you say? Well, we'll save that for future discussion, but I can assure you that both bodies were cremated, leaving their deaths beyond dispute. I hear there remains physical evidence, as well. I understand how difficult this must be for you, having to share such tragic news with your brother. Please give Ryan my sincere condolences. I'm aware of the special bond he shared with that woman." Kohl rose abruptly from the desk and walked to the door. "But now, if you'll excuse me, I have more important matters to attend to. Just let Ryan know he's being watched."

Kohl opened the door and signaled to the waiting soldier. "See this gentleman to the lobby." The soldier clicked his heels together.

Ed's mind was numb with the tragic news. Erika and Leo both dead? What physical evidence could there be after cremation? What can ashes prove? And why warn Ryan he was under Gestapo watch when you've just been trying to kill him? Too many questions. Too much manipulation and deception.

He looked out across the Place de la Concorde. The vast surface glared under a blazing sun and across the Seine the Dôme Church glistened like a beacon. Traffic was mostly bicycles and a few German staff cars. An occasional taxi or troop transport rumbled by.

Waiting for the cop in the center of the square to wave the pedestrians on, Ed saw a man in herringbone jacket leave the shadow of the Crillon to join Ed curbside. He nodded politely, then began perusing a folded newspaper. Once they reached the Tuileries gardens the two men walked nearly side-by-side until the stranger peeled off toward the Pont du Carousel.

Ed moved on mechanically, his thoughts now centered solely on how to break the news to Ryan.

CHAPTER NINETEEN

Demarcation Line to Saint-Nazaire, Occupied France
2 - 4 September 1941

Reaching Nantes proved far easier than the previous day's journey to Morlanne. The taxi driver made a few inquiries in a border village and Erika greased a few palms with sizeable banknotes before finding the home of a sprightly grandmother. The widow was making ends meet in difficult economic times by helping both the desperate and the smuggler cross in and out of Occupied France. After a restless night in a cheap *auberge*, Erika and the children climbed into the back of a horse-drawn wagon, the old women took up the reins, and the cart creaked up a dirt road under a canopy of ancient pines.

The border passage brought only one encounter with authorities. A graying customs official at a dilapidated shed greeted the *grand-mère* with a kiss to both cheeks, accepted a gratuity from Erika's handbag for his part in the illegal crossing, and directed them onto a side path ignored by the German guards stationed over the hill. Within minutes their wagon emerged from the deep woods into an overgrown field in the Occupied Zone. A slate-roofed village with a rail line lay in the hazy distance and a northbound train was scheduled to arrive within the hour. The widow wished them well and Erika offered a further gratuity, at first refused. Only when Erika insisted it was "to feed the mare" did the woman accept. The sorry horse had obviously suffered during the hour-long journey and Leo drew attention to her prominent ribs and swayback.

The one disturbance in an otherwise smooth train passage stemmed from the woes of a fellow passenger on the train to Nantes. When police inspectors boarded, the nervous young man seated across from Leo began to sweat profusely. He repeatedly ran a finger beneath his collar as if it were about to choke him. The man's eyes darted about the compartment and the boy finally took pity. "Do you need to pee, monsieur? There's a *toilette* at the back."

The young man smiled nervously. "No, but thanks, kid." He took a deep breath. "It's just so infernally hot in this car." Again he stretched his collar and finally loosened the necktie a fraction.

Leo gave the man a sly grin. Erika held her breath, terrified he would draw attention with some unexpected move. The inspectors were already approaching their seats. She took charge, abruptly lifting Sophie onto the nervous man's lap. The girl burst into tears, her wail of protest affecting all within range.

Throwing Erika a grateful smile, the young man attempted to comfort the child by hugging her closely and kissing the top of her head. Sophie reacted by pushing away and protesting even more loudly. With a baleful look at Leo, Erika joined in the charade, assuring Sophie she should quiet down on "*Papa's*" lap. She then began to chastise her "husband" for his poor parenting skills when comforting a tired and obviously distressed daughter.

Taken aback by a howling child desperately seeking to escape her father's embrace, the inspectors took pity on the long-suffering parents. One took a brief look at Erika's papers, exchanged a sour smile with his comrade, and both moved on to escape the chaos. When the officials stepped out into the vestibule, the stranger handed Sophie back to Erika and offered a simple "thank you."

"We know how to handle inspectors," Leo replied.

In Nantes they were able to find a taxi willing to drive them out along the Loire. At the doctor's house overlooking the river Erika asked the driver to wait. She led the children to the door and immediately spotted yellow police tape barring the entrance "under order of the civil authorities." Now she understood the unanswered calls. Given the circumstances it was just as well, since the phone line to the house had likely been tapped by the Gestapo. She looked quickly in all directions. The surroundings appeared quiet and deserted, and the doctor's dust-covered Peugeot still sat beneath its shelter. Someone had finally denounced the compassionate old widower.

A quick search of the portico area yielded nothing, so they followed the flagstone path around to the rear garden fronting the Loire. While Leo showed Sophie the flower garden, Erika carefully searched the rear of the house. Above the back door she spotted something protruding from the wooden trim. To the casual eye it appeared to be nothing but a shard of flaking paint, but Erika and René had long ago planned for unexpected separation. With a sliver of wood she carefully coaxed out the cardstock and exhaled in relief. René had found the time to prepare for his departure so was likely still free.

The message made her heart leap: *Héloise should seek refuge where silver fish gather at the sea.* Héloise, her current code-name. "Silver fish" surely the targeted U-boats at

Saint-Nazaire. She would search out a place with a name implying refuge, likely close to the submarine bunkers. There she would find her husband and never let him go it alone again.

Le Dernier Refuge was an ancient tavern tucked beneath a narrow, five-story building barely a room and a staircase wide. The inn was shoehorned between similar buildings near the Avant-Port in Saint-Nazaire. The Old Town bar itself was clearly a sailors' dive, its walls adorned with roping and nets and old lithographs of fishing smacks and tall-masters. A rusty anchor hung from a rough-hewn rafter above the zinc bar. With the fishing fleet still out to sea and the stevedores not yet off the afternoon shift, the place was nearly empty. Two grizzled mariners with tattooed skin like worn leather smoked in a corner. A checkered board sat between them, the white chessmen so smudged by time they differed little from the black pieces.

The men looked up from their game as Erika entered with the children in tow. Before they could greet her, a middle-aged woman rushed forward from behind the bar, dishtowel still in her hand. "Ah, my dear, we've been expecting you!" She dried her hands on her apron, shook Erika's, then looked to the door in surprise. "Isn't there another woman, as well?"

Erika breathed a sigh of relief, sensing a friend at last and knowing she'd found René. "I regret she couldn't make it, madame." The mention of Nicole brought a fresh wave of sorrow. "But we are most grateful to find you."

The friendly demeanor was in sharp contrast to the woman's downturned mouth and harsh creases lining her face, evidence of a demanding life. "But of course, my dear. The children must be exhausted after your journey, and you might appreciate some time to rest and freshen up. I'll show you to your room."

Erika reluctantly surrendered the valise. The hostess entered a doorway half-hidden behind the bar. The checked curtain parted to reveal a narrow staircase rising steeply to the next floor. Erika took a last look at the old men, who seemed to have lost all interest in the new arrivals. One tapped an angry finger on the newspaper now lying between them, the chess board shoved aside. Erika put Sophie on her hip. With Leo on the woman's heels, they ascended the stairs.

Off the third landing their hostess opened the door to a small room. A double bed hugged the wall and an alcove held a daybed. In the corner, an electric hotplate and tiny sink. Mullioned windows bearing multiple layers of chipped paint looked to the basin beyond. In the distance spread the vast Loire estuary flecked with military and civilian vessels.

Only after the door closed firmly behind them did the woman speak again: "Your husband described you well and said you could show up at any time. He and my man are working side-by-side on a business matter of value to France, so you're to be our guests for as long as you wish."

"You can't imagine how grateful we are, madame." Erika recognized René's pipe sitting in an ashtray on the dresser. *How lightly we travel these days*, she thought. The woman handed back the heavy suitcase and Erika set it on the quilted bed, eliciting a creak of protest from the ancient springs. "Allow me to pay rent for the next week." She opened her handbag.

"Oh no, my dear. Put that away, please! We all fight for the same cause so there will be no talk of money. Just make yourselves at home and I'll send a message to your man."

"How rude of me—" Erika reached out to shake the woman's hand again. "My name is Héloise."

"Not rude at all, Héloise. So much on our minds these days, *n'est-ce pas?* Please call me Geneviève, and a pleasure to meet you." Her grip was firm, a working woman's hand. "Now if you'll excuse me, I must attend to my guests down below before they kill each other. Those two always argue politics the minute my back is turned. They know I forbid it." She smiled at the children, who already stood at the window, Leo pointing out the swooping seagulls to Sophie. "It's been a long while since I had little ones here. You're very lucky, Héloise. Lucky indeed."

Erika saw loss in the woman's eyes but didn't feel the time was right to inquire. Instead she silently acknowledged her own good fortune and again shook the woman's calloused hand. "Thank you so much for your gracious hospitality, Geneviève."

The innkeeper disappeared down the staircase and returned moments later. She carried a tray of fatty sausages, some butter and cheese, a half-empty bottle of red wine and a chunk of dark bread. A pitcher of milk for the children completed the unexpected and welcome meal. Setting the tray on the dresser beside René's pipe, she smiled at last and left as quickly as she had come.

Now came the anxious waiting. While the children devoured bits of sausage wrapped in butter-smeared bread, Erika sipped at the wine. Her stomach had troubled her since Bayonne and nothing seemed to sit well. Concerns about her husband had been her first thought, and Ryan out there somewhere with Horst still on his tail.

From the window she watched the activity on the streets and docks and waited for René to make his way home. A certainty was growing within and forcing her to rethink their life ahead. She'd hoped to seek confirmation from Doctor Ballineux but it wasn't needed after all. A second missed menstrual period now, and they'd always come like clockwork. Except that one time, of course, with Ryan back in America and Leo growing inside her. Nevertheless, she'd wait a few days before telling René, just in case. He would have enough on his mind. The raid must be getting close.

"Uncle René!" Leo hopped down and flew into René's open arms.

He gave the boy a big kiss on the top of his head. "And this little beauty must be Sophie." He swung her around the room, much to the delight of both children. "Ow," he said, rubbing his shoulder, "need to take it easy a bit longer." He smiled again. "But where's Nicole? Has she gone out?"

Erika embraced her husband. She kissed him and rested her head against his chest. "Little Sophie's ours now." Her voice was barely audible. "But more about that later, *d'accord*?"

René's face clouded, his grin gone. "Are you all well, my love?" She nodded, and he bent down to put an arm around Leo. "And have you looked after your mother, my little man?"

"We've been really busy, with nice ladies we first thought were mean, and soldiers who were brothers and saved us from the Nazis, and Monsieur LeBlanc, who really is mean, but I put stuff in his gas tanks and let air from his tires and we rode with some old lady on a horse-cart, and then I fooled the German inspector with Sophie's help—" he paused for a breath, "—and then…" his steam running low, "and then…oh yes, Musette's finding lots to eat in the barn so she's getting along without us."

"Quite a story, Leo, but for now do you suppose you might look after Sophie? Your mother and I have grown-up things to discuss down in the tavern."

Sophie stood beside Erika, grasping her skirt. "Yes. Sophie and I will read some more." Leo helped her up onto the mattress. "But don't let *Maman* tell you all the story or I won't have anything more for later." Erika was pleased he hadn't mentioned the death of Nicole in front of the girl. Such a thoughtful boy!

They found the bar filling with customers and claimed a small table in the farthest corner. Erika told of Horst's inexplicable survival and the tragic suicide of Nicole. "So the girl is our responsibility now, my love," she said at last.

René smiled wanly. "But my God, Erika, I thought Ryan forced cyanide down his throat!"

"I've given it a lot of thought, but we'll never know how it happened. The poison supposedly came from a British agent. That might have been another of Horst's deceptions. Maybe it wasn't a kill pill at all. Horst might have planted both the dying spy and the fake poison." She took his hand in hers. "Listen, darling, it really doesn't matter now, does it? What's important is that the sadist is still very much a danger. He drove Nicole to suicide, and should now believe Leo and I are dead, but he's sure to come after you and Ryan. Go give his brother a call right away!"

René reached a receptionist at the consular number given him by Ryan. He crafted a simple message: *Extreme urgency. Tell RL Le Masque alive in Berlin.* RG. He included the name and number of the inn. Erika waited impatiently for him to finish and return from the phone in the alcove. From time to time she eyed the front door as each new patron arrived. Even if Horst was in Berlin, his agents could be lurking out there somewhere. René returned with two glasses of beer. "It's done."

Almost an hour passed as she detailed Madame de Brassis' unexpected death, the episode at the border crossing and finally the treachery of LeBlanc.

"I'm the one who phoned that bastard and told him to expect you," René confessed. "Then the partisans told me the Gestapo picked up the doctor the day we all left. The bastards must have just missed us. I knew you'd be worried if you tried to reach me through Ballineux and got no answer. There's no way you'd stay put in Morlanne—I know you too well—so I snuck back and hid the note." He bent over and kissed her. "When I called LeBlanc again, hoping to let you know what had happened, he said you'd already come and gone. I got suspicious when he insisted on a way to reach me, so I hung up. Then I started worrying, but I knew you wouldn't rest until we made contact again."

While René brought her current on the group's sabotage plan, her thoughts drifted to Ryan, out in the field and believing himself free of a target on his back. Her stomach again unsettled, she emptied the rest of her beer into René's glass.

God, how sick I am of this war!

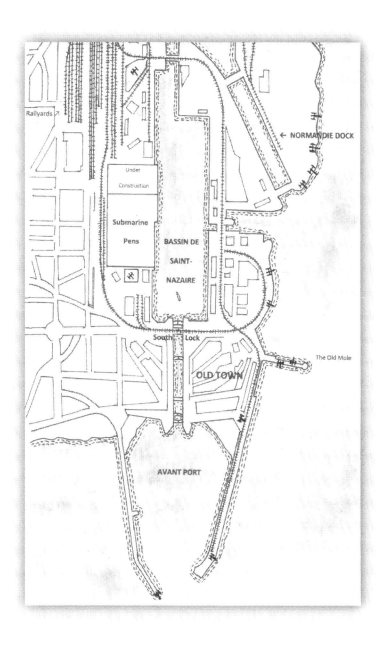

CHAPTER TWENTY

Saint-Nazaire, Occupied France
9 September 1941

René and Malraux entered Old Town just as dawn broke over the hills to the east. Daylight raced across the broad estuary, but barely penetrated the tight labyrinth of stone buildings surrounding the headquarters of the 7th Submarine Flotilla.

René's dark beard was gone. Young partisan Raymond, apprenticed to a barber, had created for him a tight military haircut befitting his new look. A black-and-silver Knight's Cross decorated the blue Kriegsmarine uniform of a *Kapitän zur See*. Awarded for distinguished valor in battle, the medal justified René's limp, clearly an old war wound.

Malraux's uniform denoted his status as René's adjutant. The British spy's first-hand knowledge of the German military had prepared both men for what to expect. The guard at the door accepted the high-ranking officer at face value. He saluted and all but ignored the forged identity papers before announcing the visitors' arrival to the commandant.

The office smelled of mold and stale tobacco, and the old stone walls glistened with moisture. *Kapitänleutnant* Herbert Steiner had just arrived from his main headquarters at l'Hôtel l'Hermitage some thirty minutes up the coast at La

Baule. He showed deference to René's superior rank as the three officers exchanged Hitler salutes.

Steiner had the bearing of a typical submarine commander—fit of body, sparing of words and accustomed to having his orders obeyed. The man appeared about René's age, slender and handsome in an unassuming way. He offered his guests tea. René politely declined for both, "determined to keep to a tight inspection schedule."

Steiner held out cigarettes in a monogrammed case and his lighter made the rounds. As smoke gathered in the low overhead beams, the commandant scanned René's letter of introduction. Ostensibly from Navy Group Command West in Paris, it directed *Kapitän zur See* "Greifinger" to inspect the entire 7th Flotilla naval facility at Saint-Nazaire and evaluate its preparedness. It mentioned potential SOE or partisan sabotage and instructed Steiner to give full access to the visitors.

René and Malraux owed the authenticity of their paperwork to a libidinous naval courier. The man had fallen for the charms of a particularly attractive prostitute whose sole mission in the cause of freedom was to attract his attention. Once the German was deep in her embrace at one of the town's notorious *maisons tolerées*, a partisan within the brothel filched a few official documents from the courier's bag. Those innocuous items gave the group's forger enough to replicate documents worthy of very close scrutiny. Whether they were missed was anyone's guess.

René checked his watch and again mentioned a schedule too tight for extended pleasantries. He took back the papers and handed them to Malraux for safekeeping. The commandant's distaste for their intrusion was obvious. "Why Command West's sudden interest in our security protocols?"

René crushed his cigarette in the tin ashtray on the desk. "It's come to our attention that saboteurs plan an action against your facility. Stolen charts and construction blueprints turned up in a recent raid in Nantes. Command West finds that discovery compelling enough to call for a closer look at your local operations."

Abandoning those papers in the warehouse had first caused great discord in the group, but Maurice and René ultimately decided on a quick and positive approach to turn their carelessness to an advantage. Assuming the incriminating documents had reached Gestapo hands, the information would surely move up the chain for risk assessment. Preemptive action seemed logical, and what better reason for an unannounced security inspection than an anticipated attack on the submarine base?

Steiner did not attempt to hide his frustration. "Yes, I'm well aware of that misguided concern. Two of the Reich's beloved secret police showed up a few days back to warn of imminent problems with partisans. So I'll tell you exactly what I told them." He crushed out his half-smoked cigarette. "This port is one of the most-heavily defended on the French coast."

Using a baton as pointer, Steiner rose to address two large maps hanging on the stone wall. "Here you see the secured port facility." He tapped key locations as he continued: "Three large, lock-protected basins, the largest carrying the town's name, and directly above it the 'Penhoët.' Over here to the east the so-called 'Normandie Dock.' Our U-boat pens," he tapped a huge rectangular block in the middle of the map, "open out into the *Bassin de Saint-Nazaire*, as you can see. We have flak towers here at the north end of the basin near the rail yards, and others to either side of the swing bridges protecting both upper basins. And still more across the river and estuary.

"By the way, this is the only Atlantic facility able to handle a battleship the size of the *Tirpitz*. We hope to berth her here soon to support our raids."

The men nodded but said nothing. They knew of that huge battleship so feared by the Allied Forces.

Steiner had moved on. "Flak towers are also sited just below the completed pens." His pointer moved down the map. "And ten gun emplacements line the eastern exposure from up by the Normandie dock, down past the East Lock into the Saint-Nazaire basin, and then south to the tip of the East Jetty. We have two additional batteries out on the Old Mole to lay down fire on anyone approaching from either the sea or the river. And finally, gentlemen, our searchlights can make day out of night over the entire docking facility at any sign of trouble."

"All fine and good," René approached the maps, "but who steps in should your guards and base crews be compromised?"

Steiner smiled indulgently. "Just look here." He moved over to the second map showing the greater coastal area. "If ever needed, we summon two naval antiaircraft battalions and two artillery battalions, stationed here and here." His pointer again designated positions close to the town. "And were that not enough, the 679th Infantry Regiment and two local labor companies are only minutes away."

Steiner set aside the pointer and lit a new cigarette before taking his chair behind the desk. "So you see, gentlemen, Command West need have no worries about our preparation." He gave a fleeting smile. "In fact, I'd love to see partisans challenge such defenses, only to be squashed like bedbugs beneath a thumbnail. You'll be equally impressed by what you find inside our bunkers, so be my guest and see for yourself. Your investigation will find us secure within the base itself and armed externally to fend off anything the enemy might throw at us. There's absolutely nothing a few partisans or British operatives might do against the forces we've aligned here."

René nodded his appreciation for the thoroughness of the defenses. "I'm sure that's exactly what we'll find inside. But you know how Command works, always demanding confirmation of what it already knows. And Berlin is also seldom satisfied, *nicht wahr*?" René had remained standing, and now Malraux followed his lead. "We all have jobs to do, and ours remains to verify personally that all these fine security measures are first-rate."

Steiner encompassed everything beyond his cramped office with one sweeping gesture. "It's all out there waiting for your appraisal, sir." His look spoke of resigned acceptance.

He buzzed in an aide and directed him to provide the visitors with a tour through the submarine complex. After a final exchange of salutes with the commandant, the two saboteurs left the headquarters and followed the young sailor toward the pens.

The plan formulated in Nantes had called for René to pose as a naval engineer from Berlin on a surprise inspection tour. They'd hoped to find some target for sabotage which might slow completion of the submarine base, but work had proceeded at such a record pace in Saint-Nazaire that only a few pens remained unfinished. Those not yet complete were under tight watch as *Organisation Todt*, the Reich's construction arm, labored day and night to meet its deadline. An alternate plan was clearly needed.

By the end of the tour René breathed a sigh of relief, happy to have avoided encountering the chief engineer of the project. His study of naval engineering under Maurice had been superficial at best. Thankfully, it had also proved unnecessary. They did wonder at the self-assurance of the local commander regarding his security measures, and looked forward to comparing notes with Maurice before meeting again with the merged partisan groups. They would find a way to make Steiner a bit less confident, a task made easier thanks to Malraux. A limited amount of Nobel 808 explosive was arriving from the Brest network he had helped establish.

The more impatient partisans from both Nantes and Saint-Nazaire had grown weary of long-range planning and worrying about reprisals against civilians. Led by Jean-Philippe and Henri, the hotheads demanded a fierce and immediate attack against the existing pens. René and Malraux had reluctantly agreed to surveil with that as a backup option.

Now the two faced the group with news that would rattle a few cages. "My friends, our sabotage plan's not going to work." René prepared himself to counter protests which immediately filled the room. "At least, not as we'd hoped."

"But we've been over this a hundred times." Jean-Philippe jutted his jaw out in challenge. "What's the problem with you two, afraid of killing your own countrymen?"

René ignored the jibe, forcing himself to remain conciliatory. "It's true we have concerns, but only because we now know what we're up against. Men, we're outnumbered by superior forces, and those fortifications are too strong and too complete for our limited explosives."

Jean-Philippe took stock of the partisans one-by-one. "Then perhaps we need someone else on the inside. Right, *copains*?" A few men nodded, but René saw little conviction on their faces. Several turned to Maurice and the respected Frenchman spoke up. "Let's allow Rénard his say, my friends. These two have been inside those walls. They know what we're facing." He gave René an encouraging nod. "Go ahead, out with it—tell the group what you've learned and what you're thinking."

René knew some action was urgently needed to retain group cohesion, but rash action would doom them. "Just take a look around," his hand swept the assembled partisans, "only a dozen of us here when a major assault would require hundreds. Let me show you what we're up against." He rapidly sketched the nine completed pens plus five additional under construction. Each opened to the massive *Bassin de Saint-Nazaire*. He designated a perimeter of barbed-wire fencing and a guarded entrance gate. "All right, here's the floor plan." He used his pencil as a pointer, and the men crowded the table for a better look. "First off, you'll find a guardroom just inside the main entry on the right. They were loose with the password—it's *"Ostpreussen."* A squad with *Schmeissers* waits there, day and night. A dozen naval police, perhaps more. Still others patrol with dogs inside the fenced perimeter."

"What about the boats?" A question from young Raymond, the barber's apprentice. "Let's destroy a few U-boats."

"It's true they're minimally-crewed overnight, primarily maintenance personnel. Most of the mariners are billeted over in La Baule and only a few stay in Old Town. Within a year they will all house on-site. By the way, the local commander scoffed at even the possibility of sabotage in such a heavily-fortified port facility."

The normally taciturn Cerberus looked pleased. "More power to us—surprise equals success."

René damped down such optimistic expectations. "Yes and no. The *Boches* do feel invincible, especially since the British have done so little since Dunkerque." That reference was sure to rile Jean-Philippe, so he moved on. "The bays berthed nine submarines when we went through this morning. Each gets its own pier and dedicated shore crew. Refueling pumps are situated along each walkway, here and here," the tip of the pencil tapping out a staccato beat, "also alarm boxes at either end of each bay."

"So where do we plant our explosives?" The question came from Félix Mercier, a trawler captain with a balding head, full black beard, and missing right ear, souvenir of a clumsy on-board misstep in his youth. Félix had helped integrate the two groups, and he was one of the few refusing to use a *nom de guerre*. "Félix means happy," he'd say when asked, "and I'm happy to give the Boche this!" There followed a rude hand gesture which invariably brought a laugh.

"The standing orders are to submerge the boats in event of attack to prevent the placing of limpet mines. And these concrete walls," René's pencil now retraced the exterior lines of the drawing, "are enormously thick, built to take anything the Allies might throw at them from sea or air." Now his pencil shaded in the entire floor plan in broad smudged strokes. "Last but not least, you'll find reinforced concrete over three meters thick capping the structure. No RAF bomb's going to breach that, and certainly no partisans armed with *plastique*, that's for sure."

Henri protested: "I say we've got all we need—the password, the interior layout, where the guards hang out.

And the explosives are due in at my uncle's dry goods store this afternoon. So let's go do some damage!"

"And just what do we do with that explosive?" Malraux's turn to stifle unwarranted optimism.

"Kill *Boches,* of course!" Henri glared at René, muttering an aside to Jean-Philippe heard by the group. "Unless *mein Herr* here hates spilling a little German blood."

René stepped forward, fists clenched, forgetting his commitment to remain calm.

Maurice placed a restraining hand on Henri's arm. "Just back off and let it go. Rénard showed his worth in Nantes, killing *Boches* with the best of us. Besides, those arms and shoulders of his would make mincemeat of you."

René smiled mirthlessly and turned aside.

Maurice wasn't through. "If all you hotheads want is to do some killing, then have at it." He gestured through the grimy windows toward Old Town and the basins. "Grab your pistol and head on down to the wharves. No shortage of Germans there." Several of the younger partisans nodded eagerly in agreement. "But innocent civilians will suffer for such recklessness, and you'll end up strung up on the nearest lamppost with nothing accomplished. Nothing at all." He appealed to the entire group: "Come on, men, we're here to weaken that smug sense of invulnerability, right? That calls for a plan with some hope of success."

"So what would you have us do?" The conciliatory question came from Félix Mercier. "Did you spot anything at all we can put a dent in?"

Malraux was most knowledgeable about munitions. "Well, the walls and roof are far beyond the Nobel explosive's capabilities. We're promised ten kilos, a generous gift but hardly enough to damage a colossus like that." He pointed to René's sketch. "And let's face it—we haven't a single demolition expert in this crew. I can teach the basics, but we haven't time, place or sufficient materiel to test that limited training."

Jean-Philippe was clearly impatient. "As Raymond suggested, what about the submarines? Any vulnerability there?"

"Even with surprise on our side, we've nothing capable of sinking a U-boat. Hell, they can handle a depth charge and keep on moving."

Now Raymond sounded discouraged. "So we just forget the whole thing and get drunk?"

Henri spat on the wooden floor, his eyes still fixed on René.

It was Maurice who spoke up. "Of course not." He turned to Malraux and René. "These two have already put together an alternate plan. I think you're going to like what they've come up with."

Malraux took the lead. "Here's our proposal, men. The three of us hope it meets your demand for action. U-552 and U-593 are scheduled to ship out tomorrow at midnight. They share a common berth here in the southernmost bay." His finger tapped at René's sketch. "Let's say a small group approaches in a skiff from the north, hugging the basin wall until they reach the northernmost portal." His finger was now positioned at the end of the completed pens adjoining the construction zone. "These men swim under the metal gates and take up positions at the rudder end of the two subs now in that bay. They carry bundled 808 with timed pencil fuses."

René interrupted to poll the assembled men. "How many strong swimmers here?" Ten raised hands, two were more hesitant. "More than enough—I doubt we need more than four actually setting the explosives and one piloting the skiff. Our fisherman Félix can handle that end. The U-boat crews will be pre-occupied with the departures at the other end of the facility, so no one should notice our incursion. But this plan calls for everyone to exit on that skiff at the end of the raid, so be prepared for the strong swimmers to come to the aid of the weaker."

Excitement spread across the room and René felt heartened. "Malraux and I show up in Kriegsmarine uniform at 23:45 hours, ostensibly there to observe on behalf of Command West. Given our *carte blanche* reception today, no one bats an eye. Meanwhile, two of you set up diversionary explosions on the basin's south caisson, as close to the South Lock's winding mechanism as possible."

Now the partisans exchanged broad smiles. Even Jean-Philippe and Henri appeared intrigued as René continued with laying out the plan: "The men handling the diversion will have set the putty to blow just as the U-boats are entering the lock. You won't do much damage—our swimmers will need most of the 808 for those rudders—but the blasts will grab attention and night patrols will double-time over once the alarm sounds. The lock operators will focus on getting those submarines out into the Avant Port. Our swimmers attach their explosives to the rudders of the two targeted submarines with fuses timed for two hours, then join us to open up for the team waiting out front. Together we finish off any remaining defenders.

Henri, always eager to die for the cause, smiled broadly. "So we hit them on two fronts?"

René pocketed his pencil. Remembering the plans inadvertently left behind in Nantes, he tore up his sketch as he answered, "Precisely. With the diversionary explosives set to blow at a quarter past midnight, that team rejoins the saboteurs waiting just out of sight up front, and everyone waits for our signal. Remember, silent killing if possible, so use your knives. Malraux and I will open the entry door from the inside, and then the two groups go for any remaining guards."

René could feel the enthusiasm as Malraux picked up the thread. "If we disable those boats for a couple of weeks, we've made our point, right?" He received animated agreement all around. "So once we've cleared the bunkers, we gather at the mouth of the north portal, swim into the basin, and Félix picks us up outside."

"What about the berthing crews?" Henri was clearly heartened by the prospect of killing *Boches* at last.

"We're told they leave through a side entrance once the subs are underway, but any stragglers are fair game."

Raymond expressed concern about the flak batteries and searchlight stations lining the basin. "Won't they just light us up and blow us out of the water? One shot from a flak battery would turn any skiff to kindling."

Maurice jumped back in: "Look, as Malraux says, the skiff will hug the basin wall. The water level is well below the reach of those lights. Besides, the enemy's going to be concentrating on the South Lock where the subs appear to be under attack. The flak crews will be watching the skies. Once we're all on board the skiff, we backtrack, clamber up the basin wall, cross the rail yards and disappear. It'll work. We still have a full day tomorrow to fine-tune the plan and scout out a rowboat."

"And just how do we get it into the basin?" Henri still had a few doubts.

"It's true, said Félix, "the fishermen keep all theirs up-river."

"We 'borrow' one of the provisioning skiffs. A half dozen or so are always anchored in the main basin to service the torpedo boats. Malraux and I confirmed that they dock along that wall just north of the construction zone. Unlikely we'll find them guarded at night, but our swimmers should be prepared with knives and garrotes. Remember, dockside security stinks—the *Boches* believe they're invincible and consider the very idea of an attack ridiculous."

The mood of internal strife had lifted, the men anxious to act at last. "And one final thing," Maurice eyed each man in the group, "let's avoid reprisals against the local population. Malraux's going to make this appear an SOE operation, so no matter what happens, if you don't speak fluent English keep your mouth shut. And carry no identification. We'll agree on hand signals tomorrow."

Raymond objected: "All well and good, but what about clothing?" He gestured to the working class garb worn all around.

Malraux spoke up, the best saved for last. "We've got that covered, *copains*. Just open those crates there." Two shabby wooden boxes sat in the corner of the tower room. Raymond pried loose a lid. The partisans gathered around to admire piles of BEF uniforms as well as two Bren assault rifles and a number of British pistols with ammo belts.

"*Mon Dieu, messieurs*, a treasure trove!" Raymond gave voice to the enthusiastic murmurs of the group. Nearly fifty thousand troops of the British Expeditionary Force had embarked on those docks the year before, abandoning their weapons and supplies to the advancing Wehrmacht. Félix and friends had squirreled this gear away for better times. Now each of the partisans received appropriate kit. Should the plan succeed, the sabotage would be deemed the work of British agents and the town might escape reprisals. And the Occupiers would waste time and resources scouring the estuary and coast for non-existent landing craft.

All participants agreed on meeting the next morning to work out individual assignments. Malraux would give both the swimmers and the two assigned to the diversionary explosions at the South Lock a quick course in setting charges and fuses. As the men donned coats before dispersing, he offered one last piece of advice: "We're going to need every available man for a challenge this daunting, so if you know anyone here in town who claims to be with us, he should step forward now, because tomorrow night we strike a blow for freedom!

Erika had come to despise the peeling wallpaper, the one-burner hotplate, and those creaking stairs leading up from *Rue Thiers*. On arrival, she'd imagined spending quiet hours in the room above the tavern, watching the swoop of the seabirds, observing the hustle and bustle on the street and waters below, and entertaining the children. Instead, the seaport traffic had become a constant daily reminder of captivity in close quarters.

The children were still interested in the parade of fishing smacks and lighters, and especially excited to spot flag-flying submarines or follow the progress of an occasional destroyer moving through the locks. But finding ways to occupy their minds for days on end had become exhausting. They wanted to explore this new world, not just observe it, but she couldn't forget that Horst's spies could be anywhere out there.

The day after their arrival Geneviève had rushed up the stairs and knocked excitedly. Someone had phoned the previous evening and asked for them. The innkeeper assured Erika she had pleaded ignorance and revealed nothing. But now a tall man in an overcoat had been downstairs asking probing questions. The stranger described them well and knew both their code names. There could be only one explanation—Gestapo sent by Horst. Thank God René had been off plotting with his partisans and not come into the bar unexpectedly! Especially frightening was the agent's clear description of her. Had the substituted fingers failed to fool Horst? It was clear she dare not venture into public until after the sabotage was a *fait accompli* and they were far away at last.

René's new proposal for attacking the bunker compound struck her as too hastily planned and ill-conceived. It was clear the partisans lacked more than a touch of common sense, but here she was, tied down by maternal obligations and out of the loop. She, too, wanted to strike some meaningful blow against the facility, but such a foolhardy gamble made no sense to her frustrated mind.

The children slept just meters away in the alcove, so she kept her voice low but her sarcasm clear. "What a glorious moment this'll be for all you men, right? You finally strike at the heart of the Reich by killing off a few guards and—if all goes well, mind you—perhaps even keep a couple of U-boats in dock for a day or two. And it'll only cost the lives of half our men, and probably your own as well!"

"Please, darling," René's tone imploring, "please try to understand." She shook him off and turned to the little sink, busying herself with washing up after supper. "Just hear me out, René insisted. "You know we can't restrain these men forever, and they're sick of doing nothing. Some of the young firebrands already speak of joining the Brest or Angers networks where partisans are taking bigger risks."

Erika dropped to the wooden chair, tormenting the ragged dish towel in her hands. She wouldn't surrender to such foolhardiness. "So you grandstand here tomorrow night just to hold your group together? Is that really why we're here?" She raised a hand to stop his interrupting. "No, let me finish. How this misbegotten plan strikes some significant blow against the Nazi bastards is something I'd love to know." She flung the towel toward the sink. It fell short, a twisted lump on the worn linoleum. "Perhaps you'd be so kind as to clear that up for me?"

René cupped her hands in his. "Listen, darling." He kissed her eyelids. "I understand what you're going through, I really do. For years we've done everything side-by-side, just the two of us in charge. But it's time we face facts. Most of Europe is already under Hitler's heel and England is fading fast. Malraux says their economy's a shambles and their major cities devastated by Göring's bombers. And what have the Allies accomplished on the Continent lately? Little more than insignificant Channel raids, he says."

"But clearly nothing that'll win this war," Erika observed.

"My point exactly." René lifted her from the chair and took her place, pulling her onto his lap. She snuggled against him, the fight leaving her, satisfied for one brief moment to be in his arms. He caressed her cheek. "Our hands are tied right now—these fascists are simply too big and brutal for the Allies. All we have are token acts of resistance until America does more than just send material support."

"She will, won't she?"

"Ryan's convinced it'll happen soon now. That's why he and his friends are back in Europe. And why Malraux agrees to an endeavor as insignificant as this one."

She took a deep breath in surrender. "So we do stupid little attacks for the same reason England makes defiant gestures on the Channel?"

"What's our choice, darling? If we show them we aren't all docile sheep, that there is active resistance, we give hope to the suffering British. Besides, many small gestures just might get some momentum going, right?" He waited for Erika's nod, grudgingly given. "And even if tomorrow only slows down two U-boats for a few weeks, it's a statement, a thorn in the bastards' side."

"*Maman?*" Leo's drowsy voice emerged from the alcove where he shared a cot. "You're going to wake up Sophie, then she'll be grumpy and a real bother. She kicks me as it is." René laughed as Leo rolled back toward the wall. "I'm sleepy, and besides, I'm sad when you two argue."

Erika kissed René, then stepped over to tuck in the boy. "Hush, my love, go back to sleep. We're not arguing, we're discussing. All is fine. Your father and I have adult business to handle, but we'll keep our voices low, all right?" She realized she'd never referred to René as his "father" before.

"I love you, *Maman*," his words already muffled by sleep. "You, too, *Papa*." René had heard it and was smiling broadly, too.

How had she gotten so lucky with this child? And then to find him a new father in dearest René, that powerful—if stubborn—man with a heart of gold. Leo had endured so much in his short life—constant danger, violent confrontations, life on the run, few peaceful moments. No child deserved such a fate. And now there was Sophie, such a combination of shy smiles and wicked naughtiness. What a hate-filled world for rearing children, and what horrors occurring across the continent as those heartless bastards made their lives a hell.

René would go into battle tomorrow without her at his side. It was the right thing to do, no matter the possible cost to his growing family. He would be brave and possibly foolhardy, as was his way whenever he thought their cause just. She would be strong, as she had learned to be.

But now, *mon Dieu*, how and when to tell him of their pregnancy?

CHAPTER TWENTY-ONE

Saint-Nazaire, Occupied France
10-11 September 1941

Beneath a bright moon the U-boat compound appeared even more daunting. René and Malraux waited beyond the train tracks for a group of sailors to enter first. The concrete structure loomed high above, a monolith longer than three soccer fields capped by a massive roof. Hooded lamp posts followed the perimeter of the guard fence and other lamps bathed the stark walls in dim wartime light. The air reeked of fresh concrete, diesel fuel, and unidentifiable chemical agents. Judging from the distant activity, the Todt Organization was still keeping its round-the-clock schedule for completing the final bunkers.

The hollow feeling in René's stomach was not hunger—he rarely ate before a mission—and it certainly wasn't fear. This sort of danger was old hat. But the enormous crypt-like structure felt menacing, and surreptitiously killing soldiers and sailors went against his grain. SS thugs preyed on innocents and Gestapo bullies destroyed civilian lives, but the targets this night would be service personnel who might as willingly have overthrown Hitler as sworn an oath to him. Many had no choice in the matter, or felt they were doing their patriotic duty to the Fatherland. He couldn't know for certain.

Perhaps his customary composure would have settled in by now had Erika's farewell been more encouraging. Leo and Sophie had already gone to bed as he'd headed for the door, his billed officer's cap stowed in a satchel, an everyday overcoat not quite hiding his uniform. A Walther P-38 semi-automatic was strapped to his waist. He would ditch the overcoat shortly before his rendezvous with Malraux.

Leo had unexpectedly slipped from bed and run to him, pulling René down to whisper in his ear: "Be careful, *Papa*," a quick smile, "and please don't get shot in the butt again."

René sent the boy back to bed with a teasing swat and a laughing suggestion: "Better keep an eye on your own rear end, young man." Leo had giggled, and René was amazed at how easily Leo accepted the family's strange lifestyle.

At the door Erika had kissed him and wished his mission success. In her glistening eyes he'd seen unspoken fears, and he worried for her. She was changing. Where was that combative spark fanned by years on the run, that determination to see any challenge through? Some part of her no longer fully engaged in their common struggle. Perhaps the events since Bayonne had simply exhausted her, following so closely on the heels of the warehouse battle. Holding her in his arms, he sensed some deeper concern, something unexpressed that might endanger the night's mission.

Erika had always been a wonder, so calm and wise in everything she undertook and willing to do whatever necessary to protect those she loved. He found her more beautiful now than that first day he'd seen her on Ryan's arm. That she had grown to love him, the "clumsy Alsatian," still baffled him. And now she had taken on the care of a second child in this insane world. Perhaps he'd read too much into her mood. Perhaps she was simply hiding her frustration at no longer fighting by his side, knowing they had always been stronger together.

Yes, perhaps it had something to do with Erika. Or perhaps he might actually be afraid. Never before had he faced such a well-armed foe, on its home territory, and with such a small crew to back him up.

But what the hell, life or death—it'll sort itself out soon enough.

Early that morning Malraux had helped the partisans construct their mines of putty explosive and practice placing the pencil fuses. The four men would work in teams of two. Each swimmer would submerge with an explosives package strapped to his waist and bind it as close as possible to a rudder shaft. A French submariner from the Great War had suggested this as the most vulnerable spot on the U-boats. René recognized guesswork supported by hope. Malraux had drawn sketches of what the saboteurs should expect to find below the waterline, and within the next hours they would know if the attempt had been worthwhile.

The directive to call on every available partisan had worked. Their assault team had increased by three, each prepared to risk his life for the cause of freedom. The leaders clarified the assignments and the squads rehearsed action plans using new diagrams sketched by René. He, Malraux and Maurice answered last-minute questions to the best of their abilities, given the many unknowns in such an operation. Now all was in play.

Their turn at the gate came and they approached with the confident stride befitting senior officers. The guards saluted and gestured them on without demanding written identification. Steiner had obviously made arrangements for his important visitors from Command West. René knew the two young men would soon lie dead, and felt a deep sorrow at what was to come.

Malraux's words distracted him from the morose and disabling thoughts. "It seems we're becoming quite well-known around here, my friend."

René straightened his shoulders, suddenly conscious of his limp and aware of having mentally cringed in the face of the coming slaughter. "And a few hours from now we'll be even better known, though not by our true names, I can only hope."

The guard at the door saluted, acknowledged the password, and stepped aside for them to enter. René found the biting odor of curing concrete even stronger inside the structure. They passed half a dozen men relaxing over a game of cards, their Schmeisser machine pistols hanging from the back of their chairs. The men didn't look up as the intruders moved past the wide opening to the guard room and followed the long corridor toward the pens. The next reinforced door opened to reveal the long bays. René felt the vastness of the building and searched the darkness above for the unseen ceiling.

The far southern bay was awash in activity—the thump and throb of pumps and compressors, uniformed men shouting orders and small squads rushing through last minute checklists and tasks. Evenly spaced pools of light led the eye out to the dark portals where the berthing channels met the waters of the basin. René counted only seven U-boats berthed along the empty piers. All appeared unmanned at this late hour. Off to their left, the two darkened craft targeted for sabotage rocked gently in the wash from the basin.

They moved south, guided by the flare of a welder accomplishing some last-minute task on the conning tower of U-593. Workers rewound fueling lines, diesel fumes soured the air, and junior officers with clipboards moved about the decks. Empty torpedo racks were already stationed on the far wall. The closest sub emitted a deafening blast as vents cleared, luminous bubbles disturbing the dark waters like so many fireflies.

René checked the time. Quarter to midnight. Sailors stood by to release the lines. Crews mustered and dropped below deck. The welder stowed his torch and rolled his equipment ashore as gangways withdrew. A whistle gave a final warning, first from the far sub, then repeated by the nearer. In a great hurry now, the sailors still topside slid into the belly of the boats as the berthing crews loosed the final lines.

Officers and two sailors remained topside as U-552 rumbled to life, its exhausts spewing fumes. It slipped away toward the entrance, trailing a gentle phosphorescent wake. Minutes later U-593 followed into the blackness of the basin. Once the boats cleared the portals the docks fell silent. The bunker crews stowed their equipment and retreated, chatting quietly. A few workers washed down the concrete before heading toward the crews' service exit.

René and Malraux remained out of the glare of the overhead lights, seemingly deep in private conversation. They would give the first submarine fifteen minutes to enter the South Lock. The lock crews would be on watch for the arrivals, a procedure Maurice had covertly observed from an Old Town window overlooking the waterway. Although U-552 had headed out a few minutes before schedule, their timetable should still hold. By now the partisan team would have placed charges at the caissons, the fuses set to blow at quarter past midnight. Those men would now be long gone from the targeted area, having joined the assault team gathering in a side street near the main entry. There they would be waiting for a signal from René and Malraux.

René again checked the time: ten after. The swimmers would have left the water, their explosive bundles now strapped to the target subs, their fuses timed to blow in less than two hours. By then the Germans would still be scouring the complex for damage after the partisans' assault. Perhaps more unsuspecting *Boches* would die when the *plastique* at the rudders finally blew.

At quarter past, with no explosion or alarm sounding outside the compound, Malraux remained calm but René tensed. They compared watches. At twenty past, having allowed time for fuse delay, the men agreed to rendezvous with the waiting swimmers. Even if the diversion had been botched, their task remained the same: open the front entry to the raiders, take out as many defenders as possible, then meet Félix's skiff at the portal.

At the northernmost bay they searched the length of the pier. The saboteurs should have left the water by now, hunkering down in the shadows, prepared for the assault on the guard room. No one responded to René's quiet signal. There were no damp footprints on the concrete. He and Malraux reversed course in silence, their pistols up as they approached the passage to the hall. René slowly lowered the handle and squinted down the empty corridor. Nothing stirred. Still no sign of their men. René exchanged a look with Malraux, who appeared equally puzzled. What had gone wrong?

They approached the guard room. The narrow corridor remained eerily silent. René led the way, his back to the wall, his limp forgotten. Leo's teasing admonition came to mind. No bullet in the rear this time. Pressing up to the door jamb, he listened for the chatter of men relaxing inside, the slap of the cards on the table. He heard nothing. A trap? He hesitated, unsure.

Muted bursts of gun fire abruptly rattled outside the compound, followed by muffled shouts and commands. René tensed as his eyes shot to the entrance. The steel door stood slightly ajar, allowing the sound to intrude into the vault of the bunker complex. He knew at once a street battle raged beyond the thick walls. They'd been compromised, a traitor in their midst.

A pistol, tapping at his shoulder, demanding attention. His first thought was betrayal. He dropped to a crouch and turned, ready to fire, but Malraux was looking away, staring at the access door to the pens. Its handle moved downward, slowly, tentatively. Malraux's voice, barely a whisper, "We're sitting ducks here—let's go for the guards!"

In one motion, René lunged into the room, dropping to the floor, his pistol raised. Malraux dived to his left, his weapon braced in both hands. The room was empty. Playing cards spread across the table, half-empty glasses of beer, a lone cigarette smoldering in the overflowing ashtray. The Schmeissers gone. No back door to the guard room. They positioned themselves to either side of the storage closet and Malraux kicked open the door. Nothing.

The exchange of gunfire had already turned sporadic, a dull popping. The partisans were going down, and he and Malraux were trapped between the enemy about to burst through that front door and others entering from the pens. They could join their comrades outside in a last-ditch stand, but what chance had P-38s against a Schmeisser fusillade? His mind raced. Those coming down the corridor might be their delayed comrades, but more likely armed *Boches* stalking them.

Was their charade already blown?

Malraux's thoughts mirrored his own. "Let's see if these uniforms still work their magic."

"Agreed." They lowered their weapons and René approached the doorway. Faint voices and hesitant footsteps came their way, perhaps three men, perhaps more. He put authority in his voice: *"Hallo! Wer ist da?* Identify yourselves now!"

A young voice, gruff yet nervous: *"Matrosen."* Sailors.

René exhaled and felt secure enough to push his luck. "Show your faces, on the double!"

The men appeared in the light, unarmed. "Seaman First Class Rögerfeld, sir." His eyes darted nervously, first to René's insignia of high rank, then toward the entrance. The occasional gunshot still reverberated beyond the barrier, but it was quieter now, mostly shouting and muted orders. Only moments remained if this was to work.

The lead seaman appeared flushed, scared. "If I may ask, sir, what's going on out there?"

René took control, demanding answers, not giving them: "You come from the bunkers—are there more of you at the pens?"

"No, *Herr Kapitän*, just us, as far as we know. You see, sir, we fell into some decent schnapps and dozed off inside our boat." René smelled the liquor, noted the unsteady stance of the three. "And then we missed the transport back to La Baule. We thought to hitch a ride and then heard that racket out there," he gestured to the door, "and, well…" His voice trailed off.

Malraux stepped forward and eyed with disgust the condition of the sailors' uniforms. "There are saboteurs out there, and your dereliction of duty shall not go unnoticed." The men turned sheepish. "You three will remain in that guard room till we've wrapped things up. Expect more than just a reprimand once this is over. Now get out of our sight! You drunks sicken me!" The sailors entered the guard room on unstable feet.

René and Malraux strode up the corridor, putting distance between themselves and the trouble. It was clear many of their comrades would be dead or captured, their own charade unmasked at any moment. Once under the cavernous ceiling of the first bunker, they ran toward the portal, waiting for gunfire at their backs, hearing only their own footfalls slapping the concrete.

Slick iron rungs descended into the basin. They clambered down, submerging to their necks in the frigid water. Taking a deep breath, they dove beneath the heavy metal doors, surfaced out in the basin, then backstroked north. The waterlogged uniforms weighed heavily. They kicked off their footwear and stayed close to the concrete wall. No skiff waited to pick them up, and the construction zone had fallen deathly silent. Alarms were sounding to the south of the complex and searchlights lit that horizon. At the north end all remained still as death.

At the swing bridge opening to the northern Penhoët Basin they climbed a metal ladder and emerged on the edge of the rail yards. Across the track loomed warehouses, atop the largest a massive flak tower, its three anti-aircraft guns silhouetted against the moonlit sky. A string of flatbed railcars hid them from sight.

Malraux, winded from the exertion in the cold water, slapped his shoulders to restore circulation. "What do you think?"

"Find our men and free any survivors."

Malraux paced, his hands shoved deep in the soggy trouser pockets. "We're outmanned, outgunned and clearly outwitted, my friend."

"But we owe the others a try!"

"Listen, Rénard, every man knew the risks. Sadly, things just didn't go our way."

"But think of Maurice—Laura's expecting!"

The two men hunkered down beside a pile of crates, seeking shelter from fog coming in off the estuary on a rising breeze. "A risk he was willing to take." Malraux hesitated, placing his hand on René's shoulder. "Let's face it—Maurice will have saved himself and anyone else he could." He removed his uniform jacket and twisted water from the sleeves. His teeth chattered as he put it back on. "But only those who get away will ever fight the bastards again. So you get the hell out of here, and now!" He blew into his cupped hands, trying to warm them. "And as far from Saint-Nazaire as possible. Steiner knows your face, everyone knows that limp of yours, and there'll be no hiding now that word is out."

"And you're any different? They know that mug of yours, too."

"Yes, but I can disappear. I've contacts across Brittany to the Channel. Not you, comrade, you've no connections here. Time to think of yourself and your family."

René had no rebuttal, gradually coming to terms with their failure. "Fine, you're right, I have to get them to safety, but first we need to dump these damned uniforms. Suggestions?"

"There's a tavern a few blocks from here, beyond those warehouses. He pointed west. "It's called *La Reveille,* in case we're separated. Closed for the night, of course, but the old gal who runs it lives above the joint. A sympathizer, so she'll help out. Secretly listens to the BBC and thinks Churchill's a saint. I've holed up there since I first hit town." He buttoned up the tortured uniform jacket. "If we stick to the backstreets and the shadows, we'll make it there fine."

René ran his hands the length of each soaked trouser leg, spreading water on the pavement at his feet. "Then let's get to it. My wife will be worried sick, and the *Boches* will have Old Town sewn up tighter than a drum. Half the coastal forces will soon be out looking for us," he wiggled his toes to restore circulation. "But we run across any of our team, we free them, agreed?"

"Of course, Rénard. We'll give it a try."

They moved out under cover of the rail cars, keeping low, the gravel underfoot torturing the soles of their shoeless feet.

CHAPTER TWENTY-TWO

Saint-Nazaire, Occupied France
10 September 1941

A firefight rattled the distant horizon, and searchlights turned night to day over the lower stretches of the *Bassin de Saint-Nazaire*. By now trucks would have thundered down through New Town and crossed the square, spitting out well-armed *Boche*s. Erika knew the partisans had failed, knew René and his comrades could die. They might already have fallen. And then the military authorities and Gestapo would search door-to-door, hear of a young family recently arrived at the tavern, and the neighbors would reveal everything, if only to protect their own.

Erika was thankful she'd abandoned Old Town early that morning the moment René had left for the final preparatory meeting. Both had agreed Geneviève's inn lay too close to the pens. Putting to use Félix Mercier's rough sketch of the northern borough, Leo had taken charge of their little exodus. He led Erika through the narrow streets with Sophie on her hip. Their circuitous route bypassed the warehouses and rail yards and Erika thought they blended well with the morning pedestrian traffic. She kept a constant eye out for a possible Gestapo tail. Only once did they draw unwanted attention, an admiring whistle from a Wehrmacht sergeant. She'd ignored him in the time-tested manner of any good Frenchwoman by holding her nose high.

Janine Mercier had welcomed them as long-absent family, immediately sharing eggs and barley coffee. A fisherman's brood ate better than most since fresh catch was always in great demand in the underground market now that foodstuffs demanded such a premium. Janine's teenaged daughters were already off in school, leaving Leo and Sophie to spend the afternoon with the girls' outgrown toys.

An anxious evening passed with no news of the raid. Leo and Sophie sat with the shy Mercier twins over a dinner of fish stew before bedding down on a braided rug near the hearth. Once the children slept, Erika gratefully accepted a sherry. The women sat side-by-side on a rough-hewn bench, talking until words no longer had purpose. They passed the hours staring into the glowing coals. Each was lost in her personal troubled thoughts when the muted gunfire brought them to their feet. The women rushed into the street to join neighbors looking toward the basins. Seeing nothing but the glow in the sky, they returned to the hearth.

Shortly after one a.m. and a knock at the front door. Erika started but remained seated. Janine opened and greeted someone by name, then spoke briefly in hushed tones before rejoining her guest. The pallor on her face sent a chill down Erika's spine. She could only listen numbly to the report: "All is lost, the soldiers were tipped off and waiting for our men. Some are dead, others believed under arrest." She stirred the embers in the hearth, raising a feeble flame. She kept her back to Erika. "Nothing on your husband."

She stepped into the adjoining room to check on her daughters, leaving Erika to consider their shared fate. A minute later Janine sat down beside Erika and grasped her hand. Erika felt the tremor before she saw the tears. "My Félix...he's gone." Erika gasped. Janine's voice remained barely audible. "Georges says the *Boches* laid them out in a row and there was no mistaking Félix's missing ear."

Erika took the distraught woman into her arms. Janine sobbed for several minutes before drawing away with a grateful nod. She blew her nose and straightened her shoulders. "I've family over at Pornichet, so we'll be heading there while it's still dark." She stared into the coals, dabbing at her eyes. "But what of you? You've nowhere to go, and they'll be all over this place once they know it's Félix."

Conscious of Janine's tragic loss, Erika still felt compelled to ask: "And no mention of a man in Kriegsmarine officer's uniform?"

"Georges couldn't see all the bodies. It was dark, soldiers everywhere. It's just that he knows...he knew my Félix. One of his deckhands, as devoted to my husband as a son." She remained silent for several moments. "Perhaps your Rénard was more fortunate?"

Erika wanted to reach out and console Janine again but knew they would both collapse in anguish if she tried. "We must now count on action and not fickle luck."

Janine seemed calmer now, resolute. "So where will you go?"

"No idea." She focused on the loudly ticking wall clock. "I have to assume the worst and waiting simply puts us all at further risk."

Janine stood abruptly and took Erika's hand. "Come, we've things to do. Our boat's at the wharf. You and your children can hide there until you decide what comes next. Look for *La Demoiselle*, a smack with rust-red trim, a two-master but with longer keel and broader beam than most. She's berthed down Rue du Rivage, third pier to the left once you reach the boardwalk."

"You're sure, Janine? What about your crew? Won't they be compromised if we hide out there?"

"The Germans will take everything, including our trawler, so the boat's already lost to us." Janine swallowed hard. "But the *Boches* will need time to track us all down. Too many locals involved. With my Félix gone, Georges and Michel will avoid the piers. The crews always meet for a quick drink before heading out, and word spreads fast at the taverns."

Janine stopped short and turned away before she spoke again. "I must wake the children, tell them their father's gone and somehow get us over to Pornichet. They're sure to be watching all roads out. You know, I'd gladly take you along, but my parents could never handle so many and strangers would grab attention in the village."

"No, of course not." Erika was already picturing hiding out on a fishing boat surrounded by river traffic. A challenge, but short term it would have to do. "The boat's a very gracious offer, and I thank you." Erika's practical side took hold. "And I hate to ask, but what of food and drink?" She gestured to the sleeping Leo and Sophie. "The children, you know."

"Dry provisions are always onboard for when the men go out, plus water and cider. Should be some beer in bottles, as well. Come to the kitchen with me. I've some fresh things you can take with you now. I'll have enough to carry, what with the girls and all." Janine filled a canvas bag with hard-boiled eggs, crackers and nuts, some hard sausage and a chunk of cheese. She added a loaf of coarse bread. "Just avoid the other crews—the curious may have loose lips."

Erika awakened her children and hushed Leo gently when he protested. "I'm still sleeping, *Maman*." His voice a mumble. "Must we go now? It's still dark outside."

"Yes, love, and see that Sophie is dressed quickly. Tell me if her diaper needs changing and I'll handle it. Morning isn't far off and then we'll get some breakfast. For now, we're going to the Mercier's trawler."

"Like the fishing boats we watched from the room?" His eyes brightened at the prospect as he helped Sophie dress while Erika quickly rearranged things in the suitcase. "Are the twins coming with us to the boat?" Leo had taken an instant liking to the Mercier girls.

Sophie, chimed in, "Boat! Boat!"

"Yes, Sophie, 'boat.'" No time now for anything but escape. "Sorry, Leo, the twins can't join us. Perhaps another time."

"How's *Papa* to know where we've gone?"

Erika bit her lip, curbing her fears. "We'll leave him a note, right?"

Leo appeared unconvinced. "Last time we had to go find him."

This time was different, but night was advancing, and René was still missing as the clock chimed two. She needed to find *La Demoiselle* before the morning crews reached the docks and they faced unwanted scrutiny.

She felt a wave of nausea. Morning sickness, not grief. Not yet. Grief could come later when she had a sound plan and the children were safe. Somewhere. She should have told René about the baby. He deserved to know.

The tavern keeper provided René with a pair of old shoes, in good shape but a size too small. The trousers and woolen sweater smelled of mothballs. René gladly accepted a faded workman's jacket and a soft cap as he stood there soaked and shivering. What she offered Malraux was a slightly better fit. Her husband had never returned from the war up north. After a year without word, she knew he wasn't coming back.

It was clear the other saboteurs had never found a skiff nor entered the pens. And the lock team had also failed in its mission. Someone had squealed, perhaps someone sharing too much with a curious neighbor. None of that mattered now. The partisans were either gone or soon to meet a noose or bullet. With luck, a few were on the run, but it was only a matter of time. The *Boches* would search everywhere: outbound trains, buses, trucks, cars, farm wagons. Whatever moved would be fair game. Malraux would head northwest on foot, working his way inland, dependent only on his own quick wits. With no family to worry about, a man traveling alone might actually elude capture. A family of four less likely.

Barely a block from the apartment a foot patrol spotted the men and ordered them to halt and identify. As agreed beforehand, each tore off in a different direction, hoping to divide the pursuers. It didn't work. René knew the patrol saw a limping man as an easier target. Though their bullets went astray, the clamor attracted a guard dog team that soon picked up the chase. Within minutes he was perspiring heavily. He ditched the jacket as he ran.

He ignored the constriction of the shoes. Blisters would heal. Finding his family was all that mattered, getting them to safety his reason for running. From moment to moment he broke out into full moonlight before finding shelter again in the shadows. The alleyways were treacherous, dark and narrow, his full concentration needed to avoid a misstep and fall. The limp caused a painful stitch with each stride but wouldn't weaken his resolve. Any delay would cost him his wife, his children.

The pursuers were closer now, the baying louder. He realized the folly in abandoning a jacket drenched in his sweat. The wolfhounds would have his scent and control the chase. Ironic for an Alsatian to be trapped by the jaws of dogs named for his heritage. Panting heavily, he paused at the intersection of three tight passages, uncertain of his next move. Hands on knees, he fought for breath.

Mercier had mapped out a route and given an address when he'd volunteered his home as refuge for Erika and the children. René had memorized the diagram before handing it to Erika. Now with the enemy in pursuit, the convoluted passageways slowed every step and worry frustrated his memory. Turning right would bring him back to the rail yards and industrial district. A left turn would take him farther from the fisherman's quarter. The center path still felt right and he ran on.

The streets were empty. A civilian breaking curfew and hearing the commotion would hole up away from prying eyes and probing questions. René thought he'd gained a bit of a lead, but perhaps the buildings only muted the sounds of the dogs. At one intersection he spotted the slits of headlamps prowling the narrow cross streets closer to the river. Soon other pursuers would join in the hunt. How he detested being prey rather than predator!

The warehouses gave way to tightly-cramped housing units several stories tall. The ground-level businesses were shuttered for the night, but he knew he was on the right track. Here a chandler's shop beside a café, over there a grocery and a rope maker with nets hanging from the eaves. He knew he was nearing the wharves. At last he spotted the street name remembered from Félix's map, *Rue du Rivage*, the house number suddenly clear in his mind. The goal was close. The stitch in his leg was steady now, his breath coming in ragged gasps as he moved from stoop to stoop. There it was—a small oval in blue and white enamel. Number 303. The dogs were barely a block or two behind. He couldn't allow the pursuers to see him stop.

No light escaped the drapes covering windows to either side of the entry. Only a wisp of smoke rose from one of the chimneys. He looked up and down the street, even more worried. He searched the door jamb for something brighter than the fading wood trim and found a scrap of paper jutting out a hair's breadth, placed so high that only a tall man would spot it, and then only if he knew to look. With the note in his pocket he took to the streets again. The yapping dogs were closer. Flashlights swept the pavement at the head of the rue.

The moon reflected off the Loire as he made the descent toward the river. He passed a narrow gap between two houses. Balling up the sweater, he heaved it deep into the confined space. The dogs might be misled and stop to bay into the recess. With luck he would find a place to read Erika's note. It would lead him to her.

Hugging the shadow of the walls as the street curved downward, René felt his energies flagging. He spotted a kerosene lantern swinging in the breeze off the water, glowing softly in the deepening fog. There the street opened to a small square bordered by nautical shops and taverns. A boardwalk branched off in both directions.

Squatting beneath the lantern, he held the note to the feeble light. In Erika's script a hastily-scrawled riddle challenged him: *Ein Mädchen in rotem Kleid, da wo Du als Junge zu Hause warst.*

The baying had risen to a fevered pitch. The dogs knew they had their prey cornered. The shouts of the men and the anxious howling of the animals echoed from up the street. He hunkered down beside a street sweeper's cart as a police car crossed the square , its siren blaring as it headed up toward the pursuers. The sweater had worked, at least for the moment.

A girl in a red dress, where you were at home in your youth.

Her clue bounced around in his head. At least the second part was clear—the only place he'd felt at home as a boy was aboard his father's Rhine boats. The girl in the puzzle he'd solve on the run, but he knew he was almost there.

Kapitänleutnant Thomas Steiner drummed his fingers on the desk. The commandant's eyes shifted repeatedly to the bunker plan on the wall, although it no longer demanded immediate attention. He checked his watch. Almost four a.m. He had learned of the partisan attack over an hour in advance and quickly taken appropriate countermeasures, but still his nerves were frayed. Little had gone as smoothly as hoped, and now all traces of this embarrassing fiasco would have to be buried.

Crediting his security plan for thwarting the sabotage would have been the easy answer, but chance alone had brought them down. Hoping to impress a local girl with details of his soon-to-be-tested courage, one young saboteur had revealed too much. That young Frenchwoman was also seeing a German submariner on the sly. Fearing for her lover's safety, she'd sent a warning and the sailor had dutifully reported the partisan plans to his superiors.

Thank God for small favors, thought Steiner.

He faced the door as Dauerheim entered with the latest report. "We believe most of the terrorists are accounted for, sir. It was just as expected: planned diversionary explosions on the lock, an armed assault on the front entry and a waterborne attack targeting the U-boats. Our men interceded on three fronts."

"How much damage if they'd succeeded?"

"They carried far too little explosive to seriously damage either the lock caisson or any of our boats." He took a seat as directed. "Amateurs, sir, not demolition experts. We defused the explosives on the South Lock once the sappers left to join the frontal assault. Our men wiped out that entire team at the front gate."

"No survivors?"

Dauerheim shrugged. "Our men had to defend themselves. The bastards didn't have a prayer."

"Casualties on our side?"

"Two, sir. Minor flesh wounds. One clumsy fellow tripped and sprained an ankle. The partisans were poorly armed so no match for a Schmeisser."

"What of the skiff?"

"Five showed up there, sir. Three dead. We've laid out the bodies inside the compound, pending your inspection and further orders."

"Any Wehrmacht involvement yet? Or Gestapo?"

"None, sir. All is under wraps for now. The flak troops and local army command were forewarned of an anticipated training exercise and nothing more. The story appears to be holding, though Old Town will certainly suspect the truth. And, of course, families of the dead. People always talk."

"And our 'visitors from Paris?' Those two are the key. Any signs of the leaders?"

"Yes and no, sir. Sailors sharing a bottle missed the evening transport back to La Baule. They met the imposters on the way out, fell for the uniform ruse, then opted to keep their soused heads down by hiding in the guard room. They report the two 'naval officers' headed back out to the bunkers."

"Your search inside was thorough?"

"Per your orders. Quite frankly, those two have disappeared."

"Well, those were no phantoms, although I wish to hell they had been! Any missing rowboats, launches, fishing vessels, anything of that sort?"

"None, sir."

"Then perhaps they both drowned but I have my doubts. They likely slipped away before we went looking." The commander removed his greatcoat from the rack. "Come, Gregor—walk with me." He grabbed his lighter and a pack of Aristons off the desk, pulled on leather gloves, and waited for Dauerheim to open the door to the street. It felt good leaving the dank office for the fresh night air.

On the stoop he adjusted his cap. The usual early-morning fog had enveloped Old Town, bringing with it the cold. A dense marine layer dampened the stone paving and turned it slick. Only those with permission to break curfew stirred in that pre-dawn hour.

Steiner offered his lieutenant one of the cigarettes and the men stopped long enough to share a light. At the compound they joined the squad of naval police smoking silently with their backs to the massive concrete wall. Dauerheim led the commandant over to the perimeter fencing where the bloodied corpses lay in a neat row. "Those British uniforms appear genuine enough—likely abandoned during last year's rout—but our men checked the undergarments. They're all locals for sure."

Steiner squatted beside the first body, turning the dead man's face toward the light. The eyes saw nothing, the corneas dulling now, and Steiner felt a twinge. Regret? Sorrow? Disgust? He wasn't sure. Experiencing the casualties of war close-up was so immediate. How different from watching an enemy destroyer or freighter sink beneath the waves. His eyes moved from body to body, some eyes closed, others staring sightlessly into the fog. "All ages, it seems. Courageous fools, but fools all the same. Papers?"

"None. But our young lover boy is filling in details, so it shouldn't be difficult putting identities to all these faces."

"Our loose-lipped partisan was at the skiff?"

"Surrendered immediately. If their leader hadn't fired, they all might have lived. The others carried nothing but knives and explosives, but our men dropped them when they made a run for it. The only other survivor took two rounds in the back and won't last. We're doing our best to keep him alive, just in case we need to corroborate details. By the way, our enamored informant still knows nothing of his girl-friend's attachment to the submariner. His fears for her safety give us excellent leverage."

"Let's keep it that way. We may have further use for her. Meanwhile, get these bodies inside before the locals spot them."

"I'm afraid that ship has sailed, sir. Two young fellows had a quick look from outside the compound before disappearing into the fog. We couldn't stop them."

Steiner said nothing. His gaze moved along the towering wall toward the construction zone. What the hell was he doing here on land when he could accomplish so much more at sea? Out there, command meant true command, with only himself to please. Now this incident might well torpedo any chance for a more active role in the war. He rose to his feet and pulled his coat tighter, then fished the cigarette pack from his pocket. Dauerheim returned almost immediately after relaying the orders. They left the compound just as a wheeled trolley came around to cart away the stiffening bodies.

They walked back in silence. Steiner lost himself in contemplation, poring over ways to make the best of a very bad situation. Entering the headquarters building he had the night duty non-com set a water pot on the hotplate. Once at his desk, Steiner became all business. "Listen, Gregor, shut that door and have a seat. What I'm about to say must remain confidential."

"Of course, sir." Dauerheim's smile showed how delighted he was with his superior's confidence in his discretion.

Steiner removed his cap and slicked his hair into place, checking his reflection in a framed citation hanging on the wall. "As you well know, nothing would give me greater pleasure than commanding a new VII-class." His eyes followed the sleek lines of the scale model on his desk. "But since Berlin sees fit to keep me land-bound, I do my best to meet their expectations." He brought the model U-boat closer, lifting it from the stand to sight along the sleek body, imagining torpedoes bursting from its tubes. "Sadly, this evening's wrinkle, and in hindsight our two 'official' visitors from yesterday, reveal a serious breakdown in our security measures. We can expect trouble from Command West."

"But sir, they presented solid credentials. Why should you have suspected them? Our captive says those two are experienced outsiders—one from Nantes, the other an SOE operative from up north now leading a local group."

"The fact remains, they duped me. You must know that Paris—not to mention Berlin—has little tolerance for gullible commandants." His fingers tapped a steady tattoo on the desktop until he forced them to stop. "We've become so accustomed to Paris hovering over our shoulders that a surprise visit seemed plausible enough, especially after those plans turned up in that Nantes warehouse. Perhaps I should have given the visit of those Gestapo louts more weight. But Command's focus is shifting quickly to the Atlantic war, security remains paramount, so I understand the concerns and I've dropped the ball on this one."

"Sir, it could happen to anyone!"

"Perhaps, but it happened under my watch, and now it's on me to make the situation go away."

The lieutenant spoke candidly: "We squelched this so quickly that very few even know of it. The local officials will believe what we tell them to believe. The last thing they'll want are reprisals against the citizenry." He hesitated, as if wary of his next thought. "But obviously, once the families get the bodies back the whole town will know otherwise."

Steiner was in no mood for mincing of words. "So spit it out, Gregor."

"The Todt people are still working around the clock."

"How's that germane? Were there witnesses among the night crew?"

"We'd ordered them off-site just before the action. The foreman and engineer bitched about timetables, but all followed orders so they saw nothing." Dauerheim clearly waited for a response which failed to come. Finally, a grin on his face, he offered a prompt: "I believe the skirmish interrupted them mid-pour on one of the final roof sections."

"Your point being?"

"Hear me out, sir. What if those bodies disappeared during that huge concrete pour? The only witnesses then would be a couple of Polish laborers reassigned immediately to a project elsewhere—let's say down in Bordeaux."

Steiner leaned back in his chair. In truth, the idea had also occurred to him but he'd refused to give it serious consideration.

Convinced his plan had merit, Dauerheim forged on: "Just imagine—we bury the fallen partisans in the bunker itself, a lasting tribute to their misguided plan to challenge the Reich. It's respectful, even if we're the only ones to ever know it."

The commandant turned the idea over in his mind. How easy that would be, bodies gone forever, the locals intimidated into silence. His own people would never break the story, and well-placed threats of retribution would easily squelch civilian rumors. But simple solutions often had unforeseen consequences. What of the young man singing his guts out to protect a girl with conflicting loyalties? And those ringleaders, the fake naval officers still on the loose?

He approached the town plan hanging on the wall, his eyes drawn to the massive complex at its center. Had this command, this power, affected his sense of right and wrong? Was he willing to do anything necessary to cover his own shortcomings? No, these partisans had lost their lives for their beliefs. Terrorists, yes, yet still men of conviction, misguided or not, and they deserved better than that. And their families deserved to know their men died bravely.

Without honor in what we do, where is the purpose and justification for our actions? He thought of Maria and his two young ones back in Kiel. Of his father, a captain who went down at the helm of his destroyer in the Great War. Steiner would hope to instill that same sense of duty and integrity in this young lieutenant waiting impatiently for a response to a bold suggestion. Perhaps he would find a principled way to save his career, but he would never compromise the ethics of a sea captain.

A knock at the door. The non-com entered with a tray, set the coffee pot and two cups on the desk, then hesitated. Dauerheim was in no mood for interruptions. "What is it, sergeant?"

"Sir, a matter of possible interest just in from a local night patrol." He handed over a slip of paper and withdrew, gently closing the door behind him as the lieutenant scanned the message.

Seeing a shift in Dauerheim's features, the commandant became impatient: "Come on, spill it!"

"About 01:00 hours a foot patrol spotted two men breaking curfew. Over in that mixed-use area west of the rail yards. Both refused to stop and identify themselves and made a run for it, so the patrol took a few shots and gave pursuit."

"Anyone hit?"

"No signs of it, sir."

"And?"

"One disappeared immediately in the direction of New Town. The other headed north. A dog patrol joined the pursuit and the fugitive gave them a run for it. It's quite a rabbit warren up there with streets switching back every which way. And the fog wasn't even in yet. Anyway, they tracked him down to the fisherman's quarter, but he gave them the slip all the same."

Steiner shook his head. "Even with the dogs?"

"Even with dogs."

"And this interests us why?"

Dauerheim looked up from the incident report, a gleam in his eye. "The man was big and ran with a limp."

Steiner released a long, slow breath. "Ah, I see…our '*Kapitän zur See* Greifinger,' perhaps? And the other one surely the purported SOE fellow, likely now well through New Town and long gone. Have we a follow-up on him?"

"Not a sign yet, sir."

"All right, here's what we do: double the road blocks and controls between here and all towns to the west and north. And search the fisherman's quarter high and low, every house, every shop, every damned boat! Have the interrogator find out if any of the terrorists had connections to the fishing fleet."

Steiner saw the slim possibility of something positive coming from this disastrous night. "Go on, Gregor, get on it now. This might be the break we need. Should we snag either of the ringleaders, I just might save my command as well as my neck."

Dauerheim was already out the door.

Erika's cryptic note would have kept anyone else guessing, but René immediately caught the nautical allusion. Only he would know to look for a boat of some kind. He searched south first, considering any number of bobbing vessels. Nothing suggested a girl in red. He retraced his steps to the square. Heading north, he finally spotted *La Demoiselle,* half-hidden in the encroaching fog and rocking gently in her faded rust-red livery. He crossed the gangway to the deck, then stopped to scan the pier for any activity. He felt his heartbeat returning to normal, but held his breath before rapping lightly on the door of the cabin.

Erika's face appeared briefly in the smudged window. The hinges creaked and she flew into his arms. "What took you so long? Are you all right? Are you hurt?" Her questions came in ragged bursts of emotion, her face buried in his chest as she sobbed in relief. "You should have been here long ago!"

"A disaster, Erika!"

"I know—it just felt wrong from the start. I love you, but what I said is true—you never listen to me!" She thumped his chest hard with both fists.

He laughed with relief at seeing her. "Now come on, we can't stay on deck." Erika pulled him into the gloom.

The lanterns from dockside cast a feeble light in the tight confines of the cabin. Leo, sitting on the floor beside Sophie, called up to him: "We're sailors now, *Papa!* We're going to sea!"

"*Papa,*" echoed Sophie, liking the word. "*Papa, Papa.*"

"Hush, you two," Erika's voice low but stern, "keep it down or we'll be discovered!"

Leo whispered to his mother, "but it's good to have *Papa* here with us, isn't it?"

René squatted down to tousle both children's heads, then tensed in surprise and bolted upright. Two figures were silhouetted against the dull glow of the forward windows.

Erika quickly defused the situation: "They're friends, my love, and here to help."

A teenaged youth eagerly extended his hand. "Georges, sir, Félix's deckhand…" His voice faltered. "But now your man, if you'll have me…have the two of us." His companion stepped forward, a girl barely his own age. Her headscarf revealed little beyond a pretty nose. "My fiancée, Lisette. She cooks and knows the ocean as well as I do, and she can mind the children."

The slender girl offered her hand. "*Enchantée, monsieur.*" Now René could see the girl had been crying. She was very young and very pretty. He turned to Erika, perplexed. "Care to fill me in on your plan?"

"Janine Mercier's given us this boat and left town. She knows the *Boches* will confiscate it soon enough, once they connect the attack to Félix." She gave Lisette a quick glance.

"Félix? You've heard from him?"

Erika's expression said it all. "But as for us, we have no choice but to run. Soon the whole quarter will teem with *Boches*. They know you and your role in the botched raid and will hang you for it!"

Erika was right, whether he wished it or not, and he finally muttered an exasperated, "I've never run from a fight!"

"But we have a growing family now, so we live to fight another day, right? That's always been our plan."

"They'll be watching the water, as well." He switched to German. "And why are these two here?"

"A gift from Janine, same as this boat. Lisette's one of the Mercier twins, and Georges has fished these waters with Félix for a couple of years. Face it, darling, you know river boats inside and out and how to navigate inland waters. But Georges here knows the Atlantic and how to guide us through the estuary to reach the ocean. It's said to be very treacherous."

René wanted to express to the girl his sorrow at the loss of her father, but the girl's gaze remained fixed on the youth. Georges pulled her closer in reassurance as they waited for René to determine their fate. "So we somehow evade both the harbor police and the shoals of the estuary, and then what?" He slumped against the cabin door.

"England. Or Gibraltar, or maybe Spain or Portugal! We can decide once we reach the sea. Georges knows the immediate coast in both directions." She reached over and lifted up his chin. "Don't you see, love, we've no choice— we have to leave town now! Once someone or something leads them to this boat, we're finished."

René turned to the youth and switched back to French. "Then it's true? You know these waters and sea navigation?"

Georges didn't hesitate. "Like the back of my hand, sir. Just let me prove it!" He squeezed the girl to him again. "And did I mention Lisette can help with the kids?"

"And you're willing to abandon your family, your country?"

"Not abandon, sir, just take a breather until Lisette's safe. I plan to sign up with General DeGaulle's Free French to win back our country." The girl's eyes remained downcast, and René understood. Having just lost her father to the partisan cause, her fiancé's plan would soon put his life at risk, too.

"That works for me, Georges." René's mind churned. "Perhaps we can make this work after all. What about provisions, fuel, charts? I presume we have a compass?"

"Félix always kept the fuel topped up. As long as we stay close to the coast and avoid patrols, it should be smooth sailing. We fishermen support each other, and there's no love lost for the *Boches* out there." Georges gestured toward the open sea. "We run low on fuel, others will share, even if only a few liters at a time. And this boat can work the wind. We won't rely solely on the engine."

Animated now, the youth slid open a flat drawer of charts. "Félix always kept everything on board, and he has friends in ports along the way. North or south, it doesn't matter." He took Lisette's hand and addressed her: "*Ça va, Chérie?*" She nodded. "There's another matter Madame wants you to know about us before you decide, sir—"

"Call me René, since we seem to be in this together."

Leo, ever watchful, spoke up: "But *Papa*, you're supposed to be 'Rénard' now!"

"We're back to René, Leo. Now let Georges speak his mind."

"It's just…you see, sir…I mean René…Lisette carries my child."

"*Verdammt nochmal!*" His curse escaping with a will of its own, René turned abruptly to Erika. Had she already known this? "That's all we really need now, right? A six-year-old kid—"

Leo couldn't let that pass: "Almost seven!"

"Very well, a *seven*-year-old kid, a little girl still in diapers, and now a girl carrying this teenager's child! Erika, how will this ever work?"

She kissed his haggard cheek and whispered in his ear, "It'll have to, for you see, darling—I'm carrying yours, as well!" Stunned by the revelation, he first found no words. Then astonishment and joy brightened his face and Erika kissed him again. "So if it's all the same to you, let's get to sea before the *Boches* show up. You can complain about it as much as you like once we've found a new home."

On the eastern horizon a narrow band of gold hinted at morning. Fog muted the rumble of the diesels as the motley fleet of trawlers left port in the pre-dawn hours. One by one the fishing smacks set out for the vast estuary and the Atlantic beyond. To the west lay Saint-Nazaire, shrouded in mist. Tiny blurs of light marked wharves to either side of the Normandie dock. The fishing boats rocked and bobbed as they met the main current of the river. The unseen shoals ahead made the river mouth treacherous to those unfamiliar with this vast expanse where Loire met the Bay of Biscay.

The fishermen went about the business of preparing nets as hungry gulls squawked overhead. Closer to shore, harbor patrol boats scoured the waters, their searchlights sending ghostly shafts of light sweeping through the fog banks. The air smelled less of earth and foliage now and more of salt, but onboard the odor of old catches tinged every breath drawn.

Their trawler was a relic from the 1890's, once outfitted with a coal-fired steam boiler but converted in recent decades to diesel. René was pleased she could still rely on sails and was anxious to learn how she handled at sea. Fresh seafood was at a premium, and the fishing fleet received a modest priority for the limited civilian fuel supply. *La Demoiselle* would need every liter she carried. A long voyage lay ahead, and opportunities to replenish remained uncertain despite assurances from Georges. René and the young man hoisted the mainsail to take advantage of an offshore breeze.

Inside the cabin Erika and Lisette sat with their backs braced to the walls. Wool blankets over their shoulders helped stave off the chill. As they compared notes on morning sickness, they worried about nausea once the trawler reached the open Atlantic. Leo recited one of his adventures to Sophie, who interrupted often with one-word responses or sentences unintelligible to anyone but her.

Off to starboard René caught a quick glimpse of a larger vessel easing up the dredged channel of the *Passe des Charpentiers*. Likely a destroyer, though difficult to be certain through the shifting swaths of fog. The outbound submarines would have taken the same passage during the night and now be well off the coast, resuming their role of stealthy killers.

The partisan attack had been a colossal waste of effort and lives. The hotheads had prevailed and the group had gone in half-cocked and ill-prepared. He should have held strong and waited for a better opportunity. The price of his weakness was dismal failure of the mission and many deaths.

The swell and roll beneath his feet brought back memories of the Rhine, a welcome distraction after the night of aggravation, loss and disappointment. Moving around the deck he didn't notice his limp, that lasting reminder of von Kredow's first act of personal vengeance. René exhaled deeply. Erika had been right. He knew river craft, the Rhine currents, the mechanics of engines and lines. He'd sailed the Bodensee on a small one-master, knew how to work the winds and handle sudden squalls. But this was a fishing trawler, and the ocean would present unknown challenges. Thank God for that kid moving confidently about the deck, anxious to demonstrate his nautical skills as he showed him the ropes.

They had reached the first chop of the open sea when trouble found them. The other fishing boats had drifted far afield, now mere tiny specks on the horizon. Some had surely already lowered their nets. The sky remained overcast as the fog lifted and the sky to the east brightened. A gunboat over a kilometer distant abruptly changed course and carved a broad radius across the swells, approaching head-on under the harsh wail of a klaxon.

Having surrendered his jacket and sweater to the guard dogs, René now wore a fisherman's smock and a woolen cap discovered in the cabin wardrobe. He reeked of sweat and fish, looking and smelling like an overworked boatman. As the launch approached, he assumed the slouch of a man beaten down by years of hauling heavy nets.

Georges was beside him, speaking under his breath. "These cops aren't the typical bastards you meet on-shore—some of these guys even know our seagoing life. They rarely hassle us fishermen, but they're *Boches* all the same. They may try to take us down a notch or two."

René nodded. "Get in the cabin and make sure everyone's hidden. Things could get rough." He felt the weight of the illegal handgun in his trouser pocket, a death sentence if found. Near the Avant Port the harbor police had been boarding a few trawlers. At René's request, Georges fished out an old revolver hidden behind the steering console, a corroded relic unsuited to a salty environment. No way to know if the piece would fire till put to use. He had four cartridges. Four chances.

The klaxon whooped again as the gunboat came alongside and the police tossed a line. The captain hailed them, demanding they cut their engine and prepare for boarding. René fastened the rope to a cleat and eased the vessels closer.

"What can we do for you, captain?" He mimicked the local inflection and hoped the harbor police weren't savvy enough to distinguish one dialect from another.

"Prepare for boarding," the officer repeated, "and get all your crew on deck!" His French correct but stilted.

"Just me and the kid today, sir. We're short one man this morning." Georges was back topside. René prayed for silence from the cabin. "My other mate came down with a helluva head cold last night, the shirker." René smiled and swept his left arm in a gesture of gracious welcome. "A bit early for fish, sir, so how about a brandy instead? Warms the bones." He hoped that was Cognac on the rack in the cabin.

The boats rocked side-by-side in the swell as the officers leapt onto *La Demoiselle's* deck.. Two enlisted men remained on the gunboat, one with a rifle at his shoulder and the other at the helm. The lieutenant's demand was brief: "Your papers, please."

Georges played ignorant and handed over the fishing permit issued by the Saint-Nazaire port authority. The junior officer scanned the document and handed it to his superior. "You this Mercier?"

René thought quickly. If these cops had a two-way radio they might already have names of the partisans. "No, sir, Mercier's the one back in port, likely nursing a Calvados. For his health, you understand."

"And your papers?" A look of impatience, perhaps revulsion at René's odiferous outfit.

He patted his pockets and shrugged. "The fish rarely ask for them, sir. Must be in my other trousers." He buried both hands deep in his pockets, as if checking one last time, and shrugged in regret. He kept the revolver in his grip. If all cartridges fired, he could possibly drop the two officers before taking down the rifleman. By then he would also have the captain's sidearm and guarantee himself the helmsmen."As for the kid," he looked over at Georges, "he's got no papers. He's barely seventeen."

Georges had stepped to the hold and dragged the hatch cover aside, keeping the peg of the lockdown in his hand. "Want to take a look, officers?"

The stench of decades rose from the depths and the captain brought a handkerchief to his nose. "Not necessary, kid—no catch yet, right? But I will take a quick look in the cabin, just in case you've hidden away a little something for the black market."

"It's all yours, captain." René stepped aside, positioning himself to make every shot count. Georges acknowledged the unspoken plan with a nod. With luck, one officer might come down a serious headache from that wooden peg.

The door abruptly swung open in the captain's face. He jerked back as Leo emerged, rubbing his eyes and yawning. He looked up and politely asked, "Is that your boat, *monsieur l'agent*?" He pointed to the police launch.

The captain nodded. "It is."

"Why are you tied to our boat?"

"We're seeing what you're up to." The captain exchanged grins with the lieutenant.

"Well, monsieur—I was sleeping, but all the noise woke me up!"

The officer made a fake bow: "So sorry, Your Majesty." Now he'd begun to laugh.

"That's all right, *monsieur l'agent*. But I've a lot of fishing ahead and need all the sleep I can get!"

The absurdity of a child's reprimand brought both officers to laughter. Once he caught his breath, the captain demanded of René: "What's the brat doing on your boat?"

"Sorry, captain." René did his best to appear contrite. "My wife's also sick this morning, so I got stuck with the boy. He can be a handful." He bent toward the captain to confide in a whisper, "The old lady's probably shacking up with Mercier for the day. Sharing his misery, right?"

Still chuckling, the captain made a deep, sarcastic bow to Leo while addressing the lieutenant, "Come on. Let's get going. We can't have His Majesty missing out on much needed sleep, now can we?"

René slowly released his grip on the revolver once Georges had tossed the line back to the launch. As the boats drifted apart, René heard the captain shout to his lieutenant: "Even the French spawn believe they still own this world!" The gunboat engines thundered and the vessel quickly left the stubby trawler in its wake.

Leo's shout of *"Bon voyage!"* was lost to the offshore wind.

René finally allowed himself to join Georges in laughter. He gave Leo a half-hearted scowl before entering the cabin. A pile of woolen blankets hid the two women, with Sophie cradled between them. On the opposite side lay the crumpled tarp which had briefly hidden Leo.

At René's encouragement, Erika threw back the covers. "Close one?"

"Too close. But Leo came through with his typical charm."

"Once he opened the door it was too late to stop him. We couldn't hear what was said out there."

"Best you didn't. But one thing's for sure—it's time our son was back in school and learning a little discipline. That boy's growing up too fast for his own good." René returned the revolver to it hiding place, hoping it would never be needed. "Until then, let's just leave him to his natural inclinations."

From the stern they watched Georges reef the sails. A line secured the wheel, keeping them on course. Leo observed every move with rapt attention and pestered the youth with incessant questions. Sophie had fallen asleep on Lisette's lap. The waves were up now, the trawler bending to the wind, froth whipping across the bow. René steadied Erika, one arm wrapped around her with his hand on her belly. "It's a baby for us, then?"

She laughed. "Yes, definitely a baby. Yours and mine."

He nuzzled her neck and smiled.

She returned his grin and leaned back into his embrace. "Yes, yours and mine." At her insistence he'd shed the smelly fisherman's gear, done a quick wash-up in the cabin, and agreed to regrow his beard. They'd rummaged around and found a passable bulky sweater. My seagoing pirate, she thought.

He nodded, clearly considering their future. She knew choosing Spain or neutral Portugal would get them to safety faster, though with many risks along the way. But England was many more dangerous days to the north, and the waters potentially more hazardous. The Saint-Nazaire estuary had dropped below the horizon, but the sad memories of the town were sure to haunt their quiet hours. "How soon?" he asked.

"Seven months is my guess. Mid-spring."

"Leo's good with little ones. Keeps him out of trouble, right?"

"He's good all right." She laughed quietly. The encounter with the harbor police could easily have gone sideways. "That boy can always find trouble but has luck on his side, just like Ryan." The nagging worry surfaced. "Darling, do you suppose he got our message about Horst?"

"If not, he will soon enough. His brother will see to that. One thing about Ryan, he's tougher now, stronger. Think of him back in Marburg, always the bon vivant, expecting all to go his way." She remembered well those simpler times before Horst had turned their lives into a living hell. "But he's matured now, more careful, so he'll be fine, trust me." He lifted her collar to shield her face from the wind. "So what'll it be, *Liebling*, port or starboard?"

"Spain or England?"

"Spain or England—time for a decision."

She didn't hesitate. "I say England. First, you won't last more than a fortnight before you're itching to knock a few Nazi heads again. More opportunities in that direction. Second, the Allies can certainly use your knowledge and talents. And third, life is rougher in Spain. We've quite a growing brood to consider, and besides, Leo needs to get back to school. I want him to learn English. He's got a gift for languages. Best of all, Madame de Brassis' posthumous generosity will keep us in food and baby clothes for some time to come."

"Perhaps the Allies can put your medical training to use."

Erika curbed her selfish desire to stay involved in the battle. She sighted up the distant coast toward Brest, singling out tiny trawlers scattered across the broad expanse. Suddenly she reached for the binoculars at his neck. "A conning tower!" She pointed anxiously.

René's brow furrowed as he took the field glasses, then grinned in obvious relief. "Nothing to worry about, love." His smile broadened. "Just a coastal freighter topping the horizon."

He held her close. She closed her eyes and he kissed her forehead. "We're going to be all right. England it is." Their lips met. "I love you so," he whispered, his words almost lost to the slap of the sail, but she knew it anyway.

"Hey, you two!" Leo was looking back before entering the cabin. "Better keep your eyes on the ocean. Just ask Georges. This boat doesn't sail itself, you know."

WIDERSTAND

1941

CHAPTER ONE

Paris, Occupied France
17 September 1941

The death house at Cherche-Midi prison was silent but for the sobbing of a prisoner in the next cubicle. A man, nameless, faceless. Perhaps one of those shackled partisans whose delivery had taken precedence over hers on the day of her incarceration. The courage of her neighbor had dissolved into terror, but perhaps he had more to lose than Marita. Rumor was that men got the rope rather than the guillotine. At least the blade of the *Fallbeil* was quick. The hangman used a narrow cord and simple knot. No snapping the neck, no clean break, just a long, agonizing struggle to assure the condemned saw the error of his ways before he perished.

In the tight confines of her death cell she sat on the narrow metal bench bracketed to the wall. No bed—it would never have fit—or even a jug of water. She wouldn't be here long enough to need either. The high, barred window to her back cast a pale light. She tracked the zig-zag course of roaches scuttling at her feet. From time to time she swatted away a fly. Giving her hands something to do, she gathered up her ragged hair. She had kept the gift from Frau Biedermann and now used the comb as a clip. The guard with the handcuffs had accepted her explanation that it would keep her hair free of the descending blade.

The damp walls reeked of urine. It made her wish she had peed before leaving her cell. There had been so little time to prepare even knowing that each hour might be her last. When they did finally come for her she was too nervous to think of any personal comfort. The other women had called out their support—"*Vive la France, vive le général de Gaulle*"—as the guards led her to this death house an hour earlier. Good women. Brave women. And now both blood and urine would soil the bed of the guillotine. Just one more mess for her captors to clean up. *I piss on all you Boche bastards!*

Her appeal for clemency had been denied, her tribunal a farce. In a barren room with the appearance of hasty preparation—a Nazi flag tacked to the wall behind the magistrates' dais, another table for the attorneys, a single chair for her—justice was served. The presiding judge obviously had better things to do. Perhaps he was late for a luncheon at Le Pré Catalan. Playing bookends to the head magistrate, the two assessors observed her from time to time over their reading glasses. Her timid attorney Bertin smelled of sweat, his collar obviously too tight, his fingers drumming incessantly on the tabletop during the brief proceedings. Nervous facing an important German judge, she guessed. She herself had remained calm, resigned to her fate, unwilling to give her persecutors reason to doubt her strength and character. A heavy chain bound her waist and confined her wrists. An armed soldier stood on either side of her. What a threat to the mighty Reich she was.

Once she had made clear she needed no interpreter, the presiding judge read the charges to the prosecutor, who then spent a mere quarter hour making his case. He emphasized the English design of the wireless set found in her office and her easy access to intelligence in a club filled nightly with Reich officers. Several times he mentioned her nefarious Jewish blood. The sole evidence to support the charges was the transmitter, on display before the tribunal.

Marita received a token opportunity to explain her purported treason. While she spoke, the presiding judge organized the stack of files before him, probably estimating how soon his odious workday would be over. After her denial of guilt, he nodded to the assessors and declared judgment and punishment in one breath: "Immediate execution by beheading for this traitor to the Greater Reich." Bertin had only an "I told you so" look to share. Marita herself shrugged off the foregone conclusion to this farce. As they led her from the room, the chief magistrate already called the next case.

Upon her return to the cell block, her fellow inmates broke loose with questions, ignoring the rule for silence in the presence of guards unless directly addressed. "It's to be death, my friends," Marita smiled with self-imposed nonchalance, "as expected." "But they never execute women!" came the response from several cells, giving empty hope to those who still denied what was happening in their midst. Then the block had fallen silent.

In the death house, a deep, throaty laugh preceded the arrival of shuffling boots and jangling keys. The voices stopped outside her cell and she heard the ancient tumbler start its turn. "No, wait! We'll do the men first." The key hesitated in the lock at the words of the man in charge. She straightened her back, her hands tightly knit to quiet the trembling. "Oh go ahead, bring the woman along, as well. It'll do her good to watch them dance." Her door creaked open. "Good morning, mademoiselle. A fine day to meet your maker." He turned to give his colleagues a smile. "But don't you worry—I am very good at my job." His comrades echoed that husky laugh. Not a German. A foreigner, his French suggestive of Switzerland.

Long ago, Ryan had spoken enthusiastically of bicycling through the Alps over snow-peaked passes and coasting down into green valleys dotted with charming farmsteads. One day they would go there together, he had promised. Or perhaps it wasn't a promise, only pillow talk of no consequence. But that was more than a decade past, a beautiful moment she would never experience. She inhaled deeply as she rose to her feet, knowing that all she had loved and lost, and whatever might have come in her future—all that was now about to end. And she refused to cry.

She smiled at the men in black uniforms: "Shall we get on with it, *messieurs*?"

CHAPTER TWO

Ermenonville, Occupied France
19 September 1941

R olf remained tight-lipped over the phone when he summoned Ryan and Argent back to the château. Two weeks had passed with no news of Marita, so both were on edge when the calls came in. He had insisted on meeting again at Ermenonville. When Edmond finally braked to a halt, Rolf was waiting in the courtyard, casually smoking a cigarette beneath the entry portico. He greeted them with a smile and handshake and asked them to follow him up the curving staircase. He refused to speak further until they reached the room with the tall French windows and a view of Paris in the distance.

"Some good news at last, gentlemen." Rolf removed a glass-stoppered carafe from the sideboard and set out three snifters. He began to pour, hesitating long enough to wipe a smudge from the rim of one bulbous glass. "Our lovely friend is doing fine for the moment, as safe as can be expected, and—"

Ryan interrupted: "Can we speak with her, see her?"

"Sadly, no on both counts. She's been in the women's wing of Cherche-Midi these last weeks. We finally found a Justice Department insider open to our bribe. He gave us what we wanted. Amazing what well-spent francs can do."

"How's she holding up?" Argent demanded.

"Your charming Mademoiselle Lesney survived inter-rogation and a typical staged trial, but it's clear powerful men still want her out of the picture, and quickly. But we got off damn well—they learned nothing of the operation at the club."

"Who gives a damn about that?" Rolf's manner infuri-ated Ryan. This was Marita he was talking about. "How do we reach her, get her out?"

"Nothing's ever that simple, Ryan. She was convicted of espionage, a capital offense. The tribunal sentenced her to death."

Argent grabbed Rolf's arm, his patience also at an end. "And with what proof? You said they didn't catch on to us!"

Ryan finally made the connection. "They convicted solely on that wireless set they planted because the whole setup was payback from that extortionist, right?"

Rolf nodded. "He's most certainly our culprit." He sipped the cognac and sighed with satisfaction. "Appears our friend Serge Bergieux disappeared into Göring's clutches, just as planned, but still found a way to get revenge on our dear mademoiselle. He was very tight with the local Gesta-po, it seems."

"So what comes next?" Ryan made no effort to hide his frustration. "We're still waiting for that good news you promised, Rolf."

"Well, things have changed for the better, thanks to our people in Berlin. There's to be no execution."

"She's to go free?" Argent's face momentarily bright-ened.

"Regrettably, they only commuted the death sentence. She's still looking at ten years in a forced-labor camp." Rolf distributed the snifters, but the others ignored them. "Depor-tation is already underway."

"She disappears into the Reich and we'll never find her!" Ryan gritted his teeth in frustration.

"It seems we're a day too late for that. According to the jailor with the greased palms, she's already on an eastbound train."

"My God," Ryan said, "there must be hundreds, maybe thousands of those labor camps by now!" He dropped into an armchair, overwhelmed by the sheer magnitude of such a task. "So how on earth do we track her down now?"

Rolf continued undeterred: "Well, that's just the thing—on our own we've no hope of finding her, but Berlin can do just that if given time and proper incentive."

"Then have your people find her and Argent and I will get the job done."

Flushed with obvious anger and frustration, Argent stopped mid-pace. "They owe us for what we've been doing here to make their lives easier."

"Again, gentlemen, certain hurdles stand in our way," Rolf set down his snifter, still untouched. "Please understand—this isn't a priority for the Abwehr, more a generous favor we're asking. But I'm told things might be expedited should one hand wash the other. Berlin will be happy to pull strings to locate her, perhaps even obtain her eventual release once the matter settles down a bit…"

Ryan waited for the other shoe: "But?"

Rolf could resist the alcohol no longer and took a sip. "But they expect something in return, something only you, Ryan, might deliver."

"If it's in my power, they've got it."

Rolf switched momentarily to English: "Ah, 'there's the rub,' as Shakespeare would say. My chief wants to discuss certain matters with you in person. He's a very private man when it comes to such things."

"Then set up the meeting—right away—and I'm there."

"Unfortunately, he's in Berlin."

Ryan drew a determined breath. "Then it appears I'm off to Berlin."

"Excellent!" Rolf appeared pleased to have that hurdle out of the way at last. "Your travel visa is only a phone call away, and powerful people will look after you once you arrive."

"And what of Argent here?"

"He'll grab a train the moment we know her location, and we'll post a coded message in all the Berlin personals so you can rendezvous with him. Should Argent arrive first, he can scout out the situation, perhaps even contact her or find guards open to a bribe. But, dear Ryan, it's first up to you to do what's necessary in Berlin."

"Whatever your man asks," he hesitated, fearful of overreaching, "as long as it's also in my country's best interests, of course. But keep me in the loop. Once we know exactly where she's held, no matter what else is on my plate, I join Argent and we get her out of Germany. We're agreed then?"

No one challenged the commitment in Ryan's eyes.

Polished by heavy traffic, the rails in the freight yards of Pantin shone amber in the light of the waning day. Several trains idled as crews finished last-minute servicing. One massive locomotive chuffed away, transporting the bounty of France to Germany. Clouds of smoke and cinders filled the corridor between drab industrial buildings and tenements as it left the yards. A passenger train rattled through next, heading north, passing the red-gold fire of the setting sun from one window to the next. The autumn fog would soon move in, stealing any last hint of beauty from this rough setting of oil-stained gravel and soot-laden air.

The women emerging from the buses took no notice of the shifting light. French police forced the prisoners up a long ramp into forty-and-eights, boxy freight cars designed to handle eight horses or forty soldiers. The carriages began to sag low as twice that many women struggled for standing room in the confined spaces. The few with foresight sought out the air vents near the roofline. Once the doors were padlocked and the train underway, no one would move for many long hours. Perhaps days.

Men in gabardine oversaw the loading. *Boches*.

A police sedan pulled trackside and braked to a halt behind the row of buses. Marita steeled her nerves and prepared to join the brutalized throng, but her guard guided her past the pitiful throng to the forward car in the train. Distrusting her luck and worried that someone would take note of his error, she numbly boarded a third-class coach and settled on a wooden bench beside a heavily-barred window. About twenty other privileged captives already waited, some with handbags, none with luggage, all staring forward, immobile and silent, keeping heads low to avoid unwanted attention.

Her guard bent close to remove her handcuffs and whispered a German wish for success: *"Hals- und Beinbruch!"* Her mother used to say it came from the Yiddish—*Break a neck and a leg*. The man left the carriage without looking back.

A sincere wish for luck, or a sarcastic commentary on a life of forced labor beyond the Rhine? Enough to know she had escaped the guillotine. Spared for some unclear purpose, she would make the most of the opportunity, perhaps the last break she would ever get.

The muted shouts and cries from the trailing freight cars faded as the train picked up steam. Behind her, two uniformed guards started a card game on the rearmost bench. The rocking of the carriage and quiet whisperings of her fellow passengers began to lull her exhausted mind.

The final horrors of Cherche-Midi prison rolled out in a ceaseless loop: that smooth metal bar spanning the breadth of the death room, that compact guillotine in the corner beneath the tall window, its angled blade glistening with a brightly honed edge. The executioner needed only to twist the handle to release her from this hell of a life.

Trembling, Marita had felt her strength ebb, her eyes returning again and again to the high window revealing a narrow courtyard warming under morning sun. She would miss sunlight filtering through foliage, groomed parks where lovers strolled, children sending toy sailboats across fountain basins as nannies and mothers traded gossip.

She had watched the two partisans prepare to die. Their eyes appeared glazed, expressions resigned, minds already distanced from the proceedings. It was impossible to say which man had been wracked by despair just minutes before. Neither resisted when the guards helped them mount the stools. She focused on the man closest to her, the one who'd shared a quick exchange of regret as they entered the chamber. The Swiss executioner fashioned simple slipknots in the cords and climbed up to attach them to the iron rod. He slid a noose over the first man. His Adam's apple bobbed nervously as the knot tightened at his ear. She stared, biting her lip as the hangman cinched the second rope tight.

The rest was simple. The Swiss hopped down and in one motion jerked the stool from beneath the first condemned. The man dangled, struggling to free his bound wrists, his eyes and jaws wide open. The second stool tumbled aside and the wide-open eyes of that victim immediately reddened as veins ruptured.

Marita had tried to look away, but a guard held her head straight. She had no choice but to watch as the men danced convulsively side-by-side. Trembling with the revulsion, she narrowed her vision to the feet jerking above the overturned stools. The stench of voided bowels filled the room. One guard laughed and said, "See, didn't I tell you these partisans are full of shit!"

The dying took what seemed a very long time. Hoarse guttural sounds emerged from deep in the men's throats, each wheeze somewhat shorter than the previous until only a pitiful whine emerged in final gasps.

Her legs had suddenly given way, her knees on the filthy floor, her arms still supported by the guard's. He offered words of encouragement as he squeezed her breasts: "The blade is so much quicker, you know, so consider yourself blessed."

She awoke with a start. The jostling train had thrown her head against the window. Exhaustion drained her body and mind, the horror of the previous morning still pulling her down.

They had brutally grabbed her arms and dragged her over to the guillotine. How clean they kept the instrument of death, how free of the filth infesting the rest of the death house. "Face-down, mademoiselle, unless you'd prefer to watch my blade fall." The eyes of the patronizing executioner betrayed his impatience. She focused on the man's words and ignored the overriding stench of death and excrement.

New voices and muddled argument invaded her mind as she surrendered to the inevitability of death. Then came a numbing of all thought and understanding as they removed her from the bed of the killing machine. They led her out across the narrow courtyard, her hands still cuffed at her back. Shouts of surprise and support greeted her return to the women's wing, but she understood little of what was said. The cell door in the house of the living slammed closed behind her.

She had collapsed on the bed. In her mind the two words from the death house had finally sunk in, concepts that made sense and yet made no sense. Commuted. Deported. She slept until the following morning, unable to respond to the offer of food, to the shift from day into night, to the clanging and shouting of guards. Commuted. Deported. She would live to see another day. To find some purpose in all her misery.

CHAPTER THREE

En Route, Paris to Berlin
20 September 1941

Ryan felt the constriction in his throat and sensed the return of the dark depression of recent years. He rocked unconsciously to the rhythm of the moving train. It was good to be alone in the first-class compartment, for he knew his state of mind made him very poor company. Two thoughts plagued him: Erika and Leo possibly dead, von Kredow still alive.

At Gare de l'Est, a German couple had opened the compartment door and asked to share the cabin. Expensive Party badges gleamed on their lapels and neatly-wrapped packages filled their arms. A shabbily-dressed Frenchman served as conscripted porter, waiting patiently in the aisle with their overstuffed luggage. Another successful plundering of the Parisian economy. Ryan's icy stare sent them on to the next compartment. He'd barely registered their murmurs of distaste at such incredible rudeness.

Ahead lay Berlin and Horst and the key to Marita's rescue. Behind lay a possible loss too horrifying to imagine. Weeks had passed since Edward told him Erika and Leo might have perished in a gun battle in Bayonne. Might have, they both had agreed. Perhaps another deception from von Kredow designed to drive him mad with guilt and fury, or a new manipulation by the equally disturbed Richard Kohl. Or had he simply failed his friends despite his best efforts?

With each passing day his melancholy had worsened. Now he was leaving France in frustrating uncertainty, heading toward the city that harbored his nemesis while distancing himself from determining what really happened with Erika and his son.

First there was the news of their purported deaths along with Kohl's warning that the Gestapo was again on his trail. Why had Kohl mentioned von Kredow as his "late colleague" if Horst had truly survived the cyanide pill?

He slumped in his seat and stared out at the passing countryside. Over two weeks since his desperate attempt to reach René after receiving the message signed "RG." *Le Masque alive in Berlin*. Ryan could clearly picture the sadist's bloodied face, those distorted lips fighting the cyanide pill, the shuddering convulsions and foaming spittle, those last ragged breaths. The bastard had died at Ryan's own hands, yet somehow come to life again? *What does it take to kill such a man?*

Ryan had immediately phoned the Saint-Nazaire number given. A woman answered with the name of the tavern but quickly turned uncommunicative. She denied any knowledge of a Rénard or Héloise and couldn't explain how he got her number. She finally hung up on him when he persisted. A second call on the heels of the first went unanswered. Next he tried the doctor outside Loire. That line also rang repeatedly until he had finally surrendered in frustration.

Attempts the following day had been equally disappointing. By ten a.m. he found himself on the way to the coast. *Le dernier Réfuge* was a landmark in Old Town and easy to find, but the initially friendly proprietress clammed up the moment he introduced himself. He saw the fear in her eyes. How should she know he wasn't Gestapo out to entrap her? He strolled past the bunker compound, seemingly ignoring the monumental structure and the fervent construction activity at the northern end. Nothing suggested sabotage, but what had he expected—a smoldering ruin? On his return trip he detrained at Nantes and took a taxi out to the home of Dr. Ballineux. Black-and-white crime scene stamps with circled swastikas sealed every entrance. Frustrated by questions without answers, he had caught the next train back to Paris.

Now he opened his notebook to Leo's final gift, the flower already turning brittle, its ghostly impression staining the pages. He thought of all the children whose ethnic "inferiority" condemned them to suffer under Nazi barbarism. Ryan chided himself for the selfish indulgence in personal grief, but his sorrow only intensified. Was grieving for a single child not grieving for all whose fate remained unknown? Across Europe, parents faced daily the uncertainties he now had to endure.

Erika's strength had protected Leo from a world hardened by hatred and bigotry. She had lost both parents in the process. He pictured her smile and his heart ached with memories of those naïve days before darkness enveloped Germany. Who dares expect happiness, anyway? He might have taken her back to the States in '34, witnessed Leo's birth, created a life distant from all this death and destruction. But he hadn't been ready for such a commitment, and Erika had yet to discover her own strength and will.

He sought distraction in his immediate surroundings. The compartment was worn and shabby, so different from pre-war carriages on this Paris-Berlin route. Half-starved to fund the Reich's aggression, France could no longer maintain her own railroads. From time to time his train gave priority to troop transports and rolling machines of war. Was it only a few weeks ago that he and Nicole sweltered under canvas as they made their way from Bayonne to Tours. Was she reunited with her child at last, guided there by Leo? Or were they two more victims of a sadist who never should have drawn a first breath?

His finger traced phantom handprints on the window left by bored children. Thinking of Leo, he again cursed the depravity of von Kredow but all the while blamed himself. He should have slit the bastard's throat, driven the dagger deep into his heaving chest. He should have stayed long enough to bring those Bayonne children to safety. Again, so many regrets. And why no further word from René after that single message of warning?

He willed the tension from his body, breathing slowly and focusing his thoughts on the coming task. He was about to help another beloved friend, one who still might survive her nightmare. Ahead lay tough new challenges with von Kredow alive and in Berlin. He already felt the target weighing heavily on his back. Learning the truth about Erika and Leo would have to wait.

The express clattered over the long girder bridge, the locomotive smoke obscuring the far bank of the Rhine. The river surged below, a broad stretch of gray and silver. Ryan was once again in the Reich.

How welcoming Berlin had once been in those first months and years a decade earlier. He wondered what changes would greet him now, what damning Gestapo file waited to hang him for espionage? Kohl and von Kredow had surely recorded all his "crimes" from the murder of that brutish agent on the train near Koblenz to Pabst's drowning in the Rhine. And now he'd killed others in the warehouse battle which should have put a final end to von Kredow's path of vengeance. Surely his foes would have justified their own web of deceit by documenting his offenses as the work of an enemy of the Reich. Rolf von Haldheim was certain his Abwehr could shield Ryan from the SD and Gestapo, but Ryan thought that highly unlikely.

Many questions, but no answers.

Rolf clearly wasn't authorized to give the name of the man to greet him in the capital. COI suggested that only the enigmatic Wilhelm Canaris, head of German military intelligence, came into question. In fact, David Bruce hoped the overture from the Abwehr would prove to be a covert peace-feeler from the highest levels in the Reich. If Rolf's man in Berlin wanted a face-to-face, Ryan would accommodate.

Long hours on the train had pushed back that cloud of depression. The uncertainty surrounding the fate of his loved ones fueled new determination as he approached the capital of the Reich. He would do whatever was needed to protect himself and Marita. Once foreign to him, violence was becoming second nature. That realization was unsettling, but he walled off the misgivings. Killing was a necessity of wartime, a tool to protect what was just and right. Once this horror was passed—assuming his survival—he hoped to regain his former self. But for now, steeling himself, he tucked away the doubts in some remote corner of his mind knowing they would resurface the moment they were given a chance.

One thing remained indisputable. Even if Erika and Leo were gone for good, he wasn't about to lose Marita. She had only to stay alive until he managed to track her down.

The clear sky above the flatlands of Prussia gradually surrendered to a dirty gray. Ryan's train rumbled into Berlin by late afternoon. At the last few stations his compartment had filled with ill-kempt passengers and the stench of unwashed clothing and neglected personal hygiene forced him into the aisle. He found a place beside an open window. The air tasted of soot and cinders, and Ryan wished for a drink to wash the grit from his teeth. With his bag between his feet, he stared out across a Berlin transformed by two years of war, deprivation and aerial bombardment.

At first, all seemed little changed from the day in '38 when he and Erika ran from the city with Leo in tow. The freight yards appeared as busy as ever, locomotives taking on coal from hulking supply towers and yard machines shuffling about like so many wind-up toys. But gradually the changes became more apparent. An anti-aircraft battery capped a broad concrete column several stories tall, and soldiers on the turret-mounted flak emplacement swept the sky with field glasses. Ryan scanned the low-hanging clouds himself, spotting only a flock of geese exiting the city. He knew the British bombers came by night, so perhaps the soldiers feigned alertness in anticipation of an imminent inspection.

The train rolled past several bomb craters, each deep enough to hold a freight car. Twisted and distorted rails ruptured outward from the blast sites. Grime-blackened workers toiled with heavy pry bars and brightly flaring cutting torches. Just beyond the nearest crater sat a railcar holding a three-legged mast, its winch-powered cable draping down to the bomb cavity. A tiny engine idled, waiting to haul away the next load of damaged rail.

The workers bent to their task under the watchful eyes of armed guards. These laborers were likely Polish or Ukrainian *Zwangsarbeiter*, "forced laborers." The Ministry of Propaganda preferred the gentler term of *Fremdarbeiter*, "foreign workers," a euphemism for the enslaved force which sustained the wartime Reich economy while most German men were away in military service.

Ryan's anger rose at the sight of the workers. What filthy tasks would wear down Marita's body and spirit, what "labor" would transform her into a worker drone for the Greater German Reich?

The train entered beneath the massive canopy of Anhalter Bahnhof. Soldiers with machine pistols stood on either side of the track, nearly disappearing in a cloud of cinders and steam. Black smoke assaulted his window. Ryan slammed it shut, grabbed his bag, and joined the queue of passengers already pressing toward the exits. Many dropped to the platform even before the train had come to a full stop.

Across the way a brass band struck up a martial air. He knew immediately the raucous reception wasn't meant for his express. On the neighboring track young children reached out open carriage windows, exuberantly waving tiny swastikas on sticks and shouting to family members below. Tearful mothers and grandmothers gave encouragement, their voices competing with the metallic oom-pah of the instruments. Adults closest to the rail cars reached up for a last touch of their child's hand. Many children seemed excited by their new adventure, though Ryan spotted tear-streaked faces, especially among the youngest. It was surely a KLV train, resettling urban children into foster homes in the German countryside far from bombs and collapsing buildings.

His heart went out to those mothers trying to hold back tears and to the few sad-eyed youngsters who sensed the gravity of the separation.

Turning away quickly, he forged a path toward the waiting police control. Emotions had surfaced at the thought of Leo. With no time for weakness, he joined the line, and when his turn came, he made a point of snorting into his handkerchief before handing over his passport and visa. "Darned head cold," he told the agent, explaining away the tears.

The policeman sounded sincere as he cautiously accepted the documents, doing his best to avoid Ryan's handkerchief. "Quite common these days," he said. He gave his colleague a wry look and handed over the passport, holding it by the edge. The second agent grimaced and compared Ryan's face to the photo before jotting something on a clipboard.

The control officer handed back the document. "So, Herr Seffer, what brings another American to Berlin?"

"Business with the Ministry of the Interior."

"Length of stay?"

Ryan was repulsed by the man's sour breath. Good dental hygiene was clearly rare in wartime Berlin, given what he'd experienced on the train. "A few days at most, then it's back to Paris for me."

The man grunted, already waving him on as he turned to the next in line. Ryan caught a muttered comment to the colleague: "He leaves Paris for this?"

Above the concourse he spotted cracked panes of glass and twisted girders in the vast arch of the ceiling. Souvenirs of British incendiary bombs, he assumed. At ground level nothing remained to remind Berliners of Göring's promise his Luftwaffe would keep their skies free of enemy bombers.

Word on the train was that raids were coming less frequently than earlier in the year, mostly nuisance and leafleting attacks in recent months. Perhaps England really was losing its will to fight, or as Goebbels yammered *ad nauseum*, the British military collapsing in the face of German might.

Ryan stopped in front of a news kiosk, taking in the headlines as he used the plate glass window to scan the hustle and bustle to his rear. He spotted no tail.

The elevated S-Bahn rumbled across the city. Here and there damaged buildings and piles of rubble caught his attention, the ragged holes in housing blocks revealing random hits. Elsewhere, whole blocks were falling under the onslaught of forced labor and heavy demolition equipment. *Germania*, Hitler's newly-minted capital of the world, was soon to rise under the watchful eye of his chief architect Speer, but first whole stretches along the East-West Axis had to go. Ryan's trainer in Toronto had described this planned rebirth of Berlin. Ancient Rome would pale in comparison to all the monuments destined to glorify both Führer and Reich, but where were the poor citizens driven out of these disappearing neighborhoods?

His train rolled to a stop at Brandenburger Tor. Camouflage netting stretched across the broad square. He walked the short distance to Pariser Platz and entered a Neo-Baroque lobby flanked by monumental square columns. The Adlon Hotel was a luxurious refuge offering an in-house restaurant, a café and bar, and an interior garden retreat serving drinks and light meals. The entry to a bomb shelter for hotel patrons and staff stood alongside the barbershop. Ranks of brightly colored bottles made the bar particularly inviting. Check-in, a quick wash upstairs, and Ryan would return for that much-needed drink.

The hotel drew a clientele of well-dressed Italians and Spaniards, German businessmen and military officers, a few Americans and a small group of Japanese in business suits. Political envoys, perhaps. Ryan knew that international journalists and celebrity guests favored the Adlon. In fact, three men smoking in the lounge were American newsmen remembered from evenings with Isabel at La Taverna, eavesdropping on top-notch foreign correspondents.

The staff hustled under the direction of well-mannered desk clerks in striped waistcoats. Everyone was exceedingly accommodating. First the reception, then the lift operator and finally the bellhop inquired about his plans in the city. Ryan knew hotel personnel were often agents of either the SD or the Abwehr, sometimes both, so he gave only non-committal replies and pretended weak fluency in German.

His suite was spacious, the furniture primarily Louis XVI. This hotel far exceeded the standard for his prior Berlin visits. The von Haldheim mansion of 1929 came to mind. He assumed the Abwehr was covering the costs, since his own wallet and expense account certainly couldn't. As the porter demonstrated the drapes, Ryan noted a neatly framed sign warning that all blackout curtains were to remain closed during hours of darkness at risk of financial and criminal penalties. A map gave directions to the cellar bomb shelter. Once the bellhop was convinced Ryan knew how to turn on a radio and draw a bath, he graciously accepted a small gratuity and backed from the room, closing the double doors behind him.

Ryan stood at the window, watching the square below. The new I.G. Farben building across the street was capped by an obvious flak installation. Across the square he recognized the American Embassy, the Stars-and-Stripes floating on a breeze. Daylight was waning and the streets growing dark, a strange sight in a city once so vibrantly lit at night.

Better to stay in the moment than dwell on the past, he thought. His summons would come via a message at the front desk, but he had no idea how long that might take. Once contacted, his orders were to learn all he could about the inner workings of the Abwehr, but what could he possibly offer Reich military intelligence in exchange for Marita's freedom? What could he do personally for this legendary Admiral Canaris?

He took time to shower and shave, then phoned down to have his travel shirt and underwear picked up for laundering. Housekeeping reported laundry services temporarily suspended due to a shortage of soap. The room phone was certainly bugged, so that would be the extent of its use.

At the newsstand he bought a *Berliner Abendzeitung.* He took a table at the far wall in the nearly empty bar. An elderly waiter with a badly-curved spine delivered a tiny plate of nuts. "And what is your pleasure, sir?" he asked.

"A gin and tonic sounds good."

"Indeed it does, *mein Herr*, but sadly, we're momentarily short of tonic water." The man nervously adjusted what Ryan could now see was a slightly frayed waistcoat.

"A gimlet, then. Either gin or vodka will do."

The bartender again expressed regrets. "Sorry, sir, no limes this time of year. An unfortunate state of affairs, but...the war, you know."

"Of course." Ryan thought for a moment. "A Scotch will do me fine. A double on the rocks, *bitte*." Ryan turned to his newspaper, already considering seeking out a different bar.

The man made another little bow. "Unfortunately, sir, our whiskey supplies are also quite limited."

Ryan gestured to the backlit bottles that ran the length of the wall behind the bar. "Well, I don't wish to appear rude, but is anything up there available to a thirsty customer?"

The barman lowered his voice to a whisper. "Only if you have a taste for colored water, sir. But do allow me to offer you a fine Cognac. Or Champagne, perhaps? Our selection from France is quite decent these days." The man winked, happy to come clean at last. "And I do have a good Berlin beer."

"A Pilsner then." Ryan feared for a moment that the man would say they had nothing but Export.

The "Personals" listed a variety of notices from those seeking matrimonial partners or missing family members, but only a few inserts memorialized local sons and brothers "fallen for the Fatherland." He was surprised that so few mentioned "fallen for the Führer," as well. He found nothing from Argent, so no news on the Parisian end. Tossing aside the paper, Ryan watched the barman top off his beer. A cool beverage couldn't come soon enough.

A man in a herringbone jacket entered the bar, caught the eye of the stooped bartender and quietly gave his order. Must be a regular, thought Ryan, to know what's available. The newcomer lit a cigarette and took a seat at the bar. He set his gray snap-brim fedora atop the polished surface.

CHAPTER FOUR

Berlin-Wannsee, Germany
20 September 1941

The airmail package from Bayonne had been waiting at Prinz-Albrecht-Strasse when Horst arrived in Berlin. He immediately tore away the wrapping paper and horsehair padding to reveal a small canning jar. Although the specimens had darkened in color, the alcohol had preserved their integrity, but such meaningful trophies deserved a more impressive container. Fine Zwiesel crystal provided a fitting vessel once he had filled it with clear grain alcohol and sealed the lid with red wax.

For the first week the souvenirs had held a position of honor in his newly assigned office, a none-too-subtle display of intimidation. A few bolder colleagues dared to inquire about their provenance, but even fewer showed what he considered an appropriate degree of appreciation for his trophies. Reinhard Heydrich, calling in old favors and currying new ones in both the SD and Gestapo, seemed determined to avoid offending during this consolidation of power. He instructed Horst to take the mementos home to Wannsee.

Seated in the desk chair of his home study, he now admired the way the light from the windows caught the facets of the crystal jar. Swirling within the container, the two fingers reached out to each other, touching but feeling nothing.

That devious Jew-bitch had come close to destroying his political future, but now greater opportunities lay ahead. He took great comfort knowing she had perished with no peace of mind or hope for her son. How devious and deceptive she'd been with that blond hair and long limbs. These darkened flesh of the preserved digits recalled her mongrel bloodline so offensive to his Germanic purity and sensibility. Such mixed breeds were only worthy of bowing to the will of their masters. The made the fingers dance in the jar as he hummed a Nazi tune.

The impressive Wannsee mansion had sat vacant during his years in France. Leasing to strangers could have left disorder and damaged its appeal. Children made messes on carpets, scratched polished oak and walnut, and filled the rooms with disturbing cries and demands. The fault lay in random procreation. All children should be the product of *Lebensborn*, offspring of pureblooded SS men and breeder mothers selected for Aryan beauty and strength. Only the state knew how to breed, educate and train the future heroes and fruitful mothers needed to repopulate the Reich's ruling class. Far better that his home had remained sealed from outside influences.

A somewhat dull-witted woman had looked after necessary housecleaning during his long absence. Regrettably, certain items no longer appeared in their customary places when he returned. Or so it seemed. The maid had protested meekly that nothing had changed, that she'd only moved objects for dusting purposes, but he'd assumed theft and sent her to the Barnimstrasse prison.

He would hand-pick new staff when time allowed. A trustworthy cook was a necessity, someone accustomed to his special eating habits, but for the moment he would get by with the groundskeeper and his wife who occupied the carriage house. The young Kähler could drive him into the city until further notice, and his pinched-faced woman could prepare meals as needed.

Soon he would search out maids to keep the place spotless and satisfy his personal needs. Perhaps Ethnic Germans from the occupied territories, fresh, untouched girls who had yet to experience genuine fear or pain. That would surely raise his spirits. He would train them to live or die at the beck and call of a powerful master. Yes, young and pure of blood suited his purposes well.

The emptiness of the house felt comforting, free of emotional taint from his previous life. He no longer saw Erika and the half-breed child in its darkened hallways. The place was now a bare canvas stripped of all old pigment, leaving him free to create new scenes to satisfy his artistic bent. He drew sketches for converting the cellar into a welcoming retreat to test the limits of those young girls from the country.

His dream of blood had followed him from France. An old friend now, it colored each night's sleep in a crimson wash. Once he was settled in at headquarters, he would turn his efforts back to the destruction of Lemmon and Gesslinger. For now, he would rely on the plodding Richard Kohl to track the bastards down.

Those first meetings with Heydrich had disappointed. His long-time mentor was clearly uncomfortable with Horst's altered appearance. The frozen grimace on the scarred left side remained unchanged since 1938, but the recent encounter with Gesslinger and Lemmon had left much of his face swollen. The yellowing bruises and tiny knife marks below his eye had not yet fully healed. Horst found the look suitably intimidating, but Heydrich had suggested a few more days recovering at the Wannsee mansion before any formal re-introduction as his new right-hand man.

"Please understand my position, Horst. We're talking monumental changes here. I need all the support I can muster." Heydrich tapped his cigarette ash on the edge of the saucer and took a sip of tea. As always, Heydrich's long face and close-set eyes reminded Horst of a nag. "In a few days I sit down with the Führer to discuss the unfortunate situation in Bohemia and Moravia. I will convince him that the weakling von Neurath is unsuited to the demands of Prague's administration. We've already compelling evidence of widespread Czech resistance and intent to destroy harvests, putting the well-being of the Reich at risk. I intend to show our Führer that only my personal control can assure stability and security in the Protectorate."

"Then you're one step closer to becoming *Reichsprotektor*, Reinhard!" Such a position granted ministerial status and direct access to Hitler. Surmising Heydrich could be grooming him to assume control of Reich security, Horst felt his excitement mounting. "Is the Reichsführer-SS on board?"

"Himmler gives tacit approval and will openly support my bid once the time comes. He can well imagine his SS in full control of the entire Protectorate, a splendid move for him, as well! Once in Prague I intend to use the full might of the SS to destroy those conniving Czechs. Ruthless suppression is all they'll understand, and I shall deliver just that!"

Horst saw his opening: "So to clarify, I am to hold your position here in Berlin and ferret out any who might oppose you, correct?"

Heydrich nodded. "Plus another important challenge. In your absence I've taken special interest in the Abwehr. There's simply no reason for duplication of our security efforts, so it's high time we incorporate military intelligence into the Sicherheitsdienst. Admiral Canaris is a charming old man, but he's as unsuited to his position as von Neurath to his. My dossier on the admiral grows thicker by the day, and now the old man's lobbying against our denial of Geneva protection to the Bolsheviks. My God, man, they're subhuman brutes! The admiral's simply too old-school, too conservative, afraid to show the strength our new world demands, and his activities border on treason. It's only a matter of time before we must rid ourselves of Canaris."

"Then I focus first on him?"

The long face of Heydrich bobbed and again von Kredow thought of a horse. "Get on it immediately. I'll send over the file this morning and perhaps you can find added leverage there for my meeting with the Führer. Removing Canaris and von Neurath will make all our tasks easier."

"One last question, then." Horst squared his shoulders. "Should you become *Reichsprotektor*, who will assume your duties here in Berlin?"

"Ah, yes…that matter." Heydrich set down his tea cup and pushed the saucer aside. "I shall stay on as head of Reich Security, as well. I find no reason not to handle both positions, do you?" Heydrich's eyes never left Horst's.

"Of course not, Reinhard. If anyone can handle such enormous responsibilities, it's you and you alone."

Fuming internally, Horst had held his tongue. Plenty of time later to change his mentor's mind.

Horst knew the rumors of Heydrich's Jewish background, and Canaris was thought to hold damning documentation to prove it. Three years earlier, Horst himself had concocted a cover story to conceal his own violation of the race laws. Perhaps Heydrich's openness to take that story at face value stemmed from concerns about his own racial heritage. Once Horst delved deeply into the Canaris case, he might discover information of personal advantage in future dealings with Heydrich.

For now, fear and intimidation would consolidate his position at Gestapo headquarters. Once Heydrich was busy decimating the Czech partisans, Horst would eliminate anyone in Berlin who failed to toe his personal line. Meanwhile, he would prove himself to both Heydrich and Himmler by helping destroy Canaris.

Who knew what might come next? What if some ill should befall his mentor along the way? Preparedness always paid dividends.

CHAPTER FIVE

Paris, Occupied France
20 August 1941

It felt good to be in charge again. Heydrich had rewarded Kohl's years of covert SD work in Washington with an assignment that put to work his vast insider knowledge of American diplomacy. As Reich liaison to the Special War Problems program, he had excellent cover for carrying out intelligence-gathering in Paris. His time had finally come for a hands-on role in running an espionage team, and he was determined to show himself the equal of von Kredow.

The young man entering Kohl's office had shown himself to be a surprisingly valuable asset. His serious demeanor and low-key personality allowed him to blend in well, and a sharp mind kept him out of trouble. The Waffen-SS had rejected his flat feet and mixed racial heritage—his mother German, his father Belgian, but Edmond Brédeaux was nonetheless a fervent Nazi. Kohl saw in him a youthful, slender version of himself, even down to the eyeglasses. Recruiting Edmond to play the mole in von Haldheim's espionage group had given his disciple the boost needed to become an effective agent.

Kohl greeted his protégé with words of commendation: "Excellent job, Edmond, excellent indeed! The phone lines at Ermenonville are now tapped, and Mirabeau is off to Berlin on Lemmon's tail. Thanks to your fine work, we've isolated the principal players in this melodrama surrounding that damsel in distress."

"They've made it easy for me, sir. Von Haldheim trusts me as errand boy for his agents. I'm hoping before long to move up to driving the spymaster himself."

"Don't sell yourself short, Edmond. Your diligence in following up on the one called Argent led us to the nightclub and the woman's arrest."

"I was as surprised as anyone to find an American conspiring with the Abwehr."

"For whatever reason, freeing that woman appears to be high priority for Canaris' local operation. We assume that's why Lemmon's off to Berlin. Our man Mirabeau will track his every move. Lemmon is sure to make a mess of things. I personally planted the suspicion in his mind that his cover's blown."

Edmond leaned forward, always the attentive student. "Why make things more dangerous for Mirabeau?"

Kohl gave a smug grin. "Nervous agents always make mistakes, because constantly watching your back runs you into walls. Mirabeau is well aware I've alerted Lemmon and will take necessary precautions, but I want him there the moment the man slips up. I'm most interested in discovering why the Abwehr is interested in this cabaret woman, a seeming nobody."

Edmond waited expectantly as Kohl used his necktie to wipe smudges from his wire-framed lenses. "So what's next for me, sir?"

"How easily could you get away on short notice?" He set the glasses back on his nose.

"I'm on-call for driving or courier needs. Any unexpected disappearance without an excellent reason would destroy the trust I've built up and could cost me my position."

Kohl spent a moment staring intently at the young agent. He raised an eyebrow. "Personally, I find you're looking a little peaked." Edmond frowned at the non sequitur, not grasping what was meant and causing Kohl to chuckle. "Perhaps a sudden grippe coming soon which might keep you in bed for a few days?"

Edmond's face brightened with understanding and considered the suggestion. "Yes, that might work."

"Here's the thing—no one's quite sure where the woman ended up. We're trying as hard as von Haldheim to track her down, but she's temporarily fallen through the cracks. The forced-labor system is notoriously inept at keeping track of all these prisoners. But using Canaris' resources, von Haldheim's bound to find her soon enough. With Lemmon in Berlin, Argent holds the key to lead us to her."

"And my role in all this?"

"Powerful local colleagues whose cooperation I value insist her life is forfeit. She put a stop to a very lucrative business arrangement of theirs. If they can't lop off her head, they'll make her life hell and break her in some labor camp. I want you on the spot, tracking every move this Argent makes and ready to step in should he interfere with that arrangement, understood?"

"He knows me too well, sir. Wouldn't a stranger be a better choice to tail him?"

"Perhaps. But you know the man, and you'll be the one to drive him to the station when he gets the call. It's high time you learned to tail a suspect, anyway. Practice for a few hours on some unsuspecting type in the streets of the city and you'll quickly get the hang of it. Not that difficult at all. Keep a non-descript coat and hat in the car with you at all times. A theatrical supply shop can provide a mustache or beard of some sort. "When Argent makes his move, you'll get him to the station. Phone your dispatch from there, make your excuses, then get on board and stay out of sight."

"Sounds exciting, sir. I'll be ready. One further thought—may I assume violent measures are appropriate should Argent attempt to make off with the woman?"

"If the Waffen-SS had been wise enough to accept your services, you would now face such challenges on a daily basis. While the SD tends more toward using its brains rather than the brute force of our Gestapo brothers, we're always ready to take strong action for the good of the Party. Does that bother you?"

"Not at all. In fact, I look forward to showing what I can do, but I will need a weapon."

"Excellent, I knew you had it in you!" Kohl slid a small pistol and a box of cartridges across the desk. "Now, get out there, practice the disguise, and familiarize yourself with the weapon. Our documents office will provide a Gestapo identity card. Keep it with you at all times, and well-hidden from our Abwehr friends. Use it on a moment's notice to board a bus or train without a ticket, understood?"

"Understood, sir. And thank you for your confidence."

"No thanks needed, Edmond. Just make sure the woman stays wherever she is."

CHAPTER SIX

Berlin, Germany
23 September 1941

Ryan joined a crowd outside a large department store on Kurfürstendamm. An incoming war report blared from the speakers above the sidewalk. The crimson-and-black swastikas flapping overhead did little to brighten the once-proud building, now as drab and distressed as the clientele. Haggard faces reflected back in the plate-glass window behind which all the goods were marked *Display only—not for sale*. He moved on past neglected food shops where customers queued out front, hoping to re-supply family pantries from the scarce items available that day. Berlin had become a city of wide-spread deprivation.

For two days he had wandered the central city on foot, noting how others eyed with suspicion his tailored suit and polished shoes. The Berliners appeared drawn and tired, their once-fashionable clothing reflecting two years of wartime shortages—shoes with wooden or cardboard soles, paper collars replacing cloth, wool worn so thin it revealed the underlying shirt. But most noticeable were the cloth patches identifying foreign workers and German Jews, the latter marked by a yellow six-pointed star and the word "*Jude.*"

His eyes met those of one such bedraggled citizen as they crossed paths. In response to Ryan's unexpected smile, the stranger quietly commented: *"Ausländer, nit?"*

"Amerikaner," Ryan conceded, not surprised the Jew knew he was a foreigner. He handed him a ten-mark note.

Ryan considered taking the S-Bahn out to Grunewald to see the former von Haldheim villa, but melancholy got the better of him. He chose instead to keep a few past memories intact. Tiring of the sulphurous odor of the city, he set out for the pine-scented air at Wannsee, but the dour faces of fellow passengers soon drained his enthusiasm. As he switched trains to return to the city, his eye caught the reflection of the man who wore the pale fedora.

Von Kredow should have him in his talons by now, yet he roamed freely with only that snap-brimmed hat on his tail. What was holding back the Gestapo? Or was the man waiting for Ryan to make contact with the Abwehr and compromise others? Having suffered through many of von Kredow's deceptions, Ryan was determined to control the next move.

Dependence on others had never been Ryan's way. Whatever the challenge, he had always trusted in his innate talents to steer him to success. The machinations of Horst von Kredow had undermined that certainty. Erika and Leo's fate plagued him, and Marita's life depended on some unknown task. It seemed a malevolent fate was setting his course, and he wondered if he could find the strength to resist should it draw him in an unwanted direction.

Having no word from either Argent or Rolf tried his nerves. Returning in the evening to the hotel, he immediately turned to the papers, searching for coded news of Marita. With nothing there, he scanned the biased news reports for some sense of the war's progress. Soon the papers lay scattered at his feet, as useless as the propaganda they spread. The radio provided only passing distraction. Fanfares interrupted the classical or popular music to announce military advances and victories, always followed by some boisterous martial song. Occasionally Hitler himself ranted against the Bolsheviks and English. Finally, with all diversions exhausted, Ryan clicked off the radio, put up his feet, and reluctantly allowed his thoughts to drift. They always returned to one indisputable fact—Marita was suffering horribly just out of his reach. Given the opportunity, he would act.

On the third night he had a quick beer at the Adlon bar and took to the streets. He carried a folded straight razor in the right pocket of his overcoat, and a hand-made garrote rose within his left sleeve from his wrist to his shoulder. He turned up his overcoat collar against the chill, crossed the square and headed into the side streets.

An air raid was expected, the citizenry forewarned. Beyond the main boulevards total darkness reigned. Whitewashed curbstones caught the slightest glow from the sky, but were of little help to the few pedestrians. He sensed rather than saw. An occasional vehicle approached, its headlamps masked to meet blackout regulations, and he could make out the block ahead. Passers-by kept their voices to a whisper, as if afraid to disturb the blackness. Some wore glow-in-the-dark swastikas in their lapels. Disembodied feet moved cautiously through the night, shoes aglow with *Lumogen* polish. An occasional quiet curse at some unseen hazard broke the stillness.

He aimed for the center of the sidewalk but often veered off course in his blindness. Once he narrowly missed a signpost, warned in the nick of time by the brim of his hat. Moments later he bumped into the wall of a public urinal reeking of piss. Two women brushed past him and he felt for his papers, suspecting pickpockets at work. As the murmured apologies faded, he strained his eyes, searching for each upcoming intersection, each alleyway.

A nightclub door swung open behind him. In the meagre shaft of light he spotted a couple exiting with arms entwined. A hunched figure a few meters back slipped behind the stoop to evade the light. The man wore a light-gray fedora. It was the man in the bar that first evening, the one who knew what to order. The same man who followed him toward Wannsee and doubled back on his tail. No longer the slightest doubt.

The slit-shaped headlamps of a sedan approached cautiously. Ryan used the illumination to confirm the stalker was still on his heels. Edging closer to a service alley while still exposed by the lights, he entered the passageway. If luck held, his follower would believe himself undetected and follow him in.

Any misstep would blow his cover. A few meters into the alley he lowered himself against the wall, removed his hat, and counted the seconds, estimating the man's progress. Out on the sidewalk a pedestrian ambled by, his flashlight shielded with colored paper. It was enough to silhouette Ryan's stalker in the mouth of the alleyway, something glinting in his right hand.

Von Kredow's orders would be to disable, not kill. Horst would want him alive. Ryan thought of tortured and missing friends, the legacy of that brutal sadist since university days. Qualms and uncertainty had clouded his judgement in Nantes, had allowed Horst to live. Erika and Leo might have paid the price for that hesitation. He would show no pity now.

The hem of the man's overcoat passed a hands-breadth from Ryan's shoulder. He drew a slow breath and rose to his feet. The muted light from another vehicle on the street allowed him to distinguish the contours of the man's back. In those brief seconds, Ryan rushed forward, arms extended, his cupped hands a meter apart. He slammed them over the man's ears, sending that damned hat flying. The target cried out and instinctively grabbed for his ruptured eardrums. A pistol clattered on the stones.

Ryan's right arm shot around the man's neck, his other wedged against the base of his skull. He jerked the stranglehold tight. "Who sent you?" His question a hissed demand. The man struggled but said nothing. Ryan could feel the tension in body and jaw, knew he was preparing a countermove. Remembering the damaged hearing, he shouted, each word emphasized, his lips pressed to one bleeding ear: "Who the hell sent you?"

With a sudden parry to the side, the man stomped toward Ryan's instep and pivoted to escape his grasp. Ryan was ready. He dropped, wrenching hard, dragging his victim to the ground. The fierce downward momentum of both bodies worked the fulcrum of his forearm.

The victim shuddered several times, then lay still. For long moments Ryan maintained the pressure. At last he rose to his knees and lowered the man's head to the stones. His search for a pulse found nothing but the trembling in his own hand.

The man's pockets revealed nothing. Ryan located the pistol a few steps from the body. Its heft and size suggested a Browning. He slipped the weapon into his pocket alongside the razor. He swept the area near the wall with his foot until he found his hat.

Pariser Platz spread out in vague, angular shapes under a sliver of moon. The drapes of his unlit hotel room were open, and the faces of Erika and Marita haunted the shadowed city before him.

One thing was clear—he would have to get out of the Adlon by morning. In broad daylight, the body in the alley wouldn't escape discovery for long.

He broke the seal on the Courvoisier. Bringing the bottle to his lips, he downed several slugs, but brandy couldn't still the fire in his gut. He thought of the man he'd just killed, the snap of his neck. War was war. As they taught in Toronto, a secret agent is a soldier like any other. Killing was killing, with no room for compassion or misgivings, and none expected from the enemy. Despite best efforts to justify his action, he struggled with doubts.

Marita is worth any number of Gestapo.

Ryan toasted the skies and took another long drink from the bottle, the cognac warming his throat but not the chill in his soul. He wished searchlights would puncture the scattered clouds and sirens wail their warning of death from above.

Heil Hitler? Go to hell, Hitler!

CHAPTER SEVEN

Berlin, Germany
24 September 1941

That morning Ryan intended to put immediate distance between himself and the Adlon. The *Kripo* would have found the body by break of day, and Horst would learn of it soon enough. He joined the hotel guests gathering at the front desk. When his turn came, he inquired about mail or messages.

"Nothing for you today, sir," the clerk solicitous, hating to disappoint. "But the *Morgenpost* just arrived. May I get you a paper now?"

Ryan accepted the morning edition with thanks, knowing he must check the Personals for word from Argent. "I'll be away for a few days," he told the clerk. "Please set aside any messages for me and I'll check in periodically."

"Very well, sir. A pleasure to be of service."

As Ryan turned to leave, an object escaped the folds of the paper and fluttered to the burgundy carpet. No writing marred the envelope's surface. In the phone alcove he broke the seal and removed a page ripped from a small notepad. The hand-written message was simplicity itself: "*Invaliden.* 15:00. Richthofen." He knew the Invalids' Cemetery by the Hohenzollern Canal, the final resting place for military heroes of the German nation. Judging by his choice of meeting spot, his contact had a macabre edge.

Ryan surveyed the lobby. A businessman appeared to be looking his way, only to disappear behind his newspaper. A spiral of cigar smoke rose above the *Morgenpost* between his hands. The front desk tallied bills and politely handled disgruntled guests, while luggage carts gathered outside the lifts and bellboys scurried about. A messenger walked through the lounge, ringing chimes to announce a telegram for one of the hotel's patrons. The clerk who'd given him the morning paper dealt with a dispute over allegedly mistreated baggage. Reaching the elevator, he finally released his breath.

At a quarter to three that afternoon, Ryan stood before a heavy monolith of granite and removed his hat. A single name on the stone evoked aviator brilliance: Richthofen. Here lay the famed "Red Baron" of the Great War, praised by friend and foe alike for unmatched prowess in the skies over France, his crimson Fokker triplane flashing a deadly warning to all who dared confront him. The aviator's eighty confirmed kills received unending glorification from the militarized German nation, but his tombstone impressed with its simplicity rather than ornament.

Ryan scanned row upon row of monumental tombstones. In all directions angels spread their wings, stone lions guarded stacked weapons, carved eagles grasped arrows in their marble talons, and still not a living soul in sight. He checked his watch. 15:10. Dried leaves skittered along the gravel pathway and an unexplained tremor ran up his spine.

Movement off to his right. A figure in black crouched low, placing something at the foot of a grave. A widow rose on unsteady feet, her cane a crutch. She hobbled back toward the cemetery gate. A sleek raven cawed after her and dropped out of sight, investigating whatever she had left behind.

Ryan replaced his hat and pulled his overcoat tighter to ward off a chilling gust. Would it be disrespectful to light his pipe? There'd been no thought of lunch, his stomach churning at the prospect of finally moving forward after days of interminable waiting. Surrounded by memorials to the dead, his thoughts drifted to Isabel, to the mutilated body police had found in the Spree. Had he alone mourned her loss in Berlin?

"Do you enjoy flying?"

Ryan jumped with a start. Caught staring blindly at the monument to Richthofen, he had heard no footsteps. A short man bundled in heavy naval greatcoat stood beside him, a gold-trimmed uniform cap under his arm. The biting wind whipped at the man's thinning white hair. Admiral Wilhelm Canaris, chief of the Reich's Abwehr.

"I do enjoy it, sir." The admiral's modest appearance came as a surprise, a friendly grandfather on an afternoon stroll rather than the spymaster charged with leading Hitler's powerful military intelligence network. He spoke educated English. "I did a bit of glider time when studying in Marburg."

"Then you should become an aviator. It pays to follow one's star, don't you think?"

"Another time and place, perhaps."

Canaris smiled. "I must confess, your enthusiasm for flying was known to me—thus this meeting spot. Personally, I prefer the roll of an ocean to dodging about in thin air." He offered Ryan his hand. "Canaris. *Guten Tag*. And you are most certainly Carl Seffer."

"Herr Admiral, a pleasure to meet you in person. I anticipated meeting one of your subordinates, at best."

"What I have to share with you, Mr. Seffer, is better done in person." Canaris gave a stiff bow of respect before the Richthofen monument. "I hope you don't mind a cemetery rendezvous. My respect for the heroes of Prussia and Germany—men of the old military school who lie buried here—knows no bounds. I invited you here to see if we might find a way to help my country recover her past glory—" Canaris set his cap back on his head. "—without putting Europe at further risk." Ryan caught a look of fleeting melancholy.

"Nothing would please me more than stability in Europe, sir."

"Well, our friends here can't eavesdrop, so we can speak freely." He tucked in a few strands of disheveled hair. "Come along, Mr. Seffer." He raised the collar of his greatcoat. "My bones aren't meant for this chill, and movement helps." Canaris took Ryan's elbow and guided him up the path.

"Forgive my boldness, but do I sense in your words diminished respect for Germany's current military leadership?"

"I make a distinction between political and military leadership. Sadly for Germany, we now find ourselves with a dangerous mix of the two."

Canaris clearly referred to the Waffen-SS, the political armed force of the Nazi Party. Ryan was intrigued. "And how does intelligence gathering fit into that mix?"

"Let me put it this way—an intelligence network should serve both its people and its leaders. Difficulties arise when the two have conflicting goals. My mandate is to protect our nation from external as well as internal threats, but the current situation puts unimaginable strain on that work."

"Wouldn't some find that statement treasonous?"

Canaris chuckled. "Treason is betrayal of the nation, which is to say its people, but not necessarily its government. Sadly, some in Germany seek to bolster their system of governance at the people's expense and have turned to the ugly business of racial suppression and ethnic domination. To me, rejection of the true cultural heritage of Germany— its humanistic ideals, its art and literature—amounts to treason of the worst sort." Their walk had brought them to the front gate of the cemetery and Canaris turned back.

"So, given your read on the current situation, what can we do about it? 'We' meaning a cooperative venture between your organization and the people I work for."

"As you must know, Germany now wields incredible power outside normal military channels. Decisions are made with the goal of hegemony and furthering political, social and racial objectives." Anger and disgust clouded Canaris' blue eyes. "These decisions will ultimately lead to the destruction of the German nation, its people, its lifeblood." Canaris stopped and raised his jaw in determination. "But thanks be to God, a few traditionally-minded military leaders fear for the future of our beloved country. These men— and I count myself among them—are determined to put a stop to this madness. Do I make myself clear, Mr. Seffer."

Ryan realized no one would believe he was hearing such candor. A trap perhaps? "Yes, sir, you do indeed."

"Good. Because that is fundamental to what I'm about to ask of you." Canaris stopped momentarily. He removed his cap and bowed his head before the grandiose shrine of Gerhard von Scharnhorst, the Prussian hero of the Napoleonic Wars. He ran a hand through thinning white hair and replaced his hat. "And I understand from our mutual friend in Paris that you desire something from me in return." .

"Yes, a matter of great personal importance."

"*Ah, la pauvre Mademoiselle Lesney. Un affaire regrettable, n'est-ce-pas?*" The admiral was said to have mastered at least six languages.

Despite Ryan's new sense of caution, he felt a kindred spirit in this potentially dangerous man. "This woman's a dear friend of many years, maliciously targeted by French gangsters and falsely persecuted by the Gestapo in Paris."

Canaris resumed his stroll. "At the urging of our mutual friend in Paris, I took the liberty of looking into this case. Her execution was commuted at my urging." His smile remained enigmatic. "Von Haldheim assured me our intelligence operations in Paris profited from her contributions." His face remained placid, but Ryan sensed the man was toying with him. "Are you asking more of me beyond keeping her head on her shoulders?" He came to a halt.

Ryan chose his words carefully: "First, please know how grateful I am for your intervention. Now I ask that she be delivered to a neutral country."

Canaris nodded. "America remains neutral, does it not? Or perhaps you know otherwise?"

Ryan imagined a hand-tied fly on the surface of a creek, slowly drifting past a curious trout. He refused to rise to the bait and comment on America's current or future plans. "I was thinking Switzerland, or possibly Spain." COI reported that Canaris was well connected in Spain, and German operatives sometimes worked hand-in-hand with British agents there to thwart Moscow's interests.

Canaris pulled his collar tighter. "Ah, yes, warm and sunny Spain—a lovely country. This Berlin chill has never suited my constitution." He shuddered. "Even a greatcoat does little against this wind." He strolled on. "But, assuming our mutual interests lie in my freeing this woman from her current distress, are you ready to help me in return?"

"There's little I can offer a man of your authority and resources." Ryan knew he was out of his depth sparring with this clever man. "Rolf von Haldheim assures me any assistance comes with strings attached." Ryan stopped. "So, I'm willing to help anyway I can, as long as it compromises neither my ethics nor my country. And, of course, assuming it's within my power."

"Well said, Mr. Seffer. You seem a man after my own heart. I admire moral courage and ethical conduct." He seemed momentarily distant. "True gentlemen are such a rarity these days, you know?"

A man near the canal observed from a distance. Canaris acknowledged him with a dismissive wave. A bodyguard. The admiral chose a side path and they continued on. "As you must know, the intelligence services value both discretion and indirectness." Ryan was again impressed by Canaris' command of English. "But there's a time and place for everything, including straight talk. As our two countries are not as yet adversaries, we may have certain goals in common. Shall we place our cards on the proverbial table?"

"Agreed." Ryan was wary. The admiral was a master of subterfuge. "So who presents the first card?"

"Since a card game is the chosen metaphor, let's set a few Hoyle's Rules, shall we? First, identities. You obviously know mine, so may we assume I'm clever enough to know why you left a comfortable university position in California for the hazards of present-day Europe? Bear in mind that Von Haldheim works for me, and at my direction he made an overture last month to your Foreign Service brother in France."

"Edward mentioned a possible peace feeler coming from certain highly-placed Germans."

"Then we are off to a very good start, and it's time for openness, our second Hoyle's Rule. Your role here in Europe, Mr. Seffer, goes far beyond your Special War Problems Division. Let's be frank. You are here on behalf of "Wild Bill" Donovan and his newly-minted COI." Ryan raised a hand in protest but Canaris continued unchecked. "And can we assume that you and your friends are laying the groundwork for America's joining the Allied cause?" Ryan said nothing. "No dissembling, Mr. Seffer. Just as you are surely well briefed on me, I too have done my homework, and frankly speaking, I'm very impressed by what I've learned about you."

Just how much of Ryan's European history was documented in the Admiral's files? "What exactly impresses you?"

"Your early years in Germany are interesting but hardly noteworthy. But you returned to the Reich in '38, drew some unwanted attention from the Gestapo, then departed somewhat hastily. There are rumors of an unsolved death or two, perhaps some intelligence material misappropriated from our SD colleagues? Details are quite sketchy, since someone has made a concerted effort to cover your tracks and perhaps those of others close to you." Canaris was still smiling. "So, Mr. Ryan Leonard Lemmon, have we done our homework?"

Ryan couldn't suppress a tight grin at hearing his full name, wondering if there was anything he didn't know of the von Kredow story. Obviously, any current cover was blown. "Your people are quite thorough."

"The fact is it matters little to me whether you committed crimes against the Nazi state. Speaking frankly, I've personally witnessed inhumanity and atrocities in Poland and

Hungary patently offensive to any God-fearing society."
Canaris hesitated, eyes downcast, and Ryan thought for a
moment the older man might be near tears, praying. When
he looked up again, only resolve filled his eyes. "What does
matter is that our nations have reached a critical juncture.
We face pressing issues which will destroy my beloved
Germany and be catastrophic for the whole world if not
quickly remedied. What interests me is your willingness to
take enormous risks for the good of mankind, not just on
behalf of the people close to you."

Ryan hid his surprise. How did Canaris know he
brought to Washington the stolen von Kredow protocol for
extermination of European Jews? Had his Abwehr somehow
intercepted the information from Kohl and the SD?

The admiral smiled serenely. "You see, Mr. Lemmon,
we share certain goals, even if our two countries handle
things quite differently."

Ryan couldn't imagine sharing any goal with Nazi
Germany. "With all due respect, Admiral, I see little in
common."

"You will, Mr. Lemmon, you will. Do keep in mind my
distinction between the people and the government. But for
now I've seen and heard enough to know I've found the
right man. If you agree to handle a little task for me, I agree
to determine the whereabouts of your Mademoiselle Lesney
and see she comes to no further harm. Meanwhile, you shall
be my guest this evening for dinner. I know the perfect spot
to entertain 'Carl Seffer.'"

"In public? If you know me so well, others might, too."
He thought of the stalker lying in that alleyway. Was Horst
already aware his man was dead?

"Keep in mind that your past misadventures are known
to only a select few, and only under your real name, not any

alias. Believe it or not," Canaris suddenly switched to German, "I will ask you to work for me here in Berlin as a banker, a man of finance, and thereby help our two nations avoid a catastrophic clash of wills."

"But, sir, if I might—"

"This evening—all will become clear this evening. My car will call for you at eight. You'll find suitable attire in your hotel room. And I assure you, my demands won't compromise your humanistic ideals or patriotic values, understood?"

"That suits me, admiral. But speaking of compromises, I do have one further request, and time is pressing. I suspect my cover at the Adlon is compromised." Canaris arched his brows but said nothing. "I may have been identified by a past acquaintance. A dangerous acquaintance. Do you have less conspicuous accommodations?"

Canaris smiled, again the kindly grandfather. "No problem at all. Tonight we dine in style, and tomorrow you l relocate within the city. Until then I shall look after your security at the Adlon, so you may rest well tonight on a full stomach."

With that, the admiral patted Ryan's sleeve in reassurance, shook his hand, and strode out of the cemetery. He joined his bodyguard at the gate, leaving Ryan wondering what his new banker's role might entail. More importantly, he hoped tomorrow morning would arrive soon enough to escape the wrath of von Kredow.

Only late September, but the car heater worked overtime to ward off the chill. Ryan cranked down the window a couple of inches and loosened his tie. Evening was delivering on the afternoon's cold promise. The driver expressed fears that the coming cold season might be as deadly as the winter of 1940, when coal supplies froze solid in the rail yards, potatoes stored in cellars turned to black mush, and distribution of goods became nearly impossible.

Ryan had gone directly to his hotel suite from the meeting at the cemetery. An expensive charcoal suit hung on the wardrobe door alongside a burgundy tie and a pale gray shirt. The fit was perfect. Someone had clearly taken measure of his clothing in his absence. He checked the labels. A Swiss custom tailor in Basel. The shoes were Bally wingtips, Geneva, a fraction tight until broken in.

The sedan slowed in front of Horcher's Restaurant, a dark mass beneath a shimmering sky. Blackout measures shielded the restaurant's signage, but the warm interior glow hinted at the activity within this dining spot favored by the Reich elite. The car entered an alleyway just beyond the entrance, moved slowly past trash bins, then barely made a tight turn before stopping at a rear door. Ryan re-adjusted his new silk tie and buttoned his overcoat before stepping out.

A junior naval officer waved Ryan in through a service entrance. The hallway passed a kitchen working at a feverish pace to fill orders. The officer had Ryan wait to the side as waiters rushed in and out with heavily laden silver platters. The constantly swinging double doors revealed a dining room filled with elegantly clad men and fashionably dressed women. Laughter and clinking glassware punctuated lively conversations. Ryan recognized Josef Goebbels, Propaganda Minister for the Greater German Reich, holding court at a far table. An attractive blonde stared in adoration, martini glass in hand. Was it Magda, the minister's wife, hanging on every word as he regaled the gathering? Perhaps not, for Dr.

Goebbels was a renowned ladies' man with little respect for his vows of marriage. Ryan assumed the other guests also held positions high on the Nazi roster of powerful movers and shakers.

The naval officer returned and asked Ryan to follow, then knocked quietly on a paneled door down the hall. He stepped aside to reveal the admiral seated at the end of the narrow room. "Mr. Seffer, so glad you could make it!" Canaris rose and turned to his aide: "Rudi, Mr. Seffer and I will need some time alone. I'll ring when we're ready to dine." The aide withdrew, closing the door behind him.

Pastoral Mediterranean landscapes and a large mirror hung on walls papered in rich carmine. The sole furnishings were the admiral's round table, four leather-covered chairs, a credenza with a phone, and a silver pail glistening with condensation. The admiral gestured to the seat opposite his. "Do make yourself comfortable, Mr. Seffer. Is champagne to your liking?" He lifted a dripping bottle from the ice bucket and filled two flutes.

Ryan smiled as he noted the label. "*Pol Roger*? I've yet to have the pleasure."

"The favorite of the great Winston Churchill, so it should certainly satisfy a lesser W.C. like me, don't you think? The world can never have too many WC's." Ryan chuckled at the allusion to initials shared by the two powerful men and the common water closet. They touched glasses across the table. "To a mutually-rewarding enterprise, Mr. Seffer."

"Agreed," he said, holding the Admiral's gaze. "May it benefit us both." He took a sip and nodded his approval.

Canaris launched right in: "Should things progress as I hope this evening, we'll arrive at an understanding and celebrate over a fine meal. Horcher's remains a rarity these days with its well-stocked larder. I hear lobster and eel are fresh tonight."

Ryan's stomach rumbled at the thought of gourmet offerings once so commonplace in Berlin's fine dining establishments. He leaned forward. "Judging by the status of the clientele out there," his head inclined toward the main room, "I can't say I'm surprised one gets the very best here."

"Then you've spotted our distinguished Propaganda Minister and his entourage celebrating some great accomplishment of the Reich?"

"Dr. Goebbels appears to be in fine form."

Ryan's recent meagre café fare came to mind, and he regretted skipping lunch following the cemetery meeting. The deprivation he had witnessed beyond those walls soured the prospect of enjoying a gourmet meal. "Would that all Europe could dine as well as we will tonight."

"So much has gone astray in Germany of late, thanks to the schemes of men such as those out in the dining room." Canaris set down his champagne flute. "You're not alone in noting these inequities or in wishing for a change."

Ryan carefully scrutinized the paintings in their heavy frames, the dark bronze lamp suspended from the ceiling, the sconces set into the walls. A listening device could be hidden anywhere. The black telephone on the corner table would be ideal. "Sir, forgive me if I'm out of line here," a finger at his lips suggesting the need for discretion, "but would it not be better if we got some fresh air?" Ryan gestured to the surrounding walls.

Canaris laughed. "You're certainly well suited to the role of spy, but let me reassure you. The only ears in this room are yours, mine, and, upon occasion, those of friends I still trust with my life. Thankfully, Horcher's remains my discreet haven despite what other customers might believe."

He switched to English. "In this room we do not risk upsetting the apple cart, right?"

"Understood." He should have known Canaris would be on top of his own security.

"Then, down to specifics. It's been a decade since you were last in international banking, correct?"

"Twelve years, to be precise."

"Your training in the field?"

"MBA from Harvard Business, entry-level position at Irving Trust in New York, then an advanced program in international finance here at the Alexander von Humboldt University. Not long enough to develop any real practical expertise, but my theoretical work was excellent and my basic skills adequate."

"Good, because once you're through the doors you'll be on your own."

"Doors, Admiral?"

Canaris leaned back in his chair. "What do you know of the Bank for International Resolutions in Basel?"

"I'm not sure I've even heard the name."

"You're not alone. Very few beyond an elite circle know of it, yet its role in this massively destructive war should not be underestimated."

"How is one specific bank directly involved in this war?" Ryan's curiosity was piqued.

"Tell me, Mr. Seffer, what is it that keeps armies on the move, ships at sea, planes in the air?"

Ryan wasn't in the mood for a guessing game. "Politics…and money, I suppose."

"Both fine answers. But at the most fundamental level, our military needs vehicles and petroleum for mobility, steel for weaponry, rubber for tires, ball bearings to keep things rolling, that sort of thing. A warring nation is only as powerful as its access to raw materials and key manufactured goods."

Ryan turned the puzzle in his mind, searching for the missing piece. "True enough, but what has that to do with some little-known bank in Switzerland?"

"Everything, Mr. Seffer, everything. You see, the Bank for International Resolutions is, to all external appearances, a neutral Swiss operation, a cooperative venture in international central banking to help stabilize the world economy in difficult times. But in point of fact, the BIR has become a branch of our Deutsche Reichsbank."

Ryan was floored. "The Reichsbank?" Here was an insight sure to grab Donovan's attention.

"Yes, our very own central bank, owned and overseen by the Führer himself," Canaris said. "And those are the doors I expect you to enter."

"I fail to make the connection, sir. I appreciate this fine suit of clothes befitting such a part, but how can an unknown and unauthorized 'banker' gain entrance to the Reichsbank? And to what purpose?"

Canaris refilled the Pol Roger and raised his glass to the overhead light, pointing out the effervescence. "It's actually quite straight-forward. Like all these tiny bubbles, stolen wealth rises straight to the top. The BIR operates as a 'neutral' clearing house for a vast fortune taken illegally in the conquest of Europe. This seemingly nonaligned institution runs an unpleasant little charade moving captured gold and treasure into the Nazi war coffers."

"But what's the connection to America."

"Patience, Mr. Seffer, patience." He set down his glass. "Off the top of your head, think of your most powerful firms involved in those commodities we mentioned—oil, rubber, chemicals, vehicles and such." He pushed a sheet of paper over to Ryan. "This partial list should jog your memory."

Ryan scanned the entries, noting major players in the American and British banking and industrial fields, names familiar to anyone who ever bought gasoline or tires, drove a vehicle, or kept up with the major banks of Wall Street. "An impressive list," he conceded. "But what exactly do these firms have to do with your Reichsbank?"

"That's where it all fits neatly together. These companies happily keep the Führer's war machine rolling along as he pursues a worldwide Reich. They don't give a damn who's buying, as long as they can rely on all sides to purchase their products. That's the brilliant economy of this war—the more materiel needed to conquer your neighbors, the more you must buy to keep them subjugated while you move on to your next great prize. And it all comes down to this—to do business with the Third Reich, you let the Führer write the rules."

"You're telling me our major banks and corporations are complicit in Hitler's megalomania?"

"Not just complicit, they're actively supportive. Take the tetraethyl lead needed for aviation fuel. It's what keeps our Luftwaffe wreaking havoc on the cities of England. Three of the major corporations on that list hold sole rights to the additive, so where do you think the Reich acquires it?"

"And somehow our political leaders don't know about this?"

"On the contrary, since when have the world's political leaders not worked hand-in-hand with their most powerful businessmen?"

Ryan pushed back in his chair, distancing himself from such a disturbing possibility. American and British business in collusion with the Nazis for the sake of wartime profits? And secret except at the very highest government levels? Mind-boggling to think that America was fueling SS tanks and Göring's bombers, that the Wehrmacht rode to victory on American tires.

"But wouldn't the press have a field day with all this?" Ryan was incensed. "Imagine the outcry from the English populace should they learn their leaders and tycoons were amassing further influence and wealth by supporting the destruction of their cities, the murder of their civilians. And when America joins the battle—and we both know that's coming—Americans would go on strike rather than give material support to Germany!"

"And Japan, Mr. Seffer. Let's not forget the rest of the Axis. Do you really think you won't end up fighting the Japanese, as well?"

"So where's the proof, Herr Admiral? Show me indisputable evidence of such complicity and I'll write the articles myself!"

The admiral offered a wry smile. "Precisely what I have in mind for you. You will insinuate yourself into an enterprise built on the backs of our suffering nations and blow the cover off this scheme."

"Let me get this straight—you want me inside Hitler's Reichsbank, getting the goods on this BIR and its partnership with these corporations?" Ryan considered the ramifications. "Assuming I make it past the front door, how do I locate that proof?"

"That should be the easy part, Mr. Seffer. All the proof you need is contained in a single source, and to insure your success we have an operative deep in the Reichsbank with access to precisely what you'll seek."

"Why doesn't your agent get the goods, then leak the evidence to the world through covert channels?"

"Unfortunately, that would also blow a cover we've spent years developing. But with proper training in the next day or two, you'll present yourself as a high-level auditor with the necessary clearance to look into limited bank records."

"And what makes you think Hitler and his banking cronies will be open to an outside audit?"

Canaris chuckled. "Because the Führer himself orders it."

"Okay, now I'm missing something."

"Herr Hitler is very concerned about his personal money-making ventures. With a bit of inside manipulation, we've raised his suspicions that one of the BIR's partner banks in America is skimming profits when arranging transfer of funds into the Reichsbank's coffers. The Führer demands clarification. We'll provide that by sending you in as a representative of the BIR."

"An economic spy, then."

"Precisely. There's rarely a difference between military and economic espionage, especially in wartime. Let's face it: conflicting ideologies or religious fervor may drive nations to war, but in the final analysis, what is war but opposing economic interests put to a military test?"

"And the risks?" Ryan set aside his empty glass. "How do I get out alive to spread the word if something goes sideways?"

"My agent will look after your safety with all the tools at our disposal, but we can't pretend there's no danger involved. One bad move and you could find yourself in an interrogation room on Prinz-Albrecht-Strasse. Not a pleasant place, I'm told."

"In all candor, I've recently had a taste of Gestapo interrogation methods. They leave a lot to be desired."

"In that case, allow me to advise utmost caution once you're inside the Reichsbank." The wry smile returned. "But, before you accept this challenge, let me be quite specific. I've been nothing but candid with you, knowing that, should you reveal anything discussed here, I would have full deniability. But should you agree to move forward, that will no longer be the case. Several of my operatives will be directly involved, and that puts many at risk."

"So I'll be on my own."

Canaris hesitated, perhaps deciding how much to share. "For some years now, I've had a less than optimal relationship with the Sicherheitsdienst and its police arm, that very Gestapo you have good reason to fear. The head of the SD and I have a long history together."

"Reinhard Heydrich."

"Yes, Heydrich. But the time has come to go our separate ways. There is no honor in brutality, persecution, assassination and mayhem, and Germany needs to restore its honor. Now more than ever. For me to facilitate change, I must remain on the job. Heydrich can never learn that I've infiltrated an American spy into the very financial institution which keeps SS tanks rolling across the steppes and the Führer's coffers full, or I'm finished." The admiral slid the empty bottle into the ice bucket with a look of regret. "There's far too much at stake, so you'll understand why we can't give him that opportunity."

Ryan creased his brow. "To be clear—I fumble this task, I get caught, the Gestapo never gets an opportunity to learn anything from me, correct?"

"I choose you for good reason, Mr. Seffer. Our file says you can impersonate a European at the drop of a hat, your

German is obviously flawless, and you can play the banker able to get us what we want. What we must have. I assure you, should the worst come to pass, our agents within Gestapa will make sure you never suffer."

Canaris had revealed matters which—if exposed—could cost the admiral his life. Hitler would clearly not be pleased to have someone, no matter how influential, threaten his personal income stream. Since Canaris had been so open about his conflict with the SD, he must truly need Ryan's expertise, and now it was clear they shared the mutual goal of bringing down the Nazis. This challenge fulfilled the commitment he had made when joining Donovan's COI.

He spoke at last: "I once loved Germany for its culture and beauty, and for the generous people who first welcomed me here. I've witnessed great kindness in the German soul, but such compassion withers under an ideology based on depravity and racial intolerance." Ryan paused and grinned, his mind made up. "So I'll go into the Reichsbank, Herr Admiral. Should I fail, all I ask is that you get my friend out of harm's way. Are we agreed?"

Canaris smiled warmly and rose from his chair. "Excellent, Mr. Seffer." He reached for the phone. "Let's pull the rug out from under these plutocrats. If the howls are loud enough, these corporations will have to back off, the Reich's war machine will grind to a halt, and you'll save American lives in the process. And then we help Germany find an honorable peace in the family of nations. Worthy goals, wouldn't you agree?"

"Agreed, Herr Admiral. Let's get it done."

"Dinner first, Mr. Seffer. Tomorrow we can begin, but the lobster here really is excellent, and I've developed quite an appetite."

Wilhelm Canaris peered into the depths of the unlit cross streets. Impossible to say who might lurk in that blackness. Only the main boulevards were lit, and those just barely. A dense fog was moving in, and few cars crept along, the narrow slits of their headlamps tentatively piercing the gloom.

The blackout restrictions hid anyone intent on mischief. Very few law-abiding pedestrians would be out at such a late hour. Just two months earlier, the guillotine at Plötzensee had finally taken the head of a serial killer who exploited the darkened city to sexually assault or kill almost fifty women. As German men fought for Nazi glory on the front, women and foreign laborers now carried the economic burdens of the city. Hurrying home at day's end they fought their own battles in those treacherous streets.

His driver, Karl, appeared relieved at the admiral's request to head home to Schlachtensee rather than return to the Tirpitzufer headquarters. Driving in these hazardous conditions was obviously a strain. Canaris leaned back in his seat. Any overnight intelligence could wait until morning. With luck, his bedside phone would allow him a few hours rest before the morning demanded his full attention. He closed his eyes to the world and sighed. Untold months of challenge were finally taking a physical as well as mental toll, and he asked himself how long he could navigate with impunity such treacherous shoals.

He thought he spied the quick flash of a match or cigarette lighter in the darkness, and strained to see more. It could have been the muzzle flash of a handgun, or perhaps just another devilish trick of his tired eyes. How difficult to place trust in anyone or anything in such troubled times!

The American chap appeared to be everything von Haldheim promised: intelligent, clever, and none of those undersized ears which made it difficult to trust a taller man. His manners were refined and his looks dashing. Best of all, how satisfying to know Lemmon placed the welfare of the cabaret woman before his own. Men with Christian ethics were a disappearing lot.

Canaris already knew plenty about Americans. Soon he would have to learn more. Back in '37 his covert operations put the Norden bombsight in Luftwaffe hands, a technological coup of the first order. And recently his signals people had broken many American and British ciphers. The United States was sure to enter the war before another year passed, a serious if not fatal blow to hopes for a negotiated and honorable peace. Once the vast economic resources of America committed to all-out war, Germany could face complete annihilation. And if her covert operatives proved as committed and resourceful as Lemmon, America would do very well at the intelligence game.

High time these fellows turned their attentions to the Communists. Those damned Bolsheviks had trashed his beloved navy at the end of the Great War, and now were intent on destroying every last vestige of European honor and tradition. He had cemented ties with the British a half-decade earlier to stop the leftist threat in Spain. Many of those bonds remained strong despite war with England, because lines of communication had to remain open, no matter the conflict. The best hope to save Germany from its suicidal path was to join forces with its current enemies in battle against a common foe.

Karl said they were nearing Schlachtensee. The admiral settled back and closed his eyes again. Lemmon seemed well-suited to the task at hand and a man of honor. He might even have uses elsewhere should this banking mission succeed. Spy craft required such assets. Military intelligence had long respected civilized rules of combat, morality and international law, a tradition unknown to degenerates like Himmler and Heydrich. Abwehr operatives had no choice but to adapt to changing times. He could not condone assassination, but the use of violent means in self-defense was now fundamental to saving the Germany he loved.

Leaving the American alone for a few days had proved its worth. Canaris needed to learn what the agent was made of, and his expectations were fulfilled. An Abwehr agent had easily spotted Lemmon's tail from the moment they arrived at Anhalter Bahnhof. The Parisian SD operative hadn't been sharp enough to realize he'd taken on a stalker of his own. By eliminating the Frenchman, Lemmon showed he had learned his lessons well. He would be reliable in a tight situation, a new requirement of the job.

Canaris forced his jaw to relax.

He was sickened by Heydrich's brutality and cunning. The cadets at the naval academy had once tagged him "The Goat," mocking that high-pitched voice and bleating laugh. But the nickname truly did reflect Reinhard's mental and emotional inclinations. He was stubbornly aggressive, ready to lock horns at the drop of a hat. In truth, the warning sign should have been that ungentlemanly conduct that got him expelled from the academy in their younger days. Immorality always led to ethical decay. Under Heydrich's leadership, the SD and Gestapo had ground human rights to dust beneath the heels of their jackboots, heaping shame on the German people, promoting blackmail, extortion, torture, and summary execution.

Now Heydrich was maneuvering, consolidating his power, intent on absorbing Canaris' Abwehr, determined to stand second only to Hitler. Perhaps he itched to replace the Führer himself. Reinhard had always envied the admiral's access to Hitler, his ability to gain exemptions from the most stringent Nazi laws. He begrudged Canaris' independent passport and visa section, his freedom to move people abroad without Gestapo oversight. The admiral felt his position weakening and knew it was only a matter of time before his own fiefdom fell to Reinhard Heydrich's machinations.

Unless a peaceful resolution with the Allies could be reached, Heydrich could take over the Protectorate of Bohemia and Moravia. If so, he would brutally annihilate the ethnic Czechs. That was his way. The SS cruelties and horrors witnessed in Poland left Canaris despairing of ever again seeing Germany respected by the world. What would become of his beloved country with such rot at its core? That accursed man flouted all rules of civilized warfare, using the Wehrmacht to carry out his criminal undertakings, corrupting the last vestiges of German military honor in the name of Nazi ideology. Heydrich had finally let loose his SS liquidation squads to wreak unrestrained terror and havoc in the East. No man despised the Communists more than Canaris, but such flagrant disregard for human rights meant Germany might never again be allowed to rejoin the ranks of the world's civilized nations.

The time for hedging bets was passed. The admiral had long played a dual role, obeying the Führer while covertly fighting on behalf of the German people. Now he would act solely on behalf of the country he loved. Powerful nations knew their strength lay in resources, manufacture and finance. Armies can only conquer when someone picked up the tab. The evidence gained by infiltration of the Reichsbank might encourage America to withdraw its financial support of the Nazi regime and force Germany to sue for an honorable peace. Then the warring nations would work together to battle the worldwide Soviet threat.

The admiral focused again on the dark streets, his jaw tense, his teeth grinding. He couldn't arrive home soon enough. What a godsend to have a good woman at his side in such troubled times! Despite the late hour, his wife would still be up, waiting to pour them a nightcap. Then she would calm his nerves with some favorite tune on the piano. Chopin's *Études* usually worked best. Surrounded by bookcases brimming with favored authors, his dogs at his side as she played, the admiral could finally let down his guard. She was always there for him, the perfect mate for a man whose every hour demanded so much focus, so much wariness, so much intrigue. A kind, patient woman, and he loved her dearly. Every man should be so lucky.

Canaris massaged his temples, working back the headache. Not from the champagne, but from the challenges still ahead. He considered asking Karl to turn down the heater, but thought better of it as a sudden chill took him. He searched the pockets of his greatcoat for the leather gloves. Memories of trekking across South America in younger days flooded back, thoughts of a warmer clime where he had total control of his own destiny.

CHAPTER EIGHT

Niedermühlen near Essen, Germany
24 September 1941

Argent scanned a file copied from the registry of the Occupation judicial authority. Abwehr intervention had finally turned up what they needed on Marita's case. His finger moved from entry to entry as he mentally relived her questioning at Gestapo headquarters Paris, her incarceration in the women's wing at the Prison de Cherche-Midi, and the subsequent guilty verdict from the tribunal. He stopped at "condemnation to death by guillotine," his hand trembling at the insanity of it all. Rolf looked on as he pulled the cork on a bottle of Château Margaux. Argent stared at a handwritten note: "execution interrupted at last moment with commutation and deportation." A transcript of the case for the prosecution lay in front of him on the table. Argent couldn't bring himself to read it through.

Admiral Canaris' operatives had finally located Marita at a huge munitions complex outside Essen. The city lay equidistant from Paris and Berlin in the industrial Ruhr region. Painful enough to imagine his lover suffering behind the notorious walls of Cherche-Midi, but now she lived and worked at heavy labor in the company of dangerous criminals.

Rolf's words jolted him back to the moment. "The admiral's managed to commute the death order, but stopping the deportation was beyond even his reach, given the challenges in Paris. Our powerful comrades in the SD and Gestapo pull plenty of weight around here, and they wouldn't budge. They want revenge for sending their favorite extortionist into Göring's clutches."

Rolf poured two glasses. Argent waved him off. "So what do we know about this ordnance plant?" He set aside the dossier, keeping only some local maps showing the Essen region, the plans for the nearest towns and the layout of the weapons facility.

"It lies not far from the massive Krupp works and specializes in smaller munitions—you know, incendiaries, shells, that sort of thing. Niedermühlen itself appears pleasant enough, except for that factory complex on the edge of town. Some seven hundred or so are employed in armaments and chemicals, some voluntary, some skilled locals, a large number of forced laborers and prisoners."

Argent rubbed his face, energizing for battle. He felt the stubble and realized he hadn't shaved that morning. The large mirror on the wall of the study reflected a brow furrowed in a perpetual frown, drawn cheeks, and eyes sunken from lack of sleep. Inactivity and mounting frustration didn't suit him. "Is she housed on-site?"

"The prisoners sleep in dormitories a few kilometers from the plant. Armed guards march them through town; the workers put in their ten hours, then march back." He wiped the tip of his cigarette holder and lit up. "We haven't determined what they have her doing, but we know she works the ten a.m. shift, at least for now. She's back in the dormitory by eighty-thirty or nine." Rolf made himself comfortable at the head of the table and took a sip, nodding his approval. "That's actually better for her, because the RAF makes its nighttime calls after midnight. That whole industrial region is a powerful magnet for British air raiders, of course."

"How close to her barracks?"

Rolf reached for the file and thumbed through the paperwork. "A few attacks fairly close to the town so far, but sporadic. And no direct hits on or even near the plant. It seems Krupp is drawing most of the attention. As of two days ago she's doing fine, but the work conditions in those places can be devastating—lots of toxic chemicals, and the forced laborers get the most hazardous assignments." His revulsion was obvious. "They're considered fully expendable and easily replaced."

Argent consulted his watch, figuring travel times in his head. "I can catch a train tonight. Can we get me identity documents by this afternoon?"

"Not so fast. We promised Ryan Lemmon a role in this mission. His concern is no different than your own." Rolf took another sip of the Bordeaux and expressed his satisfaction. "Such a brilliant vintage, this one. Puts most of our home-grown plonk to shame. Are you sure you won't give it a try?"

Irritated, Argent continued, "I'll post the notices in the Berlin classifieds as agreed, but only for two consecutive days. If Lemmon's not back to me within seventy-two hours, I'm going for her without him!" He rose abruptly, bumping the table and spilling some wine as Rolf poured Argent's untouched glass into his own.

"Easy, my friend," Rolf warned, and Argent half-expected him to complain about the lost Bordeaux. "Two play at this game better than one, so wait for Ryan's support. Canaris can't provide the manpower—his plate's full with other matters. There's something big going on thanks to Ryan's efforts. But Tirpitzufer is already preparing paperwork to facilitate her release. They're on it, so give them a chance."

"With all due respect, sir—this isn't the time to wait for Berlin. For all we know, Marita may be suffering horribly, and it won't take a genius to rescue her. They march the prisoners to and from work on a regular schedule. No one will expect my intervention, and I can use the cover of darkness."

"All well and good, but should you succeed, how will you get her out?"

"Take a look at this, Rolf—" He removed something from his breast pocket. "It's the only photo I have." Rolf examined a fuzzy snapshot taken at the club, obviously amateur work, likely by a German officer on leave. Marita looking directly at the camera, Argent's eyes on her. "Can our people use it to come up with an image for an identity card?"

"No guarantees." Rolf tucked the photo into the dossier. "They might have better luck with her prison photo."

"I'm not asking for guarantees, just an opportunity to get her out of that hell hole."

"I'm told love makes people do strange things, Argent. Never had the opportunity to find out personally, but I do worry about your judgement, given your deep infatuation with this lovely woman." Rolf raised a hand to stop Argent's protests. "No, please hear me out. I'm simply suggesting extra caution. Give Ryan time to make contact. Then once done, get back here. We've important work brewing and I need you in Paris, understood?"

Rolf returned to his wine, and Argent knew he was now on his own.

CHAPTER NINE

Berlin, Germany
25 September 1941

A courier arrived as dawn broke over the city. Ryan barely found time to hang up the phone and dress before the man was knocking at the door to his suite. He used the password Canaris had given the night before. The nondescript man offered no name. He instructed Ryan to pack quickly and meet him out front where a car was waiting. The grand lobby was quiet at this early hour and the night clerks paid no attention when he departed with his valise in hand. His guide must have handled the sizeable bill.

The courier shifted into first and eased into the flow of morning traffic. They soon veered southeast. The streets were still dark but the sky was a wash of pewter. Few automobiles appeared on the boulevards. Bluish sparks rained from overhead wires as trams navigated the turns of the avenues. The passengers hunched forward, faces blurred by breath-fogged windows. Buses lurched from curb to curb, disgorging the morning workforce. The sidewalks slowly filled with pedestrians, collars up against the cold, furled umbrellas anticipating rain showers.

Ryan saw they were heading toward Neukölln, a borough far less affluent than the central Mitte district. Questions for the chauffeur elicited only a grunt and a curt "Wait and see." Twice he took unexpected turns with his eye on the rear-view mirror, switching direction at least four times before working his way back to their original route. The man appeared unconcerned, so Ryan assumed the maneuvers were strictly precautionary. When the car braked to a halt midway along a proletarian housing block, he couldn't suppress his surprise at the disparity between the shabby tenement and his previous residence in the heart of the city.

"My new home?"

"You'll learn soon enough. Now follow me."

The man grabbed Ryan's valise and a worn satchel, removed a paper bag from the trunk, and unlocked the front door to the apartment house. They climbed to the second landing. Apartment 31B had no nameplate beside the door. Ryan spotted two screw holes at eye level, vestiges of a *mezuzah* case. A Jew had lived here before "resettlement." The courier unlocked the flat and handed the key to Ryan. No provision was made for the downstairs entry. He was clearly to stay put until further notice.

Furnishings were sparse but serviceable—a metal bedframe, several chairs including an old rocker, a battered sofa and a square kitchen table. The mirror over the sink was cracked. Some folded linens lay on the bare mattress. The first rays of the sun cast a milky light across the cracked linoleum of the cooking niche, where Ryan spotted a hotplate with fraying cord beside an icebox. A wall calendar still showed April beneath a photograph of a tropical island. Deep in an unlit alcove squatted a rust-stained toilet. Two windows framed by dusty drapes revealed a facing brick wall and a courtyard below.

"Better than many," the courier said, "but certainly no Hotel Adlon."

Ryan couldn't argue. "Just what am I supposed to do here?"

"Wait and learn."

Ryan stared down into the narrow courtyard, his eyes adjusting to the deep shadows. A bent man pounded derelict crates into scrap wood, the blows echoing in dull thuds. An old woman, her hair bound up in a scarf and her skirt dragging on the bricks, searched through a rubbish bin. She periodically shouted something unintelligible to the man making the racket. Two ramshackle privies occupied the far corner of the quadrangle. A line was forming for residents lacking toilet facilities in their rooms or flats. Other residents washed up at standpipes, the spent water seeping down to a centralized drain.

He turned back to the room. A solitary bulb hung from the ceiling above the table and the tilted shade of a floor lamp hovered over the worn rocker. No newspapers, magazine or books. No radio. "And how long here?"

The courier seemed anxious to be on his way. "Just sit tight. This will keep you occupied." He handed Ryan the satchel. A quick review of the documents showed Canaris had planned out every aspect of his infiltration into the bank. Clipped at the top of the sheaf of papers was a roster of the managers and employees he might encounter once inside. He also found a diagram of the management structure, an in-depth description of the inner workings of the organization, and a synopsis of how it coordinated with other central banks through the BIR to hide illicit plunder.

The man was waiting for his attention before he spoke again. "You'll hear from us soon enough."

"You'll be back?"

"No. Someone else. This evening around six, I'm told." Placing the sack on the table, he offered his first smile as he buttoned up his coat. "A woman. More your style, I'd say."

Ryan spent the first hours memorizing Canaris' materials. By afternoon he was satisfied he could pass any test. He dropped onto the couch. He couldn't help thinking of the men he had killed—the Gestapo on the night train, the stalker in the alleyway. Those were one-on-one, kill or be killed. But the policemen at the warehouse, they were faceless attackers who threatened those he loved. Could he have found a better way out of Horst's trap? He caught himself unconsciously rubbing his forehead, trying to stop a nervous itch, and stuffed his hands into his trouser pockets.

The bag contained bread, cheese and a bottle of beer. He ate as a distraction, finally setting the scraps aside and returning to the couch with the half-empty bottle. He thought of Marita, so close now. And then of Erika and Leo, running to greet him beside the Tiergarten canal. What if they'd stuck to the express for Amsterdam in '38 rather than turning south? Would things have worked out differently? He tried out the creaking bed, pushing aside the stack of linens and dropping his head to the pillow. He pictured sad Nicole, and wondered again if she'd found her child at last. He fought back the recurrent image of Erika and Leo, dead in Bayonne. Just malicious handiwork of Kohl's, he told himself, another trick to trouble his mind. His thoughts returned to Marita, slaving in a prison camp just beyond his reach. He prayed she would hold out until he came to her rescue.

The afternoon dragged on. Footsteps sounded on the landing and he overheard a muted conversation, something about ration coupons. Later a woman called to her young son for a good-bye kiss. A door slammed under a flurry of profanities. Exhausted by introspection and worry over his friends, Ryan feared the long day would never end. At dusk the lines again formed for the privies. His wristwatch read a quarter to six.

A threadbare hallway runner led to a small window with a view to the street. The anticipated rain had petered out after a few cloudbursts, leaving the pavement glistening. Pedestrians hurried by with mesh sacks of provisions, anxious to reach home before dark. A few minutes after six, a woman in a beret appeared at the head of the street and walked toward his apartment house. She hesitated briefly at the front stoop, looked around, then let herself in without buzzing. He waited at the second landing, watching her move up the staircase.

Damn, he thought. *Here's the last thing I need right now.*

Her trench coat emphasized a slender waist and full hips, her knock-out looks reminding him of Marita. Long legs teased as she ascended the stairs. Her breasts swayed gently with each step. Such a classy look put the rundown tenement to shame. He tried to ignore his libido and reproached himself for base urges when his life was in such turmoil. And yet, he'd gone months without the touch of a woman. The night with Nicole had been something else entirely. He longed for a caress, soft lips pressed to his, the warmth of someone sharing his bed.

The young woman caught sight of him and returned his smile, her hazel eyes flashing beneath thick auburn hair and that blue beret. He pictured her head on his pillow, those breasts moving to his urgent thrusts, and he silently cursed his own weakness. Again he pictured Marita. *Let it go—there's too much at stake.*

She introduced herself with a businesslike handshake. Johannah Federer. He surmised Johannah wasn't her real name. She must have removed gloves in the vestibule, for her hand was still warm and he'd expected the touch of cool flesh. Her cheekbones were high, almost Slavic, and a hint of carmine brightened her lips. Yes, those working at the Reichsbank did well despite the war's privations, and this attractive woman obviously had good connections.

He gestured to the open door. "Welcome to paradise, *Fräulein*."

"I've seen far worse—" Her voice as warm as her hand as she took in the space before turning back to him. "—and far better."

Ryan shut the door and turned the key. "Sorry, but I've little to offer a guest." He gestured toward the kitchen. "Unless stale bread, dry cheese and rusty tap water are appealing."

"I'm not here as a guest. I'm to be your tutor."

"Then I'm in your hands." His thoughts refused to behave, this lovely newcomer a welcome relief from his melancholy. "You'll find me a willing learner."

Despite her indulgent smile, Johannah Federer remained all business. She declined his offer to sit beside him on the sofa, gesturing instead to the kitchen table. "Better suited to our immediate business," her eyes revealing she hadn't mistaken his frame of mind. "Time is short, and we've much to cover."

Ryan surrendered. "You work for the Reichsbank, then?"

"I do."

"And also for the Abwehr?"

"We play many roles these days, if only to survive."

He admired her cheekbones and chanced a question. "This flat—it belonged to Jews."

"One Jew, at least. Gone now."

"To one of the camps? 'Resettled,' as they phrase it so neatly?"

"No, he's one of the luckier ones." Her finger traced a line on the dusty tabletop, her thoughts obviously elsewhere. She set down her handbag. "This particular gentleman now works for us abroad."

"And the Nazis allow that?" Ryan knew no Jew could hold a government position, much less be involved in espionage for the Reich.

"Our mutual benefactor holds a unique position vis-à-vis the Führer. The Abwehr enjoys certain exemptions from the Arianization laws."

"So I gather we're safe using this flat?" Rumor and denunciation were mainstays of Gestapo power, yet no one had shown interest in his sudden presence in the apartment. Surely they'd heard his creaking floorboards, his cough, the tap running, the toilet flushing. The walls were thin enough. He'd tested the windows—they opened easily—and scouted out a potential escape via a brick ledge, a rain pipe to the roof, and what appeared to be an easy leap to the neighboring building.

"As safe as any in Berlin." She smiled weakly. "The building's ours, the block warden and concierge specially chosen, and the residents all have something to hide or someone to protect. Everyone keeps quiet in self-defense. We've a few safe houses and small hotels scattered around the city."

"Another hotel would be nice." He thought again of that large Adlon bed with its crisply-ironed sheets, and suppressed that vision of auburn hair spread across his pillow. "So much more comfortable there, you know."

"Let's get one thing straight." Johannah demurely crossed her legs. "No one must ever know of this meeting. The hotels are simply too public. I work quite closely with the Reichsbank's vice president, and what I share with you can never be linked back to me. Our admiral has people in all the major corporations, at board level in many cases, but I'm lower fruit on the branch," those full lips softly smiling again, "yet my position is of value to our cause."

"So what's the plan?"

"I have access to the files which will prove your case to America and England. The internal security is very tight; they've so much to hide. Briefcases are controlled at the end of the day, so it will be up to you to spirit out what you need."

"You mean actual files?"

She slid a Minox across the table, a twin to the tiny camera used by Erika a lifetime ago. "You're familiar with its use?"

"Very familiar," he said, memories flooding back.

She must have noticed his distant look. "Is there a problem?"

Ryan returned to the present. "No, it's nothing. Film cartridge?"

"Already loaded—more than enough exposures for what you'll need." She removed a sheet of paper from her handbag and began to sketch, diagramming suites of rooms and offices. "As you know by now, the Reichsbank is under the Führer's direct control. The man I assist is Gustav Prahl. You'll have seen him on your list as Managing Director and Vice President of the bank. He's also on the board of the BIR. You'll find what you need in his office here." She pointed to a large square block with two smaller spaces to either side of the entry. The pencil raced across the diagram. "I work as his secretary in this space on the left, and his assistant works across the foyer from me."

Ryan quickly memorized the layout. "And how do I reach these offices? There must be other secretaries, guards, that sort of thing."

"You'll present yourself as a BIR auditor assigned to look into the transaction records of the First Federal Bank of Manhattan. They'll be expecting you on orders from the Führer. I made that arrangement personally." She smiled shyly. "Your credentials will be perfect, including passport and travel visa showing arrival this week from Basel. Our own documents section guarantees they'll pass any review. You will carry a letter of introduction from the head of the Bank of International Resolutions, but don't surrender it. The phone number on the letter will be a secure line answered by our people, in case someone in the bank does due diligence."

"And what exactly am I hoping to photograph?" The whole scheme struck him as hit-or-miss.

"Herr Prahl is obsessive with his books—he insists on having everything within arm's reach." Johannah removed her beret, pushing her hair behind her ears as she sketched again. She laid out a precise plan of the president's office. "The left-hand desk drawer holds a blue ledger in an expanding folder. It records the bank's direct control over the Basel operations and identifies corporations currently helping fund the Reich's military operations and launder its ill-gotten gains. Photograph every entry over the last year, the most recent twenty pages or so of the ledger. They document the hoarding of fortunes stolen from conquered countries, as well as…" her matter-of-fact recital faltered and she looked away.

Ryan's brow furrowed. "Would you like that glass of water now?"

She shook her head and resumed: "You will also find verification of a stockpile of gold bullion rendered from wedding rings, jewelry, eyeglass frames and dental work, all 'confiscated' in the Reich's internment camps. They melt it down into nice, pristine gold bars. You'll see the entries."

Ryan sat back abruptly. The von Kredow protocol in operation. "So they've begun to kill—"

"By the thousands, hundreds of thousands, perhaps more." Johannah had tears in her eyes. "Just look for accounts designated '*Reinhardtfonds*' or '*Max Heiliger.*'" He saw hatred in her eyes. "A little cynical Nazi blasphemy, you see."

Ryan understood: "*Heilig.*" German for "holy."

He rose from the table. At the window he looked out into the bleak courtyard. Across the way, a mother on a stiff-backed chair nursed an infant at her breast. Without turning, he spoke again, "Why can't *you* photograph this ledger? You're on the spot, have access to his office, have seen it, and you could get me the film to take to my people."

"I'd do it at the drop of a hat, but the risk is too great if I'm to remain in place." She joined him at the window. "But there's more to it than that. If we leak it through our English contacts, those making their fortunes from sales to the Reich might get their hands on it first. The corruption goes high up."

Ryan nodded, remembering how Kohl had destroyed the evidence of von Kredow's protocol before it could reach Roosevelt's eyes.

"But more important, should we be the ones to leak it— should we be connected in any way to obtaining this information—many powerful Americans will dismiss it as propaganda, a red herring, intended to weaken America's will for war." The words came faster. "But if you make it public, you and your "Wild Bill," it comes from a reputable source and gains the credence needed, don't you see?"

"Here's what I do see. I get proof of this complicity to my people in Washington, they'll use it as leverage. The American people are already torn between those who want nothing to do with another European war and those who fear for democracy and want to stop Nazi tyranny. The isolationists will say that our financial support for Hitler's war proves what's best for the Reich is also best for the United States. They'll point to the need to keep economic momentum going as things are finally improving after the Great Depression. This would feed right into Nazi hands."

"What will the other side do with the information?" Johannah looked worried.

"It's a tough call. If this goes public in America and Britain, the outcry against the industrial bigwigs and the politicians who support them might rally the people to throw the bums out. The corporate and financial giants will have to back off to prevent major labor strikes or even a popular revolution, Hitler loses his material support for the military push, and—who knows?—his own generals toss him out on his ear. It's anybody's guess how this will play out." Ryan made no effort to hide his concerns. "Whichever way it goes, we're going to rattle a lot of cages."

"So, are you still up for it?"

Ryan looked into her eyes, but saw only the suffering of Marita. "I've made a commitment."

Her smile dazzled. "Just as the admiral says—it's who you are." She patted his hand. "So let's get busy on details. We want you there tomorrow morning, so we've little time."

"What about Prahl? Won't he be suspicious, since he spends time in Basel?"

"He's down there now with his personal assistant for a BIR board meeting, so the coast should be clear."

Ryan was all business now. "This desk drawer remains locked, I presume?"

"Yes."

"Day and night?"

Johannah nodded. "Prahl keeps the key in the coin pocket of his trousers."

"I'm supposed to pick his pocket in Basel first?"

She gave a wry grin. "No need." She withdrew from her purse a tiny manila envelope and handed it to Ryan.

He shook a small brass key into his palm. "Won't he be missing this?"

"It's taken from a wax impression. It'll work, I've tested it."

A picture formed in his mind, an image he hoped was wrong. "You took it from his trousers?"

Johannah's blush was slight, but said it all. "Listen carefully, Herr Seffer. We've only just met, but there's something people in our line of work must accept, something you undoubtedly already know. A covert assignment has few limits, few boundaries. We sacrifice whatever we must for a greater good, even do things which go against our natural inclination."

Ryan did understand, but couldn't hide his concern. "I'm sorry that you're forced to—"

She shook her head fiercely, her hair coming loose to frame her face. "No, don't you dare pity me!" Her glare was uncompromising. "I do what I must to keep this position, and it isn't always pleasant and I'm not always proud, but I promised my family never to let these monsters win, and if that involves surrendering my reputation, then so be it! Need I say more?"

Her icy response encouraged no further discussion, and he felt ashamed of his recent libidinous thoughts. "Fräulein Federer, no justification of any sort is needed. If you knew all I've done that counters my true nature, then you'd know I would never judge anyone committed to fighting this evil." Now he was the one to lay a reassuring hand over hers. "Whatever it takes, *nicht wahr?* Now, shall we continue? Show me how to get past the guards and find my way into his office," he held up the Minox and gave his most reassuring grin, "so I can put both key and camera to good use."

CHAPTER TEN

Berlin, Germany
25 September 1941

Waiting for von Kredow on the observation terrace at Tempelhof Airfield, Richard Kohl's nervous stomach had nothing to do with the bumpy flight on the Junkers U-52 just in from Paris. At the end of a phone conversation the previous evening, von Kredow had ordered Kohl immediately back to Berlin. Richard knew his associate was incensed, perhaps rightfully so. Kohl's attempt to demonstrate espionage acumen had gone awry with the disappearance of both Lemmon and Gesslinger.

Kohl observed the control officers vetting travelers waiting for boarding. Most moved on through the gate after inspection of papers. Others found themselves cordoned off in a special interrogation area. A female guard took a pregnant woman into custody for a full-body search. The husband loudly insisted on accompanying his wife, and a second agent obliged him by slapping on handcuffs and leading him off. Everyone knew an "expectant" mother could easily hide contraband beneath a maternity dress.

Von Kredow appeared in the crowd and headed up the staircase. As usual, his distorted face revealed nothing, but Kohl had no expectations of a calm reaction to the unfortunate news about losing the targets. At least the public meeting place should preclude Horst's turning violent. With his new, higher profile in the Gestapo, von Kredow might well have chosen the rendezvous spot to help keep his temper in check. Kohl slid aside his untouched beer and steadied himself for a verbal assault.

The oddly cordial greeting raised Kohl's suspicions. "Richard, it's good of you to come all this way." They shook hands. "Please forgive my brusqueness over the phone, but your news took me by surprise and left me a bit bewildered."

"Believe me, I also find it most distressing that all hasn't gone as planned, but I've good reasons, as you'll see soon enough. We can head over to Prinz-Albrecht-Strasse." He reached for the valise at his feet.

"Please, Richard, sit back down. This spot will do just fine for now. Tell me where things went wrong and together we'll remedy the situation." Horst chose a chair facing the dining area, his back to the railing.

Kohl breathed slowly to calm himself, knowing Horst might lose control without warning. "Well, first off, I sent agents from Nantes to find Gesslinger in Saint-Nazaire, just as you recommended." Kohl avoided the word "ordered." Despite von Kredow's domineering personality, they held equal rank, and Kohl felt obliged to subtly remind his partner of that parity. "The commandant at the bunker compound assured them his security measures made sabotage impossible. They returned empty-handed."

"That warehouse fiasco nearly cost me my life, and would have been a success if not for those Gestapo imbeciles in Nantes. I let their captain know in no uncertain terms what I thought of such incompetence!"

"That may explain the lack of further cooperation from that office."

Von Kredow ignored the comment, causing Kohl even more consternation. He couldn't quite put a finger on Horst's unpredictable behavior.

"Has there been any partisan activity at the submarine compound?" Horst scanned the crowd, his eyes never coming to rest for more than a moment. His face remaining rigid, unreadable. Perhaps his morphine gauge was on empty.

"A nighttime security drill got the attention of a few locals, but that's the only excitement reported." Kohl dreaded the next questions, sure to involve Lemmon.

Horst absent-mindedly traced the long dueling scar on his cheek. "We'll let that go for the moment. On to Lemmon."

"I had the older brother tailed. He led us directly to the American's hotel in Paris."

"And for some reason you ignored my specific instructions to phone once you'd located him." A threatening undertone was now clear. "You disobeyed my orders."

"Hear me out, Horst. There's more going on here. I knew you'd first want to know what Lemmon's up to. I used Edward Lemmon to rattle Ryan's cage, revealing the deaths of the woman and boy and making obvious that the Gestapo knows Ryan's covert role."

Von Kredow glared. "He still believes me dead, correct."

Unable to hold that fierce gaze, Kohl glanced away. "Of course he does. My goal was to destabilize Ryan and thereby expose any others involved. We both know how much he valued that woman and child. I figured the more disturbed he became, the more likely to lose his footing and reveal something or someone of value."

"You seem to forget that the *Arschloch* is of supreme value to me personally." Von Kredow's eyes remained impenetrable. "You had him in your sights, yet you let him go."

"Of *personal* importance, yes, but I suspect his espionage activity has meaning for the SD, as well."

"In my hands, the bastard would have sung like a bird."

"Which might have been too late, Horst. Why not spread a wide net from the beginning and pull in all the conspirators at once?" Kohl found his logic persuasive. "I know we've had this argument before, but isn't it time to set aside your personal vendetta and concentrate on the bigger picture? We may be onto a national security matter of great importance here."

Horst appeared to consider the implications. "All right, get on with it. Give me a reason to care about Lemmon's espionage assignment?"

"Here's what we know: Dannecker and his Gestapo boys raided a Montmartre night club last month. The *Mischling* owner, a woman named Lesney, sent a good friend of theirs into Göring's meat grinder. It killed a profitable joint business venture. Dannecker is understandably pissed and pulled strings to guarantee her death sentence, but someone high in the Abwehr intervened, quite possibly Canaris himself. Now the bitch is doing forced labor somewhere in the Ruhr."

The mention of Canaris grabbed von Kredow's attention. Sensing movement in his favor, Kohl laid out the rest of his case. "Anyway, I'd already recruited a young driver working for a Canaris spymaster in Paris, a certain Rolf von Haldheim. Turns out that both Lemmon and an agent called Argent are in league with this von Haldheim, and the three are determined to locate that same cabaret owner."

Horst seemed intrigued. "I vaguely recollect an effete sort by that name in Berlin SD some years back. Any idea why they're after this Jewess?"

"She must know something of importance to Canaris' people, so that makes her important to us. I put a tail on Lemmon and another on this Argent fellow."

"Lemmon first. Where is he now?"

"That's why I called last night, Horst. My man Mirabeau was on Lemmon's trail, night and day. The American met with no one, just wandered around the city on his own and sleeping at the Adlon in an expensive suite under the name 'Seffer.' "

"Was?"

"Lemmon's gone missing. The hotel has no idea where. And I've heard nothing from my man in two days."

"So you've lost them both."

"Only for the moment. I was preparing to come here to track them down. That's why I called."

"Of course you were. And why wasn't I informed that the American bastard was in the city?" Von Kredow crushed out the freshly-lit cigarette.

Kohl met the dreaded question head-on: "Because you would have done your worst to him and we would have lost the Abwehr connection. Come on, Horst, you know me better than most. I've helped you go after personal enemies for years and never said a word in protest. But my commitment to the Party knows no equal. I wasn't about to risk the biggest case I've worked since coming to the Reich simply to give you the pleasure of flaying that American."

Horst seemed unappeased. "Everyone eventually talks. I would have his whole story by now."

For the first time, Kohl couldn't restrain a slight smile of satisfaction. "Three years ago he came whining back to me in Washington with a few burns, a broken nose, and a stolen protocol that might have compromised Reich security."

Horst ignored the jibe. "Tell me more about this Argent and the woman in the Ruhr?"

"My man's still following him and checks in daily. All we know for certain so far is she's outside of Essen at one of the industrial or munitions plants. It's taken forever to get an exact location from the Office for Forced Labor."

"And your man's instructions?"

"Keep her imprisoned, whatever it takes. Dannecker still wants her dead, but figures the *Zwangsarbeit* should do it in time. He insists she pay for spoiling his retirement plan."

"Then I need to get to her first and extract all she knows. Perhaps there's something on Canaris I can use."

"Hold on, Horst. This Lesney matter is my case. That's already cleared with Heydrich. Ryan Lemmon can be all yours. Use the Adlon connection and you're sure to find him again. One thing's for certain—he hasn't turned up in Essen or my agent would know, so he's still here in the city. But this Lesney woman is my show. Her interrogation file indicates one tough cookie, so she'll require more finesse than you're accustomed to."

"Well, well. Finally found your balls, eh?" Horst leaned back in his chair, forcing a lopsided grin. "Congratulations. Good for you." He snapped his fingers. "So let's wrap this up."

Kohl never saw the two burly agents approaching from his rear. They yanked him to his feet and the cold steel snapped over his wrists. "How dare you?" he shouted, his voice gone shrill. "What's the meaning of this? You can't arrest me! I'm your equal and—"

"And I do whatever I like, my old friend." Horst rose from the table, towering over Kohl. The arrest caught the attention of the nearby tables. Most witnesses immediately looked away and lapsed into silence. Others gathered up luggage and distanced themselves from the arrest. The waiters withdrew behind the bar, their backs to the disturbance.

"But Heydrich authorized—"

"Yes, Heydrich himself has authorized me to root out corruption in our ranks, no matter how far up the rot reaches. And it seems to have reached you."

"I am not corrupt and you know that full well! You're the one who's always given our mission short shrift with your lust for vengeance!"

"Please, Richard, accept the reality of your situation. It's house-cleaning time in Berlin. Heydrich demands a clean slate as he moves up in the Party, and a purge is good practice for Prague."

Kohl refused to cooperate as the agents shoved him toward the staircase. "You'll never get away with this, Horst!"

Von Kredow's voice boomed over the now silent cafeteria. "Halt!" The agents turned, Kohl braced between them. "One final word—"

Kohl hoped he'd changed his mind. Perhaps this had all been simply a gesture of intimidation. "Yes, of course—"

The back of Horst's hand sent Kohl's glasses skidding across the floor. The agents jerked him back to his feet and von Kredow grabbed him by the necktie to hiss in his ear. "You remain my lackey and puppet, just as you've always been, you poor excuse for an Aryan. Your parents and grandparents were Jews, for all we know. How dare you think yourself my equal? Just know this, you blubbering fool—you will share all you know of this Parisian matter with no one but me, and once you're of no further use, I shall kill you personally." Again that grimace of a smile before he calmed, his voice returning to normal. He straightened Kohl's tie and adjusted the knot beneath his trembling chin. "But out of respect for years of friendship, I will grant you an easy death. Fair enough?"

Von Kredow strode away, leaving Kohl to consider his radically altered future.

CHAPTER ELEVEN

Berlin, Germany
26 September 1941

The sedan came for Ryan shortly after eight-thirty. They headed west toward the Spree River. The anonymous driver of the previous day suggested a light breakfast. Ryan agreed to a cup of ersatz coffee at a café before they rolled on through morning traffic toward the Reichsbank administrative offices.

"You'll find a briefcase on the floor beside you, sir." The driver caught Ryan's eye in the rearview mirror. "Inside are identification documents and files that will pass for authentic. I threw in a writing pad, pencils and pens, just the thing for a bank auditor." Ryan scanned the paperwork. All appeared in order.

His nerves were already on edge when he closed the door behind Johannah the previous evening. His dreams had been exhausting. Waking, he'd half-expected daylight would find his cover blown and von Kredow outside his door. But now as they entered the Mitte district and neared the bank, he began to calm in the face of immediate challenges.

The camera fit neatly beneath the bottom flap in the case. Ryan replaced the papers, confirming the tiny apparatus was undetectable beneath the files. "Please tell the admiral I appreciate the attention to detail by you and all his staff. Will you be picking me up when I'm finished?"

"Parked nearby and watching for you. As you leave the bank, look to your left and you'll spot me. Signal all went well by setting the briefcase on the sidewalk and adjusting your necktie. I'll pick you up. Should things be dicey, immediately head right, then take the second alley on your right. Back-up support will be waiting. Either way, if you have what you're after, we take you directly to Tempelhof and the admiral's plane brings you to Switzerland."

Within minutes they reached the Haus am Werderschen Markt, a sleek, modern structure across from the old Reichsbank building on Kurstrasse. Prahl's offices occupied the highest level of this auxiliary building. Ryan received a cordial welcome in the spacious reception area, his cover documents paving the way to the top floor. The layout was just as Johannah had sketched. He casually looked around, hoping to spot her. Instead, an efficient receptionist handed him off to an impeccably-dressed young man. The clerk led him to a private office and asked him to wait. In passing he noted the mahogany doors fronting Prahl's office. On the left would be Johannah's workspace, directly across from the office of the personal assistant.

Ryan tested the leather-on-steel chair behind the sleek table and nervously lit one of the cigarettes thoughtfully provided by the bank. The top floor seemed remarkably quiet for an institution charged with financing all aspects of Hitler's war. Within moments the clerk returned with a stack of bound files. He carefully arranged them in chronological order. Ryan politely refused his offer of coffee or tea, requesting instead an undisturbed hour to work through the records.

He started perusing tiresome entries, making meaningless notes on the lined pad, and repeatedly checking his watch. He wondered what was keeping her. Crushing out a second cigarette and wishing for his pipe, he approached the metal-framed windows and caught sight of the black sedan waiting curbside up the street from the massive building. A soft knock quickly returned him to the chair. The door edged open and Johannah stuck in her head, a finger to her lips. A quick nod and she was gone.

Ryan sprang to his feet. Finding the corridor empty, he moved into the hall and approached the door to Prahl's office. Johannah appeared to be searching a filing cabinet and didn't look up as he moved past her half-open door. The assistant's office remained closed.

The burnished steel handle gave way silently and the door swung open. Once behind closed doors, he removed the target ledger from the desk drawer. The bank of windows provided excellent lighting and the Minox clicked with the turn of each page. He worked his way backward through a year or more of entries. The names of all those powerful corporations, industries and institutions stunned him. *How do these bastards live with themselves?* Each second seemed an eternity.

With the ledger back in the drawer, he cached the film cartridge in a seam of the Swiss trousers provided by Canaris. He hid the key and camera beneath moss in a potted palm, just as she had instructed. At the door he listened for activity in the foyer but heard nothing. The door closed softly behind him.

Subdued sounds were coming from her office and he tensed. She was no longer alone, and her door was slightly ajar. He picked up a male voice and her responses. Through the narrow opening, Ryan could see long, stockinged legs encircling Prahl's bare ass and lunging hips. Trousers pooled at his ankles. The vice-president had clearly missed her in his absence, but she ignored him, her head turned instead toward the door to confirm Ryan's escape. Their eyes met. Hers held no shame, but rather a fleeting smile of victory. She had averted a catastrophe, allowing Ryan to move on, free.

A guard examined his briefcase at the administrative reception desk. Another took similar precautions on the ground floor before he left the building. As Ryan stood on the street, watching the dark sedan approach, he felt no elation. Only sadness.

The silver six-passenger Junkers banked east over the Rhine and prepared to land at a small airfield near Freiburg. The flight from Berlin via Leipzig had gone as smoothly as the bank mission. The other five seats sat empty. His waistband still hid the incriminating film cartridge. How many international corporations would love to destroy proof of their complicity in Hitler's war? Within hours an Abwehr sedan with diplomatic credentials would ease him through customs and border controls, then it would be on to Geneva. Ed was waiting to bring the cartridge to Washington via diplomatic pouch and a long Clipper flight. Over the weekend, Canaris' courier would deliver the paperwork needed to free Marita.

Horst von Kredow fumed, his jaw clenched as tightly as his fists. Leaving the basement cells in Gestapo headquarters, he stormed up to Reinhard Heydrich's formal office and demanded an immediate meeting with the chief of Reich security, who left him cooling his heels in the antechamber for a quarter hour before finding time to speak.

"Horst, how good of you to drop by." Heydrich non-chalantly lit a cigarette and offered one to Horst. "All settled in downstairs?"

Von Kredow declined with a shake of the head. He was doing his best to rein in his fury, but couldn't bring himself to utter pleasantries. "I am told you released my prisoner Richard Kohl." Horst found his hands trembling. "The man's a danger to the Reich, irresponsible on all counts and a flagrant liar, and I personally intend to make a lesson of him for others here at Gestapa."

"Come, Horst. Take it easy, have a seat and we can dis-cuss the matter." Heydrich sat behind his polished desk and leaned back in the chair. "Allow me to be frank with you. I know things haven't been easy since you lost your wife and child to the terrorists a few years back. That's why I gave you free rein in France. You were in no condition for the bureaucratic rigors required here in the Reich Security Of-fice. But believe me when I say that you have done an excel-lent job in counter-intelligence. Those terrorists and traitors you returned to Berlin have provided outstanding infor-mation, and I thank you for it."

Von Kredow tried to temper his anger. "I intend to give you the same results here, Reinhard."

Heydrich seemed disinterested in Horst's reassurance. "Tell me this—did you ever locate the monster who allowed that lovely wife and young son of yours to drown in the Rhine?"

Horst hesitated. Had Kohl spilled his guts to Heydrich to win his release? He never should have given the weakling a day to simmer in fear and regret! He should have killed the bastard when he had the chance, but now he had to focus on the matter at hand. "Sadly, no, despite our best efforts to track him down. That treacherous Frenchman still runs free, but I intend to bring him to justice when time and duty allow."

"Exactly my point—time and duty foremost, right? Listen, Horst—I find myself on a short fuse right now, what with needing to bring Prague in line. I need reliable people here who think before they act, and I can't afford to leave my offices here in a shambles." He ran one finger along the smooth blade of his engraved letter opener, admiring its sheen. "This isn't France, Horst—this is Berlin, and I insist that my security services work diligently and without distraction."

"The punishment of traitors isn't a distraction, is it?" Horst gripped the chair arms in frustration, wishing he needn't restrain his words.

"It's obvious you're upset with Kohl's release, but I fear you've allowed some personal dissatisfaction to get in the way of an important Reich matter. If I had time, I would personally delve into the error of his ways. But the Führer needs every trained asset who understands the American mentality. Donovan's SOI operatives are beginning to cause us some problems. Richard Kohl knows how these Americans think, how their government functions, all vital information in understanding the weaknesses of a future enemy. We'll face them on the battlefield soon enough. They're already in flagrant disregard of so-called neutrality with their support of the Allies, and that means we'll need men like Kohl to help with countermeasures. Do I make myself clear?"

"But sir, the man disregarded my direct orders for the sake of self-aggrandizement!"

"If we filled our cellar with everyone around here who put personal gain ahead of an order, we'd quickly run out of basement cells, don't you think?" Heydrich released that despicable braying laugh of his. *The Jewish goat!* "Look at the broader picture, Horst. I'm leaving soon to put right the Czech situation. I brought you here to manage what I've built in Berlin, not put it at risk, and personal vendettas and disputes will make your success impossible. Have I bet on the wrong horse?"

Von Kredow forced calm. "Not at all, Reinhard." He attempted a smile. "As always, I do as you say."

"We're clear, then." Heydrich rose from his chair and Horst recognized the dismissal. "Here's my suggestion— you are not yet fully accustomed to how things have changed in your absence. Travel and distance drains a man, you know. Kohl returns immediately to his intelligence work in Paris, so he'll be out of your hair. You will let him be, and that's my direct order, understood?"

"Of course, Reinhard."

"If he continues to cause us problems, I'll be the first to know and can turn you loose on him, but absolutely nothing without my direct command. Meanwhile, spend this next week at that fine home with the view of the Wannsee. Take the Canaris files with you, relax over a few drinks and some good food, put that brilliant analytical mind of yours to good use and find me something I've missed to use against Canaris and his Abwehr."

Horst nodded. "Allow me to offer an alternative suggestion, Reinhard. It fits right in with your recommendation. What if I get some rest down in the Ruhr while looking into something that might point directly to Canaris' treason?" Horst hoped this would be the clincher. "I believe he may be involved with one of Donovan's spy teams."

"All in good time, Horst, all in good time." Heydrich crushed his cigarette in the ashtray and took von Kredow by the elbow, guiding him across the red carpet. "But for now, I must say no. I want you here in the city and available the moment I call. Meanwhile, I insist you get rest and recover from that last run-in with the French saboteurs. No insult intended, but you still appear a bit under the weather. When next we meet, you'll be back in the game and prepared for the most challenging of tasks, understood?"

Horst understood all too well but saw no point in further argument. He was momentarily side-tracked, his hands tied, if only for the moment. Heydrich would have an eye on him, so he would demonstrate his loyalty. Then, when time and opportunity permitted, when Reinhard was in Prague, he would show the strength of his own will.

CHAPTER TWELVE

Berlin, Germany
27 September 1941

The citizens of Niedermühlen took pride in their community. The flower boxes overflowed with red blooms, the water fountain splashing on the square remained reasonably clean, and the shutters on the houses were all neatly painted. But nothing could prevent the surrounding foundries and industrial plants from polluting the sky with smoke and ash, casting a pall over the small Ruhr town.

Argent sat on the Wattenauerstrasse, the main thoroughfare linking the prison dormitories and the huge ordnance complex to the north of town. He watched absentmindedly as a layer of gritty dust gathered on the café table wiped clean only an hour earlier. Attempts to accelerate the passage of time by reading local papers failed in a matter of minutes. He ate with no appetite, his stomach in knots since arriving in town three days earlier.

It hadn't been easy spotting Marita in the crowd of exhausted women trudging home after a long shift. The street was barely lit and the prisoners so shabbily dressed they all looked alike. He had matched their pace from the dark side of the street until her column passed beneath a streetlamp. Marita appeared even smaller in those ugly clogs, plodding along in the dark, her step uneven, her shoulders hunched.

Walking near the end of the column, she quietly encouraged a woman stumbling along ahead of her.

Two days had passed since that first glimpse, and the delay was killing him. Dressed as a civilian, he had taken a room in the Gasthaus zur Post. According to his travel papers, a soldier on leave. He told the owner he was vacationing here since travel to Ostpreussen was too problematic to risk a visit home on so short a leave. Even he found the story unconvincing.

His wait for Lemmon had been fruitless. The Personals in the Berlin newspapers contained all the agreed-upon code words, so twice daily Argent had taken the local bus to the Essen train station to wait beneath the clock at the pre-arranged times. The American agent never showed. It was a frustrating ritual, and Argent had finally had enough. He'd done his duty to Rolf and Lemmon, but seeing Marita slogging to work and back again to the barracks tortured him. That night he would act.

His plan was simple. Two armed guards led the parade of prisoners, another two brought up the rear. Each night she marched near the end, so he planned accordingly. Having Lemmon's help might have been useful, but he was now determined to go it alone. He'd walked the entire route several times and believed he had the ideal solution.

At the city hall the column made a turn onto the *Rathausplatz*. Directly across the square was a narrow alleyway where he would wait and watch for her approach. Just behind the city hall was a labyrinth of narrow streets where they could quickly disappear together under cover of darkness. He memorized the path to his getaway vehicle, the old Ford truck of a local grocer who—for a sizeable bribe— agreed to leave the key in the ignition, a tarp and woolen blanket in the cab, and his mouth shut for eight hours before reporting the rust bucket stolen. Behind the seat, Argent hid a few items of her clothing he'd brought from her Paris apartment.

Without Lemmon to distract the guards, Argent would have to time things perfectly. At the moment Marita made the turn onto the square, the rear guards would still be at least ten meters back on Wattenauerstrasse. For a minute or two she would be out of their sight. The blackout conditions would allow him to remain virtually invisible until the moment he spirited her away.

The guards shouldn't miss her until evening roll call at the dormitory. By then he and Marita would be well underway to Essen and freedom. Rolf's forger had fabricated a Swiss passport for Marita and an exit visa to leave the Reich for her "homeland."

Already ten-thirty, the air cold and still. He shivered in the alleyway and longed for a smoke, but knew the cigarette would shine like a beacon from his hideout. He paced up and down the tight passage, unconsciously memorizing each paving stone beneath his feet.

The radium dial of his wristwatch showed a quarter to eleven, and still no sign of the workers. Two hours overdue. He should have heard long ago the tramping of feet in the darkness, the calls of the guards keeping the women in line and moving along. Instead he heard little more than each frustrating quarter hour tolling high on the city hall tower.

What could be keeping them? He wandered briefly onto the square and stared toward the industrial complex. Smoke tumbled from the distant stacks silhouetted against the sky. A skinny dog nosed around the gurgling fountain. He returned to the hiding spot to wait. He wanted to pound his fist against the wall in frustration. Instead he sat with his back to a dust bin. *Easy, easy,* he told himself. *Give it time. Just some delay at the plant—she'll come soon.*

By midnight several more excursions into the square had confirmed no movement in the street. He began to consider postponing until the next night. For whatever reason, the workers weren't coming, and he saw little purpose spending more time in the cold, driving himself crazy. He heard a few sirens far to the north. At a quarter past twelve he would call it quits. Tomorrow he'd have to bribe the grocer again and pray the man hadn't changed his mind, given the clearly suspect nature of his requests.

Argent found a new spot on the damp cobblestones, his eyes tearing from the constant strain of watching for movement. Then he was certain he heard it—the shuffle and thump of feet approaching in the distance. And almost immediately, the distant thunder of an air raid from the direction of Essen and moving closer. The narrow patch of sky above seemed to glow a bit brighter. He was up and moving when something hard jammed into his back and he heard a low growl: "That's far enough, *mein Herr!*"

He pivoted, dropping to his haunches, knocking aside the man's gun arm while slamming a blow to his gut. The assailant grunted and parried, rising with the pistol lodged at Argent's belly. All at once the sky lit up with searchlights and a nearby siren screamed its alarm. Argent kneed the attacker in the groin and he went down. Tracer fire webbed the sky overhead before the alley returned to black.

Beneath the siren's wail—three long blasts, the warning signal—people rushed from all directions onto the square, a flurry of frightened voices and air raid wardens shouting over the din. The column of women was at a standstill, giving way to the civilians anxious to enter the shelter below the city hall. With only moments to act, he could waste no more time on the bastard who'd tried to rob him. Pulling out his Browning, he released the safety. The prisoners were now waiting outside the cellar, the guards preoccupied in all the confusion, and he could see Marita. A better moment would never come to grab her and run.

Racing onto the square, he heard a pop and felt a searing pain across his flank. He stumbled, his left hand grabbing his side and coming away wet and clammy. He found his footing and kept on moving, dodging an older couple but refusing to look back, Marita his sole focus. More explosive bursts rattled his body, now from front and rear, and a blinding flash brought him down. He thought it was a British bomb, but then he saw someone approaching, rifle raised to fire again, and Argent knew the certainty of his own death.

CHAPTER THIRTEEN

Niedermühlen near Essen, Germany
27 September 1941

Colder weather made each day's march even more demanding. Only a few lucky women had a coat or shawl. The prisoners' ragged clothing contrasted sharply with the neatness of the workplace. Marita's companions were equally mismatched, some dredged from the lowest criminal milieu—thieves, murderers, swindlers. A few were chronically manipulative and cruel. Others suffered her own fate—condemned to hard labor for crimes ranging from using forged ration cards to hiding a Jewish boyfriend or husband—that is to say, for any crime against the Reich not quite worthy of summary execution.

And then there were the Polish, Ukrainian and Balkan girls, many still in their teens. They paid the price for belonging to a "subhuman" race occupying territory vital to Germany's *Lebensraum*. Torn from their families, the girls endured unspeakable cruelties on their way to the factories that drove the Reich's conquests, or to brothels set aside for foreign workers. Marita cringed at stories told in broken German or translated by multilingual inmates. When all else failed, they used sign language to clearly express the degradation of their young lives. Marita's personal suffering paled in comparison.

Physical contact was forbidden. In rare unguarded moments a girl might touch Marita's hand in passing or lean into her, and she knew they longed for the comforting touch of mothers or sisters they would never see again. In self-recrimination for failing her own family, she was determined to do whatever she could to ease their plight.

For the first two weeks in Germany she had housed in an actual prison. The newcomers entered a concrete structure upon arrival, where male guards forced them to strip naked and spread their legs over a drain. The men poured a greasy de-lousing agent over their bodies, laughing all the while at their humiliation. Next she found herself assigned to a cell designed for six but holding nine. She slept on a filthy pallet on the floor. The meagre rations of gruel at breakfast and thin soup in the afternoon were often stolen from her bowl.

All new arrivals were subject to the brutality of the career criminals. One woman took a particular dislike to Marita, labeling her a French whore. The assailant grabbed at what was left of her hair, shorn before the mortifying delousing. When the scuffle ended with new bruises to her belly and throat, she found her bowl contaminated with urine, a gift from the assailant's companion. She'd taken to gulping down her meal before the bully could get to her ration.

Her transfer to a dormitory nearer the ordnance plant was a blessing. While the barracks were old and the sanitary facilities poorly maintained, she had an upper bunk and the cruelest offenders had remained behind in the prison. The breakfast fare, better and cleaner than that in the prison, still left much to be desired, but she learned quickly that the midday offering in the plant cafeteria would give her needed strength.

She'd lost weight from her slender frame. The frayed dress and stained pinafore seemed more suited to the rag-man's wagon than to daily wear.. She thought nostalgically of the beautiful clothes she had worn for years and yearned for the woolen overcoat she would never see again. Each morning she forced her swollen feet into wooden clogs. The left shoe was one size larger than its mate, giving her a shuffling gait as she marched. A wad of newspaper in the toe aggravated the blisters she rubbed raw daily. She jokingly wished for red paint to give the footwear a fashionable look.

After breakfast—bread and barley coffee, and once a week oatmeal gruel with a dab of margarine—the women made a rushed latrine visit before lining up for roll call and their march to the plant. Their route took them through the center of the small town of Niedermühlen. The well-maintained storefronts and houses amazed her, the flower-boxes blooming with geraniums, the shopkeepers washing down the sidewalks with water clearer than what flowed from the dormitory taps. Mothers pushed baby carriages and old men met and greeted with a tip of the hat as German life continued at its ordered pace. The town burghers paid little attention to the parade of workers, far too common a sight to interest anyone.

Marita spotted her reflection in a shop window, a hobbling crone with a bandanna on her head, shoulders stooped with exhaustion. How vain she had been back in Paris, checking her makeup and admiring her fashionable dress in the shop windows of Montmartre! She quickly wiped away tears of self-pity.

Many women suffered, their arms covered in open sores from the white phosphorus used to fabricate the incendiary bombs. Despite the gloves and eye shields provided at the factory, accidents occurred almost daily. After a week,

Marita's arms were also burned from exposure to the caustic chemical. One afternoon something had gone very wrong in the huge workroom adjoining hers. Popping and sizzling, white smoke and biting stench, women crying out in panic, an alarm sounding, first guards and then medics on the run. The injured left the building on stretchers, their faces and upper bodies heavily swathed in bandages. That night several women missed the trek back to the barracks, but the ranks soon filled again with new recruits.

Her daily shift started at ten. At two in the afternoon a whistle sent the workers to the lunchroom, a modern facility with high glass walls looking out to a garden atrium. Servers in white caps and uniforms ladled food onto their trays and the laborers found places at long tables. Only during the lunch break were they able to exchange a few quiet words. Given the scarcity of good foodstuffs in Paris, Marita was amazed to see the Reich serving all workers, forced or voluntary, a thick lentil or pea soup with sausage, dark bread and real butter. Marita followed the lead of others by using her ration of the precious fat to soothe the burning sores on her arms.

The women received one toilet break during the ten-hour shift, and the overseers allowed few exceptions. Marita pitied the poor girls with dysentery. Accidents brought harsh punishments, often a punch to the suffering gut or withdrawal of all lunch privileges. The supervisors often conscripted nearby workers to help clean up the mess, and occasionally everyone shared the punishment, depending on the mood of the shift overseer. It was not uncommon to note the stench of unreported accidents as the prisoners lined up each evening for the trek home.

Marita heard stories of women and girls impregnated by voluntary workers and guards. She wondered how anyone found a private moment, given the tight controls on the laborers' movements and time. A veteran worker confided that mothers-to-be continued working until labor pains, then gave birth elsewhere in the facility before returning the following day to the plant floor. Women spoke of a "dying room" where newborns perished in unattended bassinets.

Air raids occurred almost nightly in the region. Marita often startled awake to the distant wail of sirens. From her upper bunk she watched the sheet lightning of bombs smearing the distant horizon and the fine lines of tracer fire piercing the clouds. Explosions rumbled like thunder. Rumors circulated that a few weeks before her arrival bombs had taken out a nearby plant. Every evening, as she and her companions gathered for final roll call before heading to the dormitory, Marita wondered if their shivering march would be interrupted by a direct attack.

The night it actually happened she was too exhausted to care. The huge clock displayed eight p.m., but the overseers ordered the women to remain at their stations and the conveyors continued to roll. After a quiet discussion with his underlings, the head supervisor announced that the current shift would extend for an additional four hours. Obviously, the overnight relief had failed to arrive. Before ordered to silence, the women traded guesses. Some claimed to have heard emergency sirens shortly before the announcement. One surmised that the Allies had finally landed again and were coming to rescue them all. Under threat of the overseers' cudgels they resumed their labors. Surprisingly, those urgently requesting a toilet break were granted a few moments in the lavatory.

A typical shift on the hard concrete floor was misery enough, but the additional hours now took a further toll. Marita braced herself against the work table, but her shin splints were agonizing. She knew she wasn't alone in the suffering. Faces all around were set in stone, the drawn cheeks sunken into permanent creases. Even the youngest girls seemed to have aged in the few weeks she had known them. She wondered how they would possibly make it back to the dormitories on foot. Perhaps the factory might provide a bus.

It was not to be. Shortly after midnight a ragged group of replacement workers finally showed up. Marita's group lined up as usual in the front hallway of the plant. Small fixtures close to the floor cast a dull gleam on the tiles. She found her place near the end of the right-hand column. Wailing sirens in the distance announced another visit from the British "sky-pirates," as her captors called them. All exterior lights at the plant were already extinguished.

The women were too exhausted to care. They set out at the guards' commands, some already near collapse, hunched over and stumbling, while others like Marita docilely limped along. The night was brutally cold under clear skies, and she trembled at the thought of a harsh winter approaching. Her body shook relentlessly with chills and she braced her arms to her chest. The girl at her side lost her footing several times and finally dropped to her knees on the pavement. Those following stumbled or pulled up short. Marita helped the fallen girl stand, and a guard, catching the movement in the dull glow of his flashlight, raced forward and ordered her back into her place. "Keep moving, no touching!" he shouted up and down the line. She obeyed. Once the guard turned back, she steadied the sufferer with a hug. She wanted to keep an arm around the poor wretch, as much for the embrace of another human as for the shared body heat. The newcomer was one of the few with a woolen wrap.

The bombers edged closer to town, and for the first time Marita heard the rumble of aircraft engines directly overhead. Those prisoners still strong enough to care searched the sky for the unseen planes. Marita wondered how many of her companions would gladly die, just knowing that the British had destroyed the hated factory. She knew she would. The guards called out for the prisoners to move along faster.

Moments passed before the local siren screamed a warning and a nearby searchlight abruptly pierced the sky. Anti-aircraft shells burst in distant puffs just to the north. She tried in vain to spot the bombers. The gunners appeared to have an equally difficult time, their rounds finding no targets. Air wardens quickly appeared in the streets, blowing whistles and shouting for order. Citizens streamed from houses and apartments to converge on the *Rathaus* square, dutifully forming up beneath an air shelter sign. Many carried gas masks and some brought baskets, presumably filled with food and drink.

Marita expected the workers to continue on to the dormitories, the prisoners forced to take their chances with falling bombs. The self-interest of the guards appeared to win out and they ordered a halt. Once most the citizens had entered the bunker, the prisoners received orders to find a place in the narrow entrance corridor rather than descend to the fortified cellar. The line slowed to a crawl, then backed up and stopped.

Shuddering from the cold, Marita awaited her turn. She watched the sky in fascination. Flashes brightened the horizon above the rooftops, followed quickly by thunderous booms which shook the ground and rattled the metal shutters of the shops. The order came to advance, and she made the turn from the main street onto the square.

The pop and flash of a gunshot grabbed her attention. A man was barreling toward their column from across the square. He staggered, caught his footing, then headed directly toward her, his ragged shout lost in the din of whistles and cries from the air wardens. To avoid his onrush, Marita leapt to the side, taking the frail girl to the pavement with her. A guard bellowed "Everyone down!" The prisoners complied, as did those few civilians still crossing the square. Three rifle shots exploded and a pistol spit twice more. Marita heard an agonizing cry. Seconds passed before one final shot echoed, then orders came down the line for all to stand again.

Marita stared as the columns reformed. Beneath the halo of a shielded flashlight the first of the men lay face-down, unmoving. A guard nudged the body with one boot, confirming the kill. Another figure lay on his back near the mouth of the far alleyway. The guard sauntered over to check out the second gunshot victim while his partner shouted at the women to get moving.

The worker obeys for the good of the Reich—a slogan on the wall above her dormitory bed.

Marita obeyed. The guards prodded the slower prisoners and everyone entered the shelter in decent order. The first women to reach the cellar had already taken seats on the floor. As their numbers grew, they stood to make room for the new arrivals. One impatient guard slapped a woman who was slow to rise.

Marita found a spot close to the entry, now guarded by the air wardens. They slammed shut the shelter door and moved a crossbeam into place. The overlapping sirens became a muffled drone. The ground shook underfoot from two nearby blasts, and dust and plaster trickled down from overhead. Some prisoners coughed, others covered their eyes. Marita wished to fall asleep and never awaken. She barely registered the murmured prayers in Ukrainian or Polish accompanying the constant pounding from above.

The erratic behavior of the man killed on the square nagged at her exhausted mind. Impossible, of course, but with sleep now dragging her down, she thought she recognized the word he'd shouted before the bullets found him. She would swear forever he'd called out to her by name.

CHAPTER FOURTEEN

Niedermühlen near Essen, Germany
29-30 September 1941

Ryan took a seat in the office of the munitions plant director. Beyond the smooth metal desk ran a wall of shelves holding colorful binders—a vision of spotless organization in a plant devoted to raining down hellfire on the world. Three highly polished ordnance shells decorated the desktop. The entire room spoke of modern design, its sleek surfaces and metal trim suggestive of the airplanes dropping the plant's armaments on enemies of the Reich.

It had been a frustrating weekend. In Geneva he had to wait for the documents for Marita's release to arrive. The courier finally turned up on Sunday morning. Next had come six hours on the train once he cleared the German border, followed by an interminable evening in Essen waiting for Monday when the plant owner would be in his office. The short train ride from the city that morning had taken him past signs of recent aerial bombardment, and the small town of Niedermühlen had recently taken several hits. Laborers were clearing rubble beside the train station when he exited the local. He breathed a sigh of relief when he found Marita's munitions plant untouched.

A wall of glass separated the director's aerie from a vast hall where hundreds toiled at long assembly lines. Ryan watched racks of upright metallic canisters move from station to station as workers measured, filled and capped the cartridges, fabricating incendiary bombs by the thousands. Signs warned of the caustic nature of the white phosphorus they handled. The workers' scruffy dress contrasted sharply with the spotless workspace. Despite the white gloves and eye-guards, many worked with forearms exposed. At each station, fire-fighting equipment hung from racks. Guards stood at the ends of the assembly lines, while neatly smocked overseers paced the rows, watching for errors in assembly or handling.

Director Obermeyer entered his office and cordially greeted Ryan. The industrialist with the jovial pig eyes appeared better suited to hefting liters of *Oktoberfest* beer than running such a fastidious munitions complex. Ryan's visit was clearly expected, and the porcine Obermeyer seemed eager to please. Taking his place behind the desk, the director reviewed Ryan's documents. A frown settled over his face and he took a moment to wipe perspiration from his brow. The power and influence of Canaris, Ryan suspected.

"It's to be our Fräulein Lesney, then?" He had quickly rediscovered his friendly manner. "She will be missed, but what can one do?" Obermeyer's shrug strained his well-cut suit and added an extra chin to the double roll at the collar. Ryan was at first surprised the director knew an individual forced laborer by name among many hundreds laboring in his plant, but Marita's charms came to mind and he understood perfectly.

"I wish to see her immediately," Ryan retrieved the documents from the desk.

"My staff will need a few minutes to prepare the release papers, so I beg your indulgence." The director rose with some difficulty from his deep leather chair. "Meanwhile, may I offer you some coffee, sir? Real beans, not that ersatz brew." His teeth were remarkably white compared to Berliners'. Perhaps a man of his wealth could afford a private dentist.

"No to the coffee, but thank you. I'll speak first with Mademoiselle Lesney, and then we're off." Affluence built on the backs of slave labor sickened him, and he wanted Marita out of here as quickly as possible. Cordiality was a strain.

"Please make yourself comfortable and I'll have her brought up immediately." Obermeyer was already at the door. "And should you change your mind about coffee, just tell my girl outside. Real coffee from beans is quite a treat these days, you know." The door shut behind him. The man was obviously anxious to distance himself from any matter deserving of Canaris' personal attention.

Ten minutes later Ryan sprang to his feet as Marita entered. He forced himself to put on a good face despite her changed appearance. Captivity had transformed her. Always slender, she was now rail-thin. Her arms were covered in raw welts and crusting scabs. Once-splendid hair was bobbed and dull, and dark circles rimmed her eyes. He was shocked and infuriated as he drew her into his arms. "Here I am, as promised!" he whispered.

Then she smiled, and the warmth and beauty he had known for years emerged. She buried her face to his chest. "You shouldn't see me like this, *mon Chéri*. I've had no time to prepare!"

He hugged her more tightly, feeling the fragility beneath the smock. "It's all over now, darling. We're getting you out of here, out of Germany altogether. Before you know it, you'll feel yourself again." She was trembling and he insisted they sit. She wiped away tears, her once-lacquered nails worn to the quick. Determined to say nothing about her appearance, he focused on her imminent freedom. "We can leave immediately. I've valid travel papers for you—a Swiss passport and German exit visa. We head directly to Basel."

"Switzerland?" Her voice weak, tentative. "Not Paris?"

He took her hands in his. "France is out of the question for now, darling. You're sure to remain a Gestapo target for some time, but Switzerland is another world—you'll love it! You'd never know there's a war on. The streets are well-lit at night, and the people sit outside in the day and enjoy the lovely surroundings—and I'll see you're well looked after." He saw the doubt in her eyes. "We can be together whenever I'm there," he added.

She took back her hands, trying to hide the damaged nails. "With Florian gone, who will look after his family?"

"Florian didn't die—he's doing fine! Argent and I got him to the American Hospital and he's recovered splendidly. The man's a beast—takes more than a couple of bullets to bring him down. And Rolf von Haldheim helps the family out with expenses, so you can forget that worry."

Her eyes appeared vacant, retrieving a memory. "Where's Argent?"

Ryan knew any reply would be upsetting. "I wish I knew. We planned to be here together but it took some time to locate you and he hasn't checked in yet. Rolf is also in the dark for now." She closed her eyes. "I'm sorry, Marita, but he's just out of touch for the moment. We're certain to hear back from him soon. It's quite common in undercover work to be out-of-touch."

She remained silent, eyes shut. Was she coming to terms with a lover who might have given up on her? Ryan tracked the minute hand on the wall clock. At last Marita looked up and spoke, now decisively. "Argent won't be coming—I'm certain of that." She sighed deeply. "It's just the way things are."

"What nonsense! He'll check in soon, and your worry will have been for nothing. But now, we forget everything except getting you out of this damned place. If we hurry, we can be leave for Basel by noon."

Marita's face suddenly filled with resolve. "My dear Ryan, I can't go with you to Switzerland." She paused as he tried to make sense of her words. "Men are always like that with women, believing they can swoop in and make everything right. You want to rescue us and make us happy. But it doesn't work that way, despite your best intentions, despite your love—and I know that at some level you do love me." She placed a finger to his lips to force his silence. "No, hear me out, darling, this decision is final." She kissed him lightly, her lips dry and cracked. "I'm so very grateful for all you've done, and I'm sure it's cost you and your friends a great deal. But now there's something I must tell you. Since that moment I unwittingly sent my family to their death, I've found only one satisfying purpose in life—helping others where I can. That's why I'm here in this place—that's why I must stay."

"Let all that go for now. You're clearly exhausted. Things will look much better once you're out of this hell." He gestured toward the work hall below. "Come on! We'll find new ways you can help. Thanks to this damned war there's no shortage of those in need." He tried to help her to her feet. "You can rely on me."

"No! You're not hearing what I'm saying." She took his hands in hers. "I can't leave. There are girls here, young girls who'll never see their loved ones again. They're enslaved and forced to do unimaginable things, all for the pleasure of the Reich! They look to me to help them through this horror, so how can I leave them for some easy life, knowing they still suffer and die? How can I?" She was in tears. "Could you?"

Dumbfounded, Ryan was still unwilling to give in. "But you'll die here, Marita! Anyone can see how hard this has already been on you!" He silently cursed himself for mentioning her appearance. "No one survives long under these circumstances—you must understand that!"

Despite the tears, a faint smile grew into quiet laughter, as if she were finally releasing a burden. "You should have seen me a few days ago, a crone with mismatched wooden clogs. This," she gestured to the drab gray of her costume, "this is *haute couture.*" She stroked his cheek with her fingertips. "No, Ryan. I can't leave them—not now, not ever. They're only children, and they're my new family."

"But look at your arms—the chemicals are eating away the skin, poisoning your body!"

"That's just it—things have changed here. The director has offered me a new position which I've accepted. Having owned a night club could serve me well and benefit his business interests, so I'm to oversee the brothel used by his foreign workers."

He was stunned. "You're to run a whorehouse?"

"Don't call it that! These girls are slaves with no choice in the matter!" She bent closer, desperate to win his understanding. "But I can help them, Ryan, show them true compassion and concern. I can't replace the mothers and sisters they've lost, only comfort them when suicide seems their only answer. This gives my life purpose again despite all this senseless suffering and horror."

He hunted for words, new arguments, but came up empty. He wanted so much to free her, and now she insisted on a different path. But what right had he to change her mind, even though she would certainly die in the end? Where was the sense in her choosing slow suicide? That vengeful Nazi in Paris would see she perished eventually. She would never leave this place. Devastated, he said nothing.

"I know you. You selflessly risked your life to save your German friends, and now you're surely risking it to help me. But I'm not here for rescue. I'm here to help others. The best thing you can do for me is to allow me to do what I must, what I want. To understand my choice."

They sat for a while, fingers entwined. At last Ryan stood and pulled her to him. "I'll wait for one day, my love. I'm staying at the Gasthaus zur Post in town. If you change your mind, or merely want to talk, I'm here for you." Her kiss tasted of salt, whether from her tears or his he didn't know. "Tomorrow at noon I'll be here in this office again. If you don't come, I'll leave. But know this, Marita—I do love you, and you will be forever in my heart."

"I've always loved you and always will. But I couldn't save my family in Paris. I won't leave my new family behind." She guided him to the door, urging him out.

Hearing it shut quietly behind him, he walked away. He didn't look back.

At the Essen station he took a seat on an empty bench, his mind numbed by disappointment. Erika and Leo missing, likely dead at Horst's behest. Now Marita had given up on life to appease some inner demon. Could he have been more persuasive, found more compelling arguments? That obstinacy would be the end of her!

He had waited at the director's office for over an hour. She hadn't appeared, not even sent a note. The travel papers won at such risk now mocked him from his jacket pocket. He would destroy them at first chance.

The express for Geneva wouldn't arrive for another two hours. Distractedly, he watched the comings and goings of the travelers. Newsboys shouted the Extras. Ticket agents went about their business as on-duty soldiers took forbidden smoke breaks, and locomotives on the platforms announced their arrivals and departures with blasts of steam and piercing whistles. Scratchy loudspeakers alerted travelers and identified platforms. Passengers greeting families, soldiers on leave, men and women in uniform, businessmen in suits, most faces serious, distracted, rushed. Time waiting for no man.

Enough was enough. Forget Geneva. His next COI assignment wouldn't come until Ed was back from Washington. Plenty of time to do what was right. He joined the line at the ticket booth. One way, second class, Berlin. Von Kredow lurked somewhere in the capital. He would track him down. Somehow. And where von Kredow prowled, he would find Kohl. Twin destroyers of lives.

Canaris might abhor assassination, find it dishonorable. But sometimes the world demanded vile means to eliminate evil. Ryan had failed once. It wouldn't happen again.

CHAPTER FIFTEEN

Berlin-Wannsee, Germany
6 October 1941

The lamp spread a small circle of light that emphasized the rich reds and golds of the Persian carpet and the blood glistening on Horst von Kredow's thighs. The rest of the study remained in deep shadow. Horst sat naked, watching the blood surface and pool between his legs before dripping to the rug. A spent syringe lay on the table beside him. Another waited, filled and ready.

His glazed eyes slowly focused on a familiar figure sitting across the room in the darkness. The hint of a distorted smile appeared on the mask of Horst's face. "So, my old friend, I can't say I'm surprised you've come." He set the blade on the leather seat of the chair. "We've been dancing this dance for many years."

"The music must stop eventually, I suppose." The visitor held the Browning lightly, its muzzle aimed at von Kredow. He wore dark clothing from head to toe. He had not removed his hat. "Forgive my intruding on your self-mutilation. To each his own, right?"

"A little diversion I picked up in France. It helps pass the hours. I hope I didn't offend, but in truth I never saw you enter."

"Oh, I've been here a while already. Don't give it a thought. It's been quite a show, but what say we put an end to all this?"

Horst nodded in agreement. "We've been through so much together, and had our fair share of confrontations along the way. I must say you've proved far more resilient than I'd have imagined possible." Horst adjusted the black lampshade to direct light on his guest. "I do give you credit for that."

"I've learned from the best, Horst."

"So my time has come, has it?"

"Inevitable, given how many lives you've destroyed with your vengeance and cruelty." The man casually crossed his legs.

"Those traits serve the Reich well. Weaklings tremble when confronted by us. Why? Because they can't grasp one simple truth—compassion is for cowards. We are masters because we have a leader like Hitler. The rest of the world makes do with gutless Chamberlains." Horst sat more upright on the chair. "You should have learned that by now, old friend."

"Well, it ends here and now, Horst. You forced my hand and turned me to violence. I've always preferred a more diplomatic approach, but tonight we see who proves the weaker when the final card is dealt."

"A little secret for you then, since you believe yourself hardened enough to kill me in cold blood. Life exists only in pleasure and challenge." Horst took the dagger and carved a line in his forearm from elbow to wrist. He held the wound beneath the lamp to show the extent of the damage. "Without those two, life is nothing but an endless slog toward an unknown demise. Once I no longer take pleasure in forcing others to acknowledge they have no control over their destiny, that their existence has no meaning, I myself will surrender to the inevitable."

The tip of his dagger played with the welling streak of blood. "Just look what I've done here—I've saved you the trouble of actually shooting me. Just sit and watch and I'll bleed out before your eyes. This evening I can prevent your becoming the monster you think I've become." A right-sided grin distorted his face. "Better yet, the one I've always been." He straightened again, as if intending to rise from the chair. "And with that said, I invite your best."

Abruptly, he slumped low and sent the blade on a straight course, pinning the intruder's arm to the chair. In that same instant, the pistol spit and three holes opened in Horst's chest. A fourth shattered his tortured jawbone. He managed to stagger toward his assailant before a fifth bullet dropped him to the carpet.

The assassin wrenched the dagger from his sleeve and gently prodded his upper arm. The wound was superficial. He approached the dying von Kredow. "You won't rise again from the dead, Lazarus." He knelt down and rolled Horst onto his back, then severed his throat with the blade. Blood spread in pulsing waves, soaking the carpet before slowing to a trickle.

He wiped the dagger on the rug before returning it to the custom case on the bookshelf. In the dim light he could just make out the brass plaque commemorating Horst's SS induction. Leaving the room, he looked back one more time. The body remained still. "You see, Horst, you have indeed taught me well. I may never take pleasure in the act, but I am fully capable of killing the best."

He switched off each overhead light until he reached the landing, leaving a corridor of darkness behind him. He descended to the foyer. In response to the blackened house, a sedan already idled at the foot of the steps, the rear door open, a driver at the wheel. The killer slid in beside the tall man who immediately demanded: "Is it done?"

"It's done." Kohl spit on the lenses of his eyeglasses and used his handkerchief to wipe away a drying splatter of blood.

"Good," Heydrich said, his eyes straight ahead. The car pulled out from the drive and headed back toward the center of Berlin. "Despite all his formidable talents, von Kredow had become too great an embarrassment. My plan for Reich and Führer requires a clean slate and a new right-hand man. You, my dear Kohl, have shown yourself equal to the task."

"Thank you, sir. I did feel a bit undervalued in my old position. With von Kredow gone, I will shine under your tutelage."

Heydrich observed the passing villas. The moon had just cleared the gabled rooftops, turning them to flashing planes of silver. "I'm sure you will, Richard, I'm sure you will."

CHAPTER SIXTEEN

Geneva, Switzerland
7 October 1941

If any morning could banish thoughts of war and the millions suffering under the Nazi yoke, this would be it. Not one cloud marred the deep-blue sky over Lac Léman. To Ryan's back, the Grand Hôtel du Lac caught the first rays as the sun crested the snow-covered Alps. Across the shimmering lake, the Jura glowed pink under a recent dusting of snow. A day to forget misery, death and the aching disappointment in his heart. A day to live for the moment, if only he could.

Ryan rose to give Ed a welcoming hug, using his glove to clear a second spot on the park bench. He gestured for his brother to sit. Just in from Lisbon, Ed had flown the Clipper from New York, bringing Ryan's new identity papers and mission assignment from COI. Ryan had awaited his return in frustration.

When he'd arrived at Potsdamer Station a week earlier, two of Canaris' men had pulled him from the crowded concourse. Preoccupied by Marita's rejection, he hadn't seen them coming, and still cursed himself for the stupidity. Despite his protests they brought him directly to Tempelhof Airfield and by late afternoon he was again airborne for Switzerland. They confiscated all the "Seffer" identity papers and Marita's travel documents, telling him only that the admiral would soon be in touch.

Ryan scraped out the bowl of his pipe, the ashes staining the crusted snow at his feet. "So, what did our Washington friends have to say?"

"That's damn nasty evidence you collected! Proves many of our most powerful are getting fat on Hitler's war." Ed was clearly angry. "But don't hold your breath on things changing quickly back home." He shook his head in disgust. "Or over here, for that matter."

A pair of swans floated by and Ryan thought of Leo in the Tiergarten, throwing crumbs to the waterfowl while a breathless Erika revealed her plan to escape the Reich.

"Somehow I'm getting used to that from Washington." He sighed, refilled his pipe and struck a match. "What's their excuse this time?"

"Same old story. Many of those big shots helped get Roosevelt re-elected, and others—not just the isolationists and their ilk—claim the economic recovery depends on huge corporate profits, no matter where they're found." Ryan shared the depth of Ed's disgust. "Once we're actually into this war with both feet, all that could change, but I have my doubts. The plutocrats will keep on making fortunes, and anyone hoping to blow a whistle will quietly disappear."

"So what the hell's the point? Military intelligence I get, but what good's economic intelligence if never used?"

"Don't feel bad. Your mission wasn't for nothing, brother. David Bruce assures me that Wednesday's coming negotiations with Canaris could undermine the Führer's future plans. Maybe even get rid of the bastard, if there's any justice in this unjust world. COI says you made it all possible. It seems the old admiral in Berlin likes your style."

Distant clouds were gathering over the Jura. The break in the fall weather had been just that, a break, and a challenging winter was heading their way. Ryan was prepared to do all he could, even if it made little difference in the schemes of nations and corporations.

"What's on my plate next?"

"It's back to Berlin you go." Edward took an envelope from his overcoat. "Latest from Washington—Donovan and Bruce have something new up their sleeves. You'll be back in Hitlerland within the week."

Ryan shrugged and stuffed the unopened envelope into his pocket, trying his best to prolong the moment of forced serenity. Berlin. Good. There he would find von Kredow and Kohl. A lake steamer chugged up to the pier, its wake churning the broken ice along the shoreline and separating the swans.

"Can't say I blame you for tucking it away," Ed said with a chuckle. "But I believe this one will be of greater interest." He fumbled in his coat and handed over a folded sheet of paper. "Arrived in the local bag last night," Ed's eyes twinkled. "Seems it reached the Paris consulate a week ago but some moron figured it could wait for my return."

Ryan opened the telegram and stared at the block letters:

SAFE IN LONDON. NEW BABY ON WAY. TILL WE
MEET IN PEACE. E. R. L.

Erika. René. Leo. He shook his head as he tried to fathom how they'd reached England in wartime. He cleared his throat as emotion surfaced. "It's true then? They're really safe, all three?"

Ed seemed as pleased as Ryan. "Yep, our wireless guy confirmed it last night. Safe, sound and anxious to help MI6.

Particularly that rascal Leo, I'm told. In any case, they made it all the way from France on a fishing trawler. Took a lot of guts! London says the Saint-Nazaire plan turned sour but the intelligence they gained has future value."

"Well I'll be damned." Ryan stared across the lake, stunned by the revelation. "They made it out. Their 'deaths' just more of von Kredow's cursed lies." He re-read the telegram, his smile spreading. "And a new baby, to boot! Maybe they'll make me godfather."

"Perhaps your friends don't always need your help after all, brother." Ed nudged him good-naturedly as he left the bench. "But I'll leave you for now with that happy report. Rolf von Haldheim arrives from Paris this afternoon to liaise with Canaris' people and prepare for our meeting." Ed set his Trilby firmly on his head. "I'm to show him around, but you and I can discuss your assignment over a drink this afternoon."

"Sounds swell. I think I'll just sit here a while and enjoy the view…and your great news." He held up the cable. "Thanks so much for this, Ed. I really mean it—a fine surprise indeed!"

"Always glad to paste a smile on that kisser of yours." Ed was several steps away when he turned back with an afterthought. "Oh, I nearly forgot. You might find this of interest, too." He handed Ryan another envelope. "A special delivery came in this morning from Admiral Canaris. His courier said the old man wanted you to have it right away." He was already up the path when he called out over his shoulder: "And take your time. This evening will be fine for that drink." He headed toward the hotel, crunching the snow, chuckling again.

"W.C." drawn in elegant script decorated the upper corner of the envelope. Ryan recalled the admiral's jest about sharing those initials with both Winston Churchill and the ever-present water closet. He split the seal and removed a hand-penned note from Canaris:

> *In a life filled with challenge and suffering, nothing*
> *can replace the love of a good woman.*
> *I know. So should you.*
> *It may be difficult at first, but never let her go again.*
>
> *In fulfillment of my promise, I remain*
> *Your lesser W.C.*

Ryan leapt to his feet. His brother had already left the sunroom terrace. A petite woman in gray overcoat and red boots hesitated at the top of the icy landing, looking his direction, one gloved hand on the rail. She took a cautious step forward.

AFTERWORD

Readers will recognize in fictional Horst von Kredow a mentally-disturbed sadist empowered by a fascist government founded on prejudice, hatred, and arrogance. The evil of many historical figures of this period far exceeds anything I might have imagined for my chief villain.

The actual Reinhard Heydrich is a fitting example. While still heading the Main Office of Reich Security, he became Acting Reich Protector of Bohemia and Moravia and immediately began slaughtering Czech partisans and nationalists, further establishing his reputation as one of the Reich's harshest enforcers of Nazi xenophobic doctrine. In 1942 British-supported Czech and Slovak partisans ambushed him in a Prague street. He died of grenade wounds several days later.

An exception was the true Admiral Wilhelm Canaris, one of the most enigmatic figures of his time. A man of apparent honor and humanity, he held a position of immense power in the Reich and yet remained a confirmed anti-Nazi. He worked diligently to undermine Hitler while protecting both his country and his powerful position as head of German Military Intelligence. He was ultimately killed by Hitler. To more fully appreciate this complex figure, I suggest Richard Bassett's fine study, *Hitler's Spy Chief.*

The Bank of International Resolutions (BIR) is a fictional institution modeled after an actual banking operation. Its collusion with Hitler's Reichsbank and top American and British corporations and industries is explored in depth in Charles Higham's

Trading with the Enemy; The Nazi-American Money Plot 1933-1949. The complicity continued even after Germany's declaration of war in December 1941.

"Wild Bill" Donovan consolidated American intelligence-gathering operations, starting in 1941 with the Coordinator of Information Office (COI). With America's entry into the war, Donovan established the Office of Strategic Services, forerunner of the Central Intelligence Agency. A good resource is Douglas Waller's *Wild Bill Donovan; The Spymaster Who Created the OSS and Modern American Espionage*.

The brutal treatment of Nazi captives in both French prisons and German labor camps is described in many first-person accounts. I recommend Lucie Aubrac's *Outwitting the Gestapo* and Agnès Humbert's *Résistance*, from which I derived much of the factual material relating to Résistance activity and incarceration.

The failed partisan attack on the Saint-Nazaire submarine pens in the fall of 1941 is pure fiction. However, a courageous and destructive raid by British commandos in the spring of 1942 served as proof that England had not given up the fight. Among many fascinating accounts of this operation is Robert Lyman's *Into the Jaws of Death: The True Story of the Legendary Raid on Saint-Nazaire*.

To you who have followed the Ryan Lemmon story from start to finish, I give my most sincere thanks and invite you to watch for future novels.

I must mention again the man whose courage, brilliance and inquisitive spirit inspired these stories. I can well imagine my late father, Leonard Lemon O'Bryon, a briar pipe in his hand and a glass of German pilsner at his side, reliving personal adventures which found reflection years after his parting in the challenges facing Ryan Lemmon.

My gratitude to my brother James E. O'Bryon, who first urged me to write a novel inspired by our father's journals, and to Roy Leighton Malone III, who encouraged me to expand upon *Corridor of Darkness* and create the trilogy.

Finally, I am most grateful for the commitment and patience of my wife Dani in the critical editing of the books. Her unyielding efforts to make them as exciting and readable as possible contribute greatly to any positive reception they may find in the eyes of you, the reader.

Patrick W. O'Bryon
Cameron Park, California

Patrick W. O'Bryon travels to Europe as frequently as possible to research his stories. He shares life's adventures with his wife and some very demanding cats.

GLOSSARY

Abwehr—German Military Intelligence headed by Admiral Wilhelm Canaris

Arianisation— (Also Aryanisation) Nazi term for expulsion of non-Aryans, primarily Jews, from all aspects of public life

Auberge—Inn

Bahnhof—Rail station

BEF—British Expeditionary Force

Boche(s)—French slang for German occupiers

Cochon—French slang equivalent to "dirty pig"

COI—Coordinator of Information Office, set up by Executive Order in July 1941, the first agency established by "Wild Bill" Donovan to centralize intelligence-gathering activities of the United States in anticipation of entry into the war

Copain—Buddy, pal

Douane—French customs

Fallbeil--Guillotine

Flak—*Flugzeugabwehrkanone*, anti-aircraft gun

Gasogène—Wood-fired vehicle engine

Gasthaus—Inn or small hotel

Gestapo—*Geheime Staatspolizei* (Secret State Police), the branch of the Nazi Party Security office tasked with rooting out enemies of the Party, sister organization to the SD headed by Heydrich

Gestapa—Berlin headquarters of the Gestapo located at Prinz-Albrecht-Strasse 8

Heer—German army

KLV—*Kinderlandverschickung*, a wartime program to bring German children out of harm's way by sending them to foster homes in the countryside

Kriegsmarine—German Navy

Kripo—*Kriminalpolizei*, investigative police for non-political crimes, sister branch to the Gestapo

Lebensraum—"Living space," Nazi justification for aggressive territorial expansion

Luftpost—Air mail

Luftwaffe—German air force

Mischling—Racist Nazi term for anyone of mixed blood

MI6—British Military Intelligence (SIS)

Panzer—Armored tank

Passeur—A person who smuggled people illegally across the Demarcation Line between Occupied and Vichy France

Patrie—French homeland

Rassenschande—Racial shame or defilement caused by sexual relations between Aryans and non-Aryans

Rathaus—City hall, town hall

Schmiss—Facial scar from academic dueling, a badge of courage

SD—*Sicherheitsdienst*, the Nazi Party Security Service tasked with gathering intelligence, headed by Heydrich and in competition with Canaris' Abwehr; Gestapo sister organization

SIS—British Secret Intelligence Services (MI6)

SOE—Special Operations, Executive. Covert British wartime organization set up to conduct intelligence-gathering, organize resistance, conduct espionage and sabotage in occupied Europe. See also SIS and MI6

Special War Problems Division— (SWP) A program developed within the US State Department to deal with, among other things, the exchange of nationals trapped behind battle lines

SS—*Schutzstaffel* (Protection Squadron), elite military unit of the Nazi Party (See also Waffen-SS)

Tirpitzufer—Berlin headquarters of Canaris' Abwehr

Waffen-SS—Armed wing of the SS

WC—*Wasserklosett*, water closet or toilet

Wehrmacht—"Defense Force," the unified armed forces of Nazi Germany consisting of the Heer (Army), the Kriegsmarine (Navy) and the Luftwaffe (Air Force)

Widerstand—German resistance to Nazism

Synopsis of the conclusion of

BEACON OF VENGEANCE, A Novel of Nazi Germany

"Eyes Only" for those who have already read
Beacon of Vengeance

Determined to put an end to his long-time nemesis, Ryan Lemmon forces a cyanide "kill-pill" into the mouth of Horst von Kredow. Ryan's French resistance comrades confine the bodies of the Gestapo sadist and his thugs to military crates bound for the Eastern Front.

After a bloody gun battle at a Nantes warehouse, the partisans regroup at a doctor's house on the Loire River. The friends intend to go separate ways. Erika and René Gesslinger will head east with their partisan group to sabotage the German U-boat pens at Saint-Nazaire. But first they must help troubled Nicole rescue her infant daughter from von Kredow's hostage house.

Ryan returns to Paris with intelligence of strategic value to the Allied Forces and America's Coordinator of Information Office. However, his personal focus is to reunite at last with a beautiful woman who has loved him for years, cabaret owner Marita Lesney.

Unknown to Ryan, Marita has incurred the wrath of a powerful Nazi by undermining the lucrative extortion racket run by his partner, a malicious Parisian gangster. A Gestapo team is heading to her nightclub to guarantee she pays with her life.

Made in the USA
Lexington, KY
27 February 2016